W9-BVT-874

DISCARD

Death Wore White

# Death Wore White

## JIM KELLY

Minotaur Books    New York

F

DEATH WORE WHITE. Copyright © 2008 by Jim Kelly. All rights reserved. Printed in the United States of America. For information, address St. Martin's Press, 175 Fifth Avenue, New York, N.Y. 10010.

www.minotaurbooks.com

Library of Congress Cataloging-in-Publication Data

Kelly, Jim, 1957–
    Death wore white / Jim Kelly. — 1st U.S. ed.
        p. cm.
    "First published in Great Britain by Penguin Books."
    ISBN-13: 978-0-312-57081-1
    ISBN-10: 0-312-57081-3
    1. Police—England—Norfolk—Fiction.  I. Title.
PR6111.E5D43 2009
823'.92—dc22

                                                    2009007911

First published in Great Britain by Penguin Books

First U.S. Edition: June 2009

10  9  8  7  6  5  4  3  2  1

# Acknowledgements

There are three women without whom this book would not have reached publication: Beverly Cousins, my editor, who has again brilliantly spotted what works, and what doesn't; Faith Evans, my agent, for her gifted interventions on character and style; and my wife, Midge Gillies, for providing a touchstone service on how to unravel knots in the plot.

Trevor Horwood has again been our talented backstop, providing meticulous copy-editing. Jenny Burgoyne was again the backstop's backstop, to great effect.

In addition, I owe a continuing debt to a team of advisers who have been generous with their time and expertise: Alan Gilbert on forensics, Martin Peters on all things medical, Paul Horrell on all things motorized – including an exquisite essay on spark plugs. Michael and Brian Houten took time to help me get my hero's passion – running – just right. Allen Frary at Wells RNLI advised on boats and the dangers of boats, Eric Boyle on the chemistry of toxic waste, Chris Pitt at the RSPCA put me on the right track to discover the shadowy world of animal trafficking. And regarding that world, I have relied on the help of Ken Goddard, Director of the National Fish & Wildlife Forensics Laboratory in Ashland, Oregon.

I have benefited hugely from two excellent textbooks: *Forensic Art and Illustration* by Karen T. Taylor, and *Crime Scene* by Richard Platt.

The novel is set in King's Lynn and along the north Norfolk coast. I have played with the geography and nomenclature of the area to enliven the language and avoid inadvertent libel. All characters, establishments and organizations are fictional, and I should point out specifically that the West Norfolk Constabulary does not exist. I hope that I have captured the genuine spirit of detection, without burdening the reader with the day-to-day minutiae of working in the modern CID.

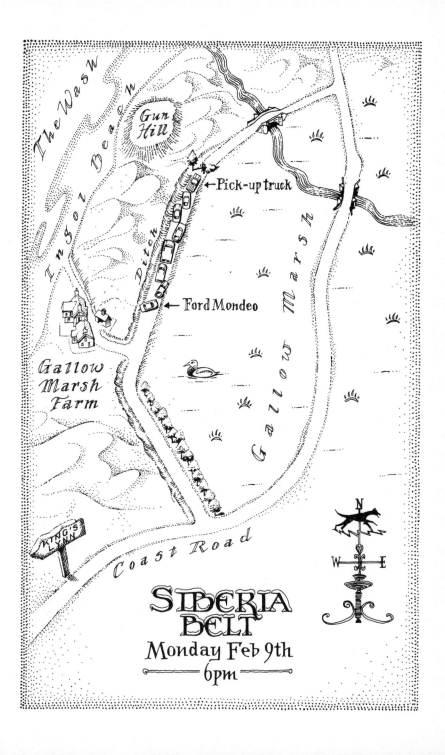

*Monday, 9 February*

The Alfa Romeo ran a lipstick-red smear across a sepia landscape. Snow flecked the sands at the edge of the crimped waters of the Wash. To the landward side lay the saltmarsh, a weave of winter white around stretches of cold black water. And out at sea a convoy of six small boats were caught in a stunning smudge of purple and gold where the sun was setting.

The sports car nudged the speed limit as Sarah Baker-Sibley watched the first flake of snow fall on the windscreen. She swept it aside with a single swish of the wipers and punched the lighter into the dashboard, her lips counting to ten, a cigarette held ready between her teeth.

Ten seconds. She thrummed her fingers on the leather-bound steering wheel.

It was two minutes short of five o'clock and the Alfa's headlights were waking up the catseyes. She pulled the lighter free of its holder. The ringlet of heated wire seemed to lift her mood and she laughed to herself, drawing in the nicotine.

A spirograph of ice had encroached on the windscreen, so she turned the heating up to maximum. The indicator showed the outside temperature at 0°C, then briefly −1°C.

She dropped her speed to 50 mph and checked the rear-view mirror for following traffic: she'd been overtaken once – the vehicle was still ahead of her by half a mile – and there were lights behind, but closer, a hundred yards or less.

She swished more snowflakes off the windscreen. Attached to the dashboard by a sucker was a little picture frame holding a snapshot of a girl with hair down to her waist, wearing a swimsuit on a sun-drenched beach. She touched the image as if it were an icon.

Rounding a sharp right bend she saw tail lights ahead again for a few seconds. And a sign, luminous, regulation black on yellow, in the middle of the carriageway, an AA insignia in the top left corner.

## DIVERSION
### Flood

An arrow pointed bluntly to the left – seaward down a narrow unmetalled road.

'Sod it.' She hit the steering wheel with the heel of her palm. Slowing the Alfa, she looked at her watch: 5.01 p.m. She had to pick her daughter up at 5.30 outside the school. She was always there, like clockwork. That was one of the big pluses of owning her own business: she kept her own time. And that's why she always took the old coast road, not the new dual carriageway, because this way there were never any traffic jams, even in the summer. Just an open road. Once, perhaps twice, she'd got caught up at the shop and phoned ahead to say she'd be late. Jillie had walked home then, but Sarah didn't want to let her down.

Not tonight, when snow was forecast. She'd make it in time, even with the diversion, as long as nothing else delayed her.

Looking in the rear-view again she saw that the following car was close, so she put the Alfa in first and swung it off the coast road onto the snow-covered track. The headlights raked the trees as she turned the car, but she failed to see that they fleetingly lit a figure, stock-still, dressed in a full-length dark coat flecked with snow, the head – hooded – turned away. But she did see a road sign.

## Siberia Belt

Ahead were the tail lights of the vehicle she had been following. There was a sudden silence as a snow flurry struck, muffling the world outside. The wind returned, thudding against the offside, fist blows deadened by a boxer's glove. She searched the rear-view mirror for the comforting sight of headlights behind. There were none. But the tail lights ahead were still visible: warm, glowing and safe. She pressed on quickly in pursuit.

## 2

Half a mile away Detective Inspector Peter Shaw stood on the beach as the snow fell, trying to smile into an Arctic north wind. The seascape was glacier-blue, the white horses whipped off the peaks of the waves before they could break. Offshore a sandbank was dusted with snow – icing sugar on marzipan. As quickly as the snow flurry had come, it was gone. But he knew a blizzard would be with them by nightfall, the snow clouds already massed on the horizon like a range of mountains.

'Tide's nearly up,' he said, licking a snowflake off his lips. 'So it should be here. Right here.' He tapped his boot rhythmically on the spot, creating a miniature quicksand inside his footprint, and zipped up his yellow waterproof jacket. 'A bright yellow drum, right?' he asked. 'Mustard, like the other one. Floating a foot clear of the water. So where is it?'

Detective Sergeant George Valentine stood six foot downwind, his face turned away from the sea. He stifled a yawn by clenching his teeth. His eyes streamed water. An allergy – seaweed perhaps, or salt on the air. Valentine looked at his feet, black slip-ons oozing salt water. He was too old for this: five years off retirement, rheumatism in every bone. They'd got the call from HM Coastguard an hour before: toxic waste, spotted drifting inshore off Scolt Head Island.

Six weeks earlier three drums had come ashore on Vinegar Middle, a sandbank just off the coast near Castle Rising. Shaw had been on the early shift at St James's, the police HQ in Lynn – his daughter Francesca played on the beach sometimes, so he'd taken a parental interest. When he got to the scene there was a five-year-old poking a stick into the top of the drum where it had ruptured. Shaw had told her to drop the stick but he hadn't been able to keep the urgency out of his voice, the note of command. Reading a child's face wasn't a textbook exercise. He'd spotted the sudden fear, but missed the anger. The kid didn't like being told what to do, so she'd waved the stick in Shaw's face as he'd grabbed her, pulling her clear of the liquid pooling at her feet. She hadn't meant to do it, but the single thrust as Shaw bent down had caught him in the eye.

The injury was covered by a dressing, secured with a plaster across the socket, the inflamed red edges of a fresh scar just visible beneath. He touched it now, moving it slightly to relieve the pressure. The chemical had proved a mystery: an unstable mix of residual sulphuric and nitric acid, the by-products of some poorly monitored manufacturing process. A 'class eight' substance; highly corrosive, with a ferocious ability to attack epithelial tissue. Skin.

'So where is it?' Shaw asked again. Standing still like this was a form of torture. He wanted to run along the water's edge, feel his heart pounding, blood rushing, the intoxicating flood of natural painkillers soaking his brain – the runner's high.

He raised a small telescope to his good eye, the iris as pale and blue as falling water, scanning the seascape.

Shaw's face mirrored the wide-open sea; the kind of face that's always scanning a horizon. His cheekbones were high, as if some enterprising warrior from the Mongol Horde had wandered off to the north Norfolk coast, pitching his tent by the beach huts.

DS Valentine looked at his watch. He'd bought it for £1 and was pretty sure the word ROLEX was fake. Its tick-tock was oddly loud. He shivered, his head like a vulture's, hung low on a thin neck. He tried to keep his mouth shut because he knew his teeth would ache if they got caught by the wind.

A radio crackled and Valentine retrieved it from the shapeless raincoat he was wearing. He listened, said simply, 'Right.' Fumbling it back inside the folds of the coat he produced a tube of mints, popping one, crunching it immediately.

'Coastguard. They lost sight of the drum an hour ago. The water's churning up with the tide.' He shrugged as if he knew the moods of the ocean. 'Not hopeful.'

Shaw ran a hand through close-cropped fair hair. They stood together, one looking south, the other north, wondering how it had come to this: Shaw and Valentine, West Norfolk Constabulary's latest investigative duo.

Some joker in admin, thought Shaw, some old lag who knew the past and didn't care about the future. They needed a new partner for Shaw, who at thirty-three years of age was the force's youngest DI, the whiz-kid with the fancy degree and a father once tipped to be the next chief constable. And they'd come up with George Valentine – a living relic of a different world, where cynical coppers waged a losing war against low life on the street.

A man who'd been the best detective of his generation until one mistake had put him on a blacklist from which he was struggling to escape. A man whose career trajectory looked like a brick falling to earth.

It was their first week as partners; already – for both of them – it seemed like a lifetime.

Shaw looked around. He'd played on this beach as a child. 'Let's get up there,' he said, pointing at a low hill in the dunes. 'Gun Hill. Get some height. We might see it then.'

Valentine nodded without enthusiasm. He turned his back on the sea wind, looking inland, along the curve of the high-water mark. 'There,' he said, taking a bare hand reluctantly from his coat pocket.

A yellow metal oil drum, on its side now, rolling in with the waves.

'Let's go,' said Shaw, already jogging; a compact, nearly effortless canter.

The lid of the drum was rusted and crinkled so that the contents had begun to seep out. From six feet he could smell it, the edge of ammonia almost corrosive. The liquid spilling down the side was Day-Glo green, the paint of the drum blistering on contact.

'I'll get the Coastguard,' said Valentine, breathless, digging out the radio. 'The boat could be out there – they'll have dumped others.'

'And call St James's,' said Shaw. 'They need to get a chemical team out to make this safe and get it off the beach. We better stay till they get here. Give them the grid reference.' Shaw read out the numbers from his hand-held GPS.

As Valentine worked on the radio Shaw squatted down, picking up ten butter-yellow limpet shells and placing them in a line on the sand. 'We could do with a fire,' he said out loud. The breeze was dropping, a frost in the air now that night was falling. He imagined the brief dusk, the fire on the high-water mark, and felt good. Pocketing the shells, he began collecting flotsam, a beer crate, a few lumps of bog oak, the dried-out husk of a copy of the *Telegraph*, then turned with his arms full.

Which is when he saw something else in the waves. Ingol Beach shelved gently out to sea, so even though it was a hundred yards away it was already catching the bottom, buckling slightly, flexing in the white water. An inflatable raft, a child's summer plaything in Disney colours. Shaw stood for a few seconds watching it inch ashore. Thirty yards out it ran aground, snagged.

Valentine watched his DI pulling off his boots and socks. *Jesus!* he thought, looking around, hoping they were still alone, hoping most of all that he'd stop at the socks. Shaw waded on, the jolt of the iced water almost electric, making his bones ache.

There was something in the raft, something that didn't respond to the shuffle and bump of the waves. A dead weight. When he saw the hands – both bare – and the feet, in light trainers swollen with seawater, he knew it was the body of a man: the black hair on the hands, a chunky signet ring. He felt his pulse suddenly thump in his ears as his body reacted to the sight of death. The atavistic urge to flee, to run from danger, was almost overwhelming. And there was the sensation that time had stopped, as if he'd been caught in the middle of an accident, unfurling around him in agonizingly slow motion.

He forced himself to observe; to step out of the scene.

Dead – but for how long? Less than forty-eight hours. The arms and legs were askew, locked in ugly angles, so rigor had yet to pass.

He put a hand on the side of the raft to steady it, his fingers gripping a raised handle at the prow. Jeans, a T-shirt, a heavy fur-lined jacket only half on, leaving one arm free. The limb was thick, knotted with muscle, the hidden shoulder broad. In the bottom of the boat there was an inch of swilling bloody seawater.

Valentine met him on the dry sand, and they pulled the raft round so that what was left of the sunset caught the dead man's head; unavoidable now, lifeless, despite the movement of the waves. The human face: Peter Shaw's passion, each unique balance and imbalance of features as individual as a fingerprint. He noted the bloated, profound pallor, like cold fat, with almost iridescent tinges of blue and green. A young man, stubble on the chin, the eyes half-open but flat, lightless, one eyelid more closed than the other. The lateral orbital lines – crow's feet – deeply scored, as if he'd spent a lifetime squinting in the sun. The muscles beneath defined the skin like the surface of a piece of beaten metal. But it was the mouth that drew Shaw's attention. The lips, uneven lines, were peeled back from teeth which were smeared with blood.

'Shit,' said Valentine, turning, taking three steps and vomiting into the sand.

He came back, dabbing at his lips. 'Sight of blood,' he

said, avoiding Shaw's eyes. He might be a copper with thirty years' experience, but it hadn't helped him get used to being in the company of the dead.

Shaw tried to reanimate the victim's face in his mind as he'd been trained to do. He tightened up the jaw, balanced the eyes, replaced the graceful bow of the lips. Not a cerebral face, a muscular face.

It was Valentine who first saw the mark on the arm. The seawater had washed it clean and so it bled no more, but there was no mistaking the shape: a bite. A human bite. The teeth puncturing the skin deeply, viciously driving into the sinew and muscle, almost meeting in a crisp double incision.

# 3

Sarah Baker-Sibley pulled the Alfa up three car lengths behind stationary tail lights. The vehicle ahead had stopped, a fallen pine tree blocking the way, lit silver by the headlights. Looking ahead she saw that it wasn't a car but a small pick-up truck, with an open back, and a covered low load. The cab had a rear window which showed a light within through frosted glass. The engine idled, the exhaust fumes spirited away each time there was a breath of wind. In a lull she heard music: something urban, jagged and loud. Then silence, and the next track, louder, even less melodic. The flurry of snow had passed, but flakes still fell.

She activated central locking and searched her handbag for her mobile. The latest model: a gift from one of her suppliers, retail price £230. Internet link, GPS, camera, video, the casing decorated with a detail from Monet's *Water Lilies*.

## NO SIGNAL
### Searching network

She threw the mobile onto the passenger seat. Ahead the snow lay three inches thick on the road, as clean as hotel linen, the two parallel tyre tracks just visible, running forward to the stranded truck.

Then she heard the crunch of a vehicle behind her and looking in the rear-view mirror she saw headlights coming up until they were so close they fell into her shadow, revealing the driver, once the glare of his lights was gone. A man alone. She checked that the door was locked.

She watched as the man levered himself out of the driver's seat, straightening, with a hand on the car for support. He struggled forward, but when the wind blew he stopped, braced, waiting for a lull.

He lowered his face to the closed driver's window. A strained smile, the white hair matted with snow, the plump fingers holding an outsized working jacket to his throat. Glasses, heavy with black frames, magnified his eyes, which were milky with age. The cold had brought some blood to his cheeks but otherwise he was pale, drained, a cold sweat on his forehead.

'You OK?' he said when she wound the window down an inch. She heard the sound of music again, louder, from the pick-up truck.

'We're stuck,' she said, briskly. 'I need to get through – I'm picking up my daughter from school. Could you check ahead, see if we can move the tree?'

He looked forward, licking his lips, reluctant, but then set out. She watched the prints he made in the snow – a single line of flat-footed impressions, slightly unsteady. He slipped at the edge of the ditch when the wind blew, his arms flying out in a crooked semaphore, the coat billowing.

'That's all we need,' she said out loud, punching in the lighter. 'Grandad in the soup.'

She rubbed clear the condensation on the windscreen and watched as he reached the pick-up's window. He bent slightly at the waist, talking, just for a few seconds, then he straightened up, both bare hands deep in the jacket's pockets.

A minute, less, and he was back, out of breath so that he had to lean on the Alfa's roof. 'OK then. We're not gonna move the tree – not now. He says we'll have to all back out. Have you got a mobile?' he asked.

'No signal.'

'Same with him. I don't own one.' He rubbed one of his eyes under the thick spectacles. Despite the cold she could see now that his whole face was wet with sweat.

Baker-Sibley pushed smoke out of her nostrils, her lips pressed in a humourless line. 'You should take it easy,' she said.

He held his jacket's lapels together. 'I'm OK. I'll try and reverse back to the turn, there was a farm track there, just give me a few minutes.' He set off before she had time to answer.

He tottered back to his car and wiped the snow from the windscreen with his sleeve before lowering himself into the driver's seat and starting the engine. He peered down at the dashboard, then at the rear-view mirror.

'Come on, come on,' said Sarah. 'It's not a fucking Space Shuttle.'

He didn't move. She threw open the door and stepped out into the night, holding a hand above her eyes to stop the snowflakes snagging her lashes. The cold made her back arch and she hunched her shoulders to try to protect the exposed skin at her neck.

Now she saw the old man's car clearly for the first time. A two-door silver Corsa, a pair of ladders neatly strapped to a roof rack.

It was what stretched behind the Corsa that made Sarah Baker-Sibley swear. A line of headlamps running back, all stranded now in the snow.

She looked up and let some of the flakes settle on her face. 'Why me?' she asked. She thought of Jillie trudging home in the snow. 'And why now?'

On cue the blizzard finally broke, the snow thickening, the wind driving it in from the sea. Visibility dropped to a few feet. She brushed flakes from her eyelids and scrambled back into the safety of the car.

# 4

In the blizzard Shaw and Valentine worked quickly, dragging the raft across the sands to the DI's black Land Rover, parked beyond a copse of hawthorns. By the time they had a tarpaulin secured, weighting the corners with rocks, the snow was settling. Then they sat it out, Shaw watching the high tide boiling on the sands through an open window. He'd been a policeman for eleven years but this was the first time he'd discovered a corpse: he was distressed to find that the emotional impact was refusing to fade. His stomach felt empty, and he kept seeing the dead man's mouth, the blood terracotta red between the white enamel of the teeth.

Valentine bent forward, his hands over the warm-air vent, his throat glugging with phlegm as the hot dust triggered his immune system. He'd binned his last packet of Silk Cut back at the station, so he closed his eyes, trying not to think about nicotine, trying not to think about the corpse in the raft. But the image of the apparently self-inflicted wound was difficult to shake off. He took a call on the radio: Control said the force pathologist was on her way and a unit of the West Norfolk CSI team was assembling, but the snowfall had brought chaos to the coastal roads, so they could be some time.

The storm itself passed in twenty minutes, rolling

inland, buffeting winds at its leading edge, while in its wake the air was still, the last of the snow falling like poppies on Armistice Day, bled white.

Shaw's patience snapped. He flung the door open and shuddered in the super-cooled air. He threw the keys to Valentine. 'Roll the Land Rover out on the beach and put the lights on – there's a floodlight there.' He leant in and tapped a red switch. 'Walk the high-water mark, see if you can find anything – clothing, a weapon, just anything. Any footprints in the sand other than ours, mark them with the scene-of-crime flags – they're in the boot – and there's some tape; try and box off the point where I dragged him ashore, although it's probably under water by now. There are evidence bags in the glove. When you see the fire brigade unit or our boys, fill them in. Scene-of-crime rules – so no smoking.'

Valentine popped another mint.

'I'm going to climb, see what I can see. I'll be ten, no more.'

'Right,' said Valentine.

Shaw detected the grudging note, a single syllable that said so much. He recalled George Valentine at his father's deathbed, a glass of malt whisky in his hand, a cigarette burning between the yellowed fingers.

Boredom, bungalow and early retirement (enforced) had killed DCI Jack Shaw. Luckily, they killed him quickly. The early exit to Civvy Street had come care of his father's last, notorious, case. Until then they'd been the force's star team: DCI Jack Shaw and DI George Valentine. A pair of old-fashioned coppers in an old-fashioned world. And so he knew what Valentine was thinking: that a decade ago they'd have wrapped this case up without all the mindless mechanics of police procedure, without a fancy degree in forensic art (whatever that was), or the check-it, double-check-it philosophy.

Valentine turned over the pair of dice attached to his lighter and keys. Ivory and green, with gold dots. 'What's that smell?' he asked before Shaw had gone ten yards.

Shaw stopped, sniffed the sea breeze. 'Could be mint, George. You crunch any more of those things you'll start scaring the sheep.' But Valentine was right, there was something else on the breeze, something laced with the ozone and seaweed. 'Petrol. An outboard?' asked Shaw.

Valentine produced a handkerchief and dabbed his streaming eyes.

'Hold the fort,' said Shaw, padding through the dunes and beginning to climb, picking a narrow ridge where the snow was just clinging to the sand and grass. At the top he pushed himself up onto an old gun emplacement, a tangle of concrete and rusted iron. The physical effort made him feel better, dissipating the stress. This high there was still a breeze, the snowflakes jostling, streamers of light like sparklers. Down on the beach he could just see the Land Rover and the spread tarpaulin.

Swinging round he looked south, to the lights of a farmhouse: a glimpse of the corrugated iron of a barn and a white spotlight illuminating a dovecote on the roof of an old stable block. They'd driven through the yard an hour earlier to get down to the beach and Shaw had noticed the name: Gallow Marsh Farm.

And then, turning inland, he saw car lights – a line of vehicles backed up behind a pine tree which was in their path, its branches twisted and broken. Exhaust fumes hung in the airless night. That was the smell on the air, not an engine at sea. Shaw got the telescope out and held it to his good eye, focusing on the vehicle in pole position. A small pick-up truck. The cab light was on, the windows flecked with snow, someone moving inside. He looked back along the line, each vehicle smoothed out by the gentle curves of snowdrifts.

Out at sea the storm clouds had unpacked themselves, revealing a wedge of clear night sky, a planetarium of lights, the moon clear of the sea. He watched the white lunar disc moving sideways along the horizon, like a prop in a child's theatre. The silhouette of a yacht, gliding east, turned in towards the coast, an engine humming efficiently, its white sail marked with a blue clamshell.

# 5

The line of eight vehicles stood as if fashioned in icing sugar, an exquisite model on an untouched wedding cake. The moon had appeared above the scene; the snow clouds had moved on after one last heavy flurry, the stars left to stretch north over the sea towards the distant pole. The marsh birds were silent, the sluices choked with ice, and the sea, past high water, tiptoed back over the sands. Closer to the marooned cars there were sounds of life: a bass note, strands of music, the rumble of vehicle engines running heating systems. From the pick-up truck in pole position the local radio now played – a jagged tinny melody which came and went with the signal.

Three vehicles from the tail of the little convoy was an off-white Astravan. Radio 2 played, a voice inside singing along loudly, a ballad about a young girl in pursuit of an older man. Fred Parlour held the final note surprisingly well, then laughed at himself. He was handsome, mid-fifties, with a compact symmetrical face, the jaw showing no signs of slackening despite the first strands of grey at his temples. His fingernails were neatly cleaned, the overalls laundered, the hair smartly trimmed.

Beside him sat Sean Harper, the firm's apprentice. His hair was sticky with product, cut short and spiky, his nose – pierced with a stud – was pressed up close to a pornographic magazine. 'You'll go blind,' said Parlour.

Harper looked at the lights of the stationary van in front. 'So what? We're gonna be 'ere all night, right? Might as well enjoy myself.'

A small dog – a Jack Russell – thrust its snout between the seats and nuzzled his fingers, the tongue making a liquid smack.

'How much you reckon they got on board?' asked Parlour, his voice friendlier. The van in front had a branded motif on the rear doors:

**NORTH NORFOLK SECURITY**
01553 121212
*There's safety in those numbers*

Sean Harper had got out when they'd first pulled up. His mobile couldn't find a signal so he'd run along the seaward side in the still falling snow to see if they had a radio. It was a refurbished Securicor van, but an old model, rust round the rivets. One guard in an ill-fitting uniform sat in the front, about as intimidating as a cinema usherette. Just a thumbs up: no window down. And no radio.

'I don't like uniforms,' Sean had said when he got back. 'Or the fuckers in them.'

Parlour shrugged. 'It's not Brinks Mat, is it?'

He got his mobile out of his breast pocket and checked the signal – one bar, but then it flickered and died. The dog sniffed at his neck so he reached back and lifted the animal onto his lap, rubbing its tummy where the fur was thinnest against the pink skin. He got a dog biscuit out of the glove compartment and fed it to her.

'All right, Milly?' Parlour thrust his head below the dog's

chin, nuzzling. 'I'll take her for a walk; she must be busting.'

He checked his watch: 7.40 p.m. They'd been stuck for more than two hours. Pushing open the door against the small drift on the driver's side he let the dog slip out. The sound of the door slamming faded, absorbed by the snow, but a pair of geese rose quickly from the marsh, creaking overhead.

The air was unnaturally still, expectant, like an empty theatre.

Parlour stood and coughed in the cold, reviewing the line of vehicles. There was no echo, the snow smothering the sound, wrapping it in silence. Sean had said he'd seen a tree ahead, blocking the road, and a car skewed across the track at the rear, behind the Morris Minor which was behind them. When he'd gone forward, beyond the security van, he'd met another driver from further up the line, a 'Chink', he said, but well spoken. Sean had asked him what he thought they should do. 'Sit tight,' he'd said, turning away. So they'd all sat tight.

Parlour stretched in the cold and stood trying to hear the sea sigh. He edged down the side of the Morris and tapped on the window. There was no light within, and no sign of life at all. Then he saw frail fingers fumbling with the window handle, one encumbered by a large amber ring. The driver wound the window down. 'Are we going to be here long?' she asked, as if he were an AA man. Make-up, a savage attempt to defy the years, made her face look artificial, her eyebrows two black pencil lines, a smudge of crimson where the lips should have been. Parlour said he didn't know how long it would be, that the sky had cleared and they'd be spotted soon. But it might be all night. And the mobiles were useless.

'I know that,' she said. 'I've always said that.'

Milly snuffled around his shoes.

'You've cut the heating?' he asked her.

She'd looked at him as if he were an idiot. 'I'm fine,' she said, and then, with what seemed like an effort, 'Please. Don't worry about me.'

He checked her fuel gauge; she had a quarter of a tank, perhaps less. 'OK. But like I say – if you get cold we're just in front.'

'I'm going to sleep now . . .' she said, winding up the window.

The next car was the last in the line, a Mondeo, stuck sideways across the track. Fred was leaning down to knock on the glass when the door opened with a jerk and clipped him on the forehead. He just had time to grab the frame, saving himself from a fall into the dark water and the reeds.

In the moonlight he looked at the smudge of blood on his fingers, touching the wound.

A teenager with a baseball cap got out of the car, the crotch of his jeans half-way down to his knees. He looked hot, his face flushed, a patch of sweat discolouring a T-shirt with the logo *Pi is God*. The rest of the fabric was covered in blue numbers. Adolescent-thin, the arms held at awkward angles, his skin clear, the narrow face dominated by thick, dark eyebrows. Parlour didn't notice the rapid shallow breathing and the trembling which made his hands vibrate in his pockets. Or the running shoes: Nike, £180 new.

'Yeah?' said the youngster, taking a hand out of his pocket before thrusting it back in.

'Don't suppose your mobile works?' asked Parlour.

He shook his head and looked up and down the line. 'Nope.' The kid licked his lips. 'What's gonna happen then, do you think?' Estuary English, but beneath it the subtle lilt of middle-class *Blue Peter.*

Parlour shrugged. 'Guess we'll start eating each other eventually.'

'No.' The kid made a noise in his throat which wasn't a laugh. 'You know . . . like, what *will* happen?' The note of pleading was unmistakable; Parlour saw the boy's eyes flooding.

'Nothing to worry about,' said Parlour, looking up at the stars. 'Police'll get a chopper out soon. We can't be the only ones stuck. You got any food? Water?' He could see a bottle of vodka on the passenger seat.

The teenager looked out over the marsh, swivelling the baseball cap down over his short, thick hair. 'Reckon I could get through? I could stop a car down on the road. Get help.'

Parlour shook his head. 'Best wait. If you fall in tonight you'd freeze to death. Isn't worth it – anyway, this thing can put out enough heat to trigger global warming. So you'll be nice and snug. How's the fuel?'

The kid got back in the driver's seat, looking blankly at the instrument panel, and held the steering wheel with both hands. Parlour noticed that the wheel had a cover – snakeskin, chevrons in black and white. He focused on the fuel gauge. 'Right. That's not so good, is it? On the red. If I was you I'd kill the lights, heat her up again and then turn off the engine. See how long you stay warm. Don't worry – if it cuts out just come in with us. OK?' Parlour held out his hand: 'I'm Fred. Your dad's car, is it?'

No answer. The boy pulled the door shut.

Parlour turned away and saw a pair of green reflecting eyes out in the marsh: a fox, watching him, smelling them all, petrified by the intrusion. It blinked first, and he followed the shadow as it slunk into the snow-capped clumps of grass. Ahead he saw someone walking back down the line of cars and trucks. A woman, forty-something, in an expensive yellow all-weather sailing jacket, waving a torch.

They met by the plumbers' van. 'I'm in the red Alfa Romeo,' she said. She produced a packet of cigarettes, fumbled until she got one between her lips and lit it with a gold lighter the size of a bullion bar.

'I should tell someone,' she said, implying that he'd have to do. 'The old guy in the Corsa behind me – that hideous little car . . .' She let the smoke circulate fully before ejecting it through her nose. 'I think he's dead.'

# 6

The tarpaulin over the body on the beach was now stiff with frost. Control had radioed to say the CSI unit was still an hour away, maybe more. Nothing moved on Ingol Beach except the tide, inching out. Valentine had taped off the toxic-waste drum and lit it with one of the portable floodlights, then he'd gone down on his knees, his thin trousers soaked, fingertip-searching the high-water mark.

Shaw told him he'd seen the cars trapped behind the fallen pine tree up on the track. Had the driver crashed? Did anyone need medical help? The coincidence made Shaw uneasy: the violent unnatural death on the sands, the fallen pine on Siberia Belt almost within sight. 'OK,' he said, refolding the map. 'The scene's secure. There's only one road in and that's blocked. We're done here for now. We'll leave the floodlight on. Let's see if we're needed on Siberia Belt.'

Valentine followed, glad to be putting distance between himself and the unseen corpse. The sight of blood made him feel the earth wasn't solid enough to stand on. Which made him want a pack of cigarettes, which he didn't have, so he spat in the snow instead.

They crossed the frosted sands until they reached a dyke which separated Siberia Belt from the beach, bridging it where a sluice gate stood, the cogs and levers of the iron mechanism choked with ice. Approaching the convoy from the south, Shaw got to the Mondeo first, but waited for Valentine to catch up. A lone figure, following Shaw's footsteps, his narrow bird-like head down. Breathless, the DS stopped when he reached Shaw, then nodded at the Mondeo. 'Latest model, SatNav as basic.'

Valentine could hardly speak for lack of breath. *Emphysema*, thought Shaw. *Fluid filling his lungs. If he's given up smoking, he's given up too late.* Shaw didn't need a SatNav to know Valentine's destination.

The bass note of a stereo system thudded from behind the misted windows of the car.

'Check it out,' said Shaw. 'I'll go along the line, see what the problem is up ahead.' A group stood beside the third car from the front of the line, lit by the interior light spilling from the open driver's door.

Valentine bridled at the peremptory tone, trying to get used to the fact that DI Shaw was the boss, not the kid in short trousers he'd once kicked a football with on the beach. It would be easier if Shaw could lay off the check-list philosophy. That's what they called him at the station. 'Check-It.' Check this, check that, check every bloody thing. Mr Politically Correct. Mr Rule Book. And Valentine knew where all that had its roots. He knew why Peter Shaw was so keen to show the world he was the perfect copper: it was because his father hadn't been, that's why. And because his father's partner hadn't been either. Jack Shaw and George Valentine had lashed up their last big case. Big time. What had the judge said? *Slipshod.*

Valentine used one foot to ease the black shoe off the other and, leaning against the Mondeo, poured out some water before putting it back on.

Shaw reached the Morris Minor and turned back with fresh instructions: 'And this,' he called. He placed his palms together and put them beside one cheek, tilting his head as if laying it down on a pillow. An elderly woman was asleep in the car, the windows slightly frosted on the inside, a tartan rug to one side where it had slipped off her body. Shaw could see her face: there was a smile on the thin lips and her hands were held slightly up from the quilt like a child's.

The door of the Mondeo opened before Valentine could tap on the roof. The teenager stood, leaning on the door. 'We getting out of here?'

Valentine shrugged. 'What's up?' He nodded forward to the group by the silver Vauxhall Corsa.

'What bastard cares?' The young man bounced on his toes and Valentine noticed that he kept putting his hands in his pockets and then taking them out, then rubbing them on the backside of his jeans.

'This one.' Valentine flipped out his warrant card. 'Why are you on this road, sir, can I ask?'

The kid took a step back and laughed inappropriately. 'Diversion. There's a sign down on the coast road – floods it said.' His accent had flattened out: he'd gone up three socio-economic classes and moved thirty miles closer to London. He looked ahead. 'Then this happened.' He put his hand on the car door and then quickly removed it as if the metal were too cold to touch, but Valentine had seen a mark on the top of his hand, the bluish remains of a stamp in the shape of a circle enclosing two letters: BT.

On the dashboard lay a mobile phone.

'Yours?'

'Shine,' said the kid. 'Two megapixel camera; hundred and fifteen grams; six point seven hours talk time.'

'Right. But does it work?'

The kid shrugged. 'I was gonna walk back to the road,' he said.

Valentine shook his head. 'A mile, and it's treacherous.'

'It's one point three miles,' he said. 'I clocked it.'

'Just stay here, OK?' Valentine was running out of patience. 'We've radioed for help but it'll be a time.' He took an extra breath and ran an eye over the Mondeo's purple paintwork – spotless. On the back seat was a blanket, a picnic basket, a shooting stick and a Frisbee. The steering wheel had a cover, black and white chevrons: an animal skin, snake perhaps. He walked on, but turned and memorized the registration number. He had a good memory, if he could be bothered to use it. The kid had annoyed him. It always did: a teenager out in Daddy's car.

Shaw was behind the plumber's van now, and through the heated rear window and the grille he'd seen a young man in the passenger seat reading a magazine. He came alongside, noticing for the first time the paw prints in the snow between the footprints, and tapped on the driver's window, then opened the door.

'Police,' he said, putting his knee on the driver's seat

and looking at the magazine. 'May I?' He took it. It was German, an illegal import at the nastier end of the hard-porn market. He held his head slightly to one side so that he could focus on the picture.

'Name?' said Shaw.

The man shrugged. '*Das Fleisch*,' he said, mangling the words. 'They got Turkish blokes on site, they bring them in from Frankfurt.'

'*Your* name.'

'I found it, the last job this morning. Building site down in the Arndale, in the Portakabin where I brewed the tea. There was loads. Worse . . .'

Shaw waited. He studied the young man's face. Noted the premature hair loss at the temples, the acne scars, and the pronounced dimple in the chin – the mental fovea.

'Sean Harper. That's my boss,' said the young man, nodding forward to the group standing in the pool of light. 'Fred.' He grinned as if this was the ultimate character reference.

'I'll keep this, Mr Harper,' said Shaw, folding the magazine inside his jacket.

'Like – it's not a crime.'

'Well, it is actually,' said Shaw. 'We'll talk about it later.'

'You go out?' asked Harper, pointing at the RNLI lifeboat motif on the lapel of Shaw's jacket, trying hard to smile.

'Yup.'

'That's cool,' said Harper, watching his magazine disappear from sight. 'I've thought of it . . . you know? Volunteering.'

For the first time Shaw noticed the blanket behind the seats ruffled into a swirled nest of tartan. He paused, sniffed the air, expecting to detect the tell-tale stench of dog, but the van was clean and neat, the overpowering odour that of the strawberry-scented air freshener stuck on the dashboard.

'You should,' said Shaw, not smiling.

Next in line was the revamped Securicor van. The driver refused to open the window until he saw the warrant card pressed up against the glass, then he cracked it an inch.

'Any trouble?' asked Shaw, knowing he'd seen the man before – in the dock of the magistrates' court. The crime? He searched his memory but couldn't pinpoint the case. Something violent, he knew that. Something violent with his hands, in pursuit of cash. Why then, Shaw asked himself, was he sitting guarding a van full of the stuff? He was twenty-five to thirty, dark good looks marred by a narrow nose which had been broken and badly reset and which only just managed to separate his eyes, the eyebrows almost meeting at the bridge. He had a half-hearted moustache and designer stubble.

'You got a control desk to contact?' asked Shaw.

The driver found his voice. 'We don't have radios – and there's no signal on the mobiles.'

Shaw stepped back, looking along the line of vehicles. 'Get my DS to radio through for you – there's enough chaos after the storm without half the force out looking for you and your bars of gold. What *is* in the back?'

The guard checked a clipboard. 'Cash. We do corner shops, the supermarkets on the estates, wholesale fish market down on the docks. About eighty thousand – not much more, anyway.'

'Sit tight,' said Shaw, wondering if his employer knew about the criminal record. He approved of rehabilitation, but putting the alcoholic behind the bar was asking for trouble.

Ahead he could see the Corsa's two nearside doors open, two figures standing back, watching Shaw. One, a man in overalls, waved and placed a hand on his heart, patting a quilted jacket. Shaw raised a hand.

'Problem?' he shouted.

The man pointed inside the Corsa, patted his chest again. 'Heart.'

He moved quickly past the next car – a Volvo, an old model estate, a hand-painted sign reading 'The Emerald Garden' on the rear window. The distinctive aroma of soy sauce was laced with petrol fumes. No driver, no passengers.

An elderly man lay tilted back in the Corsa's front seat. Shaw guessed he was sixty-five, perhaps seventy. He had heavy spectacles, with black plastic rims, and thin white hair stuck to his skull. His face was the colour of the streaks in Stilton cheese, saliva catching the light at the corners of his mouth. Vomit covered his chin and the front of the heavy jacket, a slimy eggshell-blue. Shaw picked up the strong scent of pine needles but couldn't see the air freshener.

A woman in a yellow jacket stood back, smoking. Kneeling, the man in clean blue overalls held the sick man's hand, his neat face screwed up with anxiety, a small wound on his forehead still wet with blood. A Jack Russell lay under the vehicle, its nose rummaging at the man's foot.

'Like I say, heart attack, I reckon,' said the man in the overalls. 'Don't suppose you've got a mobile signal? You stuck too?'

'I'm a policeman,' said Shaw. 'We've radioed. Can I see, please?'

He bent down and found that another man was on the passenger seat. Chinese features, his knees drawn up beneath him. 'Can't find a pulse,' he said, the consonants dulled by his accent.

Shaw took out a pocket knife and cut the tie which had become fiercely knotted at the man's throat. Then he pulled both sides of his heavy oversized jacket and shirt apart, the buttons popping clear. He turned the collar away from the neck and noticed a name tag: RFA. He leant in close to the man's face, putting a hand to his forehead. He knew instantly that the man was alive: the drops of water in his eyebrows were warm, and although his lips were blue and didn't move they were moist with the breath that was passing between them, like the draught under a door.

He backed out and shouted to Valentine, who was down on his haunches by the Morris, talking through the driver's window.

'George,' he shouted. Valentine stood slowly, one hand on the Morris for support. 'Get a chopper. Medical emergency – cardiac arrest, male about sixty-five years of age. They'll see us from the air, tell 'em to come down on the seaward side – it's flat sand under the snow.'

Shaw ducked back into the Corsa and, feeling inside

the man's pocket, he found a wallet with a driving licence in a plastic see-through compartment. John Blickling Holt. Born 30 December 1941. An address was given on Devil's Alley, King's Lynn. Shaw knew it well: a narrow cobbled street running down to the quay, reeking of fish and the tide. Mostly poor, run-down warehouses, a warren of Medieval buildings.

The man on the passenger seat said he was called Stanley Zhao. Even folded on his knees Shaw could see he bucked the racial stereotype by being the best part of six feet tall. He looked fifty, but his hair was still as black as a penguin's feathers. Shaw told him to stay in the Corsa, run the heating at half blast and sound the horn if Holt came round or got worse.

Shaw shut the door and straightened his back, bringing his face up level with the roof rack, the two sets of ladders strapped up neatly with webbing. The woman in the yellow coat and the man in the blue overalls stood between him and the first two vehicles in the convoy.

'My name's Baker-Sibley; Sarah Baker-Sibley,' said the woman. 'I need to get a message to my daughter. I should have picked her up from school – St Agnes' Hall – and I'm worried. I'm always there on time – or I ring. She won't have Clara with her – that's her best friend. She has a clarinet lesson after school,' she added. 'She'll walk home. She'll try to walk. Two miles, she's done it before and she has a key, but never in winter . . . in this,' she said, looking out over the snowfield. 'She's thirteen. So she won't think twice about trying.' She laughed, then dropped the half-finished cigarette and fumbled for the packet. 'I'm sorry – can I see your warrant card again?'

'My colleague DS Valentine will take the details, Ms Baker-Sibley,' said Shaw, holding his warrant card slightly too close to her face for comfort. 'He can radio ahead.

'This your Alfa?' Shaw asked her, walking forward. 'I'd stay put for now,' he added when she didn't answer. 'And the vehicle in front?'

'The man who's ill went forward and checked when we first got stuck,' she said. 'The driver hasn't been out. Perhaps he's getting some sleep; he had some horrendous racket at full blast to start with.'

The radio still played, but the volume was now low, the sound reedy.

Looking forward along the causeway Shaw could see an unsteady line of footprints weaving its way to the pick-up truck beside partially filled tyre tracks, the return line an uncertain attempt to retrace the same steps. Paw prints, crisper, zig-zagged between the tracks. The observation window in the rear of the cab still showed a light within. The pick-up's headlights burnt yellow, and Shaw guessed the battery was low. He walked forward, the hair on his neck bristling as a breeze took his skin temperature down a degree. Something moved in the sky and he looked up in time to see a meteor fall, a flashing line of silver that died before it reached the sea.

The truck was wide enough to block the track almost completely, leaving just the narrowest of paths down the driver's side. Shaw held on to the side and took the chance to lift the tarpaulin cover to see the load beneath: plasterboard, sheets of it for cheap walls.

Leaning forward he grasped the door handle, breaking the silence with his voice for the first time.

'Hello? Police.'

He turned the handle and swung the door open, stepping forward quickly to get a grip on the stanchion. He was less than two feet from the driver and it took him three seconds, perhaps less, to know that he was looking at a corpse.

# 7

The sight of death. For Shaw the shock was no less profound for being the second time he'd faced it in a few hours. If anything the sudden sense of living in a slow-motion world was even more pronounced. He felt his fingertips tingle as the blood rushed to his heart.

'Crime scene,' he said to himself, reassured by the calm resonance of his own voice. 'Let's stick to the book. He's dead, so there's no hurry, no imperative but observation.' He stood outside himself, watching himself follow procedure. His voice sounded good. Very good. But despite the sensation that he'd taken control a persistent thought intruded, like the buzzing of a fly around a wound: what would his father have done? An odd sensation: missing someone who'd hardly been there.

'Don't look for links,' he told himself, thinking of the body still freezing under the Land Rover's spotlight down on Ingol Beach. 'Let's take them one at a time.'

He looked at his hands, checking. 'Gloves,' he said, double-checking.

The radio signal was weak, the volume hardly audible now, but he leant in none the less and turned the radio off, leaving himself some silence in which to think.

His training had been repetitive but clear: there were procedures to follow, and a single broken rule could destroy vital evidence.

So: first, secure the scene. He stepped out, looking back along Siberia Belt to where Valentine was taking a note from the woman in the Alfa Romeo.

'George.' He said it as calmly as he could, but Valentine was experienced enough to pick up the coded charge of adrenaline. He looked up sharply. 'Make sure everyone stays put. And get that dog on a leash. Crime-scene rules. Then come forward – to the Alfa. Wait for me there.'

Now, observations. The corpse. First, the face. From a kneeling position Shaw could look up at the victim, the chin resting on the chest, a pair of off-white workman's overalls buttoned high with a white T-shirt beneath. The skull was slight, almost child-like. The features – eyes, lips and eyebrows – were large and seemed to crowd the face. The nose was small, snub and under-developed. He checked the skin at the ankles and hands. Hypostasis, the telltale pooling of blood after death, was incomplete. The man was small – a guess, five foot six or seven.

The cause of death was brutally obvious: a thin-necked chisel projected from the dead man's left eye socket. Shaw touched his own wounded eye, feeling his pulse in the blood behind the retina. The chisel had been forced in up to the hilt of the rounded wooden handle. There was remarkably little blood, but blood there was: a rivulet, now congealed, ran from the caked eye socket across the cheek to the neck and shoulder, and then behind the body, pooling on the seat. Rigor had begun to set in; both hands were held palm up, showing signs of soil stains, one with grass under the fingernails, fingers stiff. The head was bare, the close-cropped cranium vulnerable, but unmarked.

The one remaining eye was open but dead of sight, and it was difficult to judge for colour now that life had gone. A thin milky membrane had closed over the eyeball. Green perhaps, shading to grey. The overalls were covered in workaday stains: several dabs of paint, and a patch where the cloth had been bleached by a chemical.

Immediate environment. He smelt the air. Heated over a period of hours, it was heavy with aromas: an acrid hint of something earthy, possibly urine, and from the engine the smell of hot plastic and warm oil. Alcohol too, sweet as death. The dashboard held a half-eaten apple, the exposed flesh already brown, and a can of Carlsberg Special Brew. The wrapping paper from a packet of Hula Hoops was in the ashtray, which was ashless. The passenger seat was obscured by a large toolbox: metal, blue and worn, with fold-back wing lids. Hanging from the rear-view mirror was a picture of three children: two boys holding a toddler, crammed into a photo booth. One of the boys had a shaven skull, the smile uncertain, the bone structure poking through translucent skin. From a suction hook in the roof hung a little plastic model of a bald eagle, which moved very slightly as Shaw's weight tipped the suspension a few inches. Kneeling, he saw that a key ring hung from the ignition, a leather fob, with gold lettering. Three words: Jake Ellis Appeal.

He stood, feeling that he'd gained firm control of the scene, the tension beginning to ebb from his neck muscles. A run through the snow would ease the stress that was making his head ache, but he knew he'd have to wait. He looked back down the line of cars. Valentine stood beside the Alfa Romeo, motionless except for the rhythmic rise and fall of his shoulders as he lifted his rib cage to draw the air into his lungs.

Between them were three lines of human footprints – John Blickling Holt's round trip and Shaw's one way. Holt's prints were still sharp, although partly filled with the snow that had fallen after the convoy had come to rest, and by the breeze which had blown flakes over the bank from the beach beyond. But they were still clear; unmissable. To the landward side the saltmarsh was dominated by sheets of black water, dotted with clumps of marram grass. There was no sign that anyone had tried to climb the bank, or drop down into the water. To the seaward side there was the dyke, six feet across, eight deep, and beyond that the snow-covered sands, unmarked except for the delicate herringbone footsteps of the marsh birds.

Which left forwards. The lights of the truck were still on and lit the fallen pine a pale yellow. There was a six-foot gap of untouched snow between the pick-up and the tree.

Shaw took a deep breath. Even the perfect murderer leaves footprints in snow. Suicide? Hardly. Stabbing yourself through the eye was not an obvious way to leave the world. Self-mutilation? Martyrdom? A message left for the living?

Shaw breathed out, watching the plume of steam hang in the air like an accusation, his knee jiggling as he tried to think. What if the temperature rose? If the snow melted he'd lose the evidence; his crime scene would disappear.

He needed fresh eyes, even if they were hooded.

'OK, George,' he called back. 'Follow my tracks.' Valentine struggled to match Shaw's confident strides in the snow but eventually he stood by the open driver's door, squeezed in beside Shaw.

'Fuck,' he said, unable to stop the recoil in his neck muscles at the sight of the victim.

'Indeed, George. Fuck it is. Let's take it carefully, shall we?'

Valentine sniffed and looked away. His guts began to contract rhythmically, his mouth flooding with saliva. But he fought the urge to vomit again, biting the inside of his cheek until he drew blood.

Shaw retrieved a small voice recorder from his pocket, checked it was working and pressed the record button. A pinprick amber light glowed.

'DI Peter Shaw. Monday, 9th of February 2009. Eight thirteen p.m. I'm standing beside a pick-up truck. Make and registration . . .'

Valentine worked his way carefully to the rear of the truck. 'It's a Vauxhall Rascal,' he said. 'Ten years old – more.' The licence plate was clear of snow and he read out the number, his voice sharp and discordant in the still air.

Shaw went on, his breath making the hand-held recorder damp. 'The driver of the vehicle is dead. Cause of death appears to be a violent stab wound to the face which has penetrated the left eye socket. The weapon used was a chisel with a wooden, worn handle. The vehicle is first in a line of eight stranded on Siberia Belt, Ingol Beach. Six feet in front of it is a fallen tree. Before I approached the pick-up the only footprints in the snow to the rear were those of John Blickling Holt, one of the other drivers, who walked forward shortly after the convoy became stranded, and then returned to his own car – a Vauxhall Corsa. Those footprints have now been supplemented by my own, and those of DS George Valentine, who has joined me to examine the scene. There are no signs of any other footprints to the offside of the vehicle, or in front. I'm asking DS Valentine to check that observation now.'

Valentine looked back into the headlights of the Alfa Romeo, along the bank above the star-studded water of the marsh, and ahead to the fallen tree.

'Check the other side,' said Shaw, handing him a heavy-duty torch.

Valentine stepped across the rear of the truck, noting a pool of urine staining the snow by the nearside rear wheel arch, paw prints scattered nearby. Immediately below him was the deep gash of the dyke ditch. Looking back along the line of traffic he could see that after about eighty yards the ditch disappeared into a brick culvert which ran into a sluice gate – the point at which they'd crossed over from the sands. The snow over the top of the sluice and around it had been untouched when they'd climbed across. The bank on the far side of the truck was a sinuous sheet of silver white, with no sign of disturbance.

He edged back. 'Nothing – no one's been in or out.'

Shaw clicked the recorder and held it to Valentine's face. 'For the record,' he said.

Valentine's hooded eyes opened a few millimetres beyond normal. He'd never quite got used to taking orders from people twenty years younger than he was. He'd been a DI himself until they'd busted him after Jack Shaw's last case, and he'd been to more crime scenes than Peter Shaw had been to university lectures.

He took a deep breath and gave a short statement: detailed, professional, a forensic précis Shaw couldn't have bettered.

Shaw cut the recording and looked Valentine in the eyes. He thought for the first time that he might have underestimated him, and he reminded himself that trust was not one of his strong suits. So he made himself ask the question. 'What do you think?'

Valentine wasn't a whiz, and he certainly wasn't a kid, but the job ran as deep in his veins as it did in Peter Shaw's. It wasn't that he couldn't analyse a crime scene. He'd done it a thousand times. He just trusted his instinct more than a fat textbook of procedural logic. So what did instinct tell him now?

'It's two crimes,' he said. 'This killing's vicious, angry, unplanned. But signs of entry and exit are non-existent. The killer just vanishes, coolly.' He took a breath, looking towards the sea. 'And then there's the other corpse – down on the beach. Two hundred yards away, a bit more. Where does that fit in?' He squatted down, looking under the truck. Nothing. 'He could have jumped, from the cab here, into the marsh . . .'

Shaw looked unimpressed, although he didn't have a better scenario. 'Why? Why risk drowning, or freezing to death, just to avoid leaving a footprint? And the splash would have caught someone's attention.'

Valentine's jaw began to vibrate with the cold.

'We need pictures,' said Shaw.

Valentine shrugged. 'Shouldn't we wait for Tom's boys from CSI?' he asked. 'What's the rush?'

'Well. Two reasons, I guess,' said Shaw, talking to himself

as much as to Valentine. 'First, I'm no meteorologist but a freezing still night doesn't last for ever. What if the snow melts? Or there's a fresh fall? Or rain? Second, and I'm sure I don't have to remind you of this, our first responsibility is to protect life. The elderly man in the car needs hospital treatment fast. The chopper's on its way and if they put her down on the sands as close as they can to limit the stretcher distance then every snowflake within a hundred yards will get a second opportunity to fall. So. We need to record the scene to the best of our abilities – OK?'

Valentine buttoned the top of his raincoat. He'd been out of serious front-line policing for a decade and was honest enough to know he needed to sharpen up his act. Shaw was right in his summary. But that didn't make it any easier to take.

From his pocket Shaw produced a small digital camera.

'Not admissible,' said Valentine, before he could stop himself. All specialist forensic photography was on film, reducing any chance of digital enhancement. No court would accept a digital image.

'Thank you for that,' said Shaw, failing to suppress his irritation at being picked up by his own DS. 'But we need a record,' he added. 'Even if we can't take it into court. I'll get what shots I can ... Meanwhile get Control. Tell 'em what we've got. We're getting CSI anyway for the victim on the beach – and the pathologist – but we need back-up. More bodies in uniforms. We need transport for the witnesses, and somewhere we can take them for the paperwork. We need statements, names, addresses, the lot.

And no one goes home until we've had independent confirmation of their ID.'

'Somewhere warm . . .' said Valentine, taking a breath, 'would be nice.'

Shaw looked along the coast towards the lights he'd seen from the beach. 'Tell 'em to try Gallow Marsh Farm. If they've got a barn we could use that, but the unit will have to bring some air heaters. And we need a catering unit.'

He patted his jacket pockets. 'What have I missed?'

There were times, thought Valentine, when Shaw looked like his father. Something in the face, but something subtle, the way he seemed to focus on the mid-distance when he was thinking. Valentine leant in the driver's window, looking around the tomb that the truck cab had become, trying not to glimpse the victim's face. The side pocket in the driver's door was empty except for a single piece of neatly folded paper. Valentine lifted it clear with his gloved fingers. It was an invoice. Beneath it was a pair of spark plugs. He leant in closer, and sniffed.

'Old plugs,' he said.

'So?' said Shaw.

'Rusted. Plugs don't rust in situ,' explained Valentine. 'Too much oil about. If they'd been taken out recently they'd give off that burnt smell . . . but there's nothing.' He pointed at the tiny question mark of the contact points. Dull metal, a blush of oxidized steel.

The pick-up's engine still ran, the heating system clattering.

'So he took them out, left them there, they rusted. What's the problem?' asked Shaw. But he knew that wasn't

44

right. The interior of the cab was immaculately tidy. A pocket road atlas, a torch in the side pocket of the passenger door. No litter, except the empty packet of Hula Hoops folded neatly into the ashtray, and the half-eaten apple, set on a tissue so that it didn't mark the dashboard. The footwells had been swept. He opened the glove compartment: a Haynes manual for the model, an AA card. The carpet had been vacuumed recently, the plastic foot mats washed.

Then two things happened at the same time. They heard the first flutter of the helicopter blades along the coast. Within seconds it was with them, hanging in the air with the stars, an RAF Coastal Rescue, the bay doors open to reveal two men in full flight gear and crash helmets. The pilot brought it down to thirty feet and then began to edge closer, trying to find a spot as close to the dyke ditch as he could get without losing his safety margin. The snow began to rise about them.

And as Shaw turned away, looking down the line of cars, he saw the teenager in the baseball cap crawling back up the bank from the marsh. He reached the top, then stood and broke into a run. Shaw watched him for twenty yards before he slipped again, almost down into the ditch on the far side. He knelt for a few seconds, looking back at the cars, and Shaw guessed he was considering a return to the warmth of the Mondeo. But instead he turned away and began to run, into the half-light first, and then into the night itself.

## 8

Gallow Marsh Farm lay sunk in the snow, as if the weight on the roof had pushed it down into the damp sandy soil. Firelight flickered in the Georgian windows of the old kitchen. Inside, Shaw and Valentine sat at a plain deal table, the statements of the six witnesses left at the scene spread out in neat piles. Attached to each was a set of CSI pictures of their vehicles; interior and exterior, plus a set of Polaroid shots of each witness. Black and white prints; Shaw always insisted on that, so that he could study the faces in stark relief. Across the hallway the living room had been set aside for the witnesses, a nervous, over-excited party, each now dressed in the plain white SOC suits they had been allocated while their own clothes were taken for forensic examination in Lynn.

The mobile police canteen, parked in the farmyard, had produced coffee, tea and soup, hot dogs and cake. The farmer's wife had donated a bottle of Johnnie Walker and what was left of the Christmas store of Gordon's gin. A small bowl of dog food had been supplied for the Jack Russell, which had been shut in a utility room behind the kitchen. A uniformed PC stayed with the witnesses to make sure the conversation did not include any discussion of the events of the evening so far.

A cheap wooden 1930s clock on the windowsill read 11.30 p.m. The kitchen was an odd amalgam of two ages:

the original Victorian Aga clashing badly with the silver fridge-freezer, a dishwasher and washing machine, which had been running since they'd first arrived two hours earlier. A plastic laundry basket held children's clothes. Over the range were two photographs: a farmer and his wife standing by a hand-pump, a horse tethered to a stone block, and a snapshot of a child – a girl aged six or seven – hugging a black kitten.

Shaw took the limpet shells from his pocket and laid eight in a line, returning two to his pocket. 'Right,' he said. 'Eight vehicles. First in line the victim – no name as yet. Pathologist is with the body on site.' He felt the familiar thrill of the hunt, the intellectual buzz of the unsolved puzzle. In the silence he could hear Valentine's watch ticking.

'Second in line . . .' He looked at the statement. 'Sarah Baker-Sibley in the Alfa Romeo.'

'Posh bitch,' said Valentine.

'Thank you for that,' said Shaw. 'Least we know who we're talking about. Third. The Corsa. John Holt – latest?'

Valentine had radioed the Queen Victoria hospital on the half hour since the helicopter had left Ingol Beach.

'The hospital says he's comfortable – comfortable for someone who's had a heart attack.' Valentine shook his head, trying to fight off the tiredness that was making his bones drag him down. 'DC Campbell's with him – if he talks, she'll shout, but she says he's drugged up to the eyeballs. Wife's with him too.'

'Right. Fourth vehicle – the Volvo. Stanley Zhao of the

Emerald Garden. That's one takeaway dinner that won't get delivered. Fifth. North Norfolk Security. His statement's clear enough. But I've seen him somewhere, and he's seen me. Criminal record – I'm sure of it. Let's check that first thing. Name again?'

'Shreeves,' said Valentine. 'Jonah Shreeves.' He hadn't checked the statement, and Shaw wondered if he'd committed all the names to memory.

'Next?'

'Express Plumbers. Fred Parlour and Sean Harper.'

'Parlour's head wound – we need to check that, double-check it.'

Valentine took an extra breath. Shaw shuffled papers. 'Then the old dear in the Morris, Cynthia Pryce, and eighth the Mondeo. That's a full house.'

Shaw stood up and moved over to the window. His eye throbbed beneath the dressing. The farmyard was packed with vehicles: the mobile canteen, the CSI mobile lab, the diving unit's van and back-up, two squad cars, and the police bus which had ferried out a steady stream of uniformed officers for the fingertip search of the beach. The yard, the snow untouched when they'd picked their way in, was now a weave of frozen tracks, and jagged ruptured ice. On the far side was the old stable block in brick with the wooden dovecote lit a harsh aluminium white on the pitched roof.

Valentine looked at his Rolex, annoyed that the second hand had suddenly started moving. 'They're sending out taxis for the witnesses, we'll start letting them go home.' He managed to squeeze in an extra breath: 'Soon.'

'We've double-checked IDs for the lot?'

'Sean Harper – the apprentice in the plumbers' van – lives alone. But Parlour – his boss – vouches for him and we've checked Parlour with his wife. Those we can check are all who they say they are.'

'Unless the dog's really a Great Dane,' said Shaw, pacing the cork-tiled floor, as reluctant as ever to take a chair, his joints screaming for the release of exercise.

The door opened and the farmer's wife, Isabel Dereham, came in, stamping on the flagged floor. She was in her mid-thirties and slight, but she hauled another plastic basket's worth of dirty clothes in front of the washing machine with no apparent effort. Her arms and hands were suntanned, the tendons taut and strong. The sleepless nights, the hard physical work, the stress of running a farm were all in her face. And a restless energy, so that she didn't look at home in her own kitchen. But there was something else too, and it wasn't far from beauty. She flexed her wrists, relieving a pain, and smiled, the line of her lips slightly crooked. Shaw noticed that the upper and lower edges of her lips were marked by a natural red line: a textbook example of the vermilion border.

'More coffee?' she asked, pushing mousey hair off her forehead.

'I'm sorry – we're in the way, Mrs Dereham,' said Shaw.

'Well – yes. Yes you are, Inspector.' She kicked the empty washing basket. 'But I guess you'd rather be at home . . .' She put her hands on her head, closing her eyes, resting, and Shaw watched her breasts rise under the rough shirt she wore. Beautiful? Yes: the body beneath unhidden despite the clothes. 'It's Izzy, by the way.'

'Izzy,' said Shaw.

'Look. I have to get down to the beach,' she said. 'The oyster beds; the storm will have rocked the cages. Oysters are money, Inspector, big money. Unfortunately, I just manage them. But I do need to check. Is that OK?'

'Sure. Just keep off Ingol Beach.'

'My daughter's asleep upstairs. Natalie. I've explained you're here. She won't be a problem.'

When she left the cold air blew in, making the fire crackle.

They checked their mobiles on the tabletop, the signal bars blank.

'So what happened on Siberia Belt tonight?' asked Shaw.

It was a rhetorical question, but Valentine didn't spot it. He checked his notes. 'The first squad car up Siberia Belt said there was no trace of the detour sign that all of the drivers swear was on the corner when they left the main road. The diving unit back-up came from Cromer to the other end of Siberia Belt and there was no sign at that end either. But the junction's opposite a cottage and the owner swears he saw a no-entry sign there at around the right time, but he didn't see it put up, or taken down. So that's it – diversion at one end, no entry at the other, then both disappear.'

'What about the AA?' asked Shaw.

'Nope. Same with County Highways, RAC, traffic control. No one put a sign out.'

Shaw poured more coffee. 'So it's a trap for the victim. They get him off the road, he never gets where he's going – unless it was the cemetery, of course.' He looked into the fire, thinking of the victim's truck, the single line of footprints there and back.

'There's one thing that works,' said Valentine. 'Holt. The old bloke in the Corsa. He goes forward. How long does it take? A single blow, then he leaves him to bleed to death.'

'Where's the murder weapon?'

'In the coat – it's big enough.'

'True. He could have had an accomplice under it, and a getaway car. But the Baker-Sibley woman's statement is clear – he kept his hands in his pockets. He didn't lean in. She watched him.'

'She could be wrong.' Valentine shrugged. 'Maybe she looked away, it only takes a second. Then chummy bleeds to death – slowly. Death throes, that's what you saw from the hill, what she saw through the back window.'

Shaw undid the top button of his shirt – he never wore a tie. 'But there's a plan. We know someone put out the signs, then took them back in. Meticulous, premeditated. Then the killer takes a chance like that? That the witnesses are looking the other way when he strikes? Makes no sense.'

'I'm just saying it's all that works,' said Valentine, his jaw set.

'It is. Which is another good reason for keeping a round-the-clock watch at Holt's bedside – so fix it. But let's not get too excited. There's no trace of blood on Holt. Not a drop. However, he is the last person to see the victim alive, so we need to interview him as quickly as possible. We'll start the spade work in the morning,' added Shaw. 'We need to re-interview them all – check for inconsistencies, backgrounds, look for links. Check again. Anyone else?'

Valentine tipped back the coffee cup, letting the last gritty granules fire up the taste buds on his tongue. 'The runaway kid. Why run? And why run then? St James's is on to the Mondeo's registration – should be an hour, less.'

'But he's not a killer, is he?'

Valentine stretched his arms aloft, the joints cracking.

'We won't get anything tonight.' Shaw stood. 'Let's touch base first thing. We'll need to come back in daylight anyway – I've told them to keep the vehicles in situ until then. But the fact is that even by daylight the problem is still the same: we've got a murder scene with no footprints in and no footprints out.'

Valentine flapped his raincoat in front of the fire. 'Let's find a motive. Worry about footprints in the snow later . . .'

There was a silence again. Shaw remembered something his father had said about George Valentine. That when it came to the textbook he worked backwards: he found the criminal first, then the evidence which linked them to the crime. Had there been an unspoken inference: that if he couldn't find the evidence, he'd make it up?

'Right – anyone else?' asked Shaw.

Valentine rubbed the pouched skin below his eyes. 'The Chinky in the takeaway Volvo?'

Shaw winced at the casual racism, wondering if Valentine had said it deliberately. As far as his DS was concerned PC was something you stuck on your desk and didn't want to use.

'The victim in the inflatable floated in off the sands,' said Valentine, wiping his nose with a grey bundle of cotton. 'That's the cockle-pickers' territory. OK – there are Lynn-based gangs out there, legit operations, but we know the Chinese run them too, and run most of the dodgy ones.'

Shaw went to speak.

'Perhaps they've got something going, the Chinese . . . people smuggling?' Valentine continued.

Shaw shook his head. 'One guy on a raft and he's European. We had illegals coming in last year, but the trade's dried up since the Coastguard started patrolling the Wash. That's stopped it – and stopped it dead.'

'OK,' said Valentine. 'Ciggies, then; drugs? We don't know what the bloke on the beach might have had in that raft before he died. So there's a welcoming party, one of the cars that's stranded on Siberia Belt. Just because there's a detour sign doesn't mean none of them wanted to be there.'

Shaw was listening now.

'So they get snarled up in the snow,' said Valentine. 'An argument about what to do. Low life, falling out. Do we stay, do we run? Who's got the money?' He stopped, hauling up his ribs to draw air into his lungs. 'Do we get paid? We know the score with these people. It's all sweetness and light until the shit flies, then they tear each other apart. Someone gets the chisel for their trouble.'

Shaw's back stiffened. 'And then the murderer disappears without leaving a footprint. How does that work?'

'Don't know,' said Valentine, checking his watch.

Completeness wasn't one of his concerns. He was a detective, not a train-spotter.

Two doors led out of the kitchen. One into the hall and to the living room beyond, the other into a makeshift office. They could hear a woman's voice: Sarah Baker-Sibley. Each witness had been offered one call on the landline, and they could hear her talking; the speech pattern oddly modulated, tiredness perhaps, blended with stress. Valentine had got a message through to her daughter's voicemail via the control room at St James's while they were out on Siberia Belt. Three messages, in fact: stay at home; check the security lights were on; pizza in the fridge.

'God,' they heard her say, stressed out. 'OK, OK. Look, pass me over . . .'

They heard the phone go down on the hook suddenly so Valentine opened the door to usher her back to the living room. But she'd picked up the phone again. 'I'm sorry – we got cut off. Do you mind? . . . I need to ring again.' She was desperate, and Shaw knew that no one could have stopped her making a second call. The tyranny of children.

Valentine shrugged. 'Then the car's ready, OK? You'll be home in twenty minutes,' he said, closing the door.

Shaw pressed his forehead against the cold glass of the kitchen window. A line of taxis was edging through the farmyard gates.

They heard footsteps on ice outside the door. It was Izzy Dereham, back from checking the oyster beds. 'Storm's turned a couple of the frames,' she said, walking briskly to the sink, scrubbing her hands.

'Is that your van? The white Ford in the barn?' asked Valentine.

'Sure. We run the oysters in it.'

'Where?' pressed Valentine.

'Shark Tooth.' It was one of the town's newest companies, commercial shellfish mainly, having started out running boats for tourists to catch North Sea dogfish, based up the coast from Lynn at Wootton Marsh.

'They own this place,' said Dereham. 'I'm just a tenant. But you know, I've got plans . . .' She looked up to where her child was sleeping. 'Bit of arable, dairy herd, it could be a decent farm this . . . but the quick money's in the oysters.'

'Your husband?' asked Shaw, knowing instantly it was the right question.

'Patrick died.'

'I'm sorry.'

Shaw touched the picture over the fireplace taken on a farm. Something crossed Izzy's face, an expression so fleeting as to be subliminal. Grief thought Shaw, and something else, expertly hidden.

'I was born there – up the coast,' she said. 'That was our farm, before the bailiffs moved in.'

The door to the back room opened and Sarah Baker-Sibley came through. She was going to say something but the phone rang behind her. Valentine went through to answer.

'I've finished,' she announced, and Shaw noticed the hard edge to her voice. 'My daughter's at home, she's fine.' She tried to look relieved but didn't get her face right. Shaw wondered what was wrong. 'Thank you,' she added, slipping out under cover of a smile.

Valentine appeared at the door, covering the mouthpiece on the phone. 'It's St James's. Bad news. I got them to match all the car regs. They did a cross-check with the day diary. The Mondeo – reported as stolen by the owner at 7.30 p.m. tonight.'

It was late and Shaw was tired, almost too tired to let the thought take shape. Valentine shuffled the papers on the kitchen table, looking at the CSI pictures, setting apart the shots of the Mondeo. A stolen car, so they might never find the young driver.

'Thought so,' said Valentine, spinning one of the CSI prints round so that Shaw could see. It was an interior shot of the Mondeo. 'The kid does a runner,' he said, his voice suddenly animated. 'Panics when he knows we'll nab him for the theft. But he makes sure he takes something with him . . .'

'What?' asked Shaw.

'A snakeskin steering-wheel cover. Chevrons, black and white. Distinctive.' He pressed a stubby finger into the shot, leaving a greasy print.

# 9

The cobblestones along St James's glistened like pebbles on the beach. Police HQ was a curved brick 1960s block with civic pretensions, the single Victorian blue lamp salvaged from its predecessor down in the old town. The snow was turning to sleet, then rain, sheets of it thrown in off the sea falling through the floodlight that still played on Greyfriars Tower, a medieval stump which stood in waste ground opposite St James's. Under the styleless portico of police headquarters, held up by four square brick pillars, two uniformed constables manhandled a half-naked youth towards the doors, the young man's knotted back a riot of illustration: an anchor, a dancing girl, a military badge.

Valentine sniffed the pungent kick of meths on the night breeze and walked down towards the quay. He'd got a lift back into town with a CSI unit, and the trip had woken him up. The pub sign outside his local, the Artichoke, swung in the rain, no lights within. He stood for a moment beside Captain George Vancouver's statue on the waterside. This was where he'd always had a cigarette, the last one before home. He took a double lungful of night air, his shoulders aching with the effort. A day without cigarettes had left him feeling no better, no worse.

He considered the bronze statue, wondering what the

explorer would have made of the condom someone had hung from his outstretched finger. In the glistening mud below a crab scuttled, leaving a complex hieroglyph in its wake.

Staring into the mud, he thought about the old girl in the Morris in the line of cars on Siberia Belt. Nice woman, old money. He'd helped her out of the car and then she said she'd forgotten her glasses. He offered to get them out of the glove compartment but she'd said not to bother, her voice edging just too high to be natural. They'd take her car into the pound tomorrow, so there was no hurry. He'd find out what she didn't want him to see. And one other thing that kept snagging his brain. The ladders on the Corsa's roof. He'd get the CSI report on those. Check the length.

He walked over the narrow wooden footbridge which crossed the Purfleet and made his way along the King's Staithe to the maze of terraced streets he'd lived in all his life. He stopped on the corner of Greenland Street. The central heating at home would be off. He hadn't understood the timing mechanism when his wife was alive, and the secret had died with her. She'd been buried in the churchyard at All Saints' and sometimes he went by on the way home. Not tonight. A cat sat in the middle of the road like a fur hat, its eyes as green as the paper dragon set in the fanlight of the end house: once a shop, its downstairs window curved around the corner gracefully, a door set within the arc. Behind the glass a handwritten sign in Chinese characters.

He knew the sound they made. *Yat ye hoi p'i.*

Here, on the corner of a rain-soaked street, a warm

light shone: a green light, shining through a paper lantern. Walking forward, he looked left and right and knocked quickly twice, then paused, then twice again. He heard footsteps and felt happy for the first time that day.

# 10

*Tuesday, 10 February*

The eight vehicles of the stranded convoy stood in the light of the rising moon, the cold blue streak of dawn in the east as raw and unwelcome as the scream of an alarm clock. Shaw had slept for three hours in the CSI back-up van. He'd been a poor sleeper since childhood. So he was used to waking up in the dark.

But he wasn't used to waking up anywhere that wasn't home. Lena, his wife, said he was a homing pigeon, always circling back towards the loft. The contrast with his father was, as always, stark. Jack Shaw had liked working nights, sleeping at St James's when a case was on, living the job. So his father's life had been a secret from him; one of the reasons he'd been drawn to the same career, to find out, in little ways, what his father's life had been like, to see how closely the real world snapped into place beside the one he'd imagined.

So when he'd woken in the CSI van he felt a familiar frisson of anxiety, the loss of something just beyond his understanding. He thought about texting home, but knew it was too early. And there'd still be no mobile signal. The night before he'd relayed a message through St James's, telling Lena he'd be out overnight. But he wanted to hear her voice.

He'd got up quickly, trudging through the snow in the dark to the mobile canteen to re-read the witness statements, drinking a pint of bitumen-strength coffee. Others came for hot soup, tea and coffee too, but little was said. Everyone was tired, looking forward to seeing the sun. But that moment was still an hour away, more.

Shaw tried to think of the day ahead as separate from that which had gone before. Day Two: a time to take stock, step back, let the adrenaline fade. But the intensity of the images from the previous evening were too strong to dismiss: the blood-caked mouth of the man he'd pulled out of the sea; the crumpled figure at the wheel of the pick-up truck, impaled. The buzz was still electric, an intensity of consciousness, which made Peter Shaw feel very alive. He suppressed the excitement, aware that this was a drug to which his father had become addicted, the living of a life through the deaths of others. He'd wondered if that was why his father had made just that one rule: that his son could do anything with his life except become a policeman.

Shaw craved his own drug: the surge of endorphins, the rush of blood, the certainty of well-being that came with pushing himself to run, to swim, and to run again. He checked his map. The coast road was almost exactly a mile away. He set the stopwatch going on his wrist and began to run, despite the lightweight boots he wore, and when he found his footing secure in the crisp deep snow, he opened up into a wide, easy pace. The lights of the road came into view all too quickly and he slowed to a halt: 4 minutes 43 seconds. His body cried out for him to carry on, to push himself until his bloodstream pumped like a central-heating system. But he had to stop, and he felt his temperature rising inside the waterproof jacket.

He bent double, his palms in the snow, then straightened. His mobile buzzed, picking up text messages he'd been unable to receive overnight within the dead zone on Siberia Belt. He scrolled down: three from Lena, all pictures. His daughter in bed, a book folded over her head where it had dropped from her hands as she fell asleep, a snowman on the beach in front of the house, and one of Lena – cowering out of the wind on the veranda, taken by his daughter.

He jogged back along Siberia Belt, looking steadily ahead, imagining the cars the previous night, edging their way through the snow towards the sharp right-hand turn just before Gallow Marsh Farm. He rounded the bend and saw the stranded convoy. Each car and van sealed with signed plastic tags on the door handles and boots – except the Alfa, where he could see the CSI team still at work, the gentle buzz of a forensic vacuum within. The victim's truck was hidden within a SOC tent, lit like a Chinese lantern. Ahead, the pine tree still blocked the road, but beyond it stood a fire rescue vehicle, and behind that an ambulance, blue lights silently flashing. Both emergency vehicles were parked in a lay-by Shaw had not noticed before, built to allow cars to pass each other on the narrow track.

The sound of a chainsaw serrated the silence and amongst the pine's branches Shaw could see movement, the last of the snow falling from the needles.

Tom Hadden, the force's senior crime scene investigator, was buried within, while a fireman cut wood on the far side. Hadden was civilian branch, a former govern-ment scientist with the Home Office. He'd taken early retirement, moved up to the coast alone, leaving a divorce in north London. He'd brought his bird-watching binocu-lars with him, and one of the best brains in the country in forensic science. He was fifty-five, red hair now turning strawberry blond, his face obscured by freckles and lesions. He'd had some ops for skin cancer, Shaw knew, and he always looked healthier in the dark. He had a curious habit of closing his eyes when answering a ques-tion he thought was important.

'Anything?' asked Shaw, knowing he could leave the pleasantries aside.

Hadden struggled to turn his head amongst the pine branches. 'Well. I'm pretty sure it's a tree.'

Shaw pressed in amongst the pine needles, which released a wave of pungent scent. 'How'd she come down?'

'Three blows,' said Hadden, reaching forward, parting branches to reveal the trunk, neatly severed by a series of axe blows. 'Instant roadblock. I'd say it wasn't the first time our woodman had swung an axe.'

Shaw recalled George Valentine's summary of the crime: on one hand a disregard for leaving clues – the victim left to die in the cab, now the axe marks – combined with the complete absence of footprints.

'Anything else I should know now?'

Hadden extricated himself, a kneecap clicking as he did so. 'Pathologist is still at work,' he said. 'I think we'll leave her to it, don't you?'

The pronoun told Shaw all he needed to know. There

was only one female pathologist working regularly with West Norfolk: Dr Justina Kazimierz; and it would indeed be best to leave her to finish her work in peace.

Edging past the pick-up they came to the Alfa, and Shaw noticed a small flag marked with an 'A' below the driver's window.

'Ciggy butt – menthol,' said Hadden, not stopping. 'Common brand.' Shaw leant in at the Alfa's open window. The interior smelt of money: soft leather and scent. A child's picture was stuck on the dashboard, a girl with long hair, the ashtray bristled with dog-ends soiled with lipstick.

Behind that the old man's Corsa. For the first time Shaw noticed the car had been vandalized: scratched lines, crossing, peaked like a hat, an angry inchoate scrawl.

'They're fresh,' said Hadden. 'A month old, maybe less. My guess is a diamond cutter – see how deeply the metal is scored. Nothing casual.'

They walked on. 'Time of death on the victim, Tom?' asked Shaw, smiling, the perfect teeth in a surfer's grin. He'd never been surprised by the fact that in ten years of CID work he'd failed to get a straight answer to that question. He didn't expect one now.

Hadden removed a pair of thin forensic gloves with theatrical care and his eyes closed. 'Not my area, clearly – as you well know. Pathologist is the expert on that and she's with the body – but you'll get less of an answer from her than you will from me. I took her to the body last night; that's the only time I've seen the victim. So – outside temperature was freezing, inside the cab perhaps twenty degrees or more. Temperature gradient like that makes estimating the time of death difficult. The rigor had set in, but was short of complete. Two to five hours is a good working hypothesis. But that only holds if the body was inside the cab for that period: outside, much longer.'

Shaw checked his watch. The CSI team had arrived at 9 p.m., the pathologist at 9.45. So death occurred somewhere between 4.45 and 7.45 that evening. The convoy had come to rest at around 5.15. Given that dead men don't drive, that meant the victim died between 5.15 and 7.45.

But no footprints except Holt's, and he didn't have the time to deliver the fatal blow if Baker-Sibley's evidence was sound. Shaw shook his head. He was missing something. He forced himself to lower his shoulders, releasing his neck muscles.

Shaw looked back up the line to the tent over the victim's truck. 'Prints in the victim's vehicle?'

'Yeah – it's like a sweet-shop counter. We need to input them all, get them on the database. You don't get many crime scenes with this many potential murderers in situ. We need to mix and match, see what comes up.'

Shaw tried to empty his head, switching crimes, trying not to make any assumptions which might derail the investigation before it had even started. 'Anything from the beach – the corpse in the raft?'

'Standard make, beach-shop inflatable – we'll check it out, but one of the uniforms said his kids had one. Argos sell them as well. Nothing else in the thing with him – except a pint or so of blood. We presume it's his blood – but it's just that at the moment. A presumption. Nothing on the tide-line, except your barrel of toxic waste. He's been dead a while, by the way. Twenty-four hours, perhaps more.'

Shaw pressed his thumb and forefinger on either side of the bridge of his nose. Finding the yellow oil drum seemed like a distant memory. 'I need to see inside the truck cab,' he said.

'Sure.' Hadden smiled. 'I'll leave you that pleasure. She'll have an ID once the jacket's off, with luck.'

Hadden set off for the beach, Shaw for the tent over the victim's truck. He approached it slowly, making sure his footfalls gave due warning of his approach. Dr Kazimierz was a woman who didn't suffer fools gladly, and thought almost everyone was a fool. She worked in silence, and valued it in others. And she worked alone, even in a crowd.

The first thing he saw was that the body was still in place. Dr Kazimierz held the head up by the chin, looking into the eyes, the chisel still in place in the left socket. For a second Shaw saw the scene differently, two lovers perhaps, folding together their personal spaces. Then she leant forward and, with a pair of tweezers, removed something from an eyebrow. She held it in the light of a torch she'd taped to the headrest: a hair. She pocketed it in a clear plastic evidence bag, quickly sealing and signing the sticky label.

She looked up, ready to dismiss whoever had interrupted her. But when she saw Shaw she nodded, the merest hint of an acknowledgement. Then she cut a short length of tape, using the sticky side to lift a series of particles from the victim's overalls.

'I'm done in five,' she said, bagging the evidence. 'Exterior's clean now if you want to circle.'

Shaw wondered what Justina Kazimierz had looked like in her youth. He imagined a school photograph perhaps, a face not yet overwhelmed by heavy middle-European features, dark brown eyes showing off her olive skin. He'd been to her fiftieth birthday party at the Polish Club in the North End, an occasion marked by blood sausage and iced vodka with all the subtlety of lighter fuel. She'd danced then, with her husband, a diminutive man with delicate hands, light rapid steps despite her sturdy build.

Shaw circled the vehicle, squeezed between the tent and the bodywork. The tax was up to date, the registration plate the right year for the model, the tyres almost new. The paintwork was off-white, with a signwritten panel: Fry & Sons, Builders, followed by a Lynn telephone number and a website address. The tailgate was chipped and scraped in places, with rust showing in the hinges. The tarpaulin had been folded back to reveal several sheets of plasterboard, some insulating board and a bundle of wooden wainscoting.

Returning to the front of the vehicle, Shaw found the pathologist sitting on a camp stool. Plastic evidence bottles were arranged in groups on a collapsible table, glass phials laid in a plastic box, a black briefcase open to reveal a line of tools, torches, tapes and camera lenses.

Through the windscreen the dead man's head could be seen, thrown back now, the chisel protruding up as if it had been an arrow that fell to earth.

'How's *your* eye?' she asked, taking Shaw by surprise.

'We'll know soon enough – it depends on the chemical type, apparently. It's still sealed. There's nothing they can do but wait. Nothing I can do. We'll know when they take the stitches out of the lids. But they're hopeful – very hopeful.'

'Good,' she said. 'Don't forget the worst might happen.'

Embarrassed by the intimacy, he looked through the truck's windscreen at the victim. 'How do you think he died?' he asked, and they both laughed. In Shaw's experience corpses fell into two distinct categories: those which echoed the human life that had recently fled, and those which seemed effortlessly to acquire the status of cold meat. This one, he reflected, was already on the butcher's counter.

'Wallet? Papers?' he asked, pushing the image aside.

'I'll have to cut through the clothes to get to the pocket,' she said. 'I need help; you'll do.' Even though she looked away, Shaw knew that the honour had been calculated, even if it had been so ungraciously bestowed. When he'd first met Justina Kazimierz Shaw had put her brutal rudeness down to unfamiliarity with a new language. That was a decade ago.

'Now. Here,' she said, indicating a bulge at chest level beneath the overalls. 'We need this?' It was his call. They could remove the body, get it back to the lab and cut the clothes off there. Doing it this way risked destroying evidence, but gave the inquiry a vital head start if they could get an ID. He knew what his father would have done, which made him hesitate.

'Go ahead,' he said at last, holding the cloth taut as she

cut down with a pair of scissors. The fabric parted to reveal the top edge of a wallet held in a shirt pocket. A single cut with a scalpel opened the pocket so that the wallet could be lifted clear. She held it in a gloved hand and transferred it to the evidence table outside the vehicle, slipping it into a large forensic envelope, then opening it. They could both read a business card in a cellophane compartment.

## Harvey Ellis

Carpenter/plasterer/builder

Two telephone numbers: a landline and a mobile. A Lynn address: a block of seventies flats on land reclaimed from the estuary.

On the flip side of the compartment was a picture. A boy, age impossible to guess, the hair shaved clean of a white skull, a feeding tube to the nose. And the kind of smile that's for other people. Shaw turned to look at the photo hanging from the rear-view mirror, the family shot. Same kid, just less of his life left to live.

Dr Kazimierz had seen something else. The corpse's right hand had fallen to the side as they'd cut into the fabric of the overalls, revealing six inches of skin above the wrist. She could see another wound, a cut leading to a puncture near the crook of the elbow, blood caked in the sleeve itself. 'Looks like he managed to ward off one blow at least,' she said.

Shaw thought about Holt leaning in at the Vauxhall window. One blow unseen, perhaps, but two?

'The distribution of blood on the victim is the first

problem. Here . . .' She used a wooden pointer from her overall pocket to indicate the ruptured eye socket. 'The blood has pooled here, and here . . .' She lightly tapped the collarbones on either side of the small depression below the Adam's apple. 'Then it flows over the shoulder and under the body. There is some blood on the seat, and in the footwell – and that's slightly scuffed by the way.'

'All of which means?'

'I think he bled on his back – and was then placed in the van where death occurred. Also, at some point he emptied his bladder – there are traces of urine in the clothes. But there's none on the seat. Again – points to the lethal attack taking place somewhere else.'

'*Outside* the van?'

'Clearly. The chisel's shaft caught the ocular bone and fractured it, then sheared off into the soft tissue at the rear of the eye, then into the anterior lobe of the brain,' she said, snapping off the forensic gloves. 'I think he lost a lot of blood then – blood that is not at the scene. Then he was put in the driver's seat, where he died.' Shaw imagined the impact of the chisel blade, the internal crunch of the bone giving way, the painless thrust into the brain.

'So,' said Shaw. 'To sum up. I've got a murder scene with no footprints and no blood.'

'Least you've got a corpse,' said Kazimierz.

Shaw parked the Land Rover in its usual slot beside the lifeboat station, triggering a security floodlight. The building was wooden, a throwback to the fifties, with Dutch gables. Beside it stood the new building, steel, with blue metal beams exposed. He unlocked the side door and slipped into the darkness.

The hovercraft sat on its deflated rubber skirt like a cat in a basket. His eyes constructed it out of the shadows and the ambient light seeping in through the high double-glazed windows. She was perfect for working out on the sands, up the shallow creeks and over the mud flats of the Wash. Shaw sniffed the air: detergent, engine oil and polish. He reached out and flicked a single switch, bathing her in light, the paintwork polished to a deep orange patina, the two rear fans gleaming in silver and black. He felt a rush of excitement and a sense of being home. The adrenaline made him want to run, so he locked up quickly and set off along the beach in the half-light of dawn.

The clouds out at sea delayed the moment when the sun would break free and start the day. The sands stretched ahead of him. In winter nothing moved here but the sand. A mile distant he could see home: a low wooden building with a long veranda, behind it a stone cottage, beyond that the old boathouse, beach stones strung over the felt roof to keep it down in the storms. Lena had taken the leasehold on the Old Beach Café a year before: a dream priced at £80,000. No access road, no mains electricity and accounts that showed an annual trading loss of £2,000. The stone cottage and boathouse were part of the deal. Both listed, both dilapidated.

A busy year. Lena was organized, businesslike in pursuit of an ambition. The stone cottage was watertight now, the café stripped pine with an Italian coffee machine gleaming like a vintage motorbike, the boathouse converted to sell everything the sporty London beach crowd wanted: surfboards to wetsuits, hang gliders to sailboards. The exterior wooden panels of the café had been painted alternate yellow and blue. Shaw could see the flag hanging limply from the pole over the shop: a silver surfer on a blue sea. His seven-year-old daughter's discarded summer swimsuit hung on a hook by the outside water tap, bleached by the rain.

He sat on the stoop, planning a dawn swim in the winter wetsuit, trying to focus only on the forthcoming rush of icy white water. But two things gatecrashed his mind: if Sarah Baker-Sibley's daughter was alone at home to whom had she passed the phone when her mother asked her to? And then there were the spark plugs in the pick-up's door pocket. Rusted. Spent. But Harvey Ellis's cab had been otherwise neat. Unless the truck was rarely used – an unlikely scenario – then the plugs had not been in an engine for several months. He saw the tiny metal question mark of the spark plug's contact points. Corroded, black, scarred by the constant electrical explosions of years bringing an engine to life. But if they hadn't been recently taken out of an engine – which the lack of oil suggested – then were they destined to be put *into* an engine? And why would anyone *plan* to do that?

He squinted at the sun, then heard the thudding steps of his daughter running down the corridor which linked the cottage and the café. He smiled, turning, prepared for his other life.

George Valentine's toast rack was almost empty, the charred crumbs scattered over the plastic tablecloth of the police canteen. He held his coffee with both hands, trying to disguise the tremble in his fingers. Toast, no butter. It was what George Valentine called 'solids', and it would have to keep him alive until he found a chip shop before going to his bed. He touched the half-finished packet of cigarettes in his pocket, tired of finding proof that he was a weak man.

Peter Shaw stood by the canteen's plate-glass window, drinking bottled mineral water and looking across the tumbled rooftops of the old town towards the sea. He'd been on time, to the minute. At home he'd cleared ice from the gutters, snow off the veranda where it had blown in off the beach, then ferried coffee to Lena, who had been up early with Francesca because they wanted to collect driftwood on the beach to decorate the surf shop before school. He'd held a weathered plank up to the wooden door of the old boathouse as Lena hammered it into place.

She was five feet two, slim, compact. Her hair was cut short, angular, rising from her scalp like a surprise. At rest her face was melancholy, although the line of the lips always hinted, at least to him, of a smile. A slight cast in the right eye, the imperfection he had noticed first. Her body was made up entirely of curves, bisecting, crossing, running in harmony. The word sensuous was hers to keep. Francesca had the essential template of her mother's face – the high forehead, steep, falling from the thick black hairline. His forensic art tutor would have called it their 'lifelong look' – the one element of the face that anchored the rest, the one facet that would stay with them both to death. In summer Lena's skin was Jamaican black, with the depth of a glazed pot. In winter a greyness undercut the lustre, so that strangers thought she was ill.

'So, George Valentine?' She'd smiled, watching her husband closely, but he didn't answer. Shaw had told her about his new partner, the dishevelled, chain-smoking toper. 'I can see the funny side,' she said, her smile widening.

'You've never met him,' said Shaw, looking out to sea.

'You mean he wasn't at the wedding?'

They both laughed at their oldest joke. No one had been at the wedding, least of all Shaw's father or his one-time partner George Valentine. Lena's family was troubled, dispersed, in an almost constant state of family warfare which ruled out any kind of concerted action. Shaw's family just didn't want to come. His father was already ill, already dying. Shaw hadn't been surprised by his father's prejudices, but he'd been saddened by his mother's. Lena had tried to forgive them, pretended that she had, but she knew it was a day in her life she couldn't have again, and they'd taken some of the joy out of it.

'You should give him a chance, you know. It's ten years, Peter – more.' 'Unforgiving' – it was a trait she'd identified in him long ago, and one she knew now he'd never be able to shake off.

'He might surprise you,' she said. 'You surprised me.'

He picked up his tea and looked at her, knowing he didn't have to ask.

'I thought you were just a copper.'

'I *am* just a copper,' he said. He looked at his watch. 'Nearly high tide – I'd better get moving.'

She stood back, admiring their work, refusing to let him go.

'It's a murder inquiry,' he said. They both knew what that meant: the late nights, the calls, the pressure to be seen at St James's. 'It won't last for ever,' said Shaw. 'But I can't take her swimming tonight – sorry. I'll text if things change.'

'It's OK. I'll do it.' Lena tried to hide her disappointment that he would still apologize for his career, as if it hadn't been his choice. 'There's an order today,' she said. 'The new wetsuits, kites, and a pair of sand yachts. I'll be busy.'

'You need help?'

She shook her head, annoyed, because he wasn't in a position to give any help. She pointed out to sea where someone was already on a sailboard, a splash of twisting orange off the beach at Old Hunstanton. 'I'm fine.'

She hadn't taken her eyes off the sea. 'Why would someone do that, Peter?' He'd filled her in on the events of the night before: the stranded convoy, the body on the raft. 'Bite into your own flesh? Why?' She put down the hammer to take up her mug of coffee, watching their daughter on the high-water mark collecting more wood.

Lena wasn't afraid of crime, and she wasn't interested in shielding Francesca from the real world, but she didn't want it to dominate their lives, to throw shadows over a sunny childhood.

Why bite into your own flesh? Shaw hadn't had an answer for her then, and he didn't have one now, an hour later, looking out over the snow-laden rooftops of Lynn from the canteen at St James's.

The reek of frying grease lay like a duvet over the Formica tables and the huddled figures of the early shift at St James's. Valentine stood, joining Shaw by the glass, watching boats threading out along the geometrically straight channel of the Cut, heading for open water. Below them a stream of red tail lights was already flowing into the multistorey shopping-centre car park. Much of the snow had melted but the rain still fell, the brief dawn sun long buried in clouds the colour of steel wool.

'Well, we've both slept on it. Fresh ideas?' said Shaw. He'd already filled Valentine in on everything he'd learned out on Siberia Belt that morning with Tom Hadden and Justina Kazimierz.

'Ellis – the pick-up?' asked Valentine, already used to Shaw's methods. No fuzzy edges, no casual assumptions.

'Yup.'

'Well – could be any fucker.'

Shaw took a deep breath, but Valentine didn't give him the chance to get in.

'So we should do the obvious,' he said quickly, straining his neck forward, massaging his fingers into the narrow bird-like skull. 'There *are* footprints at the scene – they're Holt's. Be fucking stupid to ignore that.'

Shaw stiffened, deciding to ignore the inference. 'Let's get someone out to double-check Baker-Sibley's statement – let's see if it's possible,' said Shaw. 'She said she didn't take her eyes off him, but let's kick the tyres, make sure. And while we're at it, check out the daughter too. She was supposed to be home alone, but we heard her mum ask her to pass the phone over. Who was that to?' He tipped the water bottle back, his Adam's apple bobbing as the liquid drained away. 'Anything else?'

'I need to go outside,' said Valentine.

'We're on the tenth floor,' said Shaw.

Valentine shrugged.

Shaw followed him down the canteen, pushed open an emergency exit and stepped out on to the fire escape. Dog-ends were scattered at their feet, stuck between the metal meshing.

The temperature took the breath away, but not so effectively as the view. Below them cars crept along in the rush-hour traffic.

Valentine lit up in a single fluid movement. 'Eight vehicles – one of 'em is a security van with eighty thousand quid in it,' he said. 'So that's what it's about – box it in, get the money, leave 'em stranded.'

'Bit of a long shot.'

'Not if you've got a man on the inside.' He paused, relishing the moment. He'd been at his desk by five, a crisp wedge of fifty-pound notes held by an elastic band making his raincoat pocket bulge. It had been a good night not to go home. A good night to visit the house on Greenland Street. He'd had no sleep, but sometimes that was a blessing.

'Overtime,' he said, producing a slim brown file from the inside pocket of his raincoat. 'You were right. Security guard's got form.' He took a breath, knowing a long sentence was coming. 'At least he didn't play silly buggers and try to give us a false name. Jonah Shreeves he is: lives out at Cromer. I checked the electoral roll. Shares the property with a Mary Ellen Shreeves.'

'And he's known to us, is he?' asked Shaw, enjoying the euphemism.

'Known? He's virtually fucking family,' said Valentine, coughing. 'GBH six years ago at Sheringham.' He ploughed on, not reading now. 'Broke his girlfriend's arms, one by one, then her jaw. Hospital for a month. She'd threatened to go to the police after he'd robbed her grandmother. Cuffed her round the head. She was eighty-six, the granny. He's been out eighteen months.' He let the dog-end fall, and it slipped through the mesh. 'Nottingham, nothing off for good behaviour. Before that the term recidivist could have been invented for him: robbery, muggings, violence in all forms, often uncontrolled. Left alone he'd probably beat himself up.'

'So that's the theory?' asked Shaw. 'They box in the security van and they've got someone on the inside too. Although one suspects we're dealing with an IQ in single figures here – because we're going to suss chummy out, are we not? Soon as we check the records.'

'Maybe,' said Valentine, knowing Shaw was right, excitement ebbing out of the day. They went back inside, leaving the rattle of the rush hour behind.

'Let's find out more. Weren't you at Cromer?'

Cromer, Sheringham, Wells, Burnham. You name a sleepy seaside town on the north Norfolk coast and George Valentine had been stationed there at some point in the last lost decade of his career.

Shaw took another mineral water from the cold cabinet. 'OK – and the body on the beach?' he asked, changing tack.

Valentine ran his fingers through the condensation on the plate-glass window. Below he could look down on the yard at the back of one of the garages in the old town, a heap of car chassis, tangled metal. 'The lab's got a passport out of the clothing but it soaked up so much seawater they can't open it – it's in the drying cabinet. Could be six hours – more.'

'It's a start – and we need one. They're setting up the emergency incident suite downstairs, George. Murder inquiry. By the end of the day it could be a double murder inquiry when we find out what killed the man in the raft. We've got eight DCs – plus any calls we like to make on manpower from squads and beat. I've got them checking the statements now – back-up calls, double-checks. And there's four civilians for the phone bank. Brief them, get them up to speed. I'll talk to them tonight. We'll split them up into teams then, nominate some lead players. But you're right. Let's do the basics first. What about the widow?'

'Family liaison have got someone at Ellis's flat.'

'OK. First post-mortem internal autopsy is six tonight. But Justina's going to walk us through an external this afternoon on both bodies. At the Ark.'

Shaw drained the mineral water, crushed the bottle, lobbed it into a bin. 'Still nothing from the diving team?'

'They found the axe in the drink, about ten foot from the victim's truck and the pine tree. Looks like zero on forensics, but they're trying to match the blade with the marks on the tree.'

'Right,' said Shaw.

'Uniformed branch got round to the owner of the Mondeo late last night,' said Valentine. 'He doesn't own a snakeskin steering-wheel cover. Never has.'

Shaw thought about that, filed it away. It was one of the things he loved about police work; the constant pressure to remember every detail at a level which didn't make it impossible to remember your own name.

'So where's the kid behind the wheel?'

'Looks like he made it down to the road,' said Valentine. 'The vodka probably saved him,' he added, delighted to highlight the life-saving qualities of alcohol. 'A lift on the coast road?'

'Or he met up with whoever put the AA sign out.' Shaw shivered, a delayed reaction to the icy-cold water in which he'd swum that morning. 'Let's try and fix up the security firm for interview late morning. We'll do the Chinese restaurant first. I'll meet you downstairs in an hour – meanwhile, get the team up and running. And we need something for the radio, local TV, the evenings. Bare outlines, George – a few juicy details, but let's hold most of it back. Next of kin still to be informed, etc., etc. Let's think about a TV appeal tomorrow if we're no further forward.' Shaw put a hand to his bare throat. 'And let's get a description of the youngster in the Mondeo out as well. You're right, someone probably gave him a lift. So local radio – quick as you can.'

'You?' asked Valentine, trying to keep the question neutral.

'Boss wants a word,' said Shaw, stealing the last piece of toast from the rack.

## 13

Detective Chief Superintendent Max Warren kept a tidy office on the third floor. He was a Londoner who'd come north with a reputation for tackling street crime in the capital. He'd played rugby until settling for weekends at the golf club, but his face was still dominated by a serially broken nose. For a man who had once succeeded in projecting a tangible sense of menace, Shaw was always surprised how slight he was, a narrow neck on narrow shoulders, the loose skin mottled with liver spots. Warren had arrived fifteen years earlier to administer an injection of adrenaline into the sleepy West Norfolk Constabulary. But the operation had backfired – allowing several gallons of sleeping draught to flood back into the superintendent's veins.

Shaw didn't sit and Warren didn't ask him to, merely eyeing the spot where Shaw's tie should have been.

'Keep it simple, Peter,' he said. 'It's not a puzzle. It's two nasty murders on the same night.'

Shaw thought about pointing out the assumptions behind that summary but let the moment pass. Warren was firmly of the school that felt police officers needed university degrees as much as they needed a diploma in tap-dancing. So smart-arse backchat was best avoided.

'DS Valentine's got a good nose for low life – unsurprisingly: let him use it. I expect him to make a major contribution to this inquiry, Peter. He's applied for a permanent transfer back to St James's every year for the last decade. I can't go on saying no. So this is his big chance. His only chance. But he needs to do more than keep his nose clean. In his day he was a bloody good copper. He needs to prove to me that he still is.'

On the wall behind Warren's desk was a framed line-up of uniformed officers at Hendon – the Met's training college. Warren was centre-stage. Shaw's father was on the row behind.

'Dad always rated him,' said Shaw, forcing himself to be fair.

Warren ignored the comment. 'I'd like a position check on the inquiry daily. From you. OK?'

'Sir.'

Warren looked up over half-moon glasses, studying Shaw's face. 'Your eye?'

'Robinson says ten days,' said Shaw. 'Chances are good.'

Dr Hugh Robinson was the force's senior medical adviser. 'Right,' said Warren. 'But what the fuck does he know, eh?'

'Sir.'

That was it. Shaw, wordlessly dismissed, left Warren reading the morning papers, the *Financial Times* spread across his blotter. He remembered what his father had always said about DCS Warren – that he'd end his days in a bungalow at Cromer, chasing kids who stole gnomes from his rockery. But then his father had been jealous of Warren's rapid rise and the aura of New Scotland Yard.

Shaw cleared his calls, reviewed his budget for the

inquiry, and then met Valentine by the front desk. They took the DS's car – a battered Mazda, the plastic dashboard engrained with ash, a week's worth of sport's papers in the footwell of the passenger seat.

'The Emerald Garden, Jubilee Parade, Westmead Estate,' said Shaw, getting in. 'And remind me – why do we think Stanley Zhao's worth a visit?'

Valentine pretended to watch the traffic, working on an answer.

'The Chinese community...' he said carefully, 'is involved in cockle-picking on the sandbanks. The bloke washed up on Ingol Beach may have died of many things – but natural causes isn't one of them. It's just worth a second look. Playing the odds. Percentages.'

Shaw raised an eyebrow, turning to watch as a gritter lorry swept past, the salt sizzling as it spilt across the road. He let Valentine drive in silence while he worked through a sheaf of papers from the murder team – calls they'd made, information gathered so far on the members of the snowbound convoy. He rifled through until he got to the file on Stanley Zhao.

DC Mark Birley, a former uniform branch man bumped up for his first CID case, had conducted a phone interview with the secretary of the Burnham & District Round Table, Zhao's regular Monday night customer. Shaw flicked through a transcript, impressed by Birley's meticulous questions and annotated answers, as Valentine swung the Mazda through the rush-hour traffic.

They got to Westmead in ten minutes. It was clear that Jubilee Parade was one that had been rained on with some persistence. At one end was a pub called the Red, White

85

and Blue, its ground-floor windows boarded and painted matt black. It was known at St James's as the Black and Blue, a reference to its owner's penchant for staging boxing matches without the formality of a licence. At the other end of the parade was a mini-market with metal grilles obscuring a plate-glass window across which meandered a single crack; a man with a dog sat on a grease mark up against the wall, his feet drawn in to keep his whole body within the lee of the overhanging flat roof.

As Shaw and Valentine pulled up the gently falling rain turned suddenly to sleet, then a peppering of snow. The Emerald Garden was in the middle of the parade, a takeaway only, bare floorboards visible through the mesh covering the glazed door. Stanley Zhao opened up for them. He didn't seem surprised to see them. He didn't seem anything to see them. Shaw tried not to let the word *inscrutable* form in his head.

Zhao led the way into the kitchen through a hanging curtain of blue beads. Spotless woks dotted a bank of gas rings, and a set of chopping boards was criss-crossed with a lifetime's worth of knife wounds. The only smell was Jeyes' Fluid.

There was one other knife wound. Zhao had a scar running from his hairline to his cheek, via an eye socket. Shaw had missed it the previous night in the half-light inside the Corsa. Zhao's eyes blinked meekly behind metal-rimmed glasses, and when his lips parted he revealed a line of identical teeth, each one as white as toothpaste. He stood with his back to one of the kitchen's metal tables, and Shaw thought he'd been right about his height: six feet two, possibly three.

'I want to help,' said Zhao, moving over to stand awkwardly by the serving hatch which opened into the shop. The accent was strong; the consonants shaved almost flat by the vowels, but free of any hint of the syntax of the comic-book Chinaman.

Mr Zhao knew why they were there. He handed Shaw his passport, and a Xeroxed copy of a birth certificate. 'I have been asked before,' he said, by way of explanation.

Shaw flicked the passport open. Born Kowloon 1959. Married Hong Kong 1991. Cook. No distinguishing marks.

Shaw raised his eyebrows and touched his own cheek. Zhao pointed at the passport. 'Inside,' he said. And it was. A clipping from the *Lynn News* for 2006. 'Takeaway owner knifed by burglar.' Zhao touched the scar. He'd been in Lynn a year, he said, straight from Hong Kong, and he hadn't expected crime to be so bad.

'Did they get him?' asked Shaw. 'The burglar.'

'No.'

'You should get the passport updated,' said Shaw, handing it back.

They heard a footfall upstairs, and then the distant mosquito-buzz of a radio.

Shaw apologized if Zhao had been asked the questions before, but they were tying up loose ends, following procedure. Zhao smiled as if he believed them.

'Remind me,' said Shaw, trying to recall the details of DC Birley's interview with the Round Table. 'Why were you on the old coast road at five o'clock last night?'

Valentine began to walk round the kitchen, inspecting

a notice board, a wall chart of the menu, some postcards of Hong Kong, San Francisco, Hamburg.

Zhao's story was a carbon copy of the one he'd given Valentine at Gallow Marsh Farm. He delivered a large takeaway dinner to a meeting of the Burnham & District Round Table every Monday evening. The order never changed: fourteen chicken chow meins, a vegetable chow mein, ten portions of prawn toast, one of vegetable spring rolls. They met in the village hall at Burnham Overy Staithe. He had a contact number. Shaw remembered the warmth in the van, the fug of soya and sunflower oil.

'It's a long drive – but good customers, a big order,' added Zhao.

'Please,' said Shaw, playing for time, looking around. 'Finish your breakfast.' On a side table stood a large porcelain cup, the light green liquid inside it giving off a thin scent. Beside it was a white plate, a fork, and the remains of an omelette, a brown smear on the china. A bottle of Daddies Sauce, catering size, stood on the counter.

Valentine took over. 'You saw the other drivers stranded on Siberia Belt, Mr Zhao, at the farmhouse? Did you recognize any of them? Customers perhaps?'

Zhao shook his head, tucking in a stray piece of omelette at the corner of his mouth. 'People all look the same to me.' Valentine didn't miss the joke, but he didn't smile either. Finished, Zhao picked up his plate and took it to a metal sink.

'Do you mix much within the Chinese community here in Lynn, Mr Zhao?' asked Shaw, aware that the question was as subtle as the Daddies Sauce. There were two

Chinese communities in Lynn. The first had come with the Londoners in the seventies and had turned out as respectable as a mock-Tudor semi. They ran restaurants, chip shops, a big dry-cleaning plant and a dozen or so of the town's cabs. The other community was transient: the cockle-pickers, gangmasters organizing agricultural picking in the summer, and an even more shadowy sub-culture of prostitution and gambling.

It was pretty clear which one Shaw meant.

'We live here, on the Westmead,' said Zhao. 'My wife was born here. I mix with my own community.'

'Staff?' asked Valentine.

'Three.'

'Also Chinese?'

Mr Zhao cleaned his already spotless fingers on his white apron.

Shaw stepped in. 'I'd appreciate it if you'd give DS Valentine the details. Names, addresses. I'm sorry, we'll need to see their papers too. And one more formality . . . A driving licence?'

Zhao raised both hands, palms up, as if nothing would be easier, but Shaw detected for the first time the hard, angry set of the man's jaw.

'A moment,' he said, opening a door into a corridor, then closing it gently behind him. They heard his footsteps on carpeted stairs, then the creak of floorboards above. The door Zhao had closed swung back again and through the opening they heard drawers being pulled out, banged shut. Shaw walked quickly into the corridor beyond. To the left the stairs rose, boxes on each step. To the right the corridor led to a door, half open. He looked in: a storeroom, the jagged shadow of a fire escape just visible through reinforced frosted glass. He wondered if Stanley Zhao had really met a burglar here. That kind of scar looked more like a premeditated punishment.

Valentine stood behind him and tried the other door in the corridor. It opened and they stood together looking in. A child's bedroom: bright yellow wallpaper dotted with Looney Tunes characters – Daffy Duck, Road Runner. A cot rested in pieces up against one wall. A mobile hung, ships, fishes and lighthouses in wood. Shaw wondered if the child had an inflatable raft for the beach.

But perhaps a child didn't live there. A single metal collapsible bed was made up with grey blankets. On the coverlet a magazine. Porn: *Das Fleisch*. Sean Harper, plumber's mate, would approve. Three copies, all different dates.

They heard footsteps too late and met Zhao in the corridor.

'The door was open – we wondered where you were,' said Valentine, taking a laboured breath. 'Whose room?' he asked, making a virtue out of being caught.

'Gangsun. My nephew,' said Zhao, closing the door and forcing Valentine to step back. 'He works the late shift at weekends and sometimes he sleeps, goes home next day.'

'Likes reading, does he?' asked Valentine, a sneer disfiguring his face.

'Young man – lonely, I think. A wife in Kowloon.'

Shaw made a cursory examination of Zhao's driving licence. They heard a key turn in the front door and a man joined them: Chinese, swollen eyes, twenty years of age, perhaps less. Mr Zhao said something they didn't understand, something rapid and edged like corrugated paper. The new arrival walked out towards the storeroom. They heard a sound like coins being poured into a bucket. The man reappeared with a large plastic tub full of frozen chips.

'And him?' said Valentine, nodding at the other man.

'My brother,' said Zhao. 'We open at noon; Edison cooks.'

'You'll tell him what we need. Papers, passport, driving licence,' said Valentine, making it clear it wasn't a question.

'Of course.'

'We interviewed the Round Table secretary this morning, Mr Zhao,' said Shaw. 'He said the takeaway meal has been a standing order for – what – eighteen months?'

'That's right.'

'Mr Beddard – I'm right with the name? He said the order was for six o'clock.'

Zhao was aware now that he was being led somewhere he might regret going.

'So you would have been early – twenty minutes or more.'

'The insulated boxes keep the food OK,' he said, too quickly. 'Sometimes I get places early, take a break in the van. Smoke. My vice.'

He seemed very keen to own up to an everyday vice, thought Shaw. He tried to imagine it, the takeaway van parked outside Burnham Overy Staithe Village Hall, engine running, Mr Zhao enjoying a well-earned cigarette, light spilling out on to the snow.

But that wasn't what the secretary of the Round Table had described.

'Mr Beddard says you're often late,' said Shaw.

'In winter, people eat early. I drop off three or four times, it gets late.'

'And Edison stays here cooking – with the others?'

'Yes.'

'So who's the other man? Mr Beddard says that a couple of times you've been with a friend. Always – almost always – he said that was when you were late.'

'Sometimes Edison is bored – he comes for the ride,' he said, his voice slightly louder.

'But in winter people eat early – so it must be too busy for Edison to leave the kitchen, right?'

Zhao cracked the window open. 'Like your job, take-away food, Inspector,' he said, and Shaw sensed the syntax had been deliberately muddled to help blur the clarity of the answer. 'Never know when busy.' He shrugged. 'Not busy.'

'Mr Beddard says the other man – your friend – is not Chinese, Mr Zhao.'

Zhao rubbed his face, then drew two circles in the air. 'Mr Beddard's eyes are not good. Always someone else signs for the food; he can find never his glasses. Who knows what he sees?'

Shaw caught Valentine's eye. Enough, for now. But they'd be back. 'Let's make a start, DS Valentine, please. Names, addresses, any papers to hand.'

He turned to Zhao and tried out his most insincere smile. He didn't like it when people lied to him, especially when they didn't seem to care if he knew.

Back in the Mazda Shaw used the radio to get through to the murder incident room. The DC on point duty was Paul Twine – graduate entry, smart, but short on street-wise coppering. He gave Shaw a one-minute briefing. John Holt's condition was fragile but improving fast. DC Fiona Campbell was in attendance again having had a six-hour half-shift off to catch up on some sleep. Holt had suffered severe bleeding from the nose during the night owing to high blood pressure and had nearly choked on his dentures, which had to be cut free to clear an airway. He'd spent three hours in intensive care before being returned to his ward. By dawn he was sleeping. Twine offered Shaw a précis of the preliminary report from the pathologist but he turned it down, preferring to ring direct.

Dr Kazimierz answered her mobile on the first ring.

'Sorry, Justina, it's me. Anything I should know?'

'It's early,' she said, but the icy formality was short of full blast. 'The chisel had a nine-inch blade – the point actually fractured the *inside* of the skull at the back of the head. Blood group's AB – which helps, yes? Bad news – Tom says no prints on the weapon.'

Shaw thought about the blood group. It was a break. AB covered just four people in a hundred. He heard a tap being turned, water gushing.

'And there was a tattoo on the chest: Royal Anglians. Otherwise that's it for now.'

'So, a soldier once?'

Silence. Shaw heard the sound of coffee now, a filter machine chugging.

'As for our man on the beach . . .' she said, 'I haven't touched him.' She put the phone down.

Shaw rang Tom Hadden in the CSI unit office. Hadden didn't like being indoors, under the artificial lights which made him look so pale, and Shaw imagined him working briskly through the paperwork so he could get back out to the scene at Ingol Beach.

'Couple of things,' he said, and Shaw heard the metal locks on his forensic briefcase snap shut. 'The Morris Minor 1000.'

'The old biddy's?'

'Yeah. Marijuana.'

'Pardon?'

'George asked me to look in the glove compartment. Brown, Moroccan, top quality. Must have blown her pension on it. She'd got a pouch stuffed with it – but there were fibres all over the floor. A regular little pothead, in fact.'

'Two favours,' said Shaw, beginning to shuffle the limpet shells he'd arranged in a line on the dashboard. 'Can you check the plugs in the Vauxhall Rascal – the ones in the engine as well as the ones in the door pocket. And can you take a dental mould from the apple on the dashboard – check it's Ellis's lunch.'

'That's a long shot,' said Hadden, aware of Shaw's reputation for painstaking police work. A visual assessment of the apple against Ellis's teeth had looked like a good match. Dental matches took time, cost money. They'd have to put the work out to the Forensic Science Service. 'OK,' he said.

Shaw looked up and saw Valentine splashing out of

the Emerald Garden, head turned away from the snow. Down the phone he heard tapping and guessed Hadden was entering a note in his palm pilot.

'And the man on the beach?' asked Shaw, as Valentine stretched the seatbelt, fired the ignition, listened to the engine race, then die.

'There are some documents but I've got them in the dry heater – give me an hour . . .'

'Passport?'

'An hour,' he said. 'We got a hat – black wool. It could be his. Washed up about five hundred yards to the north-west. No name tag, but there are hairs. We can get a match if they're his. Nothing else on the high-water mark except the drum of chemicals – that's gone back to the yard at St James's They'll get us a fix on the contents, but if you want to trust my nose I'd say sulphuric acid. When we got the lid off it smelt like a thousand rotten eggs with a gangrene sauce.'

'Thanks for that image,' said Shaw. 'Speak later.'

Valentine fired the engine again, which coughed and then roared. The snow was falling steadily now, tempering the bleak greyness of the Westmead Estate.

'You asked Tom to check out the Morris Minor glove compartment?' said Shaw. 'Pot – brown Moroccan.'

The DS popped a mint, crunched it immediately. 'Blimey,' said Valentine. 'Takes all sorts. I'll check her out.'

'And Zhao? What d'you think?'

'I think he's dicking us about.'

'The real question,' said Shaw, 'is what is he dicking us about *about*. Illegals? Smuggling fags? VAT fraud? Porn?

Prostitution? Gambling? . . . There's something, I'm just not sure it's got much to do with this inquiry.'

He checked his watch: 10 a.m. They had an appointment at North Norfolk Security at eleven and it was a half-hour run to Wells-next-the-Sea and the company's headquarters.

The snow was draining the light out of the sky, leaving the day stillborn. The grey monolith that was the twenty-one-storey tower block at the heart of the Westmead Estate was just visible above them, the top lost in low cloud. Snow flecked the north-east face of the flats, clawing at windowsills and downpipes. They could hear a helicopter hovering over the traffic on the ring road.

'We've got twenty minutes,' said Shaw, and he knew he couldn't stop himself now, couldn't leave the scab of the past unpicked. He turned in his seat so that he was facing George Valentine and realized there was another reason he found his company so unsettling. It was the fact that Valentine knew more about Shaw's own father than he did. That all those hours Jack Shaw should have been with his family, he'd been in an unmarked police car, just like this battered Mazda, with George Valentine.

'I'd like to see the scene of crime,' he said.

'Siberia Belt?'

'No. Dad's last case. Your last case. I've never seen the spot where you found him – the child. I'd like to see it now. It's close – yes?'

Valentine too knew it would come to this. In fact if it hadn't come to this he'd have wondered what kind of son Peter Shaw was. He put a dry cigarette between his lips and clenched his teeth. 'It's close,' he said.

## 14

Mid-morning and the Westmead Estate was coming to life: low life. An elderly man in carpet slippers shuffled along a covered walkway between two blocks of flats hugging a dressing gown, a copy of the *Daily Express* and a single can of white cider. A woman, dressed neatly in a see-through plastic raincoat and matching hat, poured milk into a line of saucers by some waste bins, her feet lost amongst a clowder of cats.

Shaw followed George Valentine through the precinct, across a triangle of open ground covered in snow, turned past a line of lock-up garages and then between a pair of the five-storey blocks which dotted the estate. Above their heads an aerial walkway linked two sets of concrete concertinas. A piece of rope dangled, two trainers strung from the end, out of reach.

Vancouver House, the estate's central block, stood alone on a tarmac island: a giant gravestone without an inscription except for the jagged multicoloured graffiti on the concrete pillars which held it clear of the ground. Shaw thought the scene almost exotic – the wastelands of Sarajevo perhaps, the sound of a mortar about to fall from hills hidden in the mist. Ramps ran up to stairwells and lifts, leaving the dark space beneath the block as a car park. Steam billowed from heating ducts along each of the twenty floors and trailed from overflow pipes, as if the whole block were boiling on the inside, ready to spill out.

They cut straight across the waste ground, then ducked into the shadows of the car park, threading a path through the pillars, passing a burnt-out VW, and skirting a huge pool of rainwater stained with oil in which two seagulls fought over a packet of chips.

Valentine felt colder once they were in the shadows. He stopped, looking around, waiting for his eyes to shift into night vision, filling his lungs now he had the chance. He'd been back many times, so that looking around was like viewing a favourite film clip. 'Used to be a park here – back in the fifties. Marsh in summer, ponds in winter. That's why they put the flats up on pillars. Didn't work: the place reeks of damp. Keep wallpaper on the walls for a year, you get a fucking certificate.'

'How'd you know?'

Valentine took out a cigarette, ran it under his nose, deciding then he'd left it too long to give up. 'Grandparents. Dad's side. They moved 'em here when they took down the houses on Dock Street – 1971.' He spat into a puddle. 'Didn't live a year, either of them.'

Shaw knew when they'd found the spot. He had a press cutting at home with a picture of the scene that first morning. A pillar behind painted in black-and-white warning stripes, a staircase leading up, a sign showing a green figure climbing steps, two women standing where the press photographer had put them, tissues pressed to their mouths. And a lift entrance, the doors battered aluminium, lights above in the shape of up and down arrows, inexplicably unbroken. And a security phone in a metal box on the wall. The phone was ripped out now, the lift refurbished, but otherwise little had changed.

Valentine kicked the pillar. 'Here.' He thrust his hands in his pockets and closed his fingers around the dice on his lighter.

'Dad always said he thought the bloke was stupid.'

'Mosse,' said Valentine. 'Robert James Mosse.'

'Right. Dad reckoned he must have panicked – to dump the kid here, under the flats. It doesn't make a lot of sense. If you'd got the body in the car, why not go somewhere? He could have taken it out on the marshes, Dersingham Woods. We'd still be looking.'

Valentine glanced down at his black slip-ons, refusing to be drawn.

The bare facts of DCI Jack Shaw's last case had never been disputed. Jonathan Tessier, aged nine, had been found dead at three minutes past midnight on 26 July 1997. He was still dressed in the Celtic kit he'd put on that morning to play football on the grass triangle by the flats. He had been given £1 to buy chips for lunch: 40p change was in the pocket in his shorts. There was no evidence at the scene, or in later medical and forensic examinations, that he had been sexually assaulted. But he had been strangled with a ligature of some sort, the condition of the body pointing to a time of death between six and eleven p.m.

DCI Jack Shaw and DI George Valentine were the first CID officers at the scene. The body had been found by a nurse, parking after her late shift a few feet from the boy's corpse. She said she'd seen a car drive off quickly – a Volkswagen Polo, she thought – as she got out of her Mini. The driver had failed to negotiate the narrow ramp to ground level and clipped one of the concrete pillars, spilling broken glass from a headlamp on the ground. She'd found the boy's body in the oily puddle.

DI Valentine had radioed an alert on the damaged car to all units. A squad car on patrol found a Polo abandoned on the edge of allotments at Wootton just after two that morning, the front offside headlamp shattered, the engine warm. A police computer check identified the owner as Robert James Mosse, a resident – like Jonathan Tessier – of Vancouver House. Back at the scene the body had been removed, revealing a glove beneath, black leather, with a fake fur cuff. Jack Shaw and George Valentine went to Flat 8 on the first floor of Vancouver House, where they confronted Bobby Mosse, a 21-year-old student reading law at Sheffield University, at home during the summer vacation.

Here the accounts of the night diverge. Jack Shaw and George Valentine's statements dovetailed: they maintained that they showed Mosse the glove in a cellophane evidence bag before obtaining his permission to search the flat. They conducted the search and failed to find the other glove. Mosse, in contrast, swore in evidence they showed him the glove, minus any protective bag, only after the search. His mother, who also gave evidence, agreed with her son's version of events and added that at one point DI Valentine had reversed the fingers of the glove, turning it inside out, and looking inside.

Mosse said his car had been stolen that evening, a crime he himself had reported at half-past midnight, a fact verified by the duty desk at St James's. He had been at the cinema alone. His mother had accompanied him to the same picture house – the Gaumont – but had seen *LA Confidential* on the small screen, whereas he'd seen *The Full Monty* on the main one. They'd walked in because it was a nice evening and it's difficult to park near the cinema. He had a torn ticket for the performance. His film had finished first and he had strolled home. Mosse always parked his car on an open-air car park a few hundred yards from Vancouver House because vandals caused a lot of damage in the underground car park. But he was still worried about the Polo – and that night he'd gone to check on it after his mother had got home and before going to bed. He found the car gone, and phoned the police from the flat.

The smashed glass at the scene was matched to pieces found still clinging to the rim of the headlamp of the abandoned car – Mosse's car. In terms of material evidence, this was as good as fingerprints. He was arrested, taken to St James's and held overnight. A preliminary analysis of skin tissue found in the glove pointed to Mosse. Usherettes at the cinema were unable to recall him in the audience that evening. It had been a packed house. Mosse was charged with murder at 3.30 on the afternoon of his first day in custody. He denied the charge. Bail was refused.

Police records showed Jonathan Tessier had been cautioned on three occasions for vandalism – twice for scratching the paintwork of parked cars. The prosecution planned to suggest that Mosse had found Tessier preparing to damage the Polo, and an attempt to administer summary justice had spiralled out of control. Hence they would be prepared to accept a charge of manslaughter. Mosse still denied the allegation. A further analysis of the skin residue was ordered through the Forensic Science Service, an agency of the Home Office. It reported that there was a chance of only one in three billion that anyone other than Mosse could have shed the skin within the glove. Mosse continued to deny that the glove was his, as did his mother. The matching glove was never found.

Shaw looked around, as if he might find it now, more than a decade later.

The court case itself had been a one-day wonder. They'd made a crucial mistake, Shaw and Valentine, by taking the glove to Mosse's flat.

Mosse's defence team reviewed the forensic evidence in the final days before the case was to open in the Crown Court. His barrister considered the error grave enough to bring it to the judge's attention in his opening address. Mosse's mother kept her flat clean, an upright vacuum stationed in the hallway like a sentry, but even the cleanest surfaces collect a thin veneer of household dust – its composition varying between 62 and 84 per cent decaying human skin. That was how Mosse's DNA had got on the glove, maintained Mosse's defence team. The two detectives had been in the flat with it for nearly forty-five minutes. More than enough time for the unbagged evidence to be contaminated.

The prosecution was forced to concede that the glove was the only physical evidence which linked Mosse to the scene of the crime. There was, of course, abundant forensic evidence of Mosse's presence in the car, but nothing that proved he had driven it from the car park that night. Moreover, several fingerprints were found in the vehicle which matched neither Mosse, his mother nor any other regular user of it. This, the defence would argue, suggested the presence of an unknown third party – the real killer, in fact. Finally, the defence claimed that the prosecution had no direct evidence to support its suggested motive, and could not disprove any element of Mosse's alibi.

The case against Bobby Mosse was thrown out shortly after lunch on the first day. The judge's closing remarks were brief, but he had time to suggest that the slipshod police work which had compromised the prosecution case left open the possibility that the contamination of the evidence might have been deliberate.

So Mosse walked free owing to a procedural error – evidence found at the scene should be bagged, tagged and remain in the custody of the scene-of-crime team until booked into the evidence room at St James's – signed in by the duty sergeant. But Jack Shaw had been too angry to think straight. And George Valentine thought he was too good a copper to have to follow the rule book. That was the explanation Shaw wanted to believe. But the judge's barely veiled suggestion that the pair had attempted to fabricate the evidence nagged at him like an aching tooth.

Outside the court Mosse posed for press pictures under the wheeling seagulls on the quayside. Shaw had often tried to imagine what his father must have felt that day: the defeat, the injustice perhaps, the impotency. Or was it more complicated than that? Resigned, perhaps, to his fate because he *had* faked the evidence? Shaw didn't know the truth, couldn't be sure of the truth, because his father had always kept him out of his world. A black-and-white world, with no shades of grey. He knew his father was an honest man by his own reckoning. What he didn't know was whether he counted as dishonest framing a suspect whom he knew – just *knew* – was a child-killer. Was that how his father's world had worked? George Valentine's too?

If they did frame Mosse then they'd paid a heavy price for it. His father was dead within the year. George Valentine was knocked down a rank and sent out to the sticks, a one-way ticket in his hand. And Peter Shaw had paid for it too: the memory of the father he'd idolized marred by the worst slur of all: *bent copper*.

'I never understood why Dad was so angry about it,' said Shaw, looking at Valentine. 'Mum said it got under his skin, right from the start. But he'd done kids before – that schoolboy strangled by his father in the North End in the seventies. But it didn't get to him – not like this.' Shaw dragged a boot through the puddle, sending a swash of water out over the pockmarked concrete.

Valentine took out his wallet, flicking it open, holding it up for Shaw to see.

The details of the Tessier case had never registered with Shaw at the time. He'd been at Hendon, with the Met. He'd met Lena. He was building his own life. So he'd never really looked at the child's face – other than a smudged black-and-white thumbnail which had appeared in the nationals in London when the body had been found. But now there it was, in colour, pin-sharp. And he could see why his father had taken the case personally:

the blond hair cut short, the wide trusting face, the blue eyes pale enough to be tap water. He was looking at an echo of his childhood self. Was that why his father had acted the way he had that night in 1997? In anger at the murder of a child who looked so much like his only son?

Jonathan Tessier's face had found a place in George Valentine's wallet, where his own family snapshot should have been. Shaw couldn't imagine what it was like being that obsessed with a crime a decade old, but he could understand it, because Valentine's career had nearly ended beneath Vancouver House that night just as suddenly as his father's.

Hiding his emotions he handed the wallet back to Valentine without a word. 'You've been back before,' he said, wishing now that he hadn't asked to see the spot.

'Sure,' said Valentine, lighting up, the sudden flare warming the cold interior. Shaw watched him draw the nicotine into his narrow chest. A car bounced down the ramp and accelerated across the tarmac before braking in a neat circle, the smell of burnt rubber instantly acrid. Valentine licked his lip where the cigarette butts had made it sore.

'And Mosse?' asked Shaw.

'Life of crime,' he replied, smiling. 'Solicitor, down at College Lane, the magistrates courts. Married, two kids – boys; Citroën Xsara Picasso, detached house at Ringsted. A conservatory, carriage lamps, crazy paving. A cat called Zebra.'

'But otherwise you're not bothered,' said Shaw.

Valentine gave him a rare direct look. 'I'm bothered.

Jack was bothered too. Before he died he made me promise I'd clear our names, get Bobby Mosse behind bars.' He ditched the cigarette in the puddle. 'So that's another failure.'

Shaw envied Valentine that promise, *if* it had ever been made.

And he stored away the slight, after all these years; the knowledge that if his own father had been innocent of fabricating evidence why hadn't he asked his son to clear his name?

'You had your own career,' said Valentine, reading his mind. 'Mine was over. I had the time. I've had the time.'

'And?'

'And we're right back where we were on that night. Your dad and I knew for a fact that Bobby Mosse killed that kid. We didn't need the forensics on the glove to be sure. If you'd been there that night you'd have known too. He was cool all right; cool as an ice-cube. But the mother was a wreck, and she really struggled to get her story straight. Then when we showed him the glove he nearly lost it – started shaking, threw up in the loo. Said he was upset – well, yeah, I guess he was. Upset he was gonna get nicked.

'He was guilty as sin. Trouble is, I still can't prove it. Twelve years going fucking nowhere. Story of my life.' He spat in the puddle and walked away, fading into the shadows.

# 15

Out on Styleman's Middle, the sandbank three miles off Ingol Beach, five cockle boats came in to land. The snow, falling from the north, melted as it touched the sands. Crews disembarked, pencil-grey outlines working in a bank of falling snowflakes, bristling with rakes and buckets and forks. One worker carried a navigation light, a red beacon in the gloom. Otherwise the view was grey: the dark line of the horizon separating the grey clouds from the grey sea. Sometimes a seagull wheeled, a tiny white tear in the monochrome canvas. The tide, edging out, revealed the surface of the sandbank; the deep trenches left by yesterday's cockle-pickers had been sucked smooth by the sea, but the lines remained. And a single bucket, filled to brimming with the fine, gritty sand; a moat at its base washed deep by the ebb and flow of the waves.

Duncan Sly, gangmaster, joined the men to haul one of the boats hard into the bank. A big man in a seaman's donkey jacket, a blue cap covering thinning hair on a skull like a cannonball.

He spotted the cockle-picker's bucket. Leaving kit on the sands was a crime. Once the tide was over them they usually got sucked down, gone for ever. 'It better not be one of ours,' he said. He'd know if it had been left by yesterday's gang because they marked all their gear: not just the buckets, but the rakes, the sieves, shovels and sacks. A single shell emblem in blue, a clam, like a pilgrim's badge. If it was their kit there'd be a fine – everyone's wages would be £20 short that day. He set out to retrieve it.

The pickers didn't watch; they were cocooned in the cotton-wool world which helped them live through the pain in their backs, the numbing boredom. The snow fell on them, heavy now, cutting down visibility like a shutter. They'd been on Styleman's Middle for less than five minutes and most had looked at their watches once already. Spread out in twos in the mist, each within sight of the others for safety, they began to dig.

Ten feet from the bucket Sly realized what he was really seeing: not sand piled high to form a dome, matted with seaweed, but a face, the distorted oval of an open mouth, the head tilted back sharply, a small green crab on the left cheek like a beauty spot. He saw that the head was not the only part of the body which had emerged from the sand: there was a foot, in a deck shoe, and to one side a hand clutching a shred of green seaweed. He took a step forward, almost falling, and saw the seawater pooled in the mouth beyond the sand-encrusted teeth, the dark coagulated red of a split in the lips. He sank to his knees ready to scream. But then came the double shock, as unexpected as the first, and he spilt bile onto the sand.

# 16

From the air Styleman's Middle was an island, ribbed with sinuous lines of sand, like a giant fingerprint. What light there was came between showers of sleet, the low clouds pearlescent, the sea a choppy green. The police Eurocopter came in low from the north, then turned to trace the waterline in a tight circle. Onboard traffic cameras recorded the view below. At the east end a group stood by the cockle boats, scuffed footprints leading away a few hundred yards to an object on the sand: from the air a bucket, a fishing buoy, driftwood.

As the whirling blades slowed Shaw and Valentine jumped down, followed by two uniformed officers they'd rescued from a traffic survey on the quayside. Shaw landed nimbly on one foot, then transferred his weight quickly to both. Valentine landed two-footed, juddering, and nearly pitched head-first. The sand was surprisingly hard and gritty, sparkling with crushed shells. They all walked quickly to the group by the boats and the two PCs began threading scene-of-crime tape in a wide arc round the beached boats, a cordon to keep the people in. The chopper rose, slewed sideways and wheeled towards Lynn.

Fifty yards off the sandbank the Harbour Conservancy's launch was approaching at speed. It pulled a sudden circle as it skimmed into shallow water, and drifted towards land side-on. Tom Hadden and a two-man CSI team jumped clear and waded ashore, each loaded with a large canvas rucksack, the poles of a forensic tent protruding from one.

'Tom,' said Shaw, shaking hands. 'I'll lead the way – let's keep a yard off the path trodden. I don't know how long we've got until the tide rubs all this out, but however long it is, it's getting shorter.'

They set out in line, Valentine at the tail, leaving one of the PCs to stand with the cockle-pickers. Shaw counted his steps. He'd got to a hundred when he stopped, then looked up, prepared to be dispassionate in the presence of death. But he hadn't expected this: the sand-filled mouth set in the skewed O of a silent scream; the rest of the victim's body, except for the single foot and hand, unseen, imprisoned in the sand. The corpse was lying in its sandy grave, the head protruding, but thrown savagely back.

He forced himself to observe, to stay out of the scene he was a witness to. Most corpses say something: revenge, lust, greed, anger. This one was mute; just a victim, almost sucked out of sight for ever.

Shaw could see that all previous footprints had stopped ten feet short of the victim. None had circled. He looked back along the path they'd made to check that no footprints left the track. Then he took in the horizon; to the west the distant shoreline of Lincolnshire, the hills still white. To the east he knew Ingol Beach was only three miles distant, the low white line of the coastal hills just visible.

'Right. Let's do our jobs,' said Shaw. 'And let's do them quickly.'

He began to circumnavigate the corpse, etching a line in the sand with his boot. 'George, organize one of the uniforms to walk the water's edge, double-check no one's landed since high tide.'

Hadden's men walked to one side and quickly erected the lightweight SOC tent over the corpse. White, flimsy, it buckled slightly in the light wind when they lifted it into place, sinking the posts at each corner.

'Is Justina coming?' asked Shaw, following Hadden into the tent.

'On the next boat,' said Hadden. 'She was over in Ely. We'll work our way out from here but it looks like he's had at least one tide wash over him – so don't hold your breath.'

They both smiled: grim humour.

The skewed O, screaming for air.

Shaw knelt on the sand six feet from the head, looking at the face, wishing his wounded eye had healed. Without stereoscopy his vision was flatter, less vivid. Hadden mirrored him, kneeling behind. Twelve o'clock and six o'clock. The air in the tent was suddenly close, making Shaw loosen the zip at his throat.

'The sand's engrained on the skin,' said Hadden. 'In the hair. And . . .' He stopped, bile rising in his throat as a small crab scuttled from the hairline, over the cheek, dropping into the pool which had formed like a moat around its neck. 'Male. Forty? Clothing – what we can see is a polo shirt; that might be a badge on the turned collar. A gold chain round the neck.'

The light in the tent was a pale white, making the dead man's skin look like meat dripping despite a tan.

'Any thoughts?' said Shaw.

'I'd guess he drowned, got washed on to the sand bar; the weight of the corpse begins to take it down through the sand after a tide or two. Another six hours and he'd have gone for ever.'

He stood, a knee joint cracking. 'But there's something else – on the back of the head.'

Shaw walked round, respecting his circle in the sand. The hair was parted at the crown, showing the scalp. Shaw took two strides forward and knelt. Hadden joined him and with a metal spatula parted the hair where blood had congealed. A wound, the colour of a maple leaf in the fall. No bone showing, but the flesh ruptured, rucked. Shaw bent closer and smelt the seawater in the man's clothes, and the first hint of decay, the sweet aroma of evaporating sweat.

Valentine brushed aside the flaps to enter the tent. 'Nothing on the sand,' he said. 'Chopper's coming in with more manpower.' He caught Hadden's eye. 'Your office radioed – they've got a portable generator from the lab.'

Shaw studied the victim's face. The skin, as dead as pork rind, was tanned lightly, the features narrow and fine with the red double claw marks of a pair of spectacles on the bridge of the nose. The hair was well cut, short but with a foppish fringe which dragged down over one eye. Given time, Shaw could bring that face alive, iron out the swelling to the left side where the blow had fallen, lift the cheekbones, repack the features which had been stretched out in the terror of the victim's final minutes.

'He's never picked cockles for a living,' said Valentine. 'Never picked anything for a living – unless it's horses. Indoor clothes,' he added.

Shaw stood, thinking that he'd missed that. 'Justina will want to see him in situ.'

'Low tide's in two hours,' said Hadden. 'This isn't a high point – it could be under water in five, six, possibly less. We'll have to lift him then?'

It was a question, but there was no doubting the answer. If they let the tide wash over again the corpse might not be there next time, sucked down perhaps, or lost in the folds of sand. Even if they marked the spot they might lose him: heavy objects drifted in the liquid sand; wrecks wandered, sinking, resurfacing.

Valentine stepped outside, his radio crackling. Shaw left Hadden in the tent and went back to the cockle-pickers.

Duncan Sly, the gangmaster, stepped forward to meet him, taking charge, displaying authority. His skin was like burnt leather, a smoked kipper, the product of a lifetime spent in the wind and rain. Despite a slight stoop which had come with age he was still the biggest man in the group – six one perhaps, but broad, a barrel chest, with fists that looked lifeless, just hanging from the arms. The seaman's blue jacket was new, the lapels uncurled.

Sly's account was straightforward. The five cockle boats were from Shark Tooth, the shellfish company that ran Gallow Marsh Farm's oyster beds.

'The sand was clean on the lee shore when we landed – no footprints, nothing. We keep an eye out for that, in case another gang's been working our patch. And we've heard about the beach . . . the body in the raft? Radio didn't say much – and that bloke dead in his car. So we had a good look. Nothing.'

Shaw buttoned up his coat and bent down to retrieve a razor shell from the sand, as sharp as a cut-throat. He considered the coincidence that Shark Tooth owned Gallow Marsh Farm and ran the cockle boats, and filed it away with the other things that worried him.

The pickers stood around an impromptu fire: driftwood off the sandbank, old newspapers from one of the boats, and something else glowing on a bed of pebbles. 'Coal?' asked Shaw, knocking the charred wood with his boot.

'Always bring a bag,' said Sly. 'It's bitter out here late afternoon, we take breaks.'

Despite the warmth from the blaze they all stood stiffly. Sly thrust his hands out almost into the flames, then back into the pockets of his jacket. 'We should work, otherwise it's a wasted day.'

'A few questions,' said Shaw, shaking his head. 'Then we're going to have to ask you to go back to Wootton. This is a crime scene, we need to secure it. It's the third unexplained death in the area in twenty-four hours, Mr Sly. It may be a while before you can work here.'

Shaw saw glances exchanged. Besides Sly there were ten of them, two to a boat with Sly presumably in the larger one – a smart inshore fishing smack which had dropped anchor about twenty feet out. It sat at an angle now, beached, the radio mast tilting towards the moon which had appeared in a clearing blue sky. Six of the men were ethnic Chinese, standing together, smoking the same brand of cigarettes, looking everywhere but at Shaw.

Another group of three stood together and Shaw guessed they were east European; one, standing over the fire, was in late middle age, a hand held to his back, an enamel badge on his lapel depicting the Czech flag. The tenth picker – a small man – Shaw recognized as a local. He'd seen him somewhere, the fish dock perhaps, but not selling, in the background counting cash. He wore a duffle coat, the hood up. It wasn't just the coat and his lack of height that made him look like a child. The hair was curly and blond where it showed. He bounced slightly on his toes, bristling with aggression. Shaw's father had always warned him about small, angry men. They only survived by getting in the first blow before the fight started. Or they carried something in their fist to even out the odds.

No one spoke.

'You can smoke now,' said Shaw. Valentine's hand jerked towards his pocket, then pulled back.

'Any idea who the victim might be, Mr Sly?' Shaw asked.

Sly shook his head, watching the flames. 'I didn't get close enough. I didn't want to.'

Valentine nudged a pebble into the fire with his black slip-on. 'Anything unusual out here in the last few days? Any other pickers? Boats?'

'This is our pitch, everyone knows that,' said the man in the duffle coat. His voice was high, thin, but didn't lack confidence.

'Sorry – and who might you be?' asked Valentine, with enough edge in his voice for them all to look up.

'Andy Lufkin.'

'So nothing?' persisted Shaw. 'Nothing unusual?'

'It's a tough season,' said Sly. 'You get other pickers – bands up from London – but they stick to the shore banks on the west side.' In the distance they could all see the coastline of Lincolnshire.

'Someone's been dumping waste in yellow oil drums,' said Shaw. He let Sly poke some more driftwood into the fire. 'What have you seen?'

Sly took a deep breath. 'We tend to keep our heads down.'

That sounded like a euphemism, Shaw thought. 'Turn a blind eye?' he said, a sympathetic pain suddenly running through the wound beneath the dressing.

'Mind our own business,' said Lufkin. Shaw wondered if he kept bouncing on his toes to try and look taller.

'How about a child's inflatable raft – a boat, in bright green colours?' asked Shaw.

'This weather?' said Lufkin, and bit his lip.

'Yes. This weather. Perhaps that's what killed the bloke inside.'

They heard the thudding progress of a motor launch, hitting waves. Shaw could see Justina Kazimierz in the prow, letting saltwater spray her face.

Then Shaw's mobile buzzed. A text message from DC Fiona Campbell at the hospital.

'HOLT'S TALKING,' it read.

## 17

They took the Eurocopter to the pad on top of the A&E department. Shaw radioed for the Land Rover to be brought there, then spent the rest of the flight with his forehead pressed to the window. He'd left Hadden and the CSI team working against the clock. Valentine had briefed the murder team back at St James's and they were checking missing persons. But for now Shaw needed to focus on John Holt. He could see how the murder on Styleman's Middle might be linked to the body in the raft – smuggling perhaps, trafficking, rival gangs fighting for a pitch. But if there was a link to the murder of Harvey Ellis in his pick-up truck then it had eluded him. Two violent killings within a few miles, and a few hours, demanded that Shaw searched for one. And Holt was his key witness.

As they swung round in low cloud over the roof of the hospital Shaw tried to re-focus on the line of cars in the snow that night. Harvey Ellis in the lead vehicle, John Holt in the Corsa behind Sarah Baker-Sibley's Alfa. He quickly re-read the statement Baker-Sibley had made when re-interviewed that morning. Yes: she'd watched Holt go forward to the pick-up truck. But had she taken her eyes off him? No. Not for a second.

But that didn't mean John Holt was not important. He

was the last man to see the victim alive. What had he seen? What had been said?

Holt's room was hospital-hot – a cloying dry warmth suffused with the aromas of disinfectant, custard and stewed tea. The metal bed, the ubiquitous NHS bedside cabinet, the single seat, the grey linen washed a thousand times. As a doctor checked John Holt's temperature Valentine tried not to touch anything, aware that his life would probably end one day in a room like this. He took a deep breath, trying to force air into shrivelled lungs, then retrieved the packet of cigarettes out of his raincoat pocket and dropped it in the bin.

The doctor finished, thrusting her hands down into the pockets of her white coat. She looked like she'd been on her feet for a week, dank hair held up in a Caribbean headscarf. 'Ten minutes,' she said to Shaw. 'No more. No arguments, please. He thinks he's as strong as an ox . . .' Holt laughed, eyes owlish behind the heavy black-rimmed spectacles, his white hair lifeless, stuck to his scalp in the hot still air of the room.

On a chair beside the bed sat a robust woman, upholstered, grey hair too thin to hide the dome of the skull beneath. Respectable was the word that seemed to sum her up – but then Shaw remembered Holt's address, the dockside slum. They'd clearly fallen on hard times.

Mrs Holt looked at her hands, then at her feet. 'He's not well. It was a dreadful night – his blood pressure's really bad. He had a haemorrhage so he's lost a lot of blood.' Shaw could see the broken blood vessels in the old man's nose and a bloodstained wedge of cotton wool. 'He's not been well for a long time,' she added.

'Don't fuss, Martha,' said Holt softly, rolling his false teeth slightly as if they didn't fit. 'The man's got a job to do. I had to put up with half an hour of Michelle – I doubt this will be any worse.'

Martha Holt flushed. 'Michelle's our daughter – she's worried about her dad. She wanted to make sure he stayed in hospital until he's well. He's sixty-eight this year – we both think he should take it easy.'

'My daughter thinks I'm going to die on her,' said Holt. 'Worried she'll have to pay a bill for the first time in her life.'

'John,' hissed his wife. She turned to Shaw. 'Families,' she said, smiling thinly.

'My wife's too forgiving,' said Holt.

Shaw wondered if he always talked about people as if they weren't there.

Valentine began asking questions. It was his interview, Shaw had said on the way up in the lift. Step by step the DS tried to find out what the witness had seen, what he'd heard, what he'd felt. So far the interrogation was faultless.

Sweat gleamed on Holt's upper lip. 'Michelle lives in Hunstanton,' he explained, the voice healthier than his body. 'With Sasha – my granddaughter. I was driving over to finish pruning some trees – they cast shadows on Sasha's window when the moon's out. It's frightening in winter. She's had nightmares.'

'A regular visit?' asked Valentine. 'Couldn't your daughter prune the tree?'

He laughed. 'Michelle's *unwell*.' He said it in a way which made them understand he didn't believe it. 'She gets an allowance from the government. For her and Sasha. A handout.'

Martha Holt stiffened, but didn't interrupt.

'I'm retired, Sergeant. Ill-health. This heart of mine,' he said, tapping a hand on his chest. 'Although I can still get up a set of stepladders. But I had to close down the business. Dizzy spells on hundred-foot scaffolding isn't a very bright idea, is it? There's no real routine. But like I said, I'd been over on Sunday to trim the sycamore – but Sasha said to leave the magnolia because she likes to climb the branches. But then Sunday night she had a nightmare – the shadows again. So I went back on Monday to finish the job.'

Martha Holt touched a card on the bedside table. A piece of folded A4 paper, a child's picture of a house. Beside it another card, more expertly drawn, of a black cat curled on an Aga.

'That's hers,' said Holt, catching the movement. 'That's my Sasha.' He touched the first card, ignoring the second. He rubbed his arm where a drip had been fed into the vein.

'You live in town?' asked Valentine briskly, keen to get the besotted grandfather off his favourite topic.

'Quayside.' He held the DS's gaze while his wife watched her hands.

But it wasn't the quayside. The quayside was renovated warehouses looking out over the water, rabbit hutches for the upwardly mobile at London prices. Devil's Alley was a world away, just round the corner.

'Is that where the car got vandalized?' asked Valentine.

'Car park at Sainsbury's,' said Holt, patting the sheet.

Valentine let that pass. 'Talk me through your journey last night, please.'

'Right.' He held his hand to his forehead, confused, trying to focus. 'I went along the quay, then out by St Anne's to the ring road. Just past Castle Rising the AA sign was out on the road so I turned down the track. Came up behind that woman.' There was no mistaking the note of dislike. 'Well spoken, in a hurry. She thought I should check if we could move the tree. She wasn't worried about the driver, mind you. She didn't seem to care about anyone else – she just wanted to make her next appointment. Like the whole world has to stop for her.'

'And in the cab you found . . .' prompted Shaw.

Holt shrugged. 'The driver.' He let his fingers drum an annoying rhythmless tattoo. 'And the passenger.'

Shaw and Valentine locked eye contact, and in the silence they could hear the Rolex ticking.

'Let's take them one at a time,' said Shaw quickly. Valentine took out his notebook.

'Driver was a young man,' said Holt. 'Nervous type, said he was doing some work at Hunstanton – a bit of extra, he said. That's exactly what he said – I've got a good memory, you see.'

His wife nodded dutifully.

'He said the tree was too heavy to move so I went back to reverse out.'

'Nervous type?' pressed Shaw, trying to slow him down.

'Yes. He had a tape on . . . Well – or one of those CD

things I suppose. I don't know. Music they call it; bilge if you ask me. But he was keeping the beat with his hand on the steering wheel – the heel of his palm, then the fingers. Fast. Clever too. He had a map out but he said he was lost. Wanted me to look, but I didn't have my glasses for reading, just driving. I tried, but nothing, it was just a blur. Besides – what was the point? We weren't going anywhere even if we could work out where we were.'

Shaw raised a finger. 'And the passenger?'

'Young girl. Twenty-odd, I reckon. I think she'd hitched a ride.'

'Why do you say that?'

'I asked where they were going and she said *she* was heading for Cromer. "Heading", that was the word. I think she was trying her luck, you know – seeing where I was off to. But as I said, no one was going anywhere for a while. She said she had a job, that she was an artist. Bubbly type. She had a bag, like a knapsack, on her lap, and she sort of hugged it when she said that – like she had something in there.'

'What kind of knapsack?' asked Valentine.

Holt looked at the DS, his eyes shifting out of focus behind the glasses as if he was seeing it again: 'Multicoloured, yellow and black patches, with a kind of drawstring. Not very big.'

'This girl – was she good looking?' asked Shaw.

'I think so, yes.' Holt re-focused on a point just above his toes. 'I didn't get that good a look because I had to bend down to see in the cab – my back's not what it used to be.' He paused. Shaw thought it wasn't a hopeful sign, a witness who wanted to make excuses. 'Sort of fair,' Holt added. 'Long hair, lank I think. Yes. Not much of her, you know, like they are these days. But leggy all right, jeans and a sort of quilted top and those big boots. She had them up on the dashboard. Cheeky really.'

Shaw gave him some time, trying not to push too quickly for information. 'How did she seem? You said Ellis – that's the driver by the way, Harvey Ellis – you said he was nervous. Was she?'

'No – bit excited if anything. Flushed.'

'Any accent – was she a local girl, d'you reckon?' asked Valentine.

'No. I'd guess the Midlands, you know – sounded like she had a bad cold.'

They laughed and Mrs Holt withdrew her hand from the counterpane.

'How did he die? The driver,' countered Holt, suddenly, the tone of voice wrong, as if he were asking a question at a supermarket checkout.

'Someone pushed a chisel into his eye socket, into his brain,' said Shaw. 'Although I'd like you to keep that to yourself at the moment – we're not giving the details out to the press.' Martha Holt looked at her husband, but his face just froze.

'Who would do that?' he asked, blinking behind the glasses.

'How about a leggy blonde?' said Valentine, coughing up some phlegm.

They stood.

'Mr Holt, it would be really helpful if we could put

together an artist's impression of this girl – the hitch-hiker. Could you help me do that, do you think?' asked Shaw. 'We need to find her.'

Holt shrugged. 'Soon as you can get your artist, Inspector, I'm happy to help.' He smoothed down the counterpane.

'I'll be five minutes,' said Shaw.

He was four. Shaw always kept his basic kit in the back of the Land Rover in a black attaché case: a sheaf of high-quality cartridge paper – Bristol, with a slight pink tint, and a rough texture like skin. Then pencils, woodless plastic-coated leads, chisel-point, and a range of H, F and B hardnesses. A piece of J-cloth for blurring, a set of tortillions – cone-shaped sticks made from compressed paper used to blend graphite lines to produce a smooth finish. Erasers, eraser shields, brushes and pastel chalk sticks. Shaw had studied art at Southampton University. He'd always drawn as a kid, an only child's escape, encouraged by his mother. What his father didn't know was that the course at Southampton offered a year out in forensic art at the FBI's college in Quantico, Virginia.

He opened his dog-eared copy of the *FBI Facial Identification Catalog*. Over the years he'd added to the basic catalogue. Thousands of mugshots compressed by category: bulging eyes, broken noses, pouting lips, lantern jaws, providing the basic building blocks for composite imagery. He'd added his own, cut from newspapers, brochures, and magazines. There was also a recorder for the cognitive interview, so that later he could reconstruct the order in which the witness had accessed their memory. Recall first, then if that failed them, the catalogues for recognition. And last a colour chart for the eyes, hair, and any distinctive clothing or jewellery.

Twenty minutes later Shaw had the basics of the face established.

'I'm not much good, am I?' said Holt. 'I just can't see her face. Not clearly.'

'You don't have to – the memory's not like that. You'll see her in flashes, we just have to wait for them. Each time try and take something new from the image. Don't force it. It'll come.'

And it did. They talked about that night, about the snow, about walking forward in the icy wind. Slowly Holt's memory gave up its secrets. Another twenty minutes and they were done. Shaw was pleased. The face looked out at him: dominated by the wide arched eyebrows, the small mouth with too many teeth.

Holt had closed his eyes while Shaw worked, sketching in the features, adding a light source from the right to add the 3D effect.

'Oh – yes, yes, that's her. That's terrific.' Holt sat up, holding the sketch book.

There were other last-minute changes. They darkened the hair at the parting, lowered the ears, added a shine to the teeth as if they'd been polished.

Finished, Shaw fetched the ward sister and she countersigned the sketch, with Holt and Shaw. They used a date stamp off the ward desk, the hospital motif underlaid by the symbol of a ship at sea – the Lynn badge. Shaw gave it to Valentine, who bagged it in cellophane and signed it as evidence received. He'd book it in with the desk at St James's, then they'd use photocopies.

They left Holt asleep on a pile of pillows.

Sitting in the Land Rover, Valentine looked at the sketch through the clear envelope, trying not to let his admiration for the skill of the artist show.

'Next step?' he asked.

'TV, papers. Posters too — along the coast. Let's give it all we've got. She's either a killer, or she knows who is. So let's find her.'

# 18

The Ark was a converted chapel across the street from St James's, a red-brick shed in the shape of the living-quarters on a child's model of Noah's boat. For nearly a century it had been home to one of the nonconformist sects. But the church had sold up in the sixties and moved out to the ring road. West Norfolk Constabulary had been the purchaser, and, despite the constraints of a Grade II listing, had quickly renovated the Victorian structure to house the force's principal forensic laboratory. This had freed up space in the main building, where the force was struggling to deal with a crime wave brought about by the influx of East Enders to the new estates. Not that the newcomers brought with them any crimes that the locals hadn't tried. It was just that there were more of them.

Most of the town's 200,000 inhabitants had no idea what went on behind the Ark's freshly sandblasted walls and bottle-green and cream stained glass. Now, in the falling snow, lights shone from the savagely sharp lancet windows.

Shaw and Valentine sat in the Mazda, parked in one of the spaces reserved for CID at St James's, waiting for the hour to strike. Being early for an appointment with Dr Kazimierz was a crime second only to being late. They had six minutes to kill. The news that Harvey Ellis had picked up a hitch-hiker, and that she was in the truck when it ground to a halt on Siberia Belt, had turned the case on its head. Valentine thought one motive was obvious. 'They're trapped in the truck, Ellis and the girl, they know they're gonna be there most of the night, she's young and sexy *and*...' he said, letting the world slur along, '*and* she stuck her thumb out at dusk for a lift off a truck on a lonely road. He thinks the hitch-hiker's up for it; she isn't.'

He stopped, watching the snow, and his shoulders rose with a breath. 'He pushes his luck, she's sat on the passenger side with the toolbox between them. She's scared, he makes a move, she flips the top, grabs a tool, and goes for his eye.'

'Then she disappears, not a trace,' said Shaw, shivering as he watched a uniformed PC running across the yard, the snow clinging to his back.

Valentine blew his nose, took a quick breath. 'If Harvey Ellis was murdered, and if the murderer isn't John Holt – then the killer left without leaving tracks. That's a fucking fact. There's no way round it – so you can't use that fact to rule anyone out, can you?'

Shaw's father had always said that George Valentine should have made DCI before any of the rest of them. But there'd been just too many rough edges.

'But there's two other corpses with no apparent link to your amorous driver,' countered Shaw. 'One on the beach – and then a few hours later our friend out on Styleman's Middle.'

Hadden's team had recovered the body from the sands an hour before full tide slipped over his grave. No forensic evidence had been found at all on the sands: no sign of a boat landing, and again – no footprints. The previous tide had wiped the scene of crime clean, leaving only the mathematical precision of the ribbed sea sand.

The Mazda's heater was pumping out warm dust into the car and Valentine sneezed, prompting a series of metronomic sniffs which Shaw tried hard to ignore.

The clock at St Margaret's on the Tuesday Market struck the hour and they got out, ducking through the snow towards the chapel's double doors. Inside they pushed open a heavy perspex hinged screen into the main body of the old chapel. A low metal partition divided the room, continuing in glass up to the vault of the wooden roof. The windows spilt underwater light into the echoing space. The floor at this end was the original parquet, polished to reflect the stained glass, and on it stood three rows of lab tables, centrifuges, a computer suite, and a small conference area to one side beside a bank of sinks along one wall. Tom Hadden's team 'hot-desked', so there were no offices as such. A filter coffee machine coughed its way to the end of its cycle and Dr Justina Kazimierz emerged from the area beyond the partition to refill her cup. Valentine was already at the machine, helping himself. The pathologist worked on contract with the West Norfolk force but she'd been on enough cases in the last ten years for the Ark to have become a second home.

'Tom's back out at Ingol Beach,' she said. 'If you want coffee, help yourself,' she added pointedly, but Valentine just sipped noisily from the mug.

Shaw saw that here, on familiar ground, she moved lightly, reminding him of her canteen dance. She led them into the second room beyond the partition. A single stone angel stood in a niche at the centre of the end wall below the stained-glass windows, and three covered bodies lay on metal autopsy tables. To one side was a desk and Kazimierz had put her black leather bag on top, flaps folded back like a large, exotic funeral flower. A mortuary assistant was hosing down a table.

Shaw could see a foot showing on the nearest table and he thought the stone angel's flesh had a more appealing colour. Valentine gulped coffee, the shock of the caffeine failing to overcome his anxiety at being in the mortuary. He didn't like death, it marked the end of the game, the moment when there was nothing left to gamble with, let alone on.

Their footsteps grated on the concrete floor, which was criss-crossed with aluminium gutters so that the room could be sluiced. Each dissection table was in polished steel. Mobile surgical lights provided an almost unbearable blaze of electricity over each occupied table, driving away shadows where shadows should be.

Dr Kazimierz leant on one of the tables, her weight on one leg, the other shoe raised behind her so that she could tap the concrete with the toe.

'OK. I said I'd walk you through what we've got. That was before the latest on Styleman's Middle. So I've got even less time than I thought. I'll start the internal autopsies with the first victim tonight – bit later than I thought – seven thirty. Be prompt.'

'We appreciate it,' said Shaw.

'Right. Let's start with the latest, shall we? Not much to say.' She swished a plastic sheet back from the first table. The man from Styleman's Middle had been unfolded, the clothes cut away, the sand gently washed from each crevice of flesh. Water droplets covered the skin, adhering to the almost invisible body hair, some of them joining forces to trickle down onto the aluminium table.

'So no prizes,' she said, sliding on forensic gloves. 'A blow to the head here . . .' She placed both hands on the skull, turned it to one side, revealing the bruised wound. Shaw's stomach shifted at the plastic sound of a click from the neck. Valentine took a step back. 'This would have resulted in unconsciousness certainly – perhaps for several hours,' she said. 'Weapon? Wound's odd – considerable force, but a cushioned effect. A blunt instrument wrapped in something, perhaps – or a rubber mallet, one of those you use to knock in tent posts? The prints are difficult to lift because of the saturation of the skin – but I've got a set. We'll check them on records. Clothes are expensive. The polo shirt is interesting – it appears to be much older than the trousers, shorts, socks. Tom can do some more work on that. I'd say 1970s. The badge on the collar is Royal Navy.'

'Just that,' said Shaw. 'Not a ship?'

'No – just the badge.'

Shaw looked at the face, trying to memorize the features. The neatly layered hair, the unblemished skin, the fine bones, the unscarred fingers, the burnless tan. He might have been handsome, he'd certainly had money. Royal Navy – that rang a bell, a ship's bell, but he couldn't place it.

'Other than being dead he's a healthy specimen,' added the pathologist. 'He's taken a whack around the liver, but nothing too serious. We'll need to get the lungs out to be sure of cause of death – but everything's consistent with drowning.'

Dr Kazimierz went to move on.

'Can you get me a set of shots?' asked Shaw. 'Black and white, frontal?'

She filed the request in her head, then let the lab assistant who'd been working at one of the computer screens draw the plastic sheet back over the body. Shaw liked the gesture, a nod to the value of life, even when someone had succeeded in brutally destroying it with a single blow.

'This is much more interesting,' said the pathologist, her fingers interlaced, then free, then laced again.

The corpse from the child's raft was as pallid as it had been when Shaw had dragged it ashore on Ingol Beach. The shadow of a tan perhaps, but one that had faded since an English summer. He lay as if asleep, the white sheet drawn up halfway across the chest, both arms extended down and over the plastic. A crusader, laid to rest in stone. Shaw had noted the muscular physique on the beach, but here, under the laboratory's unforgiving lights, it was even more apparent that this man's body may well have been his business. The shoulders were wide and muscle tissue largely obscured the angle where the neck met the flesh of the shoulder blades.

Dr Kazimierz stood, contemplating the face, a smile on her lips.

'You've got a passport?' said Shaw. 'Prints?'

She touched a small metal cabinet where a red light winked. 'The paper's virtually disintegrated so Tom's drying it as slowly as he can. Again, prints were difficult. You need to be patient.'

Shaw studied the face of the victim again. The hair was black and thick, dark stubble on the chin and neck, blood vessels broken in the nose and cheeks. The brown eyes were flat and fish-like, the nails on the fingers and feet grimy despite the scrubbed skin. There was a signet ring on the right hand. A black stone with a carved surface. Shaw bent closer, trying to see it clearly.

'It's the figure of a man,' said the pathologist. 'With a dragon's tail.'

'Chinese?' asked Valentine. He sniffed, aware that some chemical in the room was attacking his sinuses. The presence of the corpses on the mortuary tables was making it difficult for him to think. He needed something inanimate to focus on. The pathologist slipped the ring off the finger and dropped it in a metal dish. Valentine prodded it with a wooden spatula.

'You'll get a picture of it, ' said Kazimierz.

'Cause of death?' asked Shaw, turning back to the body.

Beside the table stood a spot lamp and a large magnifying glass mounted on a flexible arm. 'Here.' She lit the lamp by switch and poised the glass over the wound on the arm. 'It's a match for his teeth, by the way, so it is his bite.'

Shaw and Valentine leant in together, the DS retreating just in time to avoid a collision.

Two interlocking sets of teeth marks – the top and bottom sets – had come together to lift the skin. The wound was an inch deep at its heart, revealing the muscle below, a single severed artery. In the middle of the double curve of the teeth was a central wound they'd overlooked at the scene: purplish, even black at the centre, surrounded by half a dozen small pustules – pimples which seemed to be full of a clear liquid, like a blister.

Shaw was unsettled that he'd missed it at the time.

'And here,' said the pathologist, resetting the lamp and glass.

Another little colony of pustules, perhaps six inches from the wound, further up the arm.

Shaw saw again the toxic yellow oil drum and readjusted the dressing on his eye. 'A burn – chemicals?'

She shrugged and took a phial from her lab coat. A few drops of an almost colourless liquid, perhaps slightly blue, lay within. 'I got this out of the wound and we did run all the industrial tests . . . but it turns out to be organic. Analysis of the organs may give us more. I've got some samples from the drum for comparison and we'll run it through the spectrometer. But my guess is it won't be a match. Do you know what I think this is?'

They shook their heads like schoolchildren.

'Venom.'

'A bite, then,' said Shaw. 'And he knew, didn't he? So he tried to suck it out, stop it getting into his bloodstream.' He imagined the pain, the panic which would make a man drive his own teeth into his flesh. 'From what?'

'Certainly nothing native to the British Isles. There are two small fang marks at the centre of the lesion, so I'd say a snake. But which one? That's more difficult.'

'Are there any databases for this sort of thing?'

'Ill try London Zoo. And Traffic, the wildlife charity.'

'So what are we saying?' asked Valentine. 'That this bloke died because he got bitten by some exotic animal he was trying to smuggle?'

'Maybe,' said Shaw.

'I should tell Hadden,' said Valentine, searching for the radio in the raincoat over his shoulder. 'He's got people out on the beach.' Above them they heard snow sloughing off the roof, thudding on to the cars parked up in the lee of the old chapel.

'But it won't be alive,' said the pathologist. 'Whatever it is. The venom that killed him is tropical. Ten minutes in zero temperatures would be enough to kill whatever animal bit him.'

'But then if he's smuggling it in – and there may be more than one – he'd have it in something to keep it alive,' said Shaw. 'That's what we need to look for, George. A canister, something that would retain the heat.' Shaw's skin crept.

Valentine retreated to the office beyond the partition.

Shaw stepped back from the corpse, trying to get the death in perspective. They heard the clock at St Margaret's chime the half hour. The pathologist took it as a cue to move on.

Harvey Ellis lay on the final table, the ruptured eye black, disfigured. Shaw noted that in death the narrow face appeared adolescent, resembling that of his son Jake, the child pictured on the photo in the victim's wallet. It was difficult to see Harvey Ellis as a father of three when he looked more like their elder brother. The shroud was drawn up to his Adam's apple, both feet exposed, a label attached to one of the toes.

'Back to no news, or very little,' Justina said.

She pulled down the shroud revealing the military tattoo in blue and red: a castle on a many-pointed starburst in silver. The badge of the Royal Anglians. 'And the defence wound.' She pulled the shroud down further and picked up the right arm.

'So our modus operandi stays the same?' asked Shaw.

'Yes. I'd say so. He died from the stab wound in the eye socket with the chisel, having fought off one earlier thrust. I think he just about bled to death on his back, or certainly with his upper body twisted down, then he was moved to the truck seat. As I said, there isn't enough blood at the scene. I'd say we were three to four pints short of a full measure. But death occurred in the sitting position, and that's where rigor set in.'

'He had a passenger,' said Shaw. 'A girl. Any trace – hairs, lipstick, a kiss? Any traces of semen on the victim?'

She thought about that for thirty seconds, more, walking slowly round the table. 'No one told me that,' she said.

'We just found out,' said Shaw quickly.

'OK. No, absolutely not, no traces at all. Which doesn't mean she wasn't there, of course. I'm looking at the body. The cab's not a pristine environment. It's a working one. There's something like thirty sets of prints on the fascia inside. CSI will check them all out. But on the body, or near the body, nothing really intrusive. And no prints on the murder weapon.'

She pulled off the forensic gloves. They looked at Harvey Ellis's face.

'You think he attacked her?'

'It's an idea,' shrugged Shaw. 'We're short of them at the moment. He had a bracelet on, anything engraved?'

She walked to a desk under one of the lancet windows and returned with a clear envelope. 'Silver. A single word – *Grace*.'

'Right,' said Shaw. He wasn't looking forward to meeting Grace Ellis.

Shaw led the way out through the swing door into the laboratory beyond. Valentine was sitting with his feet up on one of the computer tables, his eyes closed. The pathologist coughed and his eyelids slowly opened.

'And this may not help either,' she said. On one of the desks beside a computer was a vacuum cupboard containing a single glass dish holding a half-eaten apple. Valentine made an effort to look interested. Forensics wasn't his forte. People committed crimes. It was all about getting to grips with people.

'Tom said you wanted to make sure the apple was the victim's last supper,' said Kazimierz. 'Not so.'

'Someone other than Harvey Ellis ate this apple?' asked Shaw. 'Don't suppose you can tell me if it was a leggy blonde, can you?'

'Given proper funding.'

Valentine peered through the glass at the apple. 'And you can tell that – just from that?'

Kazimierz's back stiffened. 'I'd put my reputation on it, Detective Sergeant Valentine.' The inference was masterful. She had a reputation worth the bet.

## 19

'Back to Siberia Belt,' said Shaw, as the Mazda pulled out of the shadow of the Ark and slipped into the traffic sweeping past on the inner ring road. It was his father's golden rule – if in doubt, go back to the scene of the crime. Walk the job, don't talk it. Shaw held a hand to the dressing over his eye, feeling his pulse behind the bruised lid.

'Everything's changed,' he said, as Valentine tried to get the hot air vent to clear the windscreen of condensation. 'There's a passenger in the murder victim's vehicle, but she's gone. There's an apple in the murder victim's vehicle, but it's not his. The corpse on the beach is involved in some form of illegal trade in wildlife, and that's gone too. It wasn't a simple inquiry to start with.'

Shaw decanted the shells from his pocket and ran eight along the dashboard. The Mazda came to a halt at a set of traffic lights by the soaring Gothic spire of St Anne's. A branch of Curry's had a dozen TV sets in the window, each showing the local news. Shaw's sketch of Harvey Ellis's female hitch-hiker flashed up. They studied it until the car behind beeped as the lights changed.

Out of town they joined the coast road near Castle Rising Castle, the snow-topped Norman keep visible over the trees of the park. It wasn't yet dusk, but already there was more light in the fallen snow than the sky. Ahead emergency lights flashed. Valentine checked with traffic on the radio. There'd been an RTA on the bridge over the River Burn – a van hit black ice and crashed through the safety barriers. They pulled a U-turn and threaded their way through the narrow lanes on the high ground until they re-emerged near Gallow Marsh.

Siberia Belt was windswept and looked deserted until they got round the bend. Ahead they could see some of the vehicles still on site, a CSI forensic tent pegged over one.

'Come on,' said Shaw, getting out. 'Talk me through it, George.'

Valentine got out, braced against the icy breeze. They walked along the bank, Valentine listing the eight vehicles from the tail end of the line, starting with the Mondeo.

'By the way – for the record.' He stopped, tapping his toe on the spot. 'The Morris. I checked out the old dear first thing this morning. Early-stage Parkinson's Disease. The weed helps, apparently. I said she should see a doctor about painkillers. She said she had.'

He shrugged, moving on, listing each vehicle.

Tyres crunched and they looked back at the farm track to see a white van at the junction. It flashed its lights once and they saw Izzy Dereham, the tenant farmer, at the wheel, two men squeezed onto the passenger bench beside her. A wave, and she pulled out, heading down to the coast road.

Just four vehicles were left of the original convoy on Siberia Belt – the plumber's Astravan, the security van, Stanley Zhao's Volvo and John Holt's Corsa. Shaw slapped his hand on the roof of the Astravan. One of Tom

Hadden's team, a woman with a forensic face mask, was vacuuming the interior where the dog had sat. 'Hi. Tom about?' asked Shaw, looking at the dashboard, door pockets, open glove compartment.

She flicked off the vacuum and lowered the mask. 'We're expecting him – he's bringing drinks.' She smiled but Shaw could see that her lips were blue, the temperature in the van low enough for her breath to hang between them.

'We're walking the line,' said Shaw. 'It's all been dusted?'

'Sure. It's signed off – help yourself. But exteriors only, please. Don't open any doors.'

They heard the vacuum again, a whine as high-pitched as birdsong from the marsh. As they passed John Holt's Corsa Valentine stopped, studying the vandalized paintwork.

'Tom says it's a proper job – a diamond cutter,' said Shaw.

Valentine ran a finger along one of the lines. 'It's a picture,' he said, shaking his head. Shaw stood at his shoulder, thinking he might be right, but he couldn't see it. Valentine took his battered notebook and sketched the six savage cuts which made up the scrawl. He had an idea what they might be, but he kept it to himself.

They walked on past the butchered pine stump, the crime-scene tape still attached, flapping in the breeze like a Buddhist prayer flag.

'Let's get a clear picture,' said Shaw. He tried to imagine it, conjuring up the scene from his memory, the cars steaming in the moonlight, white and red light splashed on the snow.

'The hitch-hiker changes everything,' said Shaw. 'For a start – if she killed Ellis we're only looking for a set of exit prints. She was in the pick-up already.'

Valentine sniffed, brushing the back of his hand across the tip of his nose. 'She could have got out the seaward side – the passenger side, a single print perhaps, lost under a drift? We could have missed it. There was plenty of wind about, even if there wasn't much snow. Then the helicopter landed and covered the lot anyway.'

Shaw walked to the edge of the deep dyke which ran the length of Siberia Belt on the seaward side. He stood on the brink and let a snowball fall at his feet. 'Where'd she go from there, George? If she jumped the ditch we're looking for a runaway teenager with an Olympic long-jump gold medal. Plus she'd leave prints on the far side on the flat sand and we know it was untouched. If she gets in the ditch she can only go as far as the sluice that way.' He pointed south. 'And we know there were no prints there. And if she went that way,' he pointed north, 'there's another sluice blocking the way after fifty yards and there was no sign of any prints there either. If she'd stayed in the water for just ten minutes, maybe less, she'd never get out. Hypothermia. There was two degrees of frost, if the dyke wasn't full of tidal water it would have been solid ice. We've got to do better than that.'

Valentine stamped his feet. Left, right, left, right. 'OK. She was hidden,' he said. 'On the back of the truck under the tarpaulin. We didn't see her and she got out when the CSI team arrived. They wouldn't know she wasn't one of the witnesses. She just walks out once the place is crawling with uniforms. CSI. Civilian branch. It was like Wembley Way.'

Shaw clapped three times, the sound muffled by his gloved hands. Perhaps that was the key to unlocking Valentine's skills: wind him up first. 'That's the best idea either of us have had since all this started.' It was just about the *only* idea they'd had since they'd found Harvey Ellis's body. 'But . . . I stayed with the body until Hadden's team arrived. I signed over to him. Then I moved back to the Alfa and waited there. When we got reinforcements from St James's I put one on duty at the rear of the pick-up. He was still there at dawn. Paul Twine – the graduate entry.'

'He's on the team.'

'He checked IDs – he looked at mine and I chaired his appointment panel for God's sake. By that point the CSIs had a forensic tent up. They'd booked the tipper load – I saw the manifest: plasterboard, building supplies and a tarpaulin. No leggy blonde.'

Valentine sighed. 'I'll talk to Twine, make sure. It's a long stint on the same spot – perhaps he slipped off for a Jimmy.'

The wind blew in off the sea, a fresh shower of snow closing down visibility to a few yards. Then, just as suddenly, it cleared and a gash of blue opened up at sea.

When they looked south again they could see a figure walking towards them. A minute later Tom Hadden was with them, shaking a flask. The three of them stood in a close triangle passing round a cup of sweet tea the colour of estuary mud.

'Anything?' asked Shaw, nodding in the direction of the vehicles left on the bank, his voice raised above the single note of the wind.

Hadden ran a hand back through his thinning strawberry-blond hair. 'Yeah. I've seen a marsh harrier, and a seal – large as life, just off the beach there.' He smiled. 'But no. Routine, you'll have a full report tomorrow first thing. But I can't think there's anything relevant, which, given the fact we've got a murder victim on the scene is relevant in itself.'

Hadden leant back, closing his eyes to think.

'We think the victim had a passenger in the pick-up,' said Shaw. 'A girl.'

Hadden opened his eyes, the whites slightly bloodshot. 'There's plenty of spare prints – could be her.'

'But nothing else on the passenger side?'

'I'll double-check,' he said.

Valentine smiled. 'There were ladders on top of the Corsa. Fifteen-foot extent – right?'

'Yeah,' said Hadden, remembering he'd put that in his initial report, in the fine print. 'So what?'

'Prints, blood, anything?'

'I did them myself back at the Ark. Clean as whistles.'

'The idea being?' asked Shaw.

Valentine shrugged. 'Nothing that makes any sense.'

Hadden laughed. 'I think one of the witnesses might have noticed the killer building a bridge out of ladders to get to his victim.'

'Like I said,' said Valentine, taking a breath. 'Doesn't make sense.' But if they were looking for a way the killer managed to get away from the scene of crime without touching the snow a full set of ladders seemed like a handy prop.

Shaw could see it too. 'But one more check – just for us?' he asked Hadden.

'OK. Sure.'

'Anything on the spark plugs?' asked Shaw.

'Got 'em here.' Hadden patted the pockets of his all-weather jacket, retrieving a plastic envelope containing a pair of spark plugs. Hadden looked drawn, sleepless, the freckles along his forehead joined up in blotches on the pale skin. 'Reckon they're a year old – more. Perfectly serviceable but the contacts are well worn. We sent them down to the vehicle pool and they reckon – judging by sight – that they'd run for another year, maybe longer.'

'Right. So not new?'

'No way. The others – the ones from the inside of the cab – they're shot. We tried them in one of the squad cars. They wouldn't spark if you put five million volts through them.'

'So that was part of the plan,' said Valentine. 'To fake a breakdown.'

'But he didn't need to, did he?' said Shaw. 'Because the tree was down – chopped down.'

Valentine shook his head. 'Right. Belt and braces? A change of plan?'

'Or two plans,' said Shaw.

## 20

Traffic control radioed them back before the news had got through to the murder inquiry room: the van which had crashed at Burn Bridge was one of North Norfolk Security's – the company that owned the vehicle stranded on Siberia Belt. There was a single fatality. The RTA unit was in attendance, the road closed for the night. The company's MD was en route to the scene.

'He's saved us the trip to his place,' said Valentine.

At the RTA checkpoint Shaw flashed a warrant card and they trundled forward to within fifty yards of the bridge; a graceful concrete arc with steel safety railings. The sun had set, leaving behind a wound in the sky. The river flowed inland, seawater filling the maze of creeks and ditches so that the mirror-like surface seemed to fill the world to the brim.

The van had crashed through the metal barriers but its rear wheels had become entangled in the sheared metal, so that it hung now, swinging slightly, the windscreen pointing down into the water. Except there wasn't a windscreen. The driver hadn't been wearing his seatbelt and on impact had been thrown through the glass. His broken legs were snagged behind the wheel so that he too hung down, his arms reaching towards the water, a snapshot of a diving man.

Amongst the police cars and emergency vehicles was a

civilian-owned BMW, the driver being interviewed in the warmth of the car.

The RTA unit had an inflatable in the water, a floodlight already set up on the bank. As they got closer Shaw could see what was left of the driver's face, lacerated beyond recognition. Blood dripped from the man's hands, carried off by the flowing river below. Valentine hung back, chatting to the senior fire officer with the RTA unit.

'Do we know who he is?' asked Shaw of a uniformed inspector in a reflective jacket. Shaw knew the officer vaguely. Ex-CID, close to retirement, with an attitude problem that age had done nothing to mellow.

He shrugged. 'Let's get him down first,' he said. 'He falls in the water we could lose the body. What's it to you?'

'Could be something, or nothing,' said Shaw, happy to keep him in the dark. He searched his memory for the inspector's name. Jennings, that was it. He'd worked with Shaw's father in what he suspected both would have called the good old days.

There was no doubt what had happened. The BMW had been overtaken by the van, touching 80 mph. It had hit the black ice in the shadow of a line of poplars which guarded the approach to the bridge. The witness said the driver had nearly regained control but had just clipped the railings, ricocheting to the opposite side, smashing through before being snagged by the ruptured metal.

A black sports car crept towards them from the checkpoint. 'This should be the owner of the security firm,' said Jennings. 'He might have an ID for you.'

The man who got out certainly looked like he owned

something. He wore a full-length cashmere coat, driving gloves and black leather shoes shined to reflect the sky.

'I'll have a word,' said Shaw, before Jennings moved. Valentine joined him.

The MD's name was Jeff Ragg. Well fed and tall, his face looked as though it had been soaking up moisture in a bucket all day; the features heavy and bloated, the fingers too, holding a cigarette with a gold band above the filter.

'It's been a long day,' said Ragg, implying he didn't want to talk. The voice was silky, like a recorded message on a cinema-ticket line. But he couldn't look at the corpse for more than a second.

'Can you identify the driver?' asked Shaw.

'It's Jonah. Jonah Shreeves,' said Ragg. He drew on the cigarette and let the smoke sting his eyes.

Shaw thought of the last time he'd seen the security guard, behind the wheel of a van identical to this one on a snow-choked Siberia Belt.

'You can't see the face,' said Valentine. He ran a hand inside his raincoat to comfort his stomach. No, you couldn't see his face, not for the blood and bone.

'The van's missing from our compound and so's Jonah. He's my son-in-law. I don't have to see his face.' Ragg gave them a cold look, as icy as the frozen reeds on the river-bank. Shaw tried to gauge his emotions; a mixture perhaps of anger and resignation, both unsullied by grief. 'Part of the family until three o'clock this afternoon,' he added. 'I rang him out on the round and told him you lot wanted a word about what happened on Siberia Belt. Then he went home, that's their home – I bought it for them – and threw some clothes in a bag, left a note for my daughter Mary.

He wasn't planning on coming back. He's got £10,000 in his wallet. They had a joint account – he's cleaned it out. He said he'd send it back to her, sometime.' Ragg laughed.

'He had a criminal record,' said Shaw. A seagull screeched and fell on the hanging body, pulling clumsily at the hair.

Ragg's eyes narrowed and he bought himself some time by taking a step closer to the water. The van creaked as it swung slightly in the tidal breeze. 'I didn't know.'

'No CRB check? That's standard, isn't it?' asked Valentine, failing to hide a note of disbelief.

'She trusted him,' was all Ragg said. 'She said it was an insult to check him out. Now we know why.'

The RTA unit had got steel cables round the van and were preparing to winch it back to the road. The vibrations set the corpse jiggling, the blood-red hands dancing like a marionette's.

'She had to marry someone,' added Ragg. 'With a kid on the way. If he was gonna be in the family he might as well be on the payroll and do some fucking work.' He turned his back on the body of his son-in-law and looked out to sea where dusk was gathering on the horizon. 'What was on his record?'

'He nearly killed his girlfriend. He'd robbed her grand-mother, and she wanted to turn him in. Broke her arms. But there were others,' said Shaw. 'Your daughter. Did he . . . ?'

'No. Nothing. If he had I'd have killed him. He knew that.'

'Why d'you think he did a runner?' asked Shaw.

'Because if you'd told me about his past I might have

killed him anyway. I'd have kicked his arse out – and he certainly wouldn't have got a ten grand pay-off.'

Valentine coughed, the cold air beginning to make his lungs ache.

'It's possible, Mr Ragg,' said Shaw, 'that the vehicles on Siberia Belt were diverted off the main road in order to set up a robbery – the contents of your security van being the target. Could Shreeves have been involved? The inside man?'

'It crossed my mind,' said Ragg. 'We operate all along the north Norfolk coast, have done for fifteen years. There are plenty of black spots for mobile signals but most of them are out on the beaches or the marsh. There's just a few stretches of road. My vans never use them. We don't have radios, so the mobile signal is crucial. Even the worst black spots can usually pick up something if you walk around a bit searching for the signal. But not Siberia Belt – there's no signal on that stretch for about three miles. It's the worst black spot on the coast. Which is why the regular drivers never use it. Ever.'

'So maybe he was involved?' pressed Shaw.

'I love my daughter, Inspector, but she's not the world's best judge of character. I told her to wait when she met Jonah – give it a year. But she wouldn't. I said she'd regret it one day. She's at home now, doing exactly that.'

The van on the bridge shuddered and they heard a joint crack in the swinging corpse. A leg had broken and Valentine looked away as the bone appeared, the shattered end glimpsed through the shredded overalls.

'I should be with her,' said Ragg. 'As for Jonah, if he *was* involved I think he's paid the penalty, don't you?'

## 21

A single blue balloon hung from the door handle of Flat 34, The Saltings, North End; the home of Harvey Ellis. From the third-floor balcony they could see over the rough lots to where a footpath was lit by a single lamp. In the dark the snow seemed to have its own glow, as if neon tubes had been sunk within. As Shaw knocked he pushed from his mind the vision of Jonah Shreeves's corpse hanging below Burn Bridge. It seemed very likely that Shreeves had met his death fleeing the certainty of his exposure as a violent criminal who lied his way into both a job and a marriage. They might never know if he'd been part of a conspiracy to stage a robbery on the isolated coast road. A plan frustrated, perhaps, by the sudden snowstorm.

Harvey Ellis's death had been no less violent than that of Jonah Shreeves – but in Ellis's case they had a murderer still to find. Shaw squared his shoulders and knocked again, a triple crack. Valentine looked at his shoes, trying to remember the last time he'd worked a thirteen-hour day. He felt shattered, almost dizzy, but good too – like he had a career again. As they waited the only sound was the swish-swish of the ring road, and somewhere a washing machine rocking in its final phase.

Footsteps within, sharp and workmanlike, coming closer on the lino. A woman who introduced herself as

Mary Tyre, a neighbour, let them in, bustling as people do when they want to fill the silence in a grieving home.

Grace Ellis was on the sofa holding her small daughter. An older boy sat at a Formica table with homework in front of him – an exercise book with special grid lines for maths. He'd been crying, and there wasn't a mark on the paper. Shaw noted the glass of water in front of him and the frayed collar of the boy's white shirt. He could see his father in his face – the large features crowding the narrow skull, the small, compact build. Valentine accepted tea in a mug and took a dining-room chair for a seat. Shaw stood, leaving the armchair free in front of the electric fire.

Mrs Ellis stared at the TV which wasn't on, her knees pressed together, until Mrs Tyre prised the toddler from her arms and let her play on the carpet. The boy left his books and knelt, spinning toys for his sister.

Shaw estimated Grace Ellis's age as late twenties, early thirties. She had what looked like natural blonde hair falling to her shoulders, and the kind of thin stretched skin which reveals the veins beneath, the bones of the forehead and cheeks threatening to break through the papery surface. He tried to conjure up Harvey Ellis's face – the adolescent features – and thought what a fragile couple they'd been.

'The blue balloon on the door . . . ?' asked Shaw.

Grace shook her head, put a hand out for a mug of tea, then took it back. 'It's for Jake.' She thought about that. 'He's got leukaemia and there's an appeal – it was Harvey's idea. Jake's mad about birds of prey – always has been. Hawks, eagles, kites . . . Harvey takes him up to the coast sometimes, to Holkham or Snettisham. But we need the money for Jake to see a bald eagle in the wild. Five thousand pounds. There's a place in America,' she added, taking a breath. 'The Iroquois National Wildlife Refuge. We had people round last night to organize a sponsored cycle – bit of a party. But Harvey missed it. There was good news – a thousand-pound donation . . .' She looked at Shaw for the first time. 'Police community fund – the local copper put a word in for us. They did a sponsored walk. Really got behind us.'

Shaw thought about the plastic eagle hanging in the pick-up's cab. 'It's a start,' he said.

Valentine was reluctantly impressed by Shaw's skills at talking to people, putting them at ease. He wondered what Shaw would say if he told him it was a skill his father had also mastered. 'Where's Jake now?' he asked, his lips suddenly coming into contact with the tea bag floating in the mug.

'The Queen Victoria,' said Grace Ellis. 'We go every day.' She looked up at a clock on the mantelpiece. 'At six. We're late.'

'I'll arrange for a car to take you,' said Valentine, putting the mug down quickly, unable to face another encounter with the wayward tea bag.

Shaw left her some silence. Then they filled in the missing life: Ellis was local, primary school in the North End, then GNVQs at the college. He'd been a boy soldier, the TA, and he still played football most weeks for an army side. Jake and his brother Michael used to go and watch. That was Harvey's big passion – although he wasn't that good. Too short, too lightweight. He'd worked for Fry & Sons, builders, right from the start. He did his own work at weekends, evenings. Hence the business card. The rest of the time he spent with the kids. Monday night he'd been on his way to an old council house at South Creake. The job had already lasted a week. The only things he did on his own were to watch *Match of the Day* and listen to his music in the truck. Prog-metal, loud.

'I can't stand it,' she said, nodding at a CD rack by the fireplace. She looked at her watch. 'I'm going to have to tell Jake.'

'The illness must have been a blow,' said Shaw, trying to get her to talk. 'When was your son diagnosed?'

'Eight months ago. Wasn't a blow, exactly. Well, course it *was*.' She pushed hair out of her eyes. 'But Harvey said it had saved us all. Made us a family. That we'd make the most of Jake, knowing he'd be gone one day. He's right. We didn't get that chance with Harvey, did we?' Anger in her voice now.

'But Jake's very ill now?' asked Shaw, knowing the question was a euphemism.

She was bright enough to see that. 'There's not much time. A few months. Maybe weeks.' She looked at the children. 'Harvey said that if Jake left us . . .' She stopped, and Michael smiled at her. 'No – *when* – he left us, then we'd still be a family. But I said it wasn't fair. Harvey said it *was* fair – that we'd got Michael and Peg and that had been a bonus because I'd had a difficult pregnancy with Jake and they said I couldn't have any more. So we'd had our luck. And anyway, life isn't fair, is it?'

Shaw knelt down on the carpet by the children.

'Someone killed Harvey, Mrs Ellis — can you think of anyone who'd have a reason to do that?'

A cutting from the *Lynn News* was fixed with Blu Tack to the wall above the tiled mantelpiece, next to a football line-up. A picture of Jake in bed at the hospice, a headline: 'Eagle appeal takes off with £100 donation.'

'Not everyone thought the appeal was good news,' she said. 'Money's short round here. Five grand is a lot for a treat. Some people are like that. But we wanted him to have the memory.'

Valentine stood, pretending to study the team photo. 'Anyone ever threaten your husband, Mrs Ellis? You? The family?'

She shook her head. 'People said things, in the street. Every time I got my purse out I could feel people watching, thinking, *Is that Jake's money?* But no — no one ever said they would hurt Harvey.'

'How much have you got?' asked Valentine. 'For the appeal?'

'About two thousand, a few pennies more. It's hard going.'

'Could we have a picture of Harvey, Mrs Ellis? It would be a big help for our inquiries,' asked Shaw. She nodded, relieved to have a task, and went out to the kitchen where they heard her sifting through a drawer.

Mrs Tyre rested a hand on Michael's head, her fingers busy, keeping time to an unheard tune. Shaw's mobile buzzed and he scrolled down to find a picture from Lena: Francesca in the council pool at Lynn, both hands on a bright red swimming hat which meant she'd passed to the next level. He clicked the phone off, slipping it quickly into his pocket.

Grace Ellis came back into the room with a set of photos.

'Thank you,' said Shaw. 'That's a big help. We'll let you get on now.'

She saw them out into the corridor in silence. Shaw waited for the lounge door to close. 'Mrs Ellis, I'm sorry, one more question.'

He produced his artist's impression of the hitch-hiker. 'Do you know this woman?'

She took a tissue from her sleeve and dabbed at her nose. She studied the image. 'No. I don't think so, no.'

'OK.' He zipped up his jacket. 'Just for the record. I have to ask. Your marriage, there must have been a lot of strain with Jake's illness. How were you coping?'

She'd heard him but she didn't understand. Valentine held his breath, shocked that Shaw had the bottle to ask now, on the first day she was a widow.

'What?' she said. 'We just coped, together.' She looked around, as if searching for a translator. 'And when it was over, we were gonna cope with that.'

Shaw smiled, Valentine pocketed his notebook and they slipped out through the front door, trying not to let the cold in.

In the murder inquiry room at St James's a Christmas tree still stood by the window. A pair of handcuffs hung from one branch, scene-of-crime tape wrapped in a spiral up to a star made from a tin ashtray. Beneath it were three crates of beer bottles where the presents should have been, all now empty, and all originally care of the landlord of the Red House, the CID's regular watering hole, a back-street boozer with a quiet snug bar and a remarkably law-abiding clientele.

The team stood in a circle, letting the phones ring, ready for Shaw's briefing. He stood, his feet spaced to match his shoulders, his voice as confident as his body language. In his hand a set of black-and-white prints from the morgue. Beside him a bottle of mineral water. The silence was respectful: they all knew Peter Shaw, and his reputation for fast, smart, exhaustive police work. And they knew he always kept his distance. Even as a young DC he'd always managed to draw a sharp line between friendship and the often excessive camaraderie of the CID.

But there was admiration, especially for his skills as a forensic artist. Until now these had been exhibited in a series of classes for recruits, and articles in the force magazine. This was the first time anyone had seen him in action on a live case. Three A-frame easels had been set out, the contents covered by blank sheets of paper.

'Right. Let's keep it short and simple,' said Shaw. 'We have three violent deaths. Two are clearly murder victims. But first – our man in the raft.' He flipped back the sheet of paper to reveal a large mug-shot of the man they'd found on Ingol Beach taken in the morgue.

'Passport ID, George?'

'Terence Michael Brand, birthplace King's Lynn. Aged thirty-one,' said Valentine.

'So,' said Shaw. 'Brand was poisoned, possibly a snake bite.'

'Sir . . .' It was DC Fiona Campbell. 'Just on Brand,' she said, standing, all six foot two of her, shoulders rounded and slightly stooped, trying to look smaller than she was. She'd come straight on to the force five years ago from school, just like her father, a DCI in Norwich, had done before her, despite having the academic qualifications to go to just about any university.

'His name was on the national database. Address in Nuneaton. Local police got a squad car straight round. Looks like our man. He's known to them. Various scams, never violent, but plenty of victims. All to finance his hobby, apparently.'

'Hobby?' asked Valentine.

'Surfing. He's got a job poolside at the municipal baths – a lifeguard. But the contract's flexible and he disappears here and there for a few weeks chasing waves – Cornwall, Australia one summer.'

'Nothing else?'

'Two things. He was due up at Lynn Magistrates end

of this month on a charge of ABH – a fight in the town centre. He was bailed at his first appearance last week – £500, paid in cash on the day by Andrew John Lufkin.'

Shaw recalled the cockle-picker's face: the childlike curly blond hair crammed under the woollen hat. He caught Valentine's eye, and they exchanged a nod. That put the cockle-pickers at the heart of the smuggling operation.

'And?'

'Currently he's away for a month. He lives with his aunt, his father's sister, a rented flat near the station. She could ID him but she's housebound. He's never said who he stays with, and she hasn't asked. She says that's how they get along. She says he takes his wetsuit. Left a forwarding address in Lynn – she says he's got friends here.' She flicked the piece of paper in her hand. 'The Emerald Garden Chinese takeaway.'

Shaw made an effort to see the links clearly: Stanley Zhao at the wheel of his Volvo on Siberia Belt, the food going cold in the back, while Brand's body floats in to Ingol Beach.

'OK. George and I will make a second visit to Stanley Zhao. It was obvious he was lying; now we know what he was lying about. And let's keep the link with Lufkin up front – that's a direct link between the raft and the cockle-pickers. Either way Brand could be the key. You don't need to be a mathematician to work out the chances that Brand's death is unconnected to our two murders. But you need to be a copper to know they might not be. So let's not tangle ourselves up with theories until we've done the legwork.'

Outside they heard a bottle smash in Greyfriars, the

first sign closing time was approaching. One of the DCs at the back stifled a yawn. It had been a long day, but Shaw knew it was vital to sum up, keep the team's objectives clear, avoid the debilitating drift into information overload.

Shaw touched the dressing on his wounded eye. 'OK. Next: the body on the sands, on Styleman's Middle. Let's call him Styleman for now.' He flipped back the next sheet of paper and there was an audible intake of breath. Shaw had taken Justina's morgue shots and 'reanimated' the face, sketching in a random expression on the features – an understated laugh, just revealing the teeth, lifting the facial skin, deepening the crow's feet. He'd used the tortillion to give the skin lustre, and then 3D lighting to give it substance. It was a face with as much life as any in the room, and seemed about to turn to look at its creator.

'Earlier tonight, George and I attended the internal autopsy.' Valentine fought not to conjure up the image that had made him retch: the lungs held up to the light. 'There was water in the airway and stomach, and the lungs were swollen, so death due to drowning – but the wound to the back of the skull was traumatic. He'd have been out cold by the time he hit the water.

'Jacky – I want you to concentrate on this.' DC Jacky Lau was ethnic Chinese, a tough operator with links well established in the local community, and an ambition to become West Norfolk's first female DCI. She was short, compact, but you'd never call her petite. She'd joined the force late, in her mid-thirties, chucking in a job with her father's taxi firm. Outside the job her life was stock-car racing, and a series of boyfriends she'd dragged along to

CID parties in the Red House, all with leather jackets, tattoos, and engine oil under their nails.

'Is he local? Or is he a floater from up the coast? Let's do a check with all forces – Lincolnshire, Tyneside, Northumberland – even Lothian and Borders. But if he's one of ours then my guess is it's something to do with the sands. We need to know what's going on out there. That's got to be what this is about. Is it linked to smuggling? Let's dig away at the cockle-pickers.'

In his memory he saw the bone-white yacht slipping into the creek the night Harvey Ellis died. A blue clam motif on the sail. He'd sketch it, see if Lau could find the yacht along the coast.

'Let's get copies of this face along the docks, the marinas, see if we can get an ID,' he said. 'We need background, context, that's your job. Check everything.'

DC Campbell dropped her chin and smiled. They'd had a sweepstake before the briefing, trying to guess how many times Shaw would use the word 'check'.

'And finally,' said Shaw. The last evidence board. A photo of Harvey Ellis, cut from the family shot his wife had provided, smiling into the sun with the sea behind, the water dotted with swimmers. CSI shots of the inside of the victim's pick-up. A close up of the dead man, slumped forward on the wheel.

'Last case – but this is where we sink the resources in the next twenty-four hours. We have a firm ID – we can do some solid work here. But it's not easy. At the moment this case makes the *Murders on the Rue Morgue* look like a traffic offence.'

Shaw let the laughter run, a few of the team refilled their coffee cups.

'According to forensics,' said Shaw. 'Harvey Ellis died sometime between 4.45 and 7.45 p.m. The convoy pulled up at around 5.15. Ellis was driving the first vehicle – with him was a hitch-hiker. John Holt talked to him. Sarah Baker-Sibley saw him moving about in the truck – saw *someone* moving about in the truck anyway. He switched to the radio from the CD about seven – according to Baker-Sibley again. I found him dead at eight fifteen. The snow around the vehicle is untouched by another human footprint. Oh – and there's a half-eaten apple on the dashboard – but Ellis didn't eat it. The hitch-hiker's disappeared and the pathologist says Ellis didn't die in the cab. If anybody can make sense out of all of that I'd like them to speak up, right now.'

He let the silence linger.

'Could Holt have done it?' asked Campbell.

'We can't rule him out but it looks very unlikely. He couldn't have known the woman in the Alfa – Baker-Sibley – wasn't watching him. Did he really risk two thrusts through the open window? She says his hands never came out of his pockets. And no blood on his clothes? And someone was still playing with the radio and CD ninety minutes later. Plus – the evidence tells us he didn't die in the cab.'

Another silence.

'We know someone was out to divert traffic on to Siberia Belt,' said Shaw. 'The two AA signs were put out, at either end, and then taken back in. The AA is sure it's not one of their crews, same goes for the police and County Highways. Plus there was no flood on the coast road.

'The question is – who was the target? Ellis? There's a pair of blown spark plugs to hand. If he'd put them in the engine he'd be going nowhere. Was that the plan? To use the pick-up to block the road? If so, why'd they change the plan? Either way it's a trap – we just can't be sure Harvey Ellis was the fly. If he wasn't – who was? The security van?'

He unscrewed the top of the water bottle and drank half of it. 'OK. We're nearly done,' said Shaw. 'We better stop soon before everyone explodes with anxiety about the approach of closing time.'

Valentine pretended to laugh with everyone else. He really could do with a drink.

'But . . .' added Shaw, 'we also need to find two missing people. First. Ellis's passenger.'

Shaw flipped the picture of Harvey Ellis back over the board to reveal his sketch of the hitch-hiker Holt had described. 'We've got this out to the media now, as you'll have seen. This is John Holt's best guess. Female, young. Sexy. She said she was heading for Cromer – let's check that. She's our first priority. She could be our killer.

'Then there's the runaway kid in the stolen Mondeo. Perhaps he's the backstop, put there to make sure no one can get out. Because the Mondeo's the last car. What do we know about the kid? He's just stolen a car. He's drunk the best part of a bottle of vodka – if you think the best part is the bit with the alcohol in it. He's not very good at driving the car – if the position of the Mondeo is anything to go by – but perhaps that's the vodka. He wears a baseball cap. He talks like he's off the estates, but George spoke to him and we think there's a middle-class kid inside trying not to get out.'

'And there's this rubber-stamp thing on the back of his hand. BT. Do we check with them?' asked Campbell.

'Telecom?' said Shaw.

'It wasn't anything fancy,' said Valentine, shaking his head. 'Kind of thing you get on your hand at a night-club.'

'We need to find this witness. He's important. So let's think of ways to find him, shall we?' said Shaw.

They heard footsteps in the corridor and the double doors swung open. Tom Hadden held a single sheet of computer paper, a tracing across it like a read-out from a seismograph.

Under the neon light he looked ill, his eyes pink, matching the strawberry-blond wisps of hair above his ears. Hadden always reminded Shaw of a laboratory rabbit, pink ears, pale flesh under thin white hair, and the eyes set back, as if glimpsed under ice.

'Sorry,' he said.

'Go ahead – just winding up,' said Shaw. 'Anything?'

'Yeah. Fred Parlour, the plumber. He hit his head on the door of the kid's Mondeo. We did all the checks. The blood on the door is Group O, as is Parlour's. But there was a smudge on Parlour's overalls . . . here.' He put his right hand over the left thigh of his cords. 'It's not O. It's AB – same as the victim.' He held up the print-out.

'I've done some checks using antigen analysis. The blood's Harvey Ellis's.'

One of the DCs clapped slowly.

'Is that definite?' said Shaw.

'Well, it's more likely you'll be hit by a meteorite on the way home, Peter, than this blood belongs to someone other than Harvey Ellis.'

Everyone started to talk but Shaw raised a hand. 'Tom. Thanks.'

'Unfortunately . . .' Hadden was looking at the print-out. 'It's never that easy. I can match the blood, no problem. But the smear isn't just blood. There's something else and I can't ID it, not 100 per cent. Spectrometer says it's organic. The nearest match I've got is bone.'

'Ellis's eye socket was chipped,' said Twine. 'The pathologist's report mentioned fragments.'

'Yes,' said Hadden. 'But not fragments of sheep bone.'

Valentine snapped a pencil.

'As I said, I haven't got it exactly right. But it's an animal bone. Possibly more than one. Anyway, you'll have it in writing in the morning.' He was already retreating through the doors. 'I'll be in the Ark if you want me.'

There was a moment of silence as the doors banged shut. Shaw took a deep breath.

'OK. That could be the breakthrough we don't deserve. On the other hand it might not be – so let's keep our heads. We do the legwork tomorrow. George and I will deal with Parlour.'

Valentine cracked the joints in his left hand. 'He's got the victim's blood on his trousers.'

'Yeah,' said Shaw. 'But the problems are still the same – only worse. No footprints. How does that work? How does he get forward, kill Ellis, get back, without being seen and without leaving footprints. Anyone?'

There was a silence that made all the other silences sound like the Hallelujah Chorus.

'And carrying a dead sheep,' added Valentine.

# 23

The murder team dispersed quickly to the Red House. Shaw had told the team not to get excited about Hadden's forensic evidence. But it hadn't worked. He could feel the almost palpable rush of adrenaline. He didn't blame them for their optimism. Parlour had lied. He'd sworn he hadn't gone further forward along the line of cars than Holt's silver Corsa. But at some point that night he'd got very close indeed to Harvey Ellis. He'd be on a murder charge by lunchtime unless he could talk his way out of it. And Valentine was right – not for the first time. Their job was to catch a killer, not solve some arcane forensic puzzle. They could work out *how* he'd done it later. But in the end Shaw knew that if they got him in front of a jury then they would need all the answers to secure a conviction. In the end they'd have to work it out.

Shaw said he'd see them there. He wouldn't, and they knew it, knowing the DI would slip home. But this night, for once, they were only half right. Shaw knew he should go home, sleep well, and prepare for the crucial interview. But first there was something he had to do. Something which, if he'd really had faith in his father, he would have done many years before. He'd avoided even thinking about the Tessier case for a decade, probably – he could admit it now – because he was afraid of what he might find. Doubting his father's honesty seemed safer than trying to find out the truth. So he'd let it be. But now things were different. Somehow George Valentine had brought it all back to life. And he wanted to trust George Valentine. But could he?

He walked down the back stairs to the ground floor. St James's had been built in 1926, on the ruins of the old city walls. Permission had been granted for the demolition of a row of Victorian lock-up shops. The problem was what was under the lock-up shops. At that precise point on the old medieval walls the original builders had dug deep to create a series of underground magazines for the storage of gunpowder. Semi-circular vaults, in local clay brick, linked like a tube train. Four carriages in all, each nearly sixty feet in length.

But it was for the last two that Peter Shaw was bound. The custody sergeant let him into the corridor that led to the stairs and the overnight cells. A drunk sang from the first, the voice light and tuneful. At the end of the corridor was an iron door, painted gloss black, with the single word RECORDS in copperplate script.

The door, unlocked, swung easily inward on oiled hinges. Here the barrel roof of the old cellar had been left in its original state, spotlights illuminating the intricate work of the medieval builders, studded now with a network of discreet piping which provided a state-of-the-art sprinkler system. The room was full of black metal shelving, stacked with file boxes, the rows arranged like a library. In each row stood a dehumidifier.

A man at a desk sat obscuring the chair which presumably was supporting him. He had agricultural bones from which hung enough weight for two people. Even seated his stature was not in doubt, his shoulders met his head without the normal intervention of a neck, and he had one massive leg up on the corner of the desk, a cup in his hand the size of a ceramic bucket.

'Peter,' he said, standing, inadvertently heaving the desk forward. 'Sir.'

'Timber.' They shook hands, laughing.

Shaw thought Sergeant 'Timber' Woods looked his age, which must have been sixty-six. Woods had retired a year earlier after a lifetime of unblemished, if uninspired, service. He'd been asked back to cover the late shift at the records office, a sinecure demanding only diligence. West Norfolk had switched to computerized records in 1995. But the St James's budget had yet to find the extra cash to transfer the backlog. Access to information and data-protection legislation demanded the files be kept, preserved, and made available to any member of the public completing the necessary paperwork – as well as for CID and uniformed branch inquiries. So nearly three thousand case box files, bound back copies of the local papers, stenographers' notes and scene-of-crime evidence boxes had been saved – the collective memory of West Norfolk Constabulary stretching back to 1934.

'So.' Woods mashed a tea bag in another mug. 'George Valentine,' he said, smiling. 'Jack would've laughed.'

Shaw had known Timber Woods all his life. He'd been one of the few of his father's friends not to fade out of the picture after the Tessier case and Jack Shaw's hurried retirement.

'We went out to the Westmead,' said Shaw. 'George and I. I'd never seen the spot, where they found the kid.' He paused. 'And I didn't know the kid looked like me – Jonathan Tessier: the hair, the eyes.'

Woods picked up the mug, effortlessly enclosing it within his fist. 'We spent three years on the beat together – Jack and me – and we broke a few rules, cut a few corners, but I never saw him plant anything, Peter. That's a rule he didn't break, *wouldn't* break. If you played by all the rules you didn't get to nick anybody. He was a good honest copper. I don't know why you can't just accept that.'

'Doesn't mean I don't want to, does it?'

Woods looked at the spot where Shaw's tie should have been. 'He'd have been proud of you.'

'He didn't want me to be a copper.'

'He wanted you to have a life. He just didn't think you could have both,' said Woods, hiding a frayed cuff. 'He'd still have been proud of you.'

'Is there a box for the Tessier case?'

'A file?'

'No. A box – a scene-of-crime box.'

Woods took some keys from a metal drawer and led the way down the room. The door set in the far wall was iron, fireproof, the black paint peeling. He reached inside and flicked a switch, a solitary light bulb illuminating the final cellar beneath an identical brick roof.

Open wooden shelving this time, metal boxes, navy blue, stacked in lines, each secured with a small padlock, each with a card inserted in a groove. Shaw turned one to the light:

ATKINS. June 1974.
DI R.G.WILLIS. CN 778/8

Shaw walked to the end of the vault and moved back in small sideways steps, his lips marking off the alphabetical order. Then he brushed his hands on his trousers and reached into the stack, pulling a box out so that the metal screeched.

TESSIER. July 1997.
DCI Jack Shaw. CN 1399/3

They each took a handle, lugging it to a wide table, scratches polished into the surface. Woods unlocked the box and tipped back the lid. Dust rose like a final breath.

There wasn't much inside. Shaw held up a plastic bag containing a single black leather glove. The label was in Jack Shaw's writing. Date. Time. Place. Countersigned by DI George Valentine.

'And there we have it,' said Shaw, wanting to believe.

Another cellophane bag. Items of clothing cut from the body in the morgue. A football top – Celtic – and a pair of white shorts. Pants, socks (odd, both football, but one green one white), a pair of football boots with the studs removed, and a red sweatshirt. Another held the contents of the shorts pocket: a 20p piece, two 10p pieces, a single wrapped Opal Fruit. A third bag had been set aside for a scrap of paper covered in oil stains.

Shaw held it up to the light. 'Chip paper,' he read off the label. 'Beef dripping – those were the days, eh, Timber?'

Next was a glass phial, empty now apart from a dirty tidemark, but the label said it had held water and oil from the puddle in which the boy's body had been found. Three bagged hairs from the shirt – again collected at the morgue – all, Shaw noted with irritation, in the same bag. A perspex box held a length of sticky tape used to lift fibres and trace evidence from the shirt and shorts. The label noted that all the items had been examined by the Home Office forensic laboratory at Bracknell. And there was another clear plastic evidence tube, this one marked 'DNA swab – victim's fingernails. Human skin.' But the tube was empty. And a tiny chip of blue paint, held in a plastic tube, inside a clear envelope.

'The original forensics report will be with the file,' said Woods, nodding as if the question had been asked. 'But this is a copy.' There was an envelope attached to the inside of the box lid, and he slid out a sheaf of papers in close type. 'You often get those empty tubes with these old cases. Nothing left after a standard set of DNA tests in those days.'

'I'd like to book the box out.'

Woods heaved a ledger round. 'Got a bit of spare time, have you, Peter? A coupla murders would keep most DIs busy.'

'Can't sleep,' said Shaw, laughing.

'Your dad was the same,' said Woods, locking up.

'I'd like the box and the copy of the lab reports taken over to forensics – Tom Hadden's attention. Get a signature there as well, OK?'

Woods checked the entry. 'You know what this place used to be?' he asked, looking round.

'No idea, Timber.'

'Before we had to bring the records down it was cells

too. Pretty grim, actually. We had Bobby Mosse in here a night or two. I ran the place then, custody sergeant. Odd kid. He killed Jonathan Tessier, Peter. Believe me.'

'So everyone says. But that's not how it's supposed to work, Timber.' Shaw couldn't keep the edge of anger out of his voice. 'I'm supposed to be convinced by the evidence. So.' He tapped the evidence box. 'Let's see what twelve years' worth of advances in forensic science can tell us, shall we?'

They walked back into the records room. 'I'd like the file too,' said Shaw, closing his good eye, resting it now that the tiredness was blurring his vision.

Woods took a big breath. 'The file on Tessier's out.'

Shaw stopped and looked at his heavy, fleshy face. 'Who . . . ?'

'According to the book it was George Valentine,' said Woods. 'You two should talk to each other.'

An hour later Shaw was walking back along the line of the dunes towards The Old Beach Café. Despite the hour Lena was still working, that day's delivery of stock spread out on the wooden floor of the old boathouse shop: wetsuits spreadeagled in lines, a rack of swimwear, and a brace of new surf boards encased in bubble wrap.

She was in a tracksuit, her hair pulled back in a stylish knot.

'Did you have a run?' said Shaw, sitting in a wicker chair by the racks of beach shoes.

'Just down to the sea at dusk while Fran was reading.' Shaw glanced at the baby monitor Lena still left on when she worked in the shop. Fran was old enough now to find her own way from the cottage down the path. But after dark, and in winter, Lena couldn't bear to snap the electronic link between them.

'Drink? I heard the latest on the radio.'

She fetched a wine bottle, the cork eased out, and two small glass tumblers.

'George Valentine told me something I didn't know about Dad,' said Shaw, holding the wine up to the light. It looked like blood. He drank it quickly and helped himself to a second glass.

Lena knelt, spreading out one of the wetsuits, testing the seams. Shaw's family was not a subject they ever discussed. When he'd come back from London after his year with the Met he'd brought Lena with him. His mother had tried to see past her skin, but Jack Shaw couldn't even do that. The atmosphere at home was toxic in the aftermath of the Tessier case. Jack Shaw had taken early retirement to protect his pension. Which meant the Tessier file was closed. The subject was never mentioned, but had permeated his father's bitter last year of life. It hadn't been the best moment to ask him to embrace an interracial marriage. The clash marked the final break between father and son. Lena couldn't believe so little could be said as a family tore itself apart.

'He said Dad asked him to clear his name. To prove that Bobby Mosse killed Jonathan Tessier.'

'And has he?' she asked.

'No. And I don't think there's any chance he ever will.' Shaw thought about what he was going to say next, knowing it revealed a cynical side to his mind which Lena hated. 'Which raises two questions. Did Dad really ask him to clear his name? If it's a genuine question it's a kind of proof in itself, isn't it? And second. He's taken the file on the Tessier case out of the records at St James's. Why? Perhaps there's something in it that incriminates them both.'

Lena stood, holding up a new suit, a sky-blue wave picked out on the stippled black chest.

'But if Jack did ask him?'

'Then I suppose I could try to help,' said Shaw. '*Should* try to help. If we could prove Mosse was the killer it would lift the cloud over the case – not entirely, of course, even if Mosse *is* guilty it doesn't mean they didn't plant the evidence. But it shifts the probabilities. They didn't follow the rules that night, nobody's going to rewrite that. But if Mosse is the murderer then it's odds on it *was* his glove, and that it *was* bagged when they took it to the flat.'

'How are you going to prove he was the killer?' she asked, ever practical.

'I've got the forensics – the original box. Valentine's a good copper, in fact he's a bloody good copper . . .'

Shaw stopped, realizing that Valentine had earned the compliment. Lena just smiled, knowing how difficult he found it to admit he'd got someone wrong.

'A bloody good copper,' he said again. 'But forensics aren't his strong point. I'll get Tom Hadden to run through, see if they missed anything. Or I can put it up to Warren, see if he'll look at the file at least.'

'Good. Do that. Don't stew in it, Peter. You don't know what happened, so find out. If you don't trust either of them implicitly then it's all you can do.'

'You think I should trust them? *Implicitly*?'

It was one of her favourite words, but only because it hid what she really wanted to say. *Faith* was the word she was thinking about. 'Maybe,' she said, toying with a simple silver cross at her neck.

'But I don't, do I? So there's no point in pretending.'

'And what do you feel about that?' she asked, smiling, balancing a toolbox on her hip.

Shaw dropped his chin on to his chest and gave her a weary look. 'Feel?'

She pulled up another chair and put her feet up on his lap. 'Yes. Feel.'

He massaged her foot, bending the toes down to flex the instep. 'Let's go to bed.'

# 24

Shaw swung the Land Rover over the Ouse Bridge, skimming above the estuary, looking back at the Lynn waterfront a mile distant, the tide running out now, revealing banks of mud the colour of Bisto. They turned north when they reached the far bank, past the canning factory and into West Lynn, a sleepy dormitory suburb with the one road in doubling up as the one road out, 1930s semis arranged in a maze of concentric cul-de-sacs, a church tower scarred by damp, and the ferry carrying commuters and shoppers over the water to the medieval quayside on the far side of the estuary.

They followed the street signs for the West Lynn ferry. 'Let's make sure we do this one by the book,' said Shaw, skirting a line of commuters' cars. He bit his tongue, knowing it had been an unnecessary reminder. It was a scab he couldn't help but pick.

Valentine sniffed loudly, the phlegm in his throat bubbling. Then he looked out of the side window, his eyes narrowed in the harsh light, making sure the DI didn't see that he'd spotted the inference.

Fred Parlour's house was just by the ferry office. Parked outside was an Express Plumbers van, identical to the one still in the pound at St James's. They'd arranged for

Parlour's apprentice, Sean Harper, to be present at the interview as well. A footpath ran down to the river beside the house and Shaw could see a long back lawn covered by a foot of snow which stretched to the river. Out on the water boats jostled on the moorings as the rip-tide cut through, ringing the bell on one of the marker buoys in mid-stream. In the snow of the garden stood a toy windmill and a signpost pointing seawards which said NORTH POLE.

'I don't like this bloke,' said Valentine, parking up.

'Great,' said Shaw, watching the net curtains twitch. 'So we can count on you for some objective observations then.'

'He's got the victim's blood on his hands.' Valentine had spent a few waking hours the night before trying to find an innocent scenario which explained the blood on Parlour's clothes. There wasn't one. Even with a fancy degree, it just wasn't there.

'Thigh actually – the left. One smear. With traces of animal bone.' Shaw liked details, because it was when they didn't fit that you had to stop and think.

'He's a busy-body. Gets his nose into everything.'

'Remind me – what's the tariff on that these days? Life, or just ten years?'

Valentine coughed into a grey cotton bundle. 'He's a liar.'

'Yeah,' said Shaw. 'So let's start with that.'

Shaw's mobile rang and he got out of the car to answer. It was one of Tom Hadden's CSI team. They'd completed the dental checks on all those in the convoy. No match to the apple biter, not even close.

'Just say it again,' said Shaw, closing his good eye, pressing the dressing down on the injured one. The CSI told him again. Shaw tapped the roof of the bonnet. 'OK, thanks.'

Valentine could tell it was bad news.

'Zero on the apple. No match to anyone in the convoy.'

'Leggy blonde, then,' said Valentine.

Fred Parlour was on the step before they got to the top of the path. He turned abruptly, leading the way along a hall into a lounge which looked out through French windows, the lawn rolling down to the river. The ferry was crossing, butting the tide, crowded with shoppers. Flags flew over the Guildhall in Lynn while an undersized barrage balloon advertised petrol on the quayside, sea gusts making it dip and dive.

'That's quite a view,' said Shaw. He ran his eyes over Parlour's face, making an inventory of salient features, including the single plaster on his forehead where the door of the Mondeo had caught him that night on Siberia Belt.

'So how can I help, Inspector? The paper's full of it — this body on the beach, and now one out on the sands . . .'

They heard a toilet flush upstairs, footsteps, and Sean Harper came in, still fiddling with his flies, then scratching the dimple in his chin. He didn't know what to do with his arms, which seemed overlong, hanging by his sides. He touched the stud in his ear and nodded by way of greeting.

A copy of the *Daily Mail* lay open on the coffee table

at a page dominated by a story on the Lynn murders. Valentine had briefed the press, and they'd all done little more than take the police statement straight, while speculating the three deaths might be linked. The headline screamed: MURDER VICTIM FOUND ON SANDS. A breathless report tried to wedge in Harvey Ellis's death, the discovery of Terence Brand's body on Ingol Beach and the half-buried body on Styleman's Middle in 350 words of clipped journalese.

'Tea?' asked Parlour, not waiting for an answer. 'Or something stronger . . . ?' He laughed, but Shaw knew he hadn't been joking.

'Tea's great,' said Shaw.

Parlour pottered in the kitchen, singing along to the faint music from a radio, the voice youthful, light. Shaw stood in the living room trying not to pick things up. A framed wedding photo stood on a shelf in the dresser; Parlour handsome in a narrow-legged seventies suit, the wife embarrassed by a once-in-a-lifetime hairdo. No pictures of children, nephews or nieces. Everything else in its place, the two armchairs: his and hers, hers with a sewing box on a small table. Coasters everywhere. Parlour found one and put down Shaw's mug of tea, then retreated to get the others. Harper pretended to read the paper.

'You'll be delighted to know, Mr Harper, that we will not be taking proceedings over the pornography found in your possession,' said Shaw.

Harper looked pathetically grateful. He held up a thumb. 'Brilliant.' But Shaw didn't return the smile. 'As long as you can tell me where you got the magazine.'

'The Skeg,' he said. 'Under the counter.'

The Skeg was a beach café at Hunstanton. In the summer it was packed, but it limped through the winter serving greasy-spoon meals to the winter surfing crowd.

They heard a thud from above, then the sound of dog's claws on the wooden stairs, dry food being tipped into a tin plate.

Parlour came back with Valentine's tea. 'Milly's a bit shy. Shy but hungry.'

'Please,' said Shaw, laughing. 'Sit down if you want – it's your front room. We wanted a quick word just to check your statement.' He rearranged a sheaf of papers on the coffee table.

They heard the dog scrabbling at the back door. 'If she needs to go out perhaps Mr Harper could take her down the garden,' said Shaw pointedly.

Harper fled, then reappeared on the lawn, lobbing snowballs at the dog as it ran in circles.

Shaw ran through the statement Fred Parlour had given Valentine at Gallow Marsh Farm. 'I just need to be clear on one thing,' said Shaw. 'And I know this is labouring the point. But you didn't, at any time, go further forward than the Alfa Romeo? I need to check that point.'

Parlour worked at a zip on his cardigan. 'Well, that's true. Actually, I didn't go any further up than that poor man's Corsa. She came back to get me – the woman – and we went to see if the old bloke was dead. Then you sent me back to the van.'

They heard Harper laugh in the garden, the dog barking like an unoiled hinge.

'Sean went forward, of course – to the security van. But that was a minute, less. Then he came back.' He looked out into the garden. 'He's not a bad lad. That's the first time I've ever seen him with one of those magazines.' He worked a finger under his collar.

Shaw wondered how his father would have conducted the interview. The frontal assault perhaps, with Valentine offering him a lighter sentence if he made a full and rapid confession. He blew on the surface of the tea.

'Anyone say much while you were all at the Corsa? There'd be you, Mrs Baker-Sibley and Mr Zhao.'

Parlour looked blank.

'She was worried about her daughter?' prompted Valentine.

'Yeah. I said kids were a lot more independent than parents thought. Like I know.' He laughed, looking round the room.

'What did she say?'

'She said I was right but she'd let her down before – that she'd promised it would never happen again. She was upset. I mean really upset. But she didn't seem bothered if the old bloke was dead or alive.'

There was silence and Parlour swished the dregs of his tea in the mug, humming an echo of the tune he'd sung in the kitchen. Out in the garden a pile of snow slid off the shed and thudded onto the lawn, burying the toy windmill. The dog dashed after snowballs.

'Why are you lying to us, Mr Parlour?'

Shaw watched Parlour's face, and saw the smile clinging to his eyes, the muscles which held the line of the mouth twitching, a sudden flush of blood to the cheeks. And behind the eyes the brain working, trying to predict the next question, trying to find the answer.

'Pardon?'

Valentine sat back, enjoying the moment, wondering how long Parlour would be able to go on denying the obvious.

'You said you didn't know Harvey Ellis. That you'd never met him?'

'That's right,' said Parlour, a hand wandering to find the edge of the armchair for support.

'Mr Parlour. Traces of Harvey Ellis's blood were found on the trousers you were wearing on Monday night. Now I'm afraid that means one of two things. Either you did go further forward, which suggests to me that you might have killed Mr Ellis. Or that you met the person who did kill him.' Shaw looked down the garden to the distant waterfront. 'Either way the course of events from this point, right now, is pretty much unavoidable.'

Shaw stood. 'I'd like you to come with us to St James's, sir – unless you have something to tell us. Did you kill Harvey Ellis, Mr Parlour?' Shaw was less than two feet away when he asked. He liked to be that close. It was one of his father's maxims: one of the few things he'd ever said about how he did his job. Get within their personal space, then you can feel the reaction.

Parlour's eyes were small and grey and they avoided his. 'I . . . I don't know how that could have happened. The blood. I didn't go forward, and I don't know Harvey Ellis. I don't.'

Valentine produced a copy of the family snapshot of

Ellis at home. He held it up to Parlour's face, uncomfortably close.

'No. They showed me the pictures . . . the constable came round, when they checked my teeth. I said no then.' He held out his hands, the wedding band catching the light on the ring finger. He looked round the room. 'I can't leave now. The wife's at work, she won't know, I need to tell her.'

'Would you like to make a call?' said Shaw.

There was a phone by the armchair, a flip-up address book. Parlour sat, and Shaw noted that his eyes had filled and his breathing had become uneven. They listened as he got through, waiting while they paged her, and Parlour fumbled through an explanation. When he put the phone down he stood up. They all watched the dog jump in the garden – the joy of the leap, the front paws extended.

'I'll put a bit more food down for the dog – she won't be back 'til lunchtime.'

Shaw went out into the garden where Harper's footprints had soiled the lawn, revealing winter grass that was straw-yellow. The apprentice dropped a snowball from his hand as if he'd been caught out breaking rules in the playground. The dog, madcap, raced headlong, fell, and went rolling through the snow.

'OK, Mr Harper, Mr Parlour is coming to the station with us. He's told us a few lies, I'm afraid, about Monday night. Have you?'

Harper searched for the right answer, looking back at the house, the French windows reflecting a picture of the two of them stood in the snow. 'Fred always tells the truth,' he said.

'Not quite. We found blood on his trousers, blood from the man who was killed in the pick-up. When he does tell us the truth, Mr Harper, we'll know, then, if you've told us lies as well.'

'I don't understand,' said Harper, following Shaw back into the house.

Inside the kitchen door the dog bowl had been piled high. A mixture of chunky meat, slightly purple, and lumps of what looked like a white biscuity meal.

Milly crunched in the bowl, her stub tail oscillating like a metronome on steroids. Shaw watched her, unblinking. His mind raced to the truth.

'Shit!' he said, and the dog cowered. He didn't know whether to laugh or cry. Valentine came into the kitchen and stood looking at the dog bowl with him. Shaw covered his eyes, one hand resting gently on the dressing, then dropped to his knees, a hand on the dog's back, the fur wiry and slightly greasy.

'It's all right, Milly,' he said.

He'd been a fool, a bloody fool.

# 25

Shaw contemplated the large plate-glass window of the Emerald Garden Chinese takeaway. It was fogged with condensation, trickles tracing a pattern like a bead curtain. A Day-Glo poster advertised chips at 50p a portion, 60p with curry sauce.

'Right,' he said. 'Let's try and get this inquiry back on the rails, shall we?'

It was a rhetorical question, because the only person he blamed was himself. They'd left Milly the Jack Russell running round Fred Parlour's garden. Valentine had taken a plastic bag of the dog food to the Ark. The CSI team was still finishing up out on Siberia Belt, so they wouldn't have the results for twenty-four hours. But in Parlour's kitchen they'd found the still unopened cans of meat he used to make up Milly's food, and the bag of bonemeal biscuits: reduced from sheep carcasses. The other organic material was likely to be the mixture of turkey and cow's offal in the dog meat.

Which only left one maddening question. How had the dog got blood on its snout, given that Ellis's car doors had been shut, with the windows up, until the body was discovered and the dog locked up in the plumber's van?

Valentine pretended to study the front window of the takeaway. He hadn't been able to work out why Shaw was so upset with the contents of a dog bowl. When he'd explained, Valentine had been forced to remind himself, not for the first time in thirty years, that he wasn't as smart as he thought he was. But Jack Shaw's son was: an uncomfortable fact Valentine was beginning to live with. Under all the tight-arsed procedural nonsense he was starting to suspect there was a decent copper trying to get out.

Shaw pressed the dressing to his eye, silently thankful that he hadn't derailed the entire inquiry when Tom Hadden had discovered the blood traces on Parlour's overalls. They did need to get back on track. Terence Brand, the man found dead in the raft on Ingol Beach, had given his aunt in Nuneaton a forwarding address: The Emerald Garden. That Stanley Zhao had been on Siberia Belt that night was a coincidence too far. Was anyone else in the little convoy involved in Brand's smuggling? Had Harvey Ellis died because he'd been part of a plan, or because he'd been cut out of a plan?

The front door of the takeaway was closed, so they walked down a side alley. There was a clatter of a wok on the high gas flame, the cracking of eggshells. They pushed open the fire exit by the storeroom and came into the kitchen from the back. Stanley Zhao didn't jump an inch, just slipped an egg on to a plate.

'Sorry,' said Shaw. 'Back door was open. A few more questions.'

Zhao didn't say a word, but led them upstairs, his six foot-plus frame slightly stooped. The sitting room was about as Oriental as a fish-and-chip supper: a shag-pile carpet, a sideboard covered in family photos, and a flat-screen TV.

Gail Zhao was Fen-white, with black hair cut short, a face which had been pretty once but now tended to fat, the skin on her arms loose around the bone. Late forties perhaps, her husband's generation, and tall too – five ten. And the teeth, too many for the mouth, the lips working hard to hide them. She looked tired, not lifetime tired but as though she'd had a fortnight of sleepless nights. Shaw noticed that one eyelid struggled to stay open, vibrating slightly.

Valentine took Zhao through his original statement, letting them think it was all routine. Shaw sat forward in a wicker chair, watching their faces.

'You're quite sure you'd like your wife to sit in on this, Mr Zhao?' he said when Valentine had finished.

Zhao adjusted the steel-rimmed spectacles, dabbed a paper tissue on his lips now that he'd finished his breakfast. 'I just want to help,' he said.

Valentine filled in their biographies. Gail had been born in Lynn, in the North End, before the old streets had come down. Her father was in the Merchant Navy and the family had gone to Hong Kong, where he'd put his savings into a boat-building business: little launches in wood for the rich to picnic on the water. She'd been sixteen. The Zhaos had built boats too: junks for the harbour trade. She'd met Stan when she was eighteen. Her father had died two years before the territory had reverted to the Chinese. They'd sold up, come home. Stan had come with her. Four years on the Westmead, four years they didn't want again.

'It's the crime we didn't expect,' said Zhao.

Valentine stiffened, taking it personally.

Shaw had run out of patience. 'Right. So why did you lie about the spare room, Mr Zhao? You said Gangsun slept there at weekends when he was on the late shift.'

'Yes.' Zhao's eyes had hardened.

'Fine. So where did Terence Brand sleep?'

'We've never heard of Terence Brand,' said Gail Zhao, too quickly, her voice an octave too high. 'Have we, Stan?'

'I'd like your husband to answer the questions, Mrs Zhao – for now at least. Mr Zhao?'

'I know the name. The local radio had a story. He was found on the beach?' Shaw spotted it that time, the fleeting micro-expression, like a shadow moving across the face's tiny muscles and tendons, a glimpse of the truth. He'd seen fear, before Zhao had reimposed a look of polite confusion.

'Yes. The beach below Siberia Belt. Where you were stranded on Monday night. His aunt has this restaurant as a forwarding address. That's quite a coincidence, isn't it?'

From the kitchen came the rhythmic rattle of the wok being shaken on the gas hob.

'Why were you helping these people, Mr Zhao?'

'I don't understand,' he said, giving up on the smile.

'Do you know what I'm going to do if you don't answer my questions truthfully?' asked Shaw, and Valentine recognized the buzz of stress in the voice, the almost imperceptible segue from patience to menace.

Zhao licked his lips.

'I'm going to get a forensic team from our headquarters at St James's and I'm going to seal off your spare room

– the one with the child's wallpaper, the one with the pornographic magazines. I think they'll start with the sheets, don't you? See what we can find: hairs, skin cells, semen, who knows? Then we'll cross check it with Terence Brand's corpse. And when we find a match I'll come back and we'll all go to the station: Mrs Zhao, Gangsun, Edison. Put a notice up in the window – Closed Until Further Notice . . .'

'I can answer if I want to,' cut in his wife, taking her husband's hand. 'We don't know what Terry did.'

'Terry?' said Valentine.

'He's my son,' she said, the chin jutting out. Downstairs they heard the sound of chips being thrown into hot oil. 'Was my son.'

She took out a scrap of tissue and began to dab at her mouth, the eyes already swimming in tears. 'Brand is my maiden name. I was just fifteen when Terry was born, here in Lynn.'

They sat in silence, letting the truth settle like dust.

'Why are you only telling us this now?' asked Shaw.

Mrs Zhao tried to look through him. 'Terry's life was his own. We didn't ask questions. I'm his mother, that's what I do. I don't ask questions.'

It wasn't good enough, but Shaw let it go.

'And I owed him, I suppose.' She buried her face in her hands. 'I went to Hong Kong for a new life. Aunt Ruth was his father's sister. She brought him up. His father didn't stick around.' She took her hands away, damp with tears. 'She never wanted to know anything about me. But I kept in touch with Terry, she was OK about that. He was unhappy at Ruth's; rebellious, I suppose. I said he always had a home with me. When we came back I kept that promise. He told Ruth this place was run by some of Stanley's family, that it was handy for the winter surf, but that I was still in Hong Kong. I guess she believed him – I don't know.'

'But the room he slept in, Mrs Zhao, it's newly decorated, for a child,' said Shaw.

'Yes. I was seven months pregnant, Detective Inspector, but I lost the child. Last year. We shouldn't have done that, tempted fate. But I guess we got excited. It was a girl,' she added, attempting a smile.

Mr Zhao was looking at the sickly pattern on the shag pile.

'OK,' said Shaw. 'I'm sorry.' He thought about it: losing two children in a year – one a grown man, the other unborn. 'But I'd still like to know what your husband was doing on Siberia Belt the night Terry's body was washed up. What did Terry do when he was staying with you – for money?'

Mr Zhao raised a hand to his mouth. 'In the summer he surfed, wind sports. He spent money, I didn't ask where it came from. We were fond of him.'

Shaw thought of the blood-caked teeth. 'Did you give him a ring, Mr Zhao? A man with a dragon's tail carved in jet?'

He nodded, his eyelids almost closing. 'Hsi, the first emperor.'

'And in the winter?'

'He had a wetsuit – and he fished at night, on the long lines. He hung around that café on the front by the fair.'

'The Skeg?' asked Valentine.

Shaw thought of the wetsuits swilling in the sea spray off Hunstanton, the fishermen huddled at night by lanterns, the magazines under the counter at the café, sticky fingerprints on the glass. Another lucrative trade for Terry Brand. A parcel on each trip perhaps, a little extra money.

'How did he get down to the beach?' asked Valentine. 'Nearest surf is – what – fifteen miles. And he's got all his kit. You're not going to get sea rods on the bus, are you?' Key question: Shaw bit his lip.

Mrs Zhao had frozen but her husband had an answer; the wrong answer. 'His friends had a car.'

'Who are they – these friends? What do they look like?' said Valentine, flipping open the notebook, biro in his teeth, playing the role perfectly.

'We didn't see them,' Zhao said.

'They'd stay in the car – sound the horn,' said Mrs Zhao, joining in.

'In the car,' repeated Valentine. 'What sort of car?'

'A white van, dirty,' said Zhao.

Shaw zipped up his coat. 'I think *you* were the transport, Mr Zhao. I think that's why you were there that night. To meet Terry. I think you'd done it before. And I think you know he wasn't sea fishing, or looking for the perfect winter wave. He was smuggling. Dangerous work – so dangerous it killed him. I think he was curious about what he was bringing in, curious to know what price it would fetch. Did he talk to you about that, Mr Zhao? Mrs Zhao? And the merchandise? Did he bring it here?'

Shaw looked around as if he was going to start the search there and then.

'Merchandise?' said Stanley Zhao, shaking his head.

'A suitcase perhaps,' said Shaw. 'Reinforced, aluminium probably, so it wouldn't weigh too much. Or plastic containers, baskets – what did they use, Mr Zhao? You tell me. Is that why you didn't contact the police when we released his name?'

Mrs Zhao rubbed her eyes and looked at Shaw for the first time. 'If Terry was dead . . . is dead . . . what's the point in contacting the police? Terry never brought anything home, Detective Inspector,' she added. 'Never.'

Shaw guessed she was telling the truth, or nearly the truth. The magazines came home. But no, he didn't bring the consignment home. So where did it go?

'Whatever he was smuggling that last night probably killed him. I'm going to have to ask you to identify the body, Mrs Zhao. Can you do that for me?'

Shaw watched her face collapse, watched her lose control of the nerves that held the line of her mouth.

'No, I don't think I can,' she said, but she reached for her coat.

# 26

Shark Tooth's plant was on the single-track road beside the Wash at Wootton Marsh. Snow at sea had smudged out the horizon, and the reed beds were frozen. The plant's buildings were flat-pack sheds, between which tractors scurried, buckets aloft, seawater draining from the shellfish within. From the main processing shed the sound of cockles rolling on a conveyor belt was punctuated by the hissing of a cheap radio. At the corner of the yard a flag flew, the blue clamshell on a white background.

Shaw watched the flag unfurl in a slight breeze, then smelt the salt on his fingers from his early morning swim. 'Terry Brand's body was found at the beach below Gallow Marsh Farm. Shark Tooth owns the farm. It also employs the cockle-picking gang which works on Styleman's Middle. It runs boats through the sandbanks off Ingol Beach. On the night of the murder I saw a yacht off the beach – a blue clam insignia on the sail.' They both looked at the flying flag. 'Part of the answer's here. Got to be.'

Valentine flipped open the file he'd got one of the DCs to put together on the late shift. He rubbed his eyes, forcing them to focus. He'd spent a second night in the house on the corner of Greenland Street but this time he'd run out of luck, and that always made him tired. Three hours sleep, maximum. He'd read the file at the kitchen table by dawn's light, and he summarized it now for Shaw: Shark Tooth had been founded in 1990. A one-boat outfit taking hobby fishermen out into the North Sea to try and hook dogfish. There'd been a landing stage at Wootton, disused for a century, so they made the best of it. Dogfish made them a small fortune.

Now the company employed between fifty and eighty people, depending on the season. They had a dozen boats, with the focus on commercial shellfish, although they still ran fishing trips in season. There'd been a wodge of newspaper cuttings in the file following the Morecambe Bay disaster – in which a gang of ethnic Chinese cockle-pickers, mostly illegal immigrants, had died when they'd been cut off by the treacherous tides off the Lancashire coast. Colin Narr, CEO of Shark Tooth, had told the press all his workforce – Chinese or other – had legal papers, a fact verified by Lynn CID. But the Conservancy Board that regulated the harbour had brought in new safety rules for the cockle boats: limiting numbers, requiring a manifest of those going out on each tide, enforcing a licensing system for gangmasters. Ownership of the privately registered company was obscure: Colin Narr described himself as a minority shareholder. Five years ago they'd bought Gallow Marsh Farm to develop the oyster beds.

'And that's what we know,' finished Valentine, taking a breath which made one of his ribs crack. He ran a hand over an unshaved chin. He felt better, keen to get in amongst the cockle-pickers. Shaw was right: somewhere at the centre of all three deaths was Shark Tooth.

Shaw got out and let the gritty snow blow into his good eye. Ahead he could just see the distant white line of surf breaking out at sea. The gates of the factory stood open, and they strolled through, following a single sign to RECEPTION.

He wasn't looking forward to the interview with Colin Narr. He'd never understood business, found the environment intimidating, antiseptic, and foreign. Plus Narr was a town worthy – an alderman, and a member of the county council's Police Committee. Which in an odd way made him Shaw's boss. Shaw felt the familiar surge of defiance in the face of authority, loosening the top button of the tie-less shirt.

The office was a Portakabin, a posh one, but a Portakabin nonetheless, with a black Jag parked outside. Inside there was a carpet and a six-bar electric fire, a secretary in a thermal jacket. Behind a partition they could hear a mumbled telephone call. A long window onto the yard stood half open. They heard a receiver crash down and Narr came out, calling them back through into the office.

'Red tape,' he said. 'That was Defra. It's a full-time career dealing with bloody jobsworths.'

Narr wore canvas trousers and a weathered oilskin jacket. He had the kind of skin that's been marinated in fresh air, the texture of overcooked bacon, the colour of a kipper. His head was small for his body, compact and round, but he held it low, as if it were dense and heavy, and he didn't quite have the energy to hold it up. One oddity: his hair was short and mousey, receding, revealing ears without lobes, which Shaw could imagine gently shrivelling away when exposed to the sun out on the sands.

The office had a desk, a metal filing cabinet and a sixties

drinks cabinet and bar. A set of golf clubs stood in one corner, a patina of dust over the wooden heads of the drivers. The single picture window stood tilted open.

'You like fresh air,' said Shaw.

Narr looked at the window as if he'd never seen it before, one hand rising, touching his ear where the fleshy pod of the lobe should have been. 'I'm in and out, there's no point.' He smiled without showing his teeth. The Norfolk accent had been ironed flat, but the ghost of it was still there, marking him out as a local.

The wall behind the desk held a large noticeboard covered in cuttings and pictures. Shaw noted one of Narr and the rest of the Police Committee on a visit to St James's to meet the Home Secretary. An old print of the Fisher Fleet, packed with the jostling masts of the herring boats. But the dominant image was a photo of a football team in blue-and-white hoops, the team badge enlarged at the foot showing the blue cockleshell and the name: Wootton Marsh FC. Duncan Sly, the gangmaster he'd met out on Styleman's Middle, stood to one side in a smart black tracksuit, carrying a physio's bag.

'Hope you two don't mind, but we're gonna have to do this on the run,' said Narr, stuffing some papers into the pockets of his jacket. As they walked out to reception he stooped down and moved the fire nearer to his secretary, closing the window. 'I'll be gone a bit,' he said. 'You might as well enjoy it.'

They all walked briskly across the yard into a large shed which reeked of ozone. Thousands of oysters lay in metal trays, water splashing over them. Shaw breathed it in, feeling his pulse rise, the stench of the sea almost narcotic.

'Brancaster,' said Narr, picking one up and turning it like a diamond. 'London order, West End.' He worked his way along the side of the table, which vibrated slightly like a prospector's pan.

Shaw kept precisely one pace behind. 'Have you seen this?' He produced his sketch of the man recovered from the sands at Styleman's Middle. 'You don't recognize the face?'

'Uniformed copper came round yesterday with it, we all had a look. There's something familiar about it – but who knows?'

Narr picked an oyster out of a bucket, took a short knife from his pocket and expertly slid the blade into the folds of the shell, twisting his wrist and opening it out to reveal the flesh within, the colour of a summer cloud. He rolled it down his throat. 'That'd be your job?' he said. 'Finding answers.'

In the next shed thousands of cockles were being turned gently in vats of water.

'Stookey blues,' said Narr, picking one out and prising the shell open to reveal the clam-like creature within, milky white with a hint of opalescence. But he didn't eat it, tossed it instead into a pail of broken shells.

Shaw was tiring of the lecture. He noticed they'd left Valentine back in the last shed chatting to one of the factory women.

'Mr Narr, is it conceivable that someone, some group, could be smuggling merchandise onto Ingol Beach without the cooperation, possibly tacit, of your men on Styleman's Middle?'

Narr picked up a handful of the cockles, turning them

over in his palms. He walked to the side of the shed and took down a short wooden plank from the wall, at each end of which were wooden handles. He put it on the concrete floor and stood on it, bending his knees so that he could grasp the handles.

'This is a jumbo,' he said. 'When you get out on the sand you put it down and then rock on it, like this.' He swayed vigorously from side to side. 'The movement sucks the cockles towards the surface, then you rake it to get 'em out.' He stood. 'You don't get a lot of time for sight-seeing. Believe me – I did it for ten years and I don't remember enjoying the view much.' The hand again, rising to touch the missing earlobe.

'But on a good day, with clear visibility, you can see ten miles out there. You only have to straighten your back once. Or do they learn to turn a blind eye?'

'Ask 'em,' Narr shrugged. 'But don't forget we don't go out in low light, let alone darkness – not since Morecambe. So unless you've got daylight smugglers – then yeah, they could miss them.'

'We did ask the men,' said Shaw.

'Then you've got your answer.'

Shaw wondered how Narr would react if he suggested they continue their conversation at St James's. If he didn't get a bit more cooperation he'd do it, and sod the consequences.

'Lufkin, Sly. How long have they been on the books? Ever had a Terence Brand on the payroll?'

Narr held up both hands. 'Duncan Sly's born and bred Norfolk fishing. Father ran oyster beds, he spent fifteen years in the Merchant Navy. Falklands War, South Atlantic

Medal. You can't buy that kind of expertise on the open market, believe me. And you can't buy that kind of honesty anywhere. Andy Lufkin? I've known him ten years, worked with him on the Icelandic trawlers. He's got a master's ticket, but there's no boats, so he can't get the work any more and we get him instead, which is our luck. It's a tight ship, 'cos he doesn't take any nonsense.'

Shaw wondered what *that* was supposed to be a euphemism for.

'And Terence Brand?'

Narr shook his head.

'That's a no?'

Narr looked him straight in the eyes for the first time. 'That's a no.'

'And the Chinese workers? The Czechs?'

'They're all legal – they've all had their papers checked by the Board. One Czech, by the way. Bedrich – he's legal, an EU migrant worker. The other two east Europeans are Serbian.'

Shaw stepped a foot closer and wiped what was left of a smile off Narr's face. 'I didn't ask if they were legal. I asked if you trusted them.'

Narr's eyes hardened. 'They're good workers,' he said, turning on his heel and heading across the yard. Back in the office he took the sheaf of messages his secretary handed him, ignoring Shaw.

'Does the company own a yacht, Mr Narr – with the blue clam emblem on the sail?'

'A yacht?' Narr laughed. 'You've seriously overestimated the profit margin on shellfish, Inspector. No – we don't own a yacht.'

'I'd like to talk to the owner of the company, Mr Narr. Can you help me there?' asked Shaw, taking the only chair.

'Why?'

'Because I'd like to ask him the same questions I asked you.'

'Why?'

'Because I might get a different answer.'

'You won't.' Narr sighed. 'There are four minority share-holders – all local men with the knowledge and the contacts and the experience. But the capital's foreign, and they like to keep their business to themselves. Any questions, try the company secretary. But I wouldn't hold your breath.'

He flipped open a wallet and took out a card; one of Lynn's long-established high-street solicitors. Shaw took it but let his eye scan the still-open wallet, a snapshot visible in the clear plastic window: Narr in a white shirt under a tropical sun, a woman's face pressed to his, plenty of make-up despite the swimsuit top. It was Sarah Baker-Sibley, smiling at the sideways kiss.

# 27

Snow fell in Burnham Market like old white five-pound notes; extravagant flakes, accruing, silently transforming the town square into a picture postcard, complete with the winking white lights of the Farmers Market. In the fishmonger's, turbot was sold out, and at the butcher's a queue had formed despite the weather to buy partridge and lamb shank. A pair of elegant Afghan hounds waited patiently outside the wine merchant's. Shaw parked outside Sarah Baker-Sibley's shop: it had just her name on the sign, with a motif of a mobile phone; the window was crowded with them: expensive, up-market models, with cameras, radios, and Bluetooth included. A flat-screen TV showed an advert for a model including GPS.

During the drive Shaw told Valentine about the picture in Narr's wallet. He wondered if any of Narr's employees thought their boss had a secret life.

'He's well liked,' said Valentine. 'Wife left last year. Nobody thought much of her. A bitch, apparently; used to swan round the place like it was her kingdom. No one mentioned a new bird on the block, so must be hush-hush.'

'Anything else off the shop floor?'

'Sly's been around for years, isn't happy unless he's out on the sands.' Valentine put a hand on his heart as if taking an oath. 'There's no love lost with Lufkin, he's only been on the payroll for eighteen months. Nasty bit of work. Last Christmas the pickers had a party in a pub – Narr put a couple of hundred behind the bar. Lufkin and Sly got into an argument and Lufkin threw a sneak punch, in the kidneys. But Sly's a big man. He didn't go down. He knocked Lufkin into the New Year, hit him so hard that when he woke up his clothes were out of style. But Lufkin is one of Narr's old mates from the deep-sea fleet, so he's here to stay, whatever Sly thinks. But the woman in the sorting shed said Lufkin was a little shit, and her mate said if they wanted someone to drown him like a rat there'd be a rush to form a queue.'

'Otherwise it's happy families?'

'And something else. One of the old blokes said there was a rumour they were going to give Izzy Dereham the push at Gallow Marsh. The oysters aren't making what they should make. She's struggling on her own, and the lease is up next year.'

'Good work,' said Shaw.

'How we gonna play this?' asked Valentine, trying not to feel pleased about the compliment.

'Baker-Sibley? Well, it isn't a crime, not telling the police you're having an affair. I presume there's a Mr Baker-Sibley – although she didn't mention anyone when she needed Jillie picking up. Divorced? So I guess we take it carefully, keeping in mind Mr Colin Narr's – excuse me, Alderman Narr's – position as chairman of the Police Committee. She doesn't have to reveal her private life. However, I think we now have cause to ask her about it. Plus I'd like to give her another chance to tell us the truth about that phone call she made from Gallow Marsh. There was someone else on the end of that line, not just her daughter.'

'Could be Narr,' said Valentine.

'Could be. Did we check on the daughter?'

Valentine pulled out his notebook. 'I had a word with the head at the school, snotty cow. Didn't want to talk. I said we'd come down with a blue flashing light on the roof of the squad car and park it in the drive at going-home time. She coughed up pretty quick then. So – Jillie Baker-Sibley.' He heaved in a lungful of air. 'Bright, wired for nerves. The pupil from hell. Disruptive, uncoopera-tive, occasionally violent.'

'Violent?'

'Bullying, mainly – always younger girls. There's been complaints but they've kept it all in-school. Parents don't want publicity either. Last time she boxed some ten-year-old round the head, broke an eardrum. Argument over who got to sit on a bench in the sunshine. Head thinks she's disturbed, has been since she got to the school two years ago. She says she's on her last chance, doesn't matter how clever she is. One more foot out of line and they're gonna bite the bullet and tell her mum where to stick the fees.'

As they threaded their way through the drifts on the pavement Shaw recalled what Parlour had said about Sarah Baker-Sibley, how nervous she'd been that night on Siberia Belt, desperate not to let her daughter down *again*. Parental anxiety, or something more?

Baker-Sibley's shop was immaculately minimalist. The walls were whitewashed, mobile phones set like jewels on polished glass shelves. The flat-screen TV was now running an advert for broadband mobile links. A display of the new iPhone range filled one wall with a giant picture, a montage of the last century's best-known musicians.

Sarah Baker-Sibley was talking to a customer but an assistant, a teenager called Abigail with long flowing blonde hair, showed them into a back office and produced a cafetière and three cups, each with a small sinuous kink in the circular rim.

When Baker-Sibley joined them she looked elated, her eyes catching the pinpoint halogen lights strung in a line across the ceiling. *A sale*, thought Shaw, taking out his notebook, despising the thrill of money.

'You're early,' she said.

She sat behind a desk, the harsh light adding ten years to the carefully made-up flesh of her face. Valentine struggled with the kinked rim of his coffee cup, slurping loudly.

'I'm sorry to take up your time, Ms Baker-Sibley,' said Shaw pointedly. 'We just wanted to check a couple of points in your statement. DS Valentine has the note, I think . . .'

They'd agreed this on the drive over. Valentine would pitch some questions while Shaw waited for the right moment. It was becoming their favoured strategy. She told them the story she'd told them that first night: she always picked Jillie up from school, always at 5.30 on Mondays, and she always drove along the coast road. She'd seen the AA sign, took the diversion, and the rest they knew.

Valentine set his cup down. 'Then you called your

daughter from the farm?' he asked. The last question, so he took the breath he was dying for, his shoulders rising painfully.

'Yes. I knew you'd only got a message through to an answer phone when we were out on the marshes so I was still worried. Jillie always looks at the incoming number before answering, so I wasn't desperate; but, you know, she's only thirteen. I caught her at home,' she added. 'I think anyone with a child would know how it feels.' She tried a smile but got nothing out of George Valentine.

'And the second call?' asked Shaw.

'I rang her back – I got cut off.'

'But you asked her to pass the phone at one point, on the first call, I think – who to?'

She shook her head. 'No. Nobody else.'

*So one lie at least*, thought Shaw. 'Couldn't have been her father, for example?'

She folded her hands on her lap, scrunching slightly the heavy velvet black dress. 'We're divorced, Detective Inspector. James lives in Greece now, when he's not in the City. He has a flat in the Barbican.'

'And your daughter . . .'

'She's thirteen and I have custody of her, naturally.'

'Right. And you pick her up each evening?'

'Yes. St Agnes' Hall at Burnham Westgate. Just along the coast road. I usually pick her up earlier but Mondays it's later because she has a clarinet lesson after school. I've always picked her up, even when James was with us.'

She made the family sound like a corporation, thought Shaw. 'But not last Monday night?'

205

'Clearly.' She didn't volunteer any more information.

'So what did she do?' asked Shaw.

'She walked home. She has a key.' She folded and unfolded her hands, a little dance of exaggerated patience.

'But your house is where?' He made a pretence of checking his notes; the address was in Burnham Overy Town, a hamlet just inland. 'There must have been three feet of snow on the road by the time she got there.'

'Did she have a choice?' she asked, the aggression in her voice misplaced.

'Is she at school today?' asked Valentine, closing his notebook.

'No.' Baker-Sibley stiffened. 'She's doing school work here, she's not well enough to go in.'

'Anything serious?' asked Shaw.

'Just a chill.'

'Can we see her then, briefly?' Shaw sat back, while Valentine leant forward, helping himself to a fresh cup of coffee.

'Why?' she asked, but Shaw guessed she regretted it immediately.

'We don't want to have to bother you again,' said Shaw, pleased at the elegance of the implied threat.

'This is a waste of time – principally *my* time,' she said.

She was gone a long time and they both wondered why, but said nothing. Shaw's pager buzzed and the call-back number was the RNLI station at Wells, along the coast. That meant their boat was out, and that Hunstanton had to stand by. Shaw was less than five miles from home so he texted the coxswain saying he was on hand and could make up the crew.

'We might have to wind this one up, George,' he said. 'There might be a shout.'

Valentine knew all about Shaw's role in the RNLI. He thought most coppers found being a DI was job enough without being a part-time hero. He wasn't the only one at St James's who thought it was out of order. He glugged some phlegm, stowing the cotton handkerchief quickly when he heard footsteps above, the floorboards creaking.

When she appeared Jillie Baker-Sibley was a walking contradiction: thin, with fragile bones, a pale face free of make-up. She was hugging a copy of *Bleak House* to her chest. But there were hints of another life. A single tattoo of a teardrop peeking out from the cuff of a crisp white collarless shirt, and the hair, cut short like a boy's, was savagely severe, with an uneven fringe. Shaw remembered the little framed picture on the dashboard of the Alfa Romeo: Jillie with long straight hair, the perfect public-school daughter. He guessed there'd been a family argument about hairstyles and that this time, at least, the teenager had won. He also noted the mobile hitched by the buckle: an expensive model in turquoise. Her face was formless, puffy, almost insolent, as if it might resolve itself into something more mature and structured by the end of the day. But the eyes were extraordinary: violet rather than blue. Film stars' eyes, an extra's face.

'Hi,' said Shaw, trying to hit the same adult tone he used with Francesca's friends. 'Studying?'

Her mother answered for her. 'GCSE English Lit. – she's years early of course, but the school seems to think she can sit it next year.' She leant forward and touched her daughter's hair, an expression crossing her face that Shaw couldn't place: she loved her daughter, he could see that, but there was something else. It might have been fear.

'You had to walk home the other night – that must have been frightening?' asked Shaw.

'I've walked before – it's not a problem.' Her eyes didn't meet Shaw's. 'There's nothing to be afraid of in the dark. Dad always says that. And Mum always checks . . .' She touched the mobile. 'Mum and I are always in touch.' Her voice was flat, emotionless, so that Shaw couldn't tell if that was a good thing.

'Clara – my best friend – we've walked home before, she lives up the lane. If you go back to school you have to work with the boarders – they do homework early. Losers.'

'Jillie,' said her mother. 'There's nothing cool about not working hard at school.'

Shaw held up a hand. 'But this time you set out on your own?'

She shook her head, thinking, so that Shaw could see the confusion behind the eyes. 'Clara has music lessons too on Mondays. But she does an extra hour. I like snow,' she added. 'It was beautiful.'

Shaw thought about the head teacher's character summary: disruptive, violent. She flicked her head as if to clear a strand of hair from her eyes, a strand of hair she didn't have. Then she crossed her legs, interlacing the fingers of both hands at the kneecap. There was something about the ease of the movement which suddenly made her seem older.

Shaw looked at her hands. There was a slight tremble in both, a vibration like a taut piano wire. On the top of the left one was a blue mark, a circle with the letters BT at the centre, identical to the one Valentine had described on the hand of the young driver of the Mondeo.

'What does that mean?' he asked pointing, unable to keep a note of excitement out of his voice.

Valentine sat forward, realizing he'd missed it. *Hands: you should always look at their hands.*

'Oh, Jillie, really – I did ask.' The annoyance in her mother's voice was partly manufactured, Shaw sensed. Ritualistic.

Jillie smiled. 'A disco at the village hall – at Burnham Thorpe. It's Sodom and Gomorrah when the lights go down.'

Her mother bit her lip.

'And when was that?' asked Shaw.

'Saturday night.'

'It's for charity,' said her mother. 'For meals-on-wheels. She never washes those things off – it's to show off at school, isn't it?'

Valentine hadn't taken his eyes off the teenager. 'Have you got a boyfriend, Jillie?'

Her mother snorted like a horse. 'She needs to rest,' she said, rising.

'One last question,' said Shaw. 'When your mother phoned you on Monday night she asked you to pass the phone to someone else. Who was that, Jillie?'

Valentine watched her mother's face, the line of the mouth setting murderously straight. Her daughter tossed her head. 'I was at home, alone. I don't remember that.' She rearranged the simple gold chain at her neck, running it back and forth, but Shaw detected a fleeting expression on her face, reluctance perhaps, even distaste.

Sarah Baker-Sibley took her daughter by the arm, gently letting her stand. 'Indeed, as I said. Now, Jillie needs to rest.'

When she returned Shaw stood up, giving her the impression the interview was over. But he'd saved two questions. 'You told Fred Parlour – the man you first informed that you thought John Holt was dead out on Siberia Belt – that you were very keen to get back on the road and see if Jillie was OK because you'd let her down before. When was that, Mrs Baker-Sibley?'

Her eyes danced around the pictures on the office wall – a poorly executed landscape of Hunstanton cliffs, a watercolour of Holkham Hall. 'It was one of the discos, at Burnham Thorpe. It was stupid of me – I fell asleep at home and when I got to the hall it was all shut up. No one. You can imagine. I just freaked out.'

'But she was all right?' asked Valentine, standing too.

'She'd gone home with Clara – she was fine. I think she enjoyed it, actually – showing me up.' A bitter smile.

'Colin Narr,' said Shaw. 'You're friends?'

It had been an act up until now, Shaw could see that, because this was the question she hadn't expected. 'Why do you say that?'

'I ask the questions.' Shaw smiled the surfer's smile.

'And why on earth do you think I should answer them?'

'I'm investigating two murders and a suspicious death.'

Valentine noted the subtle shift again. The voice shedding its polite sugar coating.

'Your car was stranded the other night near Ingol Beach; Gallow Marsh Farm owns the land, and Mr Narr's company both owns Gallow Marsh and runs the cocklepicking business out on Styleman's Middle, where another corpse was discovered yesterday morning. Plus you're insisting on telling me lies about the call you made that night at Gallow Marsh Farm. I heard you ask to be passed to someone else. So I can ask that question, and if you choose to not answer it, you can choose not to answer it down at St James's. Was Mr Narr at home with Jillie?'

She gave him the full 100-watt stare. Then she led the way to the plate-glass door at the front of the shop, opening it to let some snowflakes blow in over the marble floor. A woman walked past outside, a pair of corgis wearing gaberdine jackets trailing on leads in her wake.

'Colin and I have been seeing each other since shortly after my marriage broke down, Inspector. I don't think we have any secrets, from either each other or the police. Any suggestion to the contrary might be of interest to his lawyers. If you insist on continuing this conversation at a police station then I will have to notify *my* lawyers.'

## 28

DC Jacky Lau stood on the rotting wooden jetty at Morston Creek, watching a pair of seals in the tidal run bobbing up, then down, like fairground ducks. In the mud the crabs scuttled, and the sound of the water draining out of the marshes was as loud as the wind. She'd parked her souped-up Renault Mégane by the National Trust information hut. A light peppering of snow was obscuring the glass lenses of her wraparound Foster Grants.

Lau had good eyes: 20:20 vision. The creek ran out through the marshes towards the open water protected by the long shingle arm of Blakeney Point. A few yachts bobbed in the tide. But one, on the edge of the marsh, looked odd – its mast set permanently off the vertical.

'Ian,' she said, not turning round.

A small man came up beside her and trained his binoculars on the sea breaking out on the distant point. Ian Norton was the harbour master at Morston, a part-time post he combined with running the National Trust booth and tea shop. Norton was stocky, powerful, like a crab on its hind legs. Jacky Lau had gone out with his son Paul for a year, and his racing Mini with outsized wheels stood on the wharf. Ian was one of her best contacts, watchful, sceptical, with an eye for detail.

'What you looking for, Jacky?'

'Good question. Guv'nor thinks the body out on the sands at Styleman's Middle had money. Yachting set. So, he figures, there might be a boat. He saw one on the night before they found the body out on the sands. A yacht, with a clam motif on the sail. How about that one?' she asked, pointing.

Norton trained binoculars on the dipped, distant mast. 'It's run aground.'

'Seen the owner?' she asked, turning to look him in the face.

Norton shook his head.

There was a gust of snow-crated wind. 'Can you run me out?' she asked, shivering, thinking about the warm interior of the Mégane, the heated driver's seat.

Norton collected his wife from a cottage on the old quay to look after the coffee shop. The NT launch was a two-man dinghy with an outboard which laboured as they nosed out into Blakeney Channel, edging up towards the yacht, the wind beginning to chop the wave tops off, spraying them with spume. Visibility dropped, the snow thickening like feathers from a pillow fight, so that by the time they came alongside they couldn't see the quay or the church up on the hill. Somewhere a foghorn sounded.

They were lucky to find it – a white yacht in a snowstorm. They could just read the name on the prow – *Hydra.*

Lau shouted, 'Ahoy,' thankful none of the stock-car-racing crowd could hear her. Norton climbed aboard using a short rope ladder which hung down from the deck. Lau followed, willing her short muscular legs to work properly in the cold. She felt relieved to get on deck, then almost instantly sick as the snowstorm rocked the boat erratically, thudding the hull against the mudbank on which it was grounded. The sail was furled but revealed a few inches of a blue motif.

A seagull stood on the varnished wooden decking, its head and bill into the wind, balancing serenely on one leg. Norton jumped into the cockpit, pulled open the double hatch to the cabin. She followed him down the three-step ladder quickly, embracing the moment when her head fell below deck level and out of the polar wind.

She slid off the dark glasses, stashed them in an exterior pocket on her leather driving jacket and let her eyes get used to the gloom. There were narrow windows at deck level, but small pleated blinds were fastened down. Norton found a switch and lambent light flooded from beneath teak panels.

The boat continued to rock, a bottle of wine rolling back and forth on the wooden decking. In the open forward galley a chopping board on the flip-down worktop held two or three pieces of cheese, a six-inch tubular piece of garlic sausage and a plastic delicatessen tub of olives.

From the forward part of the cabin she looked back towards the cockpit and saw a small TV screen, inlaid in the wooden bulkhead, the sound down, the channel showing BBC News 24. Interference zigzagged across the picture like lightning.

Beside it was a framed photograph. A man hugging two children – a young girl, an older boy – on the deck of the yacht. The sail was catching some breeze, billowed out, with a blue motif on it of a clamshell. And a hand-written legend: *Hydra*, 2005.

Norton was checking the map on the chart table – a stretch of the north Norfolk coast, from Lynn round to Wells. He traced a pencilled route with his finger around Blakeney Point and out to sea. 'Some summer sailor's got caught out by the weather, doesn't know the local waters, drops his anchor in deep water and then rows ashore. It happens. He's probably tucked up in a nice hotel asleep in his bathrobe.' Norton shivered as the hull rocked under them. 'Lucky bastard.'

'We need to double-check,' said Jacky Lau, knowing what Shaw would do. 'Find a name.' The boat lurched, and she fell on to one of the padded benches. 'Where do you sleep on one of these things?'

Norton showed her a small door in the forward bulk-head. 'Through here,' he said, flicking a switch.

Two bunks, only one of them disturbed. But it was what was lying across the other one which made Jacky Lau's pulse quicken.

She leant in and touched a skein of human hair. Thick, like a horse's tail, but soft. Holding some to her nose she caught a hint of scent, a soapy aroma. She ran it between her hands as if she were carding wool. Two feet of human hair, natural blonde streaks, brushed to a sheen like a liquid mirror.

Norton stood back now, his shoulders pressed against the panelled bulwark. Jacky lay the hair back on the bed, knowing now she shouldn't have picked it up.

'That's weird,' she said. 'Just take a seat, Ian – don't touch anything.'

She worked her way back into the cabin. There was an attaché case in a space under the map chart. She slid it out with gloved hands and found that the lock had been forced. Inside, business papers, bank statements, a set of company accounts. The boat lurched. 'Tell me this isn't going to sink, Ian,' she said.

'We're fine,' he said. 'What d'you reckon?'

'I reckon this might be it.' She moved into the galley. A small bowl, the water stained pink, a heavy wooden gaff for stunning fish standing in it. The light from the galley porthole caught the sticky matt surface of it, a stain in black, with a hint of red as subtle as the flush on a medium-rare steak. And a piece of skin the size of a stamp stuck to the stain, its surface pitted like goose flesh, but with a single hair attached.

## 29

A hearse purred in the dark outside the Ark, like a black cat with the milk. A body in a grey bag was slid in from a gurney by two lab assistants, the tailgate closing with a visceral, oily click.

'Goods out,' said Valentine, lighting up on the step as they watched the hearse creep out of the yard. 'Anyone we know?'

'Styleman,' said Tom Hadden. 'Next stop, undertaker's morgue until you sign it off. Can't bury him without a name, right?'

Shaw stubbed the toecap of his boot against the kerb. 'So no progress – any forensics off the boat?' he asked. The yacht at Morston Creek discovered by DC Jacky Lau had been towed into Lynn's Boal Quay, where a full forensic examination was under way.

'Bit early,' said Hadden. 'But Jacky's got a briefcase off the boat – she's inside.'

DC Jacky Lau had a pile of documents on a trestle table, a pair of anglepoise lamps burning into the pages. She was working with gloves, sifting into piles, a mobile-phone mic at her lips. She looked confident, in control, every micro-movement charged with adrenaline.

'So far?' said Shaw.

She held up a finger, finishing a call. 'Thanks – that's great.' She unhitched the earpiece and threw it on to the table. 'Boat's registered in the name of . . .' She read from a clipboard, treble-checking. 'James Baker-Sibley.'

She paused for a second, long enough to let them know that she'd made the connection too.

'Address in the Barbican, London. Electoral roll puts him in a house in Burnham Overy Town in 2005. Local family, one of them was something big in the Royal Navy back in the sixties. Documents back up the ID – including a passport. A British passport – with plenty of Greek entry stamps from the nineties. But most of this stuff . . .' She pushed a glossy company report aside to reveal a set of faxed figures. 'Looks like business transactions – there's a due diligence report on a company purchase, share certificates. But it's a maze. Yard's offered us a forensic accountant, so I'll get it all down to London by courier.'

Shaw and Valentine exchanged looks.

Hadden had made the link too. 'She drove the Alfa, right – Baker-Sibley?'

'Yeah,' said Shaw. 'Wife, ex-wife. Widow. Ex-widow.'

'Ex-wife?' asked Hadden. 'She won't be that upset, then.'

'She'll have the fucking flags out,' said Valentine. 'And a band.'

'If it's him,' said Shaw, unable to resist the note of caution. 'Passport?'

Lau handed it to him. He flicked to the picture. 'That's him, even if I say so myself.' Shaw's sketch had caught the 'lifelong look' – the bland, handsome symmetry of the face's main features. At last, he thought, they'd stopped finding pieces of the jigsaw, and started fitting them together.

Hadden took them through the plastic doors into the morgue. On an aluminium bench he'd got the washing-up bowl from the yacht, the fish gaff separately bagged.

'First off, there's plenty of evidence at the scene. The side of the yacht's got some pretty bad scratching and a smear of paint – heavy-duty marine, dark blue. I'd say there was a collision, something coming alongside in rough weather? Maybe. Anyway, something big. A sea boat. Trawler? Not a yacht – the marks are too high, and the paint's all wrong.

'And there's what we've got here . . .' He held the plastic envelope up to the light and Shaw could see the sickly glint of strawberry smearing the sides, the fish gaff a deadly black.

'Same blood group as our man on the sands, and the hairs match on colour.' He tapped a glass demijohn full of rose water. 'This has got plenty of blood in it too – contents of the washing-up bowl. I'll try and match DNA for you.'

He'd had the skein of blonde hair bagged too. He passed it to Shaw, who weighed it in his hand. He thought of brushing Francesca's hair before school, the subtle smell of the natural oils, the irritable tugs as his daughter wriggled at the imposition.

'We're still doing the tests on that,' said Hadden. 'Nothing yet – but it clearly isn't the dead man's.'

Shaw remembered the pink plastic frame attached to Sarah Baker-Sibley's dashboard in the Alfa. The snapshot of her daughter with luxuriant, nearly waist-length hair.

'Rest of the boat?' he asked.

'Some blood, certainly – on a rug that's been turned

over on the cabin floor. The top side's got stains too. And another piece of scalp, on the steps up to the deck.'

Hadden pulled off his forensic gloves. His hands were as pale as his eyes, the freckles anaemic, the nails short and white.

The final bag: the framed snapshot unscrewed from the wooden panelling of the *Hydra*'s cabin. The sky an Aegean blue, a single white domed chapel on the rocky hillside beyond a beachside taverna.

Shaw held his thumb on the girl. 'That's Jillie Baker-Sibley. Who's the boy – question one. Where's Mum – question two. Taking the picture? Maybe.' He held the picture closer, studying Jillie's face, the tomboy's shorts and T-shirt, the hair cut back to shoulder length. The boy was darker, older, the stance – one forearm across his knee – a mirror to his father. The son shared the father's facial keystone, the balanced features. The girl had inherited the eyes and nose, but the bone structure was Sarah Baker-Sibley's.

He handed the picture to Valentine. 'Let's get Baker-Sibley in first thing for interview,' said Shaw. 'And Jillie. Let's do it out in the sticks – Burnham Market. That way she might not panic. Then we'll bring her back here to ID the body from the sands.'

They heard the bell at St Margaret's mark ten o'clock.

'And I'll pick you up at seven, George – your house.'

Valentine stood his ground, irked to be dismissed, sensing there was something else to say that he wasn't going to hear. Hadden worked at a PC. Shaw helped himself to coffee.

'Sir,' he said, turning on his heel, slamming the door.

# 30

'I owe you for this,' said Shaw, stretching, bending his spine back so that he could see the Ark's wooden vaulted ceiling.

'It's OK,' said Hadden. 'I don't sleep much. Usually I read books about birds I don't have time to see. I've made a start on Tessier – it's intriguing work – but it's just a start.' He dragged a heavy black metal box out from under one of the work benches and placed the contents, all bagged, out on the conference table.

The last time Shaw had seen them they'd been crushed in the cellophane evidence bags. Now, laid out, following the order of the body, the sight was more intimate. The green-and-white Celtic football shirt, the white shorts, the odd socks, the studless football boots. The red sweat-shirt had been laid to one side, on top the contents of the shorts pocket: the 40p change, the wrapped Opal Fruit – the paper discoloured with age.

Shaw produced two bottles of mineral water from his overcoat and offered one to Hadden, who took it, drinking in silence. Under the neon light his skin looked ghostly – especially the narrow scar just below his hairline where the last operation had removed a melanoma.

'Right.' Hadden closed his eyes. 'I don't have the case file but there were notes with the forensics and I've access to copies of the Home Office reports. They're thorough, actually – given the state of the science at the time.' He touched the keyboard of his PC and the screen flooded with colour, the wallpaper a scene of flamingos in flight over an African saltpan. At the centre of the screen was an open folder containing a single document.

'I made some notes. Here.' He opened the document, read for a second, clicked some more, then leant back in the seat. 'This was one of your father's cases, wasn't it?'

'Just tidying up.'

Hadden trusted him enough not to ask any more, or to wonder where the case file had gone. 'There's plenty of physical evidence that we could re-examine – but most of that would take time. But my first thought is that there is a real miss here . . .' His face had flushed slightly, and his eyes for once caught the light radiating from the screen which now showed a series of microscope slides. Each picture was black, with a central image in a buttery yellow. Each one appeared to be a small distorted globe – some almost perfectly round, most smooth but asymmetrical.

'These are really small – this is at 10,000 times magnification. You couldn't get a pinhead into one of these shots, it would be too big.'

'Where'd you find them?'

'Everywhere – all surface clothing anyway – the Celtic top, the shorts, both socks outside the boot, but just the arms of the sweatshirt, and in bands. I've got a theory there – kids often wrap jumpers round their waists, the arms knotted. That would be consistent.'

'What are they?'

'Balls of paint. Thousands of them – in fact . . .' He

shuffled the sheets of printed report. 'Approx two thousand.'

'From an aerosol can?'

'No. There are traces of an industrial lubricant and a thinner. So I'd say the child was standing near some sort of paint-spraying operation at some point between the last time the clothes were washed and his death.'

'A wash would have got rid of them?'

'No – but these are distributed in a very fine mesh-like pattern over the clothes. Washing would have disrupted that – there'd be pools of them, they'd get caught up in the seams, the stitches. There's no sign of that. The case file should have details on the last time the clothes were washed, but judging by the shorts I'd say they were clean on.'

'And the paint?'

'That's why it really is your lucky day. It's not a car paint at all – it's a kind of yellow sealant paint used on tractors. It's hardwearing and withstands chemicals used for spraying. It's listed in the national database but the company that made it – Roncal – went bust in the mid-nineties.' He picked up a printed list and gave it to Shaw. 'This is a list of their customers – mostly agricultural engineers. Only local one is out at Castle Rising, on the edge of town. Outfit called Askit & Sons.'

Shaw held the list in his hand. 'Thanks.'

'That's OK. I'm not done yet – and I won't get done this week unless you push this up the priorities list. We've still got three vehicles out on Siberia Belt. And the basics from the *Hydra* will take us forty-eight hours at least.'

Shaw held up both hands. 'No, no. Tom, I can't justify

asking you to do this. Not now. The chances of taking any case forward twelve years down the line are a thousand to one – we both know that. So, if you can, you can. It's a favour, and I owe you one already.'

'OK – when I can I'll get back to it. One thing would make things quicker . . .'

Shaw nodded. 'Go ahead.'

'The original case file.'

'I'll get it for you,' said Shaw. It was a confrontation he'd been avoiding. An emotional tussle over his father's memory. 'Give me twenty-four hours.'

# 31

It had been someone's birthday in the Queen Victoria, on Mary Seacole ward. A blue balloon, detached, stirred and rushed ahead as Grace Ellis pushed through the doors of the children's ward, nodded to the nurse on night duty, and headed for Jake's room, the linoleum sticky with disinfectant under her feet. A child laughed in one of the rooms, and through an open door she saw a small girl lying on top of the sheets, one leg kicking out straight in her dreams.

Grace Ellis knew Jake would be awake. Normally he slept in the afternoon, and then early evening, something to do with the drugs. But since his father's murder he'd struggled to find deep sleep, enmeshed instead in a series of fitful nightmares. His TV was on, the sound down, a video playing, *Harry Potter and the Chamber of Secrets*, the flickering picture making the room's walls jump forward and back. At the foot of the bed was a cuddly toy, a present from the Police Benevolent Fund.

Her son turned his head on the pillow. 'Mum,' he said.

'Sorry,' she said, kissing him roughly, cradling the head. She didn't take another breath. 'Look. Dad's not here to tell you this.' The boy killed the film with the remote control, just using his fingers, not even flexing the wrist. 'The appeal, Jake. We're not going to raise the money, love. Without Dad, there's just me. I can't do it...'

She went to stand, but forced herself not to run away. 'Mrs Tyre's looking after Michael and Peggy, I can't stay long. Only I couldn't sleep thinking ... thinking you'd be looking forward to it. Because it isn't going to happen.' She began to cry. 'What is it about this bloody hospital?' she said. 'I never cry at home. I walk in here and it feels like my whole life wants to run out through my eyes.'

They both laughed. 'S'OK,' said Jake. 'It was Dad's idea really.' He hauled in another breath, an effort which distorted his face. 'He said it'd give you something to look forward to.'

'Me?'

'So you could cope,' said Jake. 'I'm OK, Mum,' he said, but his voice was desperately weak.

'Me?' she said again.

But he'd turned away, with his eyes open.

John Holt sat in his favourite armchair, the lightweight overnight bag on his lap full of his kit from hospital – pyjamas, toothbrush, toothpaste, towel, soap, reading glasses. The front room of his daughter's bungalow was overheated and he worked a finger between the collar of his shirt and his neck. His daughter Michelle sobbed on the sofa, clutching and unclutching his granddaughter's thin body. 'They won't be back,' said Holt, sipping tea, aspirating to cool the surface. 'It was a mistake – they'll get their money. We'll be OK, Micky, so stop crying.'

'She was out in the snow,' said Michelle, dabbing at her eyes. 'Playing snowballs.' Michelle was in her mid-twenties perhaps, but obesity obscured her age. Flesh hung from her arms and a collar of fat lay below her chin. On the table beside her a bottle of pills stood open beside a mug of hot chocolate. 'She was terrified, Dad – they had knives for Christ's sake!'

She'd almost screamed and Holt held up both hands. 'Micky – not in front of Sasha, OK? It's over. I was in hospital – I couldn't pay them. I'm OK now – they'll get their money.'

'They left that mark on the door.'

Holt's voice betrayed his anger. 'I've said they won't be back, Micky. Sasha's fine now. This is her home, and she's staying here. All right? I've sorted it. The sign on the door's just a reminder. It's done.' Holt blinked behind the thick lenses, adjusted the heavy black frames.

'If I lost the house I'd lose Sasha,' she said, tears welling up again. 'I'd be out on the street. They'd take her away, Dad.'

'That's rubbish,' he said. 'We'd stick together.'

But Michelle shook her head.

He took a breath. 'Look. They're not going to take Sasha away,' he said. 'I promise. We're always here for you. Now – shhhhhh . . .' He held a finger to his lips.

His wife stood at the window, parting the curtains, looking out on the snow-covered sports ground opposite her daughter's cottage.

'We'd better go,' said Martha Holt. 'Your dad needs to rest. He should still be in hospital, he knows that. If he won't go back then he should be at home.' She put a hand to her forehead, the fingers shaking. 'Discharging yourself is stupid,' she said, biting her lip.

'What? For God's sake, woman, I had to. They want

their money. I need to cash the cheque, get it to Joe.' He covered his eyes.

Michelle felt under the armchair cushion and found a packet of cigarettes, taking one out and lighting up.

'Jesus!' said her father. 'Let's go.'

Holt stood on the step after he'd shut the door. He ran a finger along the marks they'd made: six savage cuts of a knife in the wood, identical to the ones on the side of the Corsa.

Sarah Baker-Sibley stood in the doorway of her daughter's bedroom. She could smell Jillie, that soap, and the stuff that she put in her hair now it was short. Her bedclothes were thrown back, the sheet screwed up where her daughter's body should have been.

When had she seen her last? Half ten, after the news, after the police had called asking for another interview.

She turned on the bedside light and pulled open the first drawer of clothes. Nothing. What did she keep in here – knickers, socks, tops? Sarah thought that she should know, and not for the first time she felt how inadequate she'd been. She pulled open another and pushed aside multicoloured tights. A book: bound in leather. She flicked it open and felt sick. A diary, full of secrets. James had given it to her for Christmas two years earlier. But every page was blank. She flicked through: nothing. That was typical of Jillie, she thought; that she should reveal nothing, but keep everything inside her head.

Sarah covered her eyes with her hand. She'd lost a son. Now she'd lost her daughter. She'd asked her to lie for her, just this once.

Running down to the front hall she found Jillie's coat was missing, the full-length with the fake-fur lining. She turned on the outdoor light and threw open the heavy wooden door. The path was white with snow, Jillie's foot-steps a confident double line, leading away from the house.

Izzy Dereham tucked her daughter Natalie into bed with an almost savage efficiency. The child was pinned down, both arms under the coverlet, her mouth breathing warm air into the patterned quilt. The head of a jet-black toy cat peeked from the counterpane.

'Now sleep,' said Izzy. 'In the morning the world will be a different place.' The farmhouse roof creaked, the timbers straining against the wind that had come with the tide. Down by the oyster beds the sea thudded on the sands.

'But why were you crying?' asked her daughter.

'Some of the oysters were lost in the storm. I love the oysters. I cried at Christmas, didn't I, when we read about the Walrus and the Carpenter.'

Her daughter watched her in the half-light. 'That was pretend.'

'I'm not so sure, young lady.'

She turned out the light, waited a second, then padded swiftly down the stairs. In the room behind the kitchen she sat down at her desk, punched a number into the handset of the phone. He'd said not to call, but she couldn't wait. She listened to the ringing tone, as her eyes filled with tears again.

\*

On Hunstanton Beach the waves fell, breaking first to the north, then unfolding to the south, like someone turning the pages of a book. Peter Shaw studied the plastered ceiling where the light played, his fingers interlaced behind his head. Lena slept now, the sheets damp between them. The wind made the roof beams creak here too, and in the gusts it threw sand at the front door. He turned over, folding his body to fit her back, tucking his knees into hers. Lena's smell was earthy, like warm skin in the sun.

His daughter was coughing. A winter cold. He'd caught her paddling that weekend, the blood just beneath the skin as blue as the inside of a mussel shell.

He rolled out of bed and pulled on his boxers.

Walking the corridor, he checked the window latches, then the front door, double-checking the latch. Had he left the cooker on? He'd boiled pasta on the gas ring. But the kitchen was cold, no flame on the hob. He checked the red light by the shower too. Nothing.

His daughter coughed again. So he went down the corridor, the sand gritty on the wooden floor, and looked in through the open door. She was coughing in her sleep now, metronomic, both hands held before her mouth.

Closing the door behind him he bottled up the sound. The chair in which he used to sit and read to Francesca was gone, so he sat on the floor, his back to the bookcase.

4.30 a.m.

He'd see her through until dawn. He hadn't done that for a long time; she'd been three, four perhaps, and he'd hoarded the sleepless nights, when exhaustion made him think so clearly, away from the distractions of the day.

He thought about James Baker-Sibley and his daughter on board *Hydra* waiting for the tide to turn. He imagined the father cutting his daughter's hair. A mirror in front of them perhaps. Did they both hear the footsteps together? The first, above their heads, as James's killers came aboard?

# 32

Burnham Market lay tucked up in the snowy hills of north Norfolk, the rooftops as white and crisp as on any Christmas card. In the police station Shaw and Valentine waited for Sarah Baker-Sibley's Alfa Romeo to pull into the car park. Jillie Baker-Sibley, it appeared, held the key to what had happened that night on board the *Hydra*. But the leading question now, as Sarah Baker-Sibley was led into the interview room, was where was she?

'I asked for your daughter to attend for interview,' said Shaw, adjusting the dressing on his eye.

A PC brought tea. Sarah Baker-Sibley sat at a table, knocking out a menthol cigarette from a fresh pack. She looked around, her shoulders rolling slightly in the chill air. Through the window she saw a fox break cover in the high hillside above the town, running over the bare furrowed earth, suddenly clear against the snow.

Shaw sensed that the elaborate display of insouciance was a mask. Her face was puffy and she kept trying to rearrange her mouth, trying to hide an emotion very close to fear.

'She's on a sleepover. Clara's – her best friend. A house at South Creake. I've phoned and left a message.

I'm not worried, and I don't see any reason for you to be.'

Valentine pulled up a chair, the legs scraping on the bare wooden floor. He'd spent three years at Burnham Market and had taken hundreds of dreary statements in this room. The stench of institutional cleaning hung about the place, the only decoration a Day-Glo poster in yellow for Neighbourhood Watch, a burglar in black slipping through an open window, and a no-smoking sign nailed to the door. Being back made him realize just how much he'd hated those ten lost years. 'Can I have the address, Mrs Baker-Sibley?' he asked, taking a note. He told Shaw he'd organize a squad car to check it out, leaving the door open when he went.

Shaw leant against the single heavy iron radiator which cracked and thudded with the strain of the hot water dribbling through clogged pipes. 'You don't mind?' asked Shaw, nodding at the tape. 'And you don't want a solicitor? Only, the last time we spoke . . .'

She shook her head and lit the menthol cigarette.

Shaw pointed to the no-smoking sign.

'Jesus.' She stubbed it out in a saucer that had been left on the table.

'Did you tell your daughter she was expected for interview?'

'Yes, yes of course I told her. What's this about?' she said, checking her watch. 'I open at ten. Sharp. I've said all I'm saying about Colin Narr, so, as my daughter would say, Inspector Shaw, let's not even go there.'

Shaw stood, switched a shell from his trouser pocket

to the tabletop. He guessed that she'd talked to a lawyer, that they'd counselled cooperation until she found out what she was up against – that's when the shutters would come down.

'Have you any idea why the *Hydra* is moored at Morston Creek, Mrs Baker-Sibley?' he asked.

Valentine had come back and he watched her face as she heard the question. She managed to construct an expression of mild curiosity.

'I have no idea. My husband's movements are of no significance to me, Detective Inspector.'

'You said you were divorced, I think?'

'Did I? Good, that's right. Legally, emotionally, spiritually, and – until you informed me otherwise – geographically. My husband lives on Kythera, a Greek island. He has a flat in the City, as I think I told you only yesterday. My happiness soars with every mile that stretches between us.'

'And Jillie?'

'What about Jillie?' The chin came out, the eyes hardening protectively.

'When does she see her father?'

'My husband is not allowed to see his daughter. There's a court order to that effect.' She touched the damp dog-end in the saucer. 'My husband killed our first child, you see, so he's not getting another chance.'

Snow fell against the window and the silence was so deep Shaw thought he could hear the muffled impact of the flakes.

'How?' asked Valentine, taking Route One.

'James always wanted a boy, someone he could leave

his money to, someone to carry on. Women don't count. But it couldn't be just any boy. It had to be a boy in his image.' She shook her head in disbelief. 'Well, in the image he has of himself: tough, self-sufficient, brave.

'Thomas was none of those things. But that didn't stop James. He took him to Greece, on the *Hydra*. They camped on the mainland, a few miles across the strait, and James taught him how to sail the little wooden dinghy she carried. Then he sent him out to sea one day. Thomas was thirteen – Jillie's age. This was three years ago. Jillie was with me at our villa. James told Thomas he had to make the crossing. A halcyon day – that's what the Greeks call it. Hardly any wind. Thomas got hot and decided to go for a swim. He just jumped in. He'd never been on his own before, so he didn't think. There was no way back onto the boat, you see, and he couldn't climb the sides.'

She sipped the tea, the cup steady.

'I found the body. It was extraordinary, actually, because the boat, when they found it, was ten miles along the coast but his body had floated back to our house. We had a stretch of beach and I saw something from the house – I was by the phone waiting for news, James was out in the *Hydra*, searching the coast. I waded in. It was summer, so the body had begun to decompose. I didn't know it was him – not for a certainty – until I was a few feet away. It's not something I'm going to forget. And it's something Jillie can't forget. I didn't see her but she followed me into the water.

'I burnt the dinghy after the Greek police had finished the inquiry. There were scratch marks all round it, cutting into the wood.'

She turned her hard face to the window again, but tears pushed themselves out of the ducts at the corner of her eye.

'An accident then,' said Shaw.

She ignored him. 'I took Jillie home. James led his own life, there was another woman. He didn't contest the divorce. But he did try to get custody of Jillie.' She laughed. 'The court threw that out. Then, last month, he tried to take her back,' she went on. 'She'd been down to London to see her grandmother – that's my mother – and she'd got back to Lynn early. She rang me for a lift. She rang her father to chat. They used to talk.' She pushed the saucer away. 'She'd forgiven him, you see. Something I didn't think he deserved. I was late; James was in town – he still has business interests here, although he never trusted me enough to tell me what they were. He drove to the station. He was flying back to Greece that after-noon; his company has a private jet, there's a landing strip on the island but no customs. Why didn't she come? He said it would be a new life for her.' She arched her pencilled eyebrows. 'There's a pool – heated.'

She crossed her legs. 'There's no choice now, you see.'

'Choice?' asked Shaw.

'A girl will have to do. James's . . .' She searched for a word, enjoying herself. 'James's *ability* to have children is restricted. A medical condition affects his fertility, and that gets worse with age. We did try for a third, but it was impossible. So it's Jillie who'll inherit. And she's a tomboy really – he always wanted that. So she'd love to go with him, Daddy's little cabin boy.'

236

'So she *would* have gone?' asked Valentine.

'That's immaterial. Because that's when I turned up. They were sat in James's BMW. I got her out of the passenger side but James came round. He hit me. Quite hard, actually. So I hit him back. Harder. There was a witness – a taxi driver on the rank. Jillie screamed, and he tried to get her back in the car. It was quite a scene.'

She forced herself to smile and Shaw guessed she'd relived it many times.

'I pressed charges, assault. ABH. He was sentenced to six months, suspended. And James was banned from seeing her, or from coming within ten miles of Burnham Thorpe. So if he's at Morston Creek he's broken the court order – I hope you'll take the appropriate action. The judge made it clear he would go to prison if he breached the conditions.' Nobody said anything so she went on. 'We've been very happy ever since,' she said, dispensing with another unasked question.

'He must love his daughter,' prompted Shaw.

'Actually, I think his feelings towards Jillie are irrelevant, Inspector Shaw. He needs her. She's his immortality. She's the vehicle for his wealth, a receptacle for his money.'

Shaw produced an evidence bag from the holdall: clear plastic with the sheaf of long hair curled within.

'He tried again, didn't he?' asked Shaw, standing at the table, his fingertips splayed on the Formica surface.

She tried to touch the hair through the plastic.

'We found the hair on the *Hydra*, Mrs Baker-Sibley.'

She ran a nail along her bottom lip. 'Yes,' she said, looking at the tape. 'I think I need that solicitor now, Inspector Shaw.'

Shaw turned off the tape as she stood up. 'I'd sit down for one more minute,' he said. He needed to tell her something, and he didn't need to do it on the record.

She sat.

'Do you have a picture of your husband, Mrs Baker-Sibley?'

She laughed, her head thrown back.

Shaw took a file from the desktop and, flicking through, found the animated sketch he'd made from the corpse retrieved from Styleman's Middle. He placed it neatly before her, put the saucer on a corner as a paperweight.

'Is that James?'

She looked at it and Valentine could see the calculations going on behind her eyes. She took a cigarette out of the packet and just held it in her hand. 'Unless he's got a twin brother.' She tried to set her lips in a line but failed.

'I'm sorry, Mrs Baker-Sibley, but this man's body . . .' Shaw tapped the drawing, 'was found on Styleman's Middle – the sandbank a few miles off Ingol Beach – on Tuesday. I'm afraid I'm going to have to ask you to see if you can identify the body later today. There is evidence your ex-husband was attacked on board his yacht. I'm sorry.'

Valentine watched as the blood drained from her face, leaving a livid patch of blusher exposed, like a death mask.

'He's dead?'

'Three o'clock,' said Shaw. 'St James's. And then we'll need to talk again. I'd like Jillie to be there.'

'Of course.' She'd worked it out now. 'I'll make a statement after I've taken advice. But I can make a few things clear. Right now. We're off the record for now?'

'Sure.'

Outside a car alarm pulsed. She placed both palms on her face and stretched the skin back, lifting the wrinkles out of her neck.

'Yes. He did try again. Which I find hard to believe because generally he's a coward, I think, and if he'd been caught – even just talking to her – he'd have gone to jail. Jillie said he was waiting outside the school in his 4x4 the night I was stranded out on the coast road in the snow. She said he just wanted to talk, that he'd get her home, so she got in. I'd told her a hundred times to text me if her father turned up. But he persuaded her to listen to what he had to say first. He drove her to Morston and said that if they wanted to they could catch the tide. He stopped in the village and posted some letters, then drove down to the quay. She wouldn't have to go back to school, that's what he told her. They could take the *Hydra* over to Ostend – he'd done it before with her when she was young. He said he'd bought a property on the Turkish coast. There's an International School in Smyrna; they wouldn't ask questions if he paid the fees. They'd disappear. Even if the police found them he had the money to tie it up in the courts. He said it'd be like Jarndyce and Jarndyce. She's done *Bleak House* at school – she thought it was funny. So she said yes.'

'She told you that when you phoned from Gallow Marsh Farm?' said Valentine.

'Yes. I called her mobile. She told me what had happened, said she'd decided to go with her father. She said it was his turn . . .' She laughed. 'I told her it didn't work like that. I said I wanted to speak to James. Then the line went dead.'

'But you rang a second time,' said Shaw, looking out at the snow, a hawk over the hedgerow.

'James answered. He said they'd sort it out together. That I wasn't to come after them and that if I went to the police I'd never see her again. That's why I told you she was at home. He said if I kept quiet then he'd work something out, I could see her abroad. Which was nice of him,' she added, not smiling. 'I could hear Jillie crying in the background. I think she realized then that it wasn't a game. That we might not see each other again.'

'Did you go after them?'

'I didn't need to. Your squad car dropped me home. I went inside, got changed and set off for the creek – it's only a mile. I met Jillie coming up the lane. She said James had rowed her ashore. She'd told him she wanted to go home, to me. She said he'd cried when she said goodbye – which is sweet, isn't it?'

DC Mark Birley knocked, came in. 'Squad car says Mrs Baker-Sibley's daughter isn't at her friend's house.' Birley's new shirt was too long in the arm so that he had to keep readjusting the cuffs. Shaw wondered if he'd kept his uniform, still hanging in a cupboard at home.

'Mrs Baker-Sibley?' asked Shaw.

She stood. 'I'll check her other friends. The school.'

'We'll give you an hour,' said Shaw. 'Then we'll put out an alert. We need to find her.'

Anger flashed across her mother's eyes. 'I know that. Christ – I know that.' She took one last look at the sketch

Shaw had made from her husband's corpse. She stabbed a finger at it. 'The eyes were crueller. Much crueller.'

It was only after Valentine had walked her to the car park that Shaw realized her perfume still dominated the interview room: an astringent citrus. Shaw watched as she drove the Alfa out into the street, the gravel screeching as she made the turn, wrestling with the steering wheel.

'It makes sense,' said Valentine from the door. 'The diversion on to Siberia Belt, the mobile black spot, everything. All set up to stop Sarah Baker-Sibley picking Jillie up, and then stranding her out of mobile contact long enough to get to sea.'

'Let's get out to the scene, see if it works on the ground.'

'Mark wants a word,' said Valentine, nodding down the corridor towards the front counter.

The DC was filling in the station logbook. He gave Shaw a black plastic box, about the size of a brick, and flipped open the hinged top. Inside was a porous pad. In the lid was a stamp. He pressed it into the ink, turned his hand over, and printed a neat BT on his skin, just like the one Valentine had seen on the skin of the driver of the Mondeo, and just like the one on Jillie Baker-Sibley's narrow wrist.

'We've had some luck,' said Birley. 'Forty-one tickets were sold for the dance. Security for the disco, and the running of the bar, was handled by a private company . . .' Birley checked a neat note, 'called SoundEvent, based in Lynn. The parish council chairman is Rod Belcher – he's outside if you want a word. He says his son went and he said there was no trouble. The bar was beer and lager only with an age limit of eighteen. Anyone purchasing alcohol had to show an ID card. Payment at the door – which is where the hand stamp was given – secured a voucher for a free drink, a soft drink for those under-age, in return for name and address. They sell the lists on to a direct marketing company involved in flogging CDs, DVD, pop-concert tickets, magazines. So there's a list – and it's complete. SoundEvent says everyone went for the voucher.'

Birley worked a finger inside his shirt collar, easing the material away from his neck. 'So: forty-one names, twenty-nine blokes. I've got the lot. One of them has to be our runaway driver.'

He unfolded a file and arranged the snapshots. Birley had dragooned two uniformed PCs from Burnham to help build the photo gallery. He laid them out in rows, then stood back, admiring his work. Valentine studied the faces. Then he did it a second time, but it was just for show. 'Nope. 'Fraid not.'

Birley blew out his cheeks. 'I don't understand,' he said.

'Our kid got in for nowt,' said Valentine.

'How?' said Birley, looking at Shaw.

'You said the parish council chairman had a son?' asked Shaw.

Birley searched the faces, found the one he was looking for, and stabbed it with his index finger. 'Gerald Belcher – known to his friends as Gee.'

'It's not him,' said Valentine. 'Believe me.'

'There was someone else at that disco, Mark. We need to find him. Let's speak to Gee's dad. He's here?'

They found Rod Belcher standing outside, smoking by a gleaming BMW. Shaw thought he looked like an incomer: trendy-bald, his head shaved, a thin well-toned face lightly tanned. The leather jacket he wore was worth a uniformed PC's monthly salary. And glasses: narrow, across the face in red lacquer, as thin as a horizon.

Birley outlined their problem with the photos but Belcher couldn't help. His son was a regular at the discos, which were monthly, and he was sure there was no one there who was a stranger.

'Bit of a mystery,' said Belcher, checking a mobile.

'You never go?' asked Valentine, his head wreathed in cigarette smoke.

'No. Well, sometimes. But kids at this age are best left to themselves. There's been no trouble.'

'We'd like a word with Gee,' said Birley. 'Just to double-check.'

'OK,' said Belcher, ditching the cigarette and getting back in the car. The dashboard bristled with the calm, sophisticated telemetry of a £45,000 motor car. The engine purred into life. The finish was teak, a SatNav unit attached to the windscreen, the seats in tan leather. Valentine reached in and turned the ignition key, killing the engine, because around the steering wheel there was a snakeskin cover, the design unmistakable – black chevrons on a silver background.

# 33

Jillie Baker-Sibley could hear the traffic in the sea mist but she couldn't see the pus-yellow headlights until they were thirty yards away; the cars whispering past, the drivers bent forward, trying to see something where there was nothing. Fossdyke, the ancient Roman bank which kept the sea back off the land, stretched out into fog ahead of her, like a drawbridge over an unseen gorge.

She was getting colder, her arms held awkwardly at her sides, her jaw aching with the effort of not shivering. Any warmth she'd gathered overnight was bleeding away. She'd slept in the shed at the bottom of Clara's garden, wrapped up in a picnic blanket, with a paraffin lamp on. Her friend had got her soup in a flask and a microwaved stick of garlic bread.

At dawn she'd crept out and left a note.

*Thanks. Don't tell them. I'll write.*
*J. x*

She picked up her first lift on the coast road, round Lynn, and west towards the Midlands. The mist had cleared for an hour and she'd seen the horizon. To the north, reclaimed land ran to the shore of the Wash, a patchwork of mathematical fields dusted with snow, a power station the only feature, catching the sunlight like a solar panel. To the south the snow lay heavier on the villages which marked the old coastline, Dutch-style lead spires rising from knots of wind-cowed trees.

The icy wind had made the legs of her jeans flap. 'Fuck it,' she'd said to herself, wishing she hadn't forgotten how to cry. In her pocket she clutched a key, but its power to still her rising panic was fading. Alone, stranded, she felt an almost overwhelming urge to scream.

She'd got a lift, finally, from a truck to Sutton Bridge where the old mechanical swing bridge loomed, a giant's Meccano set crossing the grey waters of the Welland. The mist closed in again beyond the town, curling over the thirty-foot-high bank like dry ice. Grey cottages built on the wide dyke came and went, but they saw no one. Villages dripped in the damp cloud which had fallen on the world.

Then another truck: Luxembourg plates, a single silver container. She'd answered the driver's questions.

Where was she heading? The M1.

Was this the right way? It was the right way.

Shouldn't she be in school? She was sixteen.

Where would she go when she got to the M1 – north or south? To the airport.

Did she have a ticket? Did her parents know?

She said she needed to get out at the next roundabout. He said that it would be best to go to a police station, they could check she was OK. She said she'd tell them he'd tried to rape her, in a lay-by, that he'd used his weight to lie on top of her, that you couldn't hear her screams because of the traffic thundering by. He didn't see her cut a thin line along her cheekbone with a fingernail.

'You hit me,' she said, her voice dead.

They drove to a service station in silence and she got out at the exit. Standing on the grass verge she'd spat on his windscreen. That made her feel better, in charge, powerful. *Empowered.* She liked that word.

He'd pulled away and she'd watched the tail lights fade in the mist, the world around her a shifting jigsaw of grey and white.

The car that picked her up was a black Jag.

It went past once. Then she heard it brake. She didn't notice it going back the other way, or hear it pulling an unseen U-turn. When it coasted out of the gloom the second time its tyres crunched in the kerb on broken glass and she recognized the umbrella furled on the back seat.

She took a step back, looking around as if trying to find a way off the bank. But the field below was a milk-white pool of mist, weaving its way between wooden posts.

The passenger side window came down electronically. She shook her head, but then she got in.

# 34

A POLICE – NO ENTRY sign blocked the way forward on Siberia Belt.

'Weird,' said Shaw. 'Tom said he'd have it wrapped up by last night. Why are they still here?' He got out and stamped in the snow while Valentine struggled into his raincoat. They heard a marsh bird's call, like fingers down a blackboard. Walking, Valentine smoked doggedly, while Shaw tried to set in order, in his own mind, everything that they'd learned.

He'd left DC Birley to interview Rob Belcher and his son Gee about the whereabouts of the BMW – and the snakeskin wheel cover – on the night of the blizzard on Siberia Belt. DC Campbell was told to get a unit down to the cockle-pickers' hostel in the North End and round them up for interview. But the big breakthrough was Sarah Baker-Sibley. Her statement would provide a corner-stone for the inquiry; laying out the foundations of the plan her ex-husband had so meticulously laid to abduct his daughter. Luring her mother into the mobile black spot, and then bottling her up like a spider in a jar for the crucial hour it would take to spirit Jillie out of the country. The sudden snowstorm had all been to the good, turning the lid on the jar ever tighter.

But to achieve that James Baker-Sibley had to put in place a conspiracy. How many? Two on Siberia Belt – Ellis in front, and a backstop. Then another two at either end of the diversion to put the signs out and take them in. He doubted that Ellis put out the diversion sign – Sibley-Baker was right behind him – and he certainly didn't take it in. And the timing had to be perfect, but then they knew Sarah Baker-Sibley ran her life by timetable. She'd always be there, on the coast road, at a few minutes past the hour, on her way to pick up Jillie. It was elaborate but brilliant. If it had worked the police would never have been involved, Sarah Baker-Sibley would have been forced to stay silent or face the possibility – probability – that she'd never see her daughter again. An almost ghostly crime. As intangible as the mist now forming on the black marsh water.

Valentine slipped on the ice, his arms flailing to keep his balance, the black slip-ons skating. The sharp right turn in Siberia Belt was still two hundred yards away. So they plodded on.

And then there were James Baker-Sibley's killers, thought Shaw. What if Jillie's mother had used her second telephone call from Gallow Marsh to reach someone other than Jillie and her father? Sarah didn't really need to phone him back at all. She knew what he planned, and as far as she knew her daughter was going to go with him. What she really needed was to stop her. What better friend to call than Colin Narr at Shark Tooth? All roads led to Narr, and to the cockle-pickers Fiona Campbell was assembling for interview.

They reached the turn in the track and, once round the corner of the high flood bank, they saw ahead a single SOC tent, lit within.

Shaw stood at the turning, braving the shock of the wind off the sea. Valentine knew what was coming, a clinically logical summary of the case so far. He was getting tired of the regular lectures. Bored with treating a murder like a set of children's building blocks. The wind wrapped his raincoat round his legs, tugging at the thin cloth of his trousers.

His radio buzzed so he took the call. It was DC Twine in the murder incident room. They'd made progress in tracing the teenager at the wheel of the Mondeo on Siberia Belt. According to parish council chairman Rodney Belcher his BMW, and its distinctive steering-wheel cover, were in use on the night of Harvey Ellis's murder – but not by him. The Belchers' eighteen-year-old neighbour, Sebastian Draper, was teaching Belcher's son Gee how to drive. By way of payment they let him have use of the BMW on occasional weekday evenings when Belcher was up in the City. Draper was on a gap year, waiting to go up to Oxford to read maths in September. Responsible, sensible, polite – according to Belcher. Draper's father had refused to allow his son to answer questions when DC Lau had called, until the family solicitor was present. An interview had been arranged for the morning at St James's. Lau could have arrested him, but Twine had counselled caution. Shaw agreed. They knew where he lived and nobody was doing a moonlight flit from a million-pound address.

Other news: John Holt had discharged himself from hospital, and was under surveillance, and Jake Ellis – Harvey Ellis's son – had died overnight at the hospital, his mother at his side. The *Lynn News* was reporting a cruel irony. When his mother had been taken home from the hospital she'd found a letter on the doorstep: an anonymous donation of £5,000 to the Jake Ellis Appeal. A cheque payable through an offshore trust based in Switzerland.

Valentine relayed the messages and then stowed the radio.

'Perhaps that's Harvey's pay-off for playing his part in the abduction,' said Shaw. 'Baker-Sibley said James stopped off in Morston to post letters – let's try and trace the trust. But if it's the Swiss they're good at hiding money.'

Shaw turned on the spot. Late afternoon: a grey sky loaded with snow, pinned up above their heads in folds, like a dreary circus tent. Siberia Belt had been churned up by vehicles, the ruts frozen.

'So we know a bit,' said Shaw. 'At last.'

They both ducked their heads as a fresh squall of snow blew into their faces.

'What we don't know is what happened out here on Siberia Belt. Why did Harvey Ellis die? Obvious scenario: he loses his nerve, one of the other members of the conspiracy kills him. So – who was the backstop? The kid in the Mondeo? Sebastian Draper. But he goes out and steals a car first? I know he's going to Oxford but he can't be that stupid. But is there another credible suspect? I can't see it. Shreeves – in the security van. I guess it's possible. Was that why he was so keen to start a new life somewhere else?'

Shaw led the way forward to the lit SOC tent. 'Let's see what's keeping Tom's boys out in the cold.'

Shaw had presumed the lit tent covered Harvey Ellis's truck, but as they got close he realized it was too far back down the line. Within it Shaw could see an ultra-violet light playing across the polythene. He pulled aside one of the plastic-flap doors and ducked inside, followed by Valentine. The space was empty, a cube of air, lit by three lights. Tom Hadden was on his knees, alone, beside him a flask and lunch box and spread out on a piece of white plastic a set of hand trowels and evidence bags.

'Ah,' he said, straightening his back. Around his neck hung several hundred pounds' worth of binoculars. Shaw guessed he'd been planning a quiet hour after the final vehicle had been towed off Siberia Belt, scanning the marshes and beach for waders. 'I'm glad you're here, Peter – George. I'm afraid this isn't going to make things any easier.' He smiled, but they didn't smile back.

'This is the spot where our friend in the security van, God rest his soul, was parked on Monday night.'

Hadden knelt and threw a switch on a light gun held in a tripod before killing the overhead halogen bulb. The light was infra-red, and the effect made Valentine's eyes swim out of focus. Shaw saw a liquid stain on the ground, glowing faintly like his daughter's Halloween mask.

'Luminol?' asked Shaw.

'Yup. I'm sure I don't need to tell you what that means. Blood – might not be human of course – but blood. And lots of it; it's soaked in – so several pints. Just the right amount.'

Shaw hugged himself in the cold, relieved at last to find an answer to part of the puzzle. This must be where Harvey Ellis had begun to bleed to death, before his body had been moved to the cab of the pick-up truck. 'And this was *underneath* the security van?' he asked.

'Lucky find, actually,' admitted Hadden. 'One of the uniformed PCs was told to do a quick fingertip along the line once we'd cleared the bank.' Hadden held his fingers up. 'Red smudges.' Hadden crouched, getting his face as close to the earth as possible. 'And there's something else.'

Shaw mimicked his position, looking across the brightly lit patch where the blood had soaked in. 'Footprint?'

'Yup. Deep – given it's frozen earth. Three centimetres. Just one – we can't find anything like it anywhere else on the bank.'

'One footprint – in the blood?' asked Valentine.

'Yes. A boot, actually. Steel toecap. We've got a cast – here . . .' He rummaged in the holdall and produced a lump of plaster with the imprint of the boot. 'This helps,' said Hadden, tapping the heel, which held the imprint of a fern, like a stencil.

'Odd,' said Shaw.

'Yes. Reckon it's a burn mark. Perhaps he stepped into the edge of a bonfire when the fern was burning and it's left its outline. Anyway, distinctive, that's the main thing. Good as a fingerprint.'

He slid the cast carefully back in the bag. 'It's not the victim's boot, by the way – that's a visual assessment but it isn't going to change in the lab.'

'Why just one footprint?' asked Shaw.

'Well – blood's warm, hot when fresh. So three pints of it – perhaps more – would melt the frost out of the earth. So the foot sank in here – but not anywhere else, which was still rock hard.' He knocked a gloved hand against the earth. 'Iron,' he said.

'Which means the footprint was in the blood, not the other way round?'

'Could be,' said Hadden, closing his eyes. 'Yeah – it's a sound scenario. I'd work with it.'

'So . . .'

'So . . . we've got all the shoes from Monday night. We'll see if we can track down a match. But if you're looking for the place where Harvey Ellis began to bleed to death then this is it. There are no scatter marks in the cab – no blood particles at all as far as we can tell. Blow like that, blood would shoot . . . see?' He crouched again. The glowing puddle of blood was shapeless except for a single plume, like a wisp of pampas grass, which shot forward in an elegant curve.

'The fact the blood splatter is a parabola helps. I'd say he was stabbed in the eye, then toppled sideways, that's why you get the pattern.'

Valentine nodded, seeing it happen, feeling the familiar nausea in his stomach.

'Another puzzle,' said Hadden. 'There's no blood trails or drag-marks. I'd say he was lifted or rolled into something here – tarpaulin, plastic sheeting, God knows, and then taken to the pick-up. Like I said, the earth was frozen, so maybe that's why there's so little evidence on the ground. That's all a working hypo – so don't quote me.'

'Could the blood have dripped through from the van above?' asked Valentine.

Hadden shook his head but said: 'I'll check it out for the record, but no way – it's a sold-on Securicor van, it's a tin can, but a bloody strong tin can. Without the vents you couldn't breathe in it. And if he was attacked in the van, why the splatter mark?'

Shaw held the conundrum, unsolved, in his head. 'So the victim was found in the driving seat of his truck – thirty feet away from the spot where he virtually bled to death. Nearly three hours before he was found dead he'd driven his own van over the same spot. That's not possible.'

'I just do the science, Peter,' said Hadden, flicking off the light. 'I need to finish up.' They took the hint, backing out into the snow.

'One step forward, two steps back,' said Shaw.

'What's the step forward?' asked Valentine.

'We know how the dog got Ellis's blood on its snout.'

## 35

Back at St James's Shaw ran up the steps while Valentine waited for the antiquated lift. He pushed open the fire door and saw ahead the long corridor which led to the murder incident room. A woman, with a pail and mop, had stopped in mid-distance, hands on hips. Suddenly a reinforced glass door thudded open and DC Twine was running towards him. Policemen never run, that's standard basic training, unless it's to save life.

Twine skidded to a halt on the damp lino.

'Officer down,' he said. 'Out at the hostel – it's Fiona.'

Twine drove Shaw, commandeering a squad car on the forecourt, Valentine's Mazda in the rear-view. The rush-hour streets were wet and splashed with the jagged colours of the town: traffic lights, headlamps, bright shopfronts, pedestrians turned away from the sea wind. The workers' hostel in the North End was tucked away in the warren of terraced streets that once was home to the town's fishing community. It had been the district's Co-op, and the distinctive red-brick façade was still decorated with vine leaves and an inlaid picture in a pale sandstone of a dairymaid carrying a yoke through a meadow. Graffiti covered it now: a curled indecipherable moniker in soot-black.

An ambulance, sirens screaming, tagged on to the

Mazda as Twine put the squad car on the pavement. A small crowd backed off, a woman clasping a huge Argos bag tripping over her own heels and falling back against the wall.

They brought Fiona Campbell out on a stretcher. Even under the amber street light Shaw could see she was as pale as a Goth. A paramedic was pressing a bandage to a wound at her shoulder, a single knife-cut from the clavicle up towards the neck, the flesh hanging open to reveal a white, chipped bone. She was doused in blood on her left side, her own hand a sticky glove of arterial red.

Shaw placed a hand on her forehead. Fear had made her eyes unnaturally bright. 'You can take tomorrow morning off if it helps,' he said. As he spoke blood oozed to fill the trench of the wound. Valentine hung back. The paramedics slid her into the back of the ambulance, set up a drip and pulled off in a cloud of sirens.

'She had a uniformed PC with her apparently,' said Valentine, stepping forward, his face a colourless mask.

'Where?'

'In the building.'

The shop area of the old Co-op had been left as a storeroom: tea crates, furniture, the old marble counter stacked with loo rolls, catering packs of detergent and light bulbs. A uniformed PC sat on a stool, holding a plastic bottle of water. Even from ten feet away Shaw could see he was shaking.

Valentine spoke to Shaw's ear. 'PC Darren Cole. It's his beat – local community liaison officer. First tour of duty. He's not having a good day.'

Shaw squatted down on his heels in front of Cole. 'Darren. I need to know what happened. Quickly.'

The PC nodded, but said nothing.

'Darren. You need to tell me.'

The PC went to unscrew the top of the water bottle but thought better of it. Vomit covered his reflective tunic. 'We went in – down there.' He looked to a single metal door – Shaw guessed it was the original entrance to the Co-op's cold store. 'We searched the place. There's some drugs – and cash: fifty-pound notes, hidden under the Czech's mattress. A lot of money – thousands.'

Shaw took the water bottle, removed the cap, and gave it to him. He drank, almost half, then handed it back. 'Fiona told them we wanted to talk, down at St James's,' said Cole. 'Most of them said OK. They'd been drinking, but not as much as the Czech. He said he wouldn't go.' The PC wiped his sleeve across his mouth. 'Like, never. Fiona tried to talk him round while I got the rest out into the van. They took a bottle with 'em. I said they couldn't have it, but they took it anyway.'

A bead of sweat ran to the end of Cole's nose. But it was cold in the old shop, and Shaw noticed a bucket full of ice under a damp patch.

'When I went back in Fiona had sat down with him – there's a table. He said he wasn't coming because he was going to kill himself. He'd got a knife, a butcher's knife. He cut his wrist.' Cole gagged. 'Fiona went to stop him and he just . . .' He couldn't find the words. 'He just chopped at her, like she was jungle, you know? I grabbed her – she was on the floor – and dragged her in here. I locked the door, then I called St James's. Officer down.'

'Well done, Darren,' said Shaw, standing. 'Get him out of here,' Shaw told Valentine. 'He needs looking after – treat him like a hero. I'll take a look at chummy.'

The door was like a ship's – iron, riveted, with a heavy-duty handle. Shaw turned the key, leant on the handle and heard a pop, as if entering an airlock. The corridor beyond was tiled, a line of blood smeared down the centre where Cole had dragged Fiona Campbell through to the old shop. On each side there were shelves. Old tin boxes rusted in the corners.

Shaw got to the second door when he heard the air pop behind him and he turned to see Valentine, an unlit cigarette in his mouth, a folder in his hand, his eyes drawn down to the arterial line.

'George,' he said.

They stood together at the inner second door. 'This was in Fiona's car,' said Valentine. 'She'd picked up the men's records from Shark Tooth. Cole says the one they haven't got down the station is this one . . .' He held up the file. 'Bedrich Fibich,' said the DS, reading. 'Forty-two-year-old from Prague. A teacher, family back home. Papers list him as a labourer. He's been in England since last summer.'

'What is this place?' asked Shaw.

'I asked in the crowd – old bloke said it used to be an abattoir for all the Co-ops in town.'

Shaw pushed the second door open and the hinges screamed. A line of camp beds ran down a room. Storage heaters hadn't taken the chill off the white-tiled walls; lots of the tiles were cracked, and Shaw wondered if the engrained black stains were dried blood. He couldn't stop himself drawing in a lungful of air, examining it for traces of the slaughterer's art: the burnt bone where the saw had cut, the raw stench of offal.

The room's brutal past was impossible to obliterate, but the men had tried. The walls were covered in random pictures: the castle in Prague, a centrefold with her legs splayed, a snapshot of a young man standing on a river bank holding up a silver fish, a family wedding. And they'd brought their own smells: sweat and stale tobacco, cheap deodorant and whisky. There was a gas stove, a single garlic sausage hanging from a nail. No windows, just grilles in the roof and beyond them reinforced glass stained green by moss.

Bedrich Fibich was sitting behind a large table facing down the room, like a lonely Christ at a deserted Last Supper. There was nothing on the table except a bottle of whisky and a single glass; but a pool of blood had spread out from Fibich's clasped hands to form an almost perfect circle. His eyes were shut, and Shaw wondered if he knew anyone else was in the room. Gravity seemed to have attacked his face, pulling down the folds of skin, the heavy eyelids, the bottom lip.

Shaw walked to the table and pulled out a metal chair, its legs squealing on the tiled floor. He heard Valentine's soft steps behind him, then to one side, and then he came into peripheral vision, standing with his back to the tiled wall, just within a lunge of Fibich. Shaw could see the single knife wound in the Czech's left wrist.

'We should get you to a doctor,' he said.

Fibich opened his eyes. They were blue but the colour was lifeless, like a vein glimpsed through thin skin. 'No.'

He produced from his lap a carving knife with which he almost casually made a second neat incision across his wrist, the flesh falling open like an uncooked sirloin steak.

Valentine took half a step forward and Shaw heard saliva glug in his throat. But Shaw raised a hand from his wrist, enough to hold him there, well within striking range.

The blade of the knife reflected the light, the bottom six inches smeared with blood. Fibich held it in his hand with the point at Shaw's face, ready to thrust.

'Why? You don't have to die,' said Shaw.

Fibich seemed to stir, rolling his shoulders, wincing as the movement reopened the gash in his wrist. 'She won't have me back. Not after what we did. I had to explain the money, why I was coming home. She said I should stay away, that I was a stranger to them now.'

'She? Your wife?'

He looked at Shaw for the first time. So this was why he was dying, because he was an exile in his own land. But what had he done? Shaw had a shrewd idea. If Sarah Baker-Sibley had called Colin Narr that Monday night and told him Jillie had been abducted he would have organized a rescue. Had he sent a boat out to intercept James Baker-Sibley's yacht? Had Fibich been aboard?

'That's the bit I don't understand,' said Shaw. 'Why did the man on the yacht have to die? Narr sent you out there to get his girlfriend's daughter back, didn't he? But why did her father have to die?'

Fibich turned his wrist to examine the wounds. 'So good to be rich,' he said. 'Other people take all your risks.'

Shaw noted that he hadn't denied Narr had sent them out to the yacht.

Fibich tried to focus on Shaw's face. 'The man on the yacht tried to pay us to leave him – to leave them, the daughter too.' He stopped, and Shaw wondered if he was thinking of his own children.

'He said we could be rich if we let them go. That was a big mistake. We took her anyway. He did not want her hurt, so he did not fight. I rowed her ashore. When I return we beat the truth from him. A desperate man, he fought too hard. So we hit him too hard. But he told us where the money was before he died. Thousands of pounds, all in cash. Then we threw him overboard.'

His head rocked back and he closed his eyes. Above them a line of hooks were still embedded in the roof where the carcasses had once hung.

'I deserve to die here,' he said.

'You said "we". Who was in charge, who else was there, Bedrich?'

Fibich's eyes spun out of focus. 'The little man,' he said. 'The little man without pity. Lufkin.'

# 36

Fiona Campbell had undergone an emergency blood transfusion at the hospital and an operation to reconnect severed arteries in her neck. Bedrich Fibich had been taken to the same hospital. He was alive when they put him in the ambulance outside the old Co-op, but dead when they took him out on the forecourt by A&E. Shaw sat in the Mazda outside the Co-op with Valentine, who smoked beside the open driver's window. Lights poured through the murky windows of the old shop façade. Three uniformed PCs ferried personal effects out to a black van: clothes, letters, a fishing rod.

Shaw shared the silence with Valentine, aware of a subtle tilt in their relationship. He'd taken the decision to go into that room and confront Bedrich. Valentine could have hung back, let him run the risks alone, but he'd chosen instead to share the danger, and the sight of the spreading blood.

Valentine was concentrating on not being sick. He'd gone into the room because he felt he should. Whatever he thought of Shaw he *was* his partner, and as such he deserved the back-up. When he'd seen Fibich's blood spreading towards the edge of the table he'd changed his mind, but by then his legs had gone, so he leant against the wall. He'd fainted standing up for a second, an image of Jack Shaw on his deathbed flashing across his memory, only to be replaced by the sight of his son sat before the pool of spreading blood.

'Let's take Lufkin at dawn – tomorrow,' said Shaw, checking his watch. 'And let's go mob-handed too – with forensics. Tonight we need surveillance on him in case he does a runner.'

'I'll sort it,' said Valentine.

'We need to tie up loose ends tonight. Narr's the key: Fibich virtually admitted he'd sent them out to get Jillie back. Narr is Lufkin's boss too – they're close, we know that. But before we go for Narr we need more evidence. Fibich is dead. Lufkin's a pro – he won't talk, not straight off, anyway. Out on the sands that leaves Sly – the gang-master. We know there's no love lost with Lufkin. We think he's honest. Let's see if he's got a tale to tell.'

Valentine turned the key, thinking that if Shaw wanted a chauffeur he should bloody well hire one.

Sly's houseboat was moored behind Boal Quay. There was an abandoned creek, an old bend in the river by-passed by the main channel which spewed into the estuary. A crescent of houseboats stood moored to a raised jetty. Each had a small hut on dry land, a gangway across the mud, access to a power point and a standpipe. It was home to a menagerie of misfits, some of the boats fashioned into fantastic shapes: one, the superstructure an old single-decker bus laid on a steel hull, another incorporating a Reliant Robin. In between the New Age fantasies there were boats from a more stately era – an old Cambridge college boat, with a veranda like a Victorian railway-station platform; an old steam tug off the set of *The African Queen*; a wooden 1930s minesweeper in Atlantic grey.

They made their way along the jetty, reading off the numbers tacked to the US-style post boxes until they got to 67 The Boal Bank.

The heavy scent of rotting wood and putrid mud was cloying. Sly's home was a wooden barnacle on a steel hull, portholes lit, a washing line on the forward deck hung with a single pair of overalls. Moored alongside was a metal-hulled inshore fishing boat with an open deck, a mast bristling with sonar, GPS, radomes, a fish-finder aerial and floodlights. Shaw recognized it as the one they'd seen anchored off Styleman's Middle on the morning they'd found James Baker-Sibley's body.

They were only halfway across the gangplank when Sly appeared. A deck light flooded them in white, catching falling snowflakes. Shaw was struck again by Sly's size – the barrel-chest, the ham fists. On board his floating home he'd lost the awkwardness that had been apparent out on Styleman's Middle. He raised a hand to his side, without looking, and clicked the light off at a switch, then ran the hand down to find a latch so that he could swing the double doors into the cabin wide open. He pulled a blue seaman's cap off his cannonball head.

Inside they could see the winter-red glow of a pot-bellied stove.

'She's new,' said Shaw, ducking inside, wrapping himself in the sudden woody heat. 'The fishing boat alongside.'

'Refurb,' said Sly, shutting the doors. 'I've done a lot of the work. The engine's giving me gyp. Which isn't funny, 'cos it's my livelihood now.'

Shaw let him tell them what he wanted to tell them.

'I chucked the job. Today. At Shark Tooth.'

Valentine didn't like the self-satisfied look. 'You'll miss your mate – Andy Lufkin,' he said.

Sly took a handful of wooden staves from a basket by the door and fed them into the pot-bellied stove.

The room was simple, furnished with just a few chairs and a single oval table in scratched mahogany. A bookcase filled the prow end. The portholes were brass, a skylight above was crated with snow. As Sly tried to find glasses Shaw looked at some of the framed prints: a map of the Falkland Islands, a picture of a tanker in the Suez Canal, one of Sly – a young man of twenty perhaps – arms round two other sailors outside a bar somewhere hot, in shorts, tattoos on their arms. He was the biggest of the three; the torso muscled like meat, the neck as wide as the thighs.

And an old leather football in a glass case, a hand-painted legend in white: 'RFA Winners: 1971/2'.

Sly gave them glasses with a shot of vodka in each.

'We heard you had a fight with Lufkin last Christmas. What was that about?' asked Shaw.

'Drink,' said Sly, tipping back the glass. 'Too much of it. He's only little, it goes to his head.' Shaw guessed Sly was a man who'd relied all his life on his power to physically intimidate. Now, with the advance of age, he'd been unable to adapt. He moved with a slightly arthritic limp.

'We've been asking around, Mr Sly,' said Shaw, studying a chart laid on the table – the Wash sands out to the navigation light on Roaring Middle. 'And there seems to be a consensus that you're honest. Is that a difference we might assume you have with Mr Lufkin? Is that why your face doesn't fit?'

Sly ran the back of his hand across his lips. 'Maybe.'

They heard a burst of sparks fizzing out in the darkness and through the porthole saw flames lick up from a fire. Out on the mud there was an island of grass and a bonfire burnt; in the shadows men moved.

'That's the social club,' explained Sly.

Valentine hadn't taken his eyes off Sly. 'And Lufkin's got the boss on his side right? That's Colin Narr?'

'And Colin Narr's been there for years,' said Shaw. 'So how come your face doesn't fit now all of a sudden?'

Sly shrugged. 'Too old to cut it. It's a young man's game.'

Shaw's temper had run its course. When he spoke, his voice had an edge like a rusty saw. 'Mr Sly, I've just left Mr Fibich – you know Bedrich?'

Sly didn't move a muscle, his glass cradled in his hand.

'We went to pull him in at the hostel down in the North End. He decided he didn't want to come, so he stabbed a police officer, then dragged a meat knife across his wrists. He's dead. Someone will have to tell his wife, his kids. It'll be someone like me. We wanted to talk to him about the man you found out on Styleman's Middle. A man by the name of James Baker-Sibley.'

They heard wood crackling out in the dark, a surge of intoxicated laughter.

'And we want to ask you the same questions,' finished Shaw, setting the drink on a ledge below a porthole.

'Nothing happens on my watch,' said Sly, helping himself to more vodka.

'Mr Sly, you seem to be labouring under a misconception,' said Shaw. 'It's immaterial to me on whose watch these crimes took place. You were out there. You're out there every day. You're in charge. I want some answers. Did you have anything to do with Mr Baker-Sibley's death?'

Sly took a decision, tipping what was left of the alcohol down his throat. 'No. I liked James, we'd known each other for many years. He was my boss.'

'In what sense?' asked Shaw, the edge still in his voice.

'In the sense that he owned Shark Tooth.'

'What?' said Valentine, flicking his notebook open and closed in irritation.

'Why doesn't everyone know that?' asked Shaw.

'Silent partner,' said Sly. 'That's the way he wanted it. Same as his dad. I did the job for him too before he died. The money's offshore. Commander Baker-Sibley set it up in the nineties. I was in the Falklands with him. Narr ran the business – but I reported over his head, straight to the family.'

Valentine sniffed. 'What about the other shareholders?'

'They're in for the local knowledge, expertise, influence. They hold the licences. But James bankrolled it. I was his eyes and ears. And I didn't like what I saw, and I didn't like what I heard.'

'Right. You knew – of course you knew. That Lufkin and Narr were smuggling, maybe dumping the toxic waste. So you told James and he wanted it stopped?'

'Sure. He had interests all over – Greece, south of France, Hungary . . . the last thing he wanted was the police crawling over some two-bit scam. So yeah – he wanted it stopped. But in life there's what you want, and there's what you get.'

'Why didn't he just chuck Narr out – Lufkin too?'

'Like I say – Narr's important, he knows the business, the licences are in his name. Chuck him out, you ain't got a business.'

'So why didn't you tell us it was James's body when you found it on Styleman's Middle?'

'I saw a lot of dead men in the Falklands,' said Sly. 'They all look the same. Like meat.' He bowed his head, knowing that wasn't good enough. 'I needed time to think. Time to work it out.'

'And you worked it out. Then you did nothing.'

'That's your job. I'm out of it.'

'We need some help,' said Shaw. 'I don't think Colin Narr was on the yacht when James died. But I think he sent Lufkin out there. I need to make that link.'

'I don't want to be part of this,' said Sly. 'Can you promise me that?'

'I can promise you only one thing, Mr Sly. That if you don't tell us what you know I'll make sure you're charged with perverting the course of justice. This investigation was severely hampered by our failure to ID the body on Styleman's Middle. That's down to you.'

Sly slugged the vodka back and refilled his glass. 'Take the ferry across at West Lynn. Take it tonight. Half-way across there's a small trawler in mid-stream, the *Skolt*.

They used it for the runs over to Belgium – for the merchandise, and for dumping the waste. She's due to sail on the dawn tide. I'd make sure she doesn't. And I'd make sure you talk to her registered owner – Colin Narr.'

# 37

They stood on the steps of St James's – Shaw and Valentine – feeling the frost on the air. A bus went past, empty, the condensation on the windows cleared in circles by passengers already safely at home. It had been a good day: they knew why the convoy had been diverted down Siberia Belt. They knew how James Baker-Sibley's plan had been foiled, and they knew why he'd died. HM Coastguard had located the *Skolt* and towed it back to Boal Quay, where it was being examined by one of Tom Hadden's CSI units. But Hadden had brought them up to speed quickly on the most promising development – a gash on the port side where the trawler had been in collision with a smaller vessel. The paint was white. Yacht white.

A good day. And so Shaw couldn't deny it to himself any more: as a partner George Valentine had proved to be worth his weight in filter tips. He'd already contributed more than his fair share to the investigation. He was a good copper, inspired even, when the moment was right. Shaw wasn't the textbook pedant everyone liked to paint him as, but he knew his limitations, so having Valentine around made him feel a lot more confident about solving the final mystery: finding Harvey Ellis's killer.

But the Tessier case stood between them. Shaw might admire Valentine's unpredictable skills, he might feel sorry for him, he might even be able, one day, to ignore his astonishingly annoying habits: but he couldn't find it in himself to trust him. Not completely, not *implicitly*. Did he have a right to let a decade-old question mark hang over the DS's career? No. But it did. And it hung over his father as well. The Tessier case was unfinished business: worse – business they kept pretending didn't exist. The elephant in the locked room. He knew Valentine's bitterness went back to those twelve lost years of his career. Shaw couldn't give them back. But he could do something about the Tessier case.

Shaw stamped his feet on the icy steps. 'I need the file on Jonathan Tessier,' he said.

Valentine looked at his black slip-ons, his toes beginning to go numb in the cold.

'Why?'

'I just do, George. By the morning. And while we are on the topic, I think you might have talked to me about taking it out. It's my father's reputation too, not just yours.'

'Jack's dead.' Valentine bit his lip, looked at his car keys in his hand, the gold on the green dice catching the electric light. He forced himself not to apologize for saying it. 'I don't get an explanation, then?' he said. 'I just hand over the file. My career, my life, but you take the decisions.' He spat in the snow. 'You're an arrogant fucker, sir.' Valentine had been wanting to say that since they'd been put together as partners. He wondered if Peter Shaw had even thought what it was like for him, taking orders from his former partner's son; a snotty-nosed kid when he was first made up to DI.

It was a calculated insubordination that Shaw was powerless to reprimand. This was personal, and ranks didn't matter. So he counted to ten in his head. 'My decision, as a matter of fact, is that *neither* of us is going to have anything more to do with the case. It goes to Warren: he decides. That's the right thing to do. And that's what's gonna happen. You like it – great. You don't. Well, then fuck you. *George.*'

Valentine shook his head. Did Shaw really think anyone at St James's was going to reopen this case? They buried it once. They were the last people likely to dig it up. That's how the top brass kept their uniforms and shiny buttons: by making sure someone else always carried the proverbial can.

'I want the file back, George. This isn't the end of it – but I need the file back.'

Valentine looked around.

'By morning.'

'Yeah, right,' said Valentine, putting a cigarette on his bottom lip.

Shaw stepped inside his personal space, close enough to smell the nicotine engrained in the raincoat. 'I want the case reopened,' he said, his voice vibrating like a reed. 'Just like you do. But we're the last people who can do that. You and I have an interest in this case which makes anything we do suspect in front of a jury. It's all going up the line. I want you to understand that. For us, the case is over.'

Valentine stuck his head forward, the weak chin grey with stubble. 'This case will never be over,' he said.

# 38

*Friday, 13 February*

Andrew John Lufkin was arrested at 6.15 a.m. in his bedsit above Josie's International Hair Salon – a lock-up on the Greyfriars Estate. The backstairs entrance reeked of singed hair and cheap scent. DS Valentine stood back as they took out the door with a shoulder ram, the splinters flying as they pushed through into the bedroom. Lufkin was naked, on top of the sheets, the room heavy with the smell of a paraffin heater and the salty tang of sex.

Shaw couldn't help thinking he looked a lot cleaner than he'd expected. His skin was slightly pink, shiny, and tussling with the fumes from the heater was something else: pine, perhaps? Lufkin asked to see the warrant, not bothering to pull the sheet across his genitals. The girl was in the bathroom. She came out wrapped in a towel, a cigarette unlit between red glossed lips.

'Suzi,' said Valentine, recognizing one of the women who worked the docks, based in a sauna off the quayside. That was the smell, cedar wood, splashed with scented water. 'I'd get your stuff; this one's done.'

'He's paid up 'til lunchtime,' she said, genuinely affronted on behalf of her client's rights.

'He's not gonna take you to trading standards, is he?'

They ran her back into town in a squad car while Lufkin dressed.

All the clothes in the flat above the shop were new – brand new, newer. Boxer shorts, socks and T-shirts still held the creases from the shop packaging which filled the kitchen bin. M&S receipts, also in the bin, put the date of purchase as the previous Tuesday. Three pairs of jeans – identical – and a waterproof jacket hung in the wardrobe. They may have been worn once. But Lufkin's watch had a green army-style corded strap, a dark stain by the buckle. A single CSI officer had accompanied them on the raid. The watch strap was bagged and dispatched to the Ark with him.

'What's this about?' said Lufkin, pulling a T-shirt over his head. But it wasn't a question, just part of a ritual.

'Let's save the questions for the station, Mr Lufkin,' said Shaw. Tom Hadden's early morning report from the *Skolt* was encouraging. The mark on her port side was an exact match for the gash on the *Hydra*'s starboard side. The paint samples matched, too. And there were plenty of fingerprints on the trawler. Shaw had little doubt he'd be able to put Andy Lufkin on board the *Skolt* the night James Baker-Sibley died.

Lufkin brushed back the blond curly hair, then covered it with the hood of his duffle coat.

DC Twine was trawling through the drawers in a bedside table; a model of concentration, methodically sliding his gloved hand around each drawer, then slipping it out to check underneath.

'I don't usually have to pay for it,' said Lufkin, hitching up his trousers and putting on a pair of platform shoes.

'Yeah, yeah,' said Valentine. He picked up a cardboard box on a windowsill and from it pulled out the plastic wrapping around a new mobile phone. 'Your phone?'

Lufkin laughed. 'It's not just a phone, Grandad.' He licked his lips. 'TV, radio, video messaging. It's the dog's bollocks.'

Valentine looked around the flat and tapped his foot against the cheap electric fire sitting in the hearth. 'You can tell me some more about it down at the nick. Like how you paid for it.'

Lufkin took a packet of gum from the bathroom and chewed loudly as they completed the search. He gave them the key for a drawer in a cheap desk set under the window, inside of which they found a passport, an HGV licence and a certificate of registration with the Trawler Association.

'Where were you Monday night?' asked Shaw.

'Poker. Regular thing – with the Serbs. They can play all right, but I still won. I always win – but they come back for more. Stupid fuckers.'

'Excellent,' said Shaw. 'Perhaps it's your lucky week. But then again, perhaps it isn't.'

'There's something here, sir,' said Twine. He was flat on his back, searching under the bed. He rolled clear, a metal canister in either hand.

Each was the shape of a pencil box but the wrong size: larger, almost a shoe-box, in brushed aluminium, with several bands of metal added for strength. Shaw had never seen objects like them.

'Shit,' said Valentine, doing up his tie as he backed away.

Twine knelt, put the canisters on the bed, withdrawing his hand quickly. They were all imagining what might be inside.

'Right,' said Shaw, his good eye scanning the room. 'Mr Lufkin – enlighten us.'

Lufkin chewed gum. 'Never seen them before.'

'Get him out,' said Shaw.

Two of the DCs searching the kitchen came in as a uniformed PC took Lufkin down to the squad car. They all stood in a circle as if round a death bed.

'That one's heavy,' said Twine, smearing his hand on his trousers, then pointing.

'OK – we need to open them,' said Shaw.

'Count me out,' said Valentine.

'You were never in,' said Shaw. He picked up the heavier canister quickly and slid the top back a milli-metre, then right back, quickly, tipping it over. A gun lay on the soiled sheet.

'Makarov,' said Twine. 'Russian-made pistol – loads come in, mainly from Serbia.'

'OK,' said Shaw. 'That explains a lot.' He'd wondered how Lufkin and Fibich had found it so easy to take Jillie away from her father when they'd boarded the *Hydra*. Now he knew.

He picked up the other canister, then applied an even pressure to the lid until the contents were revealed, placing it on the bed.

What was inside began to expand, like a time-lapse

film of an orchid. Red, gold, and purple. Leaves uncurling.

Shaw picked one out and held it against the light. A £50 note. He tipped the canister over and prised the bundles out, and they each began to unfurl on the soiled bed; blossoming, like exotic flowers.

# 39

By noon the snow clouds had gone, the sky a depthless blue, the only blemish the full moon and the contrails of two 747s leaving a neat cross at 25,000 feet. Another storm lay beyond the horizon at sea, waiting to slide over the coast like a coffin lid. But for now the world was windless, the tide rising in the creeks and marshes as if percolating up, rather than flooding in; the seawater as sluggish as mercury.

Shaw and Valentine stood on the old wooden wharf at Thornham Harbour, a sheet of water as polished as a mirror between them and Nelson's Island – a tear-shaped bank of gravel in the wide creek on which the Victorians had built a suburban villa, as out of place as Valentine's black slip-ons. Red brick, with a single Gothic tower, embraced by a copse of pine trees cowed into shape by the north winds. A black Jag was parked in the shadow of the house.

'Narr lives here?' asked Valentine, suppressing a series of coughs which shook his narrow shoulders.

'Moved in ninety-one. So there must be some money in shellfish.'

Since their confrontation the night before they'd kept it like this – professional, distant, and cold. It didn't seem to bother either of them.

Shaw walked to the wooden dock's edge and looked

down into the water. The clarity was heart-stopping. He could see the black mud beneath, an eel sliding sideways raising a small whirlpool of silt, a rotting ship's timber arcing out of the river bed like a whalebone.

Shaw's mobile throbbed. It was Twine, passing on the latest from the Ark. Shaw took it all in, cut the link, brought Valentine up to speed. 'The bloodstain on Lufkin's wristwatch band looks like a match for Baker-Sibley. Twine says Lufkin's sweating so fast he's losing weight. And he's started talking. Claims Baker-Sibley went for him on the yacht, they fought, he fell and hit his head.'

'Right,' said Valentine, laughing. 'Has he named Narr?'

'Not yet. Says they heard Baker-Sibley had cash on board. They didn't know about the girl. But he knows that doesn't work. He's talking to the solicitor now. If he's going down he'll take Narr with him.'

Valentine nodded.

'And more progress on Terry Brand. Lufkin's already named names for the suppliers in Belgium – exotic pets for illegal import – snakes, scorpions, you name it. Claims he doesn't know what they were bringing in the night Brand died on the raft. But it was something lethal because they were specifically warned about opening the canisters. Lufkin says Brand had been lobbying for more cash for months – reckons he tried to go freelance, took a look, and paid the price.'

'He's in the bag,' said Valentine.

'Yeah. He is – but he's the monkey. We're here to see the organ grinder.'

Shaw raised a hand, pointing to a spot about fifty yards

offshore, in the middle of the flooded creek. A single flat stone had broken the surface. 'Causeway,' said Shaw. 'Twenty minutes, we can walk across.'

Over the water they heard a sound from the house.

*Eeeeeer Acttttttttt.*

*Eeeeeer Acttttttttt.*

Like a door in the wind; but there was no wind.

Shaw fetched his telescope from the Land Rover and studied the house. In the shadows he could see bay windows, a summer house, and a movement: rhythmic, like a metronome, amongst the pine trees. 'Narr's got an alibi, right? We've checked it, double-checked it?'

'Council meeting at the Guildhall – Police Committee,' said Valentine, reading from his memory. 'Half the senior officers in the county round the table. Didn't finish 'til gone midnight. The snow was falling by then so he stayed – wait for it – at the assistant chief constable's house. Guest room.'

'As alibis go that's pretty tight,' said Shaw. 'Makes a duck's arse look like a string vest.'

Shaw walked along the bank of the creek, giving himself some space to think. Jonathan Tessier's file had been on his desk that morning at 5.45 a.m.

Shaw's conversation with DCI Warren, if he could call it that, had been terse. Shaw didn't mind the confrontation with authority, in fact he'd rather enjoyed it once Warren had lost his temper. He'd learned the subtle art of defiance with his father, and he was good at it. What worried him was not the theoretical threat of reprisal, but the skill with which senior levels of the police force could literally close ranks.

When the Tessier case was thrown out of court they'd moved swiftly to make sure it was soon forgotten. Jack Shaw had been eased into early retirement, while George Valentine had been quietly docked a rank and sent to the backwaters of north Norfolk. The case had been allowed to disappear under dust, despite the fact that Tessier's killer was still at large. Nobody at St James's, least of all DCI Warren, would want to know the truth if it meant reliving the past.

Shaw had put the file on Warren's desk. 'Murder case from 1997 – Jonathan Tessier.'

Warren didn't touch it. 'What's that to me, Peter? That was Jack's case, and he made a hash of it; it's off the books.'

'Right. We've uncovered some fresh information, sir.'

'We?'

'DS Valentine and –'

Warren hit the desk with his fist, a ballpoint spinning off onto the carpet and a picture of his wife and two boys falling flat on their faces. 'For fuck's sake, Peter. Leave it – OK? That's an order. Do you really think the reputation of the West Norfolk needs a fresh dunk in the cesspit? The judge pretty much accused the depart-ment – yes, by implication, the whole fucking department – of planting the evidence. Now that may be run of the mill down in the Met, but it isn't up here. So why do I want to remind anyone of that?'

He'd started off shouting and hadn't been able to lower his voice, so when he finished he was breathing heavily, a line of sweat on his upper lip.

'I'm making a formal request, sir,' said Shaw, unable to

resist the tactic of lowering his voice so that Warren had to strain to hear him. 'On the grounds of a re-examination of the forensic evidence – I've included a summary in the letter. I can put that before you, or go directly to the chief constable's office. I believe this new information warrants a fresh inquiry. It at least warrants a review. That's my recommendation.'

'Is it?' said Warren, standing. They both heard the helicopter at the same moment, and looking out the window they saw it coming in to land beyond the perimeter trees, snow swirling, the chief constable returning from a security briefing in Brussels. The blades began to slow, the circular blur separating out as the pilot edged the machine down, below the treetops and out of sight.

'All right,' said Warren, placing both hands on his blotter. 'I will review the evidence, DI Shaw. Then you will have my decision.'

'Thank you. I'd like it in writing, either way,' said Shaw, turning his back before he got an answer.

Standing now by the cold sea Shaw examined the moment. Yes, he felt he'd discharged a responsibility at last. But what if Warren declined his request? He watched Valentine shivering on the water's edge. Maybe he'd been right about Warren. Would the DCI really have the guts to pick the scab off an old sore? A seagull dive-bombed Valentine, trying to pull an unlit cigarette from his hand. He flailed at it, then lit the cigarette in the cup of his hand with his back to the sea.

Shaw's mobile throbbed again. A picture from Lena. The sudden image made Shaw's hair stand on end. A pencil drawing of a face, the heavy lower lip and the high forehead marking it out as his wife. But the artwork was his daughter's – he recognized the way she always tried to draw each and every eyelash. She was her mother's daughter in so many ways except, perhaps, in this fascination with faces. She'd watched him drawing at home, his party trick, catching the likeness of friends, relatives, the odd customer in the café. But she had her own talent for it too. He couldn't work out why he found it unsettling. Perhaps it marked a coming of age, a signal that one day she might live in the same world that he did.

He snapped the phone shut. The causeway had begun to appear from the water, a curving path towards Nelson's Island, so he led the way. Although the uneven path was still under water in places, it was easy enough to pick their way forward on stepping-stones.

'We could drive,' ventured Valentine, looking hopefully at the Land Rover.

'It's fifty yards, George – not a walk in the Hindu Kush.'

Shaw set out, his boots splashing. The causeway ran in an elliptical path, resting on the tail of the original gravel bar, so that as they walked they began to see the front of the house, built to face the open sea. There was a lawn, a flagpole freshly whitewashed, a wooden veranda.

Valentine saw her first. He was moving slowly, picking a dry path. He stopped to take a breath and looked up: there was a shadow moving in the stand of old pine trees, where a swing had been hung from the great branches. Someone on the swing, moving in time with the metronome.

*Eeeeeer Acttttttt.*
*Eeeeeer Acttttttt.*

Across the lawn their footsteps were silent, but even when they went under the trees, crunching through iced twigs, she didn't take her eyes off the sea. She was bare-headed, close-cropped. Shaw was struck again by the contradictions in her: the swinging carefree playtime of a child, but the fixed gaze, the self-possession of the adult.

'Jillie?' he asked.

She didn't stop, didn't look at them. Shaw caught the swing by the rope and the seat, setting her back to the vertical.

Through a break in the dunes they could see white water, a dog running on a beach a mile wide on the mainland.

'We need to take you home,' said Shaw.

She fished in a quilted jacket decorated with sewn flowers, then held up a mobile.

'I've phoned. Mum's coming. She was waiting for the tide.'

'Mr Narr?' asked Shaw.

She snapped out of it, jerked her head back as if throwing the long hair she'd once had out of her eyes.

'He's home.'

'Where have you been?' asked Shaw. 'Your mother's been worried. We all have.'

'I was going to see Dad,' she laughed. 'But Colin spotted me on the road. And now I know that I'll never see Dad.' She looked at Shaw for the first time and he saw that the incredible violet eyes were dimmed, as if sunk beneath water. Something about the girl's calm voice made his skin creep.

Valentine stayed with her while Shaw went to check the house. When he opened the door he smelt food. Pork? And something else, a fused plug, a shorting wire?

He called for Narr. From the garden he heard the return of the swing's rusted motion.

*Eeeeer Actttttttt.*

*Eeeeer Actttttttt.*

He climbed the stairs, the smell of the cooked meat getting stronger, knowing that must be wrong. A stained-glass window lit the central stairwell. A fisherman on a biblical boat, hauling in silver fish. On the landing a bedroom door stood open. A double bed, both bedside tables holding alarm clocks, books, a mobile phone on one.

He called again. The bathroom door was open too and he could see into a mirror set above the washbasin, clear, cold, unblushed by steam. In the corridor outside a mug stood on the carpet, full of tea, a thin scuddy film on the surface, and a plug in the socket, the lead trailing away into the bathroom. Shaw pushed at the door and walked in. A shower unit stood empty. The stench of meat was tangible, as if he'd bent forward to get the Sunday roast out of the oven. He turned to look down into the bath.

'Jesus.' He took a single step to the toilet bowl and vomited.

Colin Narr lay in the bath, his limbs contorted into an agonizing semaphore. In the water lay a toaster: silver, with a marine blue side decorated with a silver anchor. His flesh was black at the extremities of his limbs, a bluish-purple on the torso, his face a ripe peach, the lips a startling blue. The flesh, cooked, swelled at the joints. Shaw forced himself to look a second time, to check the ears, the shrunken lobes.

The only sound was the swing in the garden.

*Eeeeeer Actttttttt.*

*Eeeeeer Actttttttt.*

# 40

Colin Narr had made many mistakes in the last week of his life, but telling Jillie Baker-Sibley that her father had died that night on Styleman's Middle was his last. In the warmth of the BMW she'd listened to him recount what had happened. How he and her mother had only wanted to protect her, to bring her home. But that her father had been stupid, to tell the men who came to get her that he had cash on board. So little money to die for: £50,000. He said she had to understand, that lies were necessary. Neither he nor her mother had planned that James should die. It had been Lufkin and Fibich's fault. Narr said he'd been horrified when Lufkin told him what had happened; and he'd kept it from her mother. But it was too late – James was dead. They had to do what was right for Jillie and Sarah. Jillie had smiled then, because it was really about what was right for *him*.

How had he found her? Mother's intuition. James had a cottage near East Midlands airport, a village close to the motorway. Sarah had never been given a key, even after they were married. But if they'd made a plan – daughter and father – then that would be it. To meet there. Jillie had some money of her own, a bank card. But they knew she'd keep clear of the trains and coaches. And Sarah knew she loved hitch-hiking, because she'd been forbidden to do it. She'd gone into Lynn once with

Clara during the summer holidays, hitching a ride. They'd been proud of it when they got home. Sarah had screamed at her, telling her she was a child.

And they were right. When those men had come aboard the *Hydra* to take her away they'd let her have a minute alone with her father. He hadn't argued with them because the little man had a gun. He kept passing it from hand to hand, the sweat glistening on the cold metal. But he'd asked for some time alone. That's when he'd given her the key, told her to get to the cottage when she could. He'd be there. Then the foreign one had rowed her ashore. She'd waited for her moment to leave home and then stuck to the plan. And she would have seen it through, up until the moment she'd climbed into Narr's black Jag. He'd told her that her father was dead. And that had changed the world. She'd lost a brother, and now she'd lost her father. It was about time someone paid the price.

They sat in silence during the rest of the ride back to Narr's house. Jillie's hands clenched and unclenched, imagining revenge. All the anger she'd harboured during her young life had finally found a target. Someone upon whom she could focus her hate.

The tide was out so they'd driven over. She'd said she wasn't in a hurry to get home, her mother would be in the shop, so he could eat, have a bath – he'd been out all night; she'd text her mum. They'd had eggs on toast. He'd broken the eggs scraping them out of the pan, but the bread had popped up nicely browned from the toaster with a silver anchor on the side.

Sarah Baker-Sibley was on her way. So he'd filled the bath and she'd made tea. He said to leave it outside the bathroom door. She'd knocked once to say it was there, waited ten seconds, then opened the door quickly, the toaster in her hands, plugged into an extension lead she'd found in the kitchen.

Had she said anything? Shaw had asked.

She'd thought about that, coolly reconstructing the moment of murder.

'No. Nothing.' She'd smiled then, running her hand through her short hair. 'I know what I thought. I thought that I had a brother once and that I'd forgiven Dad for killing *him*. But I couldn't forgive anyone any more, not for anything. Either of them. You can't spend your whole life forgiving people.' She'd crossed her hands on her lap. 'That's taking advantage.'

There was silence round the table in the Red House. The jukebox had run dry while Shaw was briefing them. DC Twine tilted his head back and finished his bottle of Chimay.

'Will she talk?' asked Mark Birley, one of his ham-sized hands wrapped round a pint.

'Sarah Baker-Sibley? She's talking already,' said Shaw. 'She rang Narr from Gallow Marsh the night of the storm. She didn't know what they'd do, of course. Her crime was not telling us what *she'd* done. Jillie's given us a positive ID on Lufkin – so it's all over for him. We can put him on the boat, the forensics are watertight, and the motive comes in fifty-pound notes. I'm recommending a murder charge tomorrow when I see Warren.'

'What happens to Jillie?' asked Twine.

'Jillie? Straight into care. Psychiatric review first, then who knows? She's not a full ticket – question is, is she still a dangerous ticket? Narr's murder wasn't some random act of violence. It was calculated, planned, executed. And she's thirteen – old enough to be charged.'

'And her mother?'

'Sedation. Then we'll see. If Jillie ever gets out she'll need her mother. She'll have to face charges, but I can't see any court sending her down.'

They all drank in silence.

'So – we started with three dead men. Two down – one to go. Lufkin killed James Baker-Sibley. Terry Brand died of curiosity while smuggling for Narr. But Harvey Ellis is still on the books. His killer is our priority. But that's for tomorrow.' Shaw finished a pint of Guinness and handed Valentine the empty glass.

They'd set up a darts tournament and were taking it in turns to ring Fiona Campbell in hospital, sending pictures by mobile. She'd had another blood transfusion, her condition was stable, but the knife wound across her neck would take a month to heal, a necklace for ever.

Pint glasses covered the pub's plywood tables. Birley put all his fruit-machine winnings in the jukebox to stop Jacky Lau playing any more Kaiser Chiefs. Twine was trying to explain the basic science behind lighting techniques to locate blood traces, using a set of beer mats. Shaw sent Lena a picture too, a pint of Guinness on the table, a shamrock in the top. A signal: he'd be late. He hoped she'd understand.

He waited until Valentine had been knocked out of the darts tournament before passing him the pub's copy of the Yellow Pages. He smudged the print on an advert with his finger.

## Askit's Agricultural Engineers
### *Established 1926*

He leant in close, taking an inch off the top of the Guinness. 'The file's with Warren. You've got a right to know what's in it. Everything that's in it.'

Valentine looked at his drink.

'What would you say if I told you I think Jonathan Tessier may have spent the last few hours of his life at Askit's factory?'

'Why not just tell me?' said Valentine, his jaw set.

Shaw checked that nobody else was within earshot. 'Jonathan's football kit was covered in a fine spray of a specialist paint. Askit's is the only local business to take that paint in 1997. Askit's sprayed on the premises. But the kit's mobile – I rang them up and talked to the foreman. You can load up a few gallons and get the air gun and gas cylinders into a van. So – maybe on the premises, probably on the premises, but maybe not.'

'I need a fag,' said Valentine.

They stood and went down a corridor that smelt of urine and out into a small courtyard. The landlord had bought a gas heater and a small gazebo. Dog-ends lay in the snow around it and through a plastic loud speaker the jukebox music played. The gas popped, flared, and popped again. Shaw thought it sounded like they were in the basket of a hot-air balloon, sailing unseen over the city of the sober.

The snow was falling softly but turned in a whirlwind in the yard, making Valentine dizzy. He gripped the back of a chair, sucking in the nicotine. If Shaw knew about the chemical composition of the paint on Tessier's clothes, thought Valentine, then he must have got CSI to check out the original forensics. He felt cheated, out-classed. He'd spent a decade worrying away at the case without making any progress. Shaw had notched up a break-through in a few days. And Valentine sensed there was more to come.

'But that isn't all you've found out, is it?' said Valentine.

Shaw closed his eyes. 'No.' He edged closer to the gas heater, turning one of the limpet shells in his pocket. 'I checked Askit's out through the files. Then I cross-checked the company with all criminal records online for West Norfolk from 1995. And I got something – a match. A witness at a juvenile court case in the summer of ninety-six. Timber Woods dug me out the file.'

Valentine didn't say anything.

'There was a child, *another* child,' said Shaw. 'Poynter. Gideon Poynter – they called him Giddy. He was twelve, lived on the Westmead. The family used to have money, before the father disappeared, so the Westmead must have been a bit of a shock. Mum had trouble because they were new on the estate and by local standards a bit on the posh side: so, standard welcome party – fire on her doorstep, dog shit through the letterbox, a late-night thud on the front door. She set up a Neighbourhood Watch scheme. She planned a public meeting and sent Giddy out with posters and fliers.'

'On the Westmead?'

'Quite. Someone suggested she might like to forget the idea. She declined. So they thought they'd teach her a lesson, by teaching Giddy one.'

'What'd they do?' asked Valentine, licking his bottom lip.

'They took him. A Sunday night, after dark. He was out playing on the landing so they bundled him down the stairwell. Four young thugs put him in one of the bins under the flats, one of the metal ones, and tied a bit of rope round the handle so he couldn't force it open from the inside.'

Shaw leant back, trying to remember that this had really happened, that it wasn't some sick plot from a TV thriller.

'But he got out?' said Valentine. 'He must have got out.' When they'd picked up Bobby Mosse that night in July 1997 they'd checked back through the files; reviewed every serious crime on the estate for the last eighteen months. Standard murder inquiry procedure. Valentine didn't remember anything about Giddy Poynter.

'Yeah, he got out. Eventually. Before they put him in the bin they showed him what was inside it.' Shaw looked at the bottom of his empty pint glass. 'Rats. Half a dozen. That's what counted as a joke on the Westmead.'

'How long was he in there?' said Valentine. The drink had wiped some of the anger and tension out of the line of his mouth, the narrowed eyes.

'The council emptied the bins at seven the next morning. The kid was traumatized, couldn't speak. He needed help, probably still does. But it was just another nasty story from a nasty place. The juvenile court dealt with it.'

'So how'd they catch them?'

'The kids wore gloves but one of them had a hole in the finger. There was enough to get a match – that was . . .' He checked his notebook. 'Kid by the name of Cosyns. He was on file, even then. Another two stepped up for it when he was charged. Proud of it in fact. Bunch of little heroes.'

'But just the three?'

'Yeah. They never got the fourth.' They both thought about that for a second, thinking the same thing, that it could have been Bobby Mosse. 'The three got suspended sentences and community service. Nothing custodial. Know why?'

Valentine jiggled his empty pint.

'Employer took the stand, said they'd all got decent jobs, prospects, and if they got sent down he'd have to let them go.'

'Askit's,' said Valentine.

'Askit's. A year later we've got forensic evidence linking Askit's to Jonathan Tessier's murder. And Tessier's body's found in the underground car park, a hundred yards from the waste bins where Giddy Poynter spent the worst night of his life.' It was the kind of coincidence, thought Shaw, that didn't happen in the real world.

'Is there a link to Bobby Mosse?' asked Valentine.

'Other than the fact Mosse lived on the Westmead – none.' He watched as Valentine's hooded eyes closed. He knew what his DS was thinking; that Warren would use that weak point in the case to ignore their plea to reopen the file.

They heard the last bell ring and went back to the party. Half an hour later they were walking through deserted backstreets towards the car park at St James's. Opposite the police station was a park, stone griffins on each gatepost, the Gothic ironwork hung with icicles. Inside a necklace of white lamps led through the darkness across unblemished snow. On a bench a tramp slept, the snow a blanket.

Shaw checked his mobile. He had one message – Justina Kazimierz. The US Wildlife laboratory in Ashland, Oregon had identified the venom she'd extracted from Terry Brand's arm. A spider: the Indian white jacket. Very rare, very nasty. On the black market they'd fetch $3,000 each.

'Justina,' he said to Valentine. 'She says our man on Ingol Beach was bitten by a spider. Rare, valuable, fatal bite.'

'Terrific,' said Valentine. British household spiders made him jump. Anything bigger and he'd be running before he knew he was scared.

Shaw looked through the park gates. 'I used to meet Dad here sometimes in the summer holidays,' he said. 'A half-hour lunch hour. I'd walk in from the North End, wait for him down by the pond. I had a sailboat. It was the one place he'd go without the radio – here and the beach. I'd bring a football, or a Frisbee, like we were by the sea. He'd sit and describe the view from Gun Hill, as if he was there. He'd bring chips. A can of beer. I'd play in the shadows, fight dragons under the trees.' He laughed. 'I miss him.'

Valentine looked the other way, embarrassed by the intimacy.

Shaw took a deep breath. 'George. I told you how this is going to be.' The snow was driving in again from the docks, so they turned their backs and looked through the ironwork gates. 'It's Warren's call. He's got everything I know, everything you know. We're off the case.'

'You too?' asked Valentine, a smile disfiguring his face.

'Me too.' Shaw tasted a snowflake on his lip, caught the acid hint of carbon dioxide. 'I'm the son of the investigating DCI. The officer explicitly censured by the judge in the original trial. Any juror would accept that I had an interest in clearing Jack Shaw's name.'

'And do you?'

Shaw clenched his fists, stamped his feet, spooking a raven which rattled into one of the snow-laden trees. He felt trapped, and that made him angry. And when he was angry he needed exercise, needed to dissipate the energy. But he couldn't run.

'I have an interest in finding out who killed Jonathan Tessier.'

'But you're not sure that's the same thing, are you?'

'No. That's right,' he said, aware that he'd been cornered into the implied accusation. Because if he didn't trust Jack Shaw, then he didn't trust George Valentine either.

'Thanks for the vote of confidence,' said Valentine, flapping the raincoat like a pair of furled wings. 'I'm done for,' he said, suddenly deflated. 'I'm going home.'

But he didn't mean it.

## 41

Valentine walked down through the town to Vancouver's statue. The day had left him confused and exhausted. They'd cracked open the heart of the case – he was sure of that. But his final confrontation with Shaw had sucked the adrenaline out of him. The thought that his future, what was left of it, was in the hands of DCS Max Warren made him feel impotent, discarded.

He wandered back towards Greenland Street, forcing himself not to steal a glance ahead to check if the light shone from the house on the corner. It did. And there, low down in the curved plate glass of the double doors of the old shop, the white piece of crisp cartridge paper.

*Yat ye hoi p'i*

'The game is open, night and day,' said Valentine, translating.

He knocked twice, waited, knocked again.

A man opened the door, the man they called the sentinel. Beyond the doors the sudden heat enveloped them both. The sentinel stood, smiling, waiting for him to choose. Which was polite of him, because although upstairs, in the loft, they played white pigeon, Valentine always climbed down to the basement for fan-tan.

In the hallway a child in pyjamas played with a radio-controlled car. A Christmas present, Valentine guessed, the car racing through an open door into a room where he knew the sentinel's woman slept. The sentinel said something brutal and short but the child ignored him. The sound of a parent trying to get a child to go to bed was the same in any language. As Valentine descended the stairs he could still hear the whirr of the little electronic motor as the car ran the length of the carpet.

He took one of the tall stools beside the fan-tan table. The cashier sat to one side, the dealer stood. There were eight players, each on stools. There was no alcohol – Valentine liked it that way, he liked his vices singly, and this way he knew that he'd really enjoy the thrill of luck.

An hour later he'd made £300. The dealer smiled at him. 'The numbers like you,' he said.

'Makes a change,' said Valentine, using the answer he always had ready.

He stood, stretching, poured himself some water and went to the far end of the room to sit. He always stopped at £300. It was his interim limit, the point when he forced himself to take stock. Fan-tan was a game of pure chance. George Valentine's grip on the laws of probability was crisp. He knew that a winning streak was no less likely to lead to another winning streak than a losing streak. But £300 up was always a good time to think about what it meant: six crisp £50 notes. After all, he *could* spend the money.

The far end of the room was a rest station. A set of

wooden chairs stood in a circle, some pretzels, nuts and crisps in bowls on a low table. A small TV showed a Chinese cable station with the volume so low it sounded like a trapped bluebottle. Convention decreed that all conversation here must be in English when a *gweilo* was present, so the three Chinese already there switched from Mandarin immediately.

The snow was keeping people in, they agreed. Even the police. They all laughed because DS Valentine had never hidden his trade; indeed his relationship with illegal gambling was fundamentally symbiotic. When the Serious Crime Squad had tried to clear up the gambling dens of South Lynn the house in Greenland Street had been mysteriously empty, the cellar crammed with broken furniture.

Valentine thrust a hand in his pocket to get his handkerchief but found, instead, a scrap of paper. He took it out, unfolded it: the six savage lines on the side of John Holt's car door. He'd recognized immediately that it wasn't just a scrawl, a mindless graffito. But now, suddenly, he was sure he knew what it was. He just didn't know what it meant.

'Anyone know what this says?' he said, flattening it out on the table.

They all looked at each other, a necklace of glances which didn't include him.

'Joe's sign,' said the man they called Paddy. He was compact, the racial characteristics of his face mixed with something subtle: Anglo-Saxon perhaps, or Celt. 'It's his name. Simple as that.'

'And who's Joe?' asked Valentine.

'You might visit him to borrow money,' said Paddy. 'But it would be a mistake.'

'A loan shark?'

'With sharp teeth,' said Paddy, running a finger along his own.

Shaw waded out onto the beach at Old Hunstanton, bare feet running over the snow on the sand above the high-tide mark, water falling off the winter wetsuit. Lena stood on the sands cradling a mug. She laughed at him, the way he lifted his feet quickly off the cold pebbles which lay in front of the café.

They walked back to the cottage and she lay on the rug in front of the wood-burning stove while he got out of the suit and found a bathrobe. She held a portable shaving mirror up while he looked at his injured eye. The scar was fading, the sutured eyelids still pressed together in the bruised socket. Lena bathed the eye in water from a bottle, then took a fresh dressing from the batch Shaw had been given at the clinic.

'It's healing,' she said. 'Francesca will be upset. She thinks you look like a pirate.'

Lena left him in the dark, watching the incoming waves, luminous on a moonless night. Swimming, he'd cleared his head, then filled it again. On his back, his arms rising and falling, he'd seen the Pole Star through a thin disc of cirrus. He'd put the Tessier case out of his mind and instead tried to piece together the first twenty-four hours of the Ellis inquiry. The answer was in the detail, he'd told himself, always in the detail.

He saw in his memory Holt again, in his hospital bed.

It had been a bad night. High blood pressure had broken an artery in his nose, and he'd lost a lot of blood. They'd had to fight to clear his airways the doctor had said, cutting away his dentures which had become lodged in his throat.

He thought of the two halves of the shattered dental work, the apple on the dashboard of Ellis's truck, and the image made him smile at last.

As he padded down the corridor and into their bedroom, Lena turned in the shadows, an arm thrown across the sheet, welcoming, and his heart skipped a beat.

At the fan-tan table Valentine had lost heavily, handing in his playing card at just after one o'clock when he'd got down to £50. He stood in the hall waiting for his coat. He could hear the boy crying somewhere and the reason was plain: the electric car lay on its side, the battery compartment open, the four AAs, presumably spent, spilt out.

The sentinel returned with his coat.

'Costs a fortune,' said Valentine. 'Keeping a car on the road these days.'

'Least he sleep now,' said the man, nodding, showing too many teeth. 'Sleeps like the dead.'

The moment he stood on the step, and the door closed behind him, the thought hit him and Valentine knew he was right. A child's toy, bereft of batteries. He saw the inside of Harvey Ellis's pick-up truck, smelt the spilt blood, listened again to the unnatural silence which always seems to shroud the dead.

The night air, the thrill of understanding, made his

skin hum, and he clapped his hands like a child. He turned left up Greenland Street and set out for St James's, knowing that he wouldn't sleep unless he checked now. The key to the CSI box would be with the desk sergeant. He'd need to drum up a witness from the canteen. He thought about running, but told himself to grow up.

# 42

*Saturday, 14 February*

George Valentine lay in bed listening to the gentle throb of a three-litre engine. It was parked below his bedroom window. The street light still showed between the curtains, and the alarm clock said seven. He wanted to sleep, to stave off the yearning for nicotine, the pillowcase still holding the dim memory of his last illicit Silk Cut.

'Well, fuck this,' he said, getting up, pulling back the curtain and running up the sash before he'd looked out. The cold air hit him like a bucket of iced water. DI Peter Shaw was standing by the Land Rover, the engine running, a police radio to his ear.

'I said early start,' he said, looking up. 'I meant very early start – sorry.' A gust of sea breeze blew off the freezing river and rippled through Valentine's pyjamas. He slammed the window shut.

As soon as Valentine opened the door Shaw knew that this was part of the DS's life he'd not imagined. The hallway was uncarpeted, but spotless, a picture on a hook of Valentine as a teenager, sitting on a beach with a woman with long legs and a smile hidden in the shadow from a stylish sun hat. Valentine at twenty, perhaps still a teenager even, a mop of hair over the narrow face, the cheekbones rakish rather than cadaverous. Did Shaw remember his

303

wife? Perhaps, somewhere back in a childhood memory, his father's friends drinking in the back garden.

The kitchen was 1950s basic. A wooden draining board, ugly taps and a stone basin. Valentine made tea, changed, then smoked while the pot brewed. He poured the liquid into two mugs, added milk from a fridge which was otherwise empty.

He hadn't said a word, and Shaw sensed he was enjoying the silence.

'No cards then?' said Shaw.

'What?'

'There's nothing on the mat. It's Valentine's Day.'

Valentine ignored him, taking a scrap of paper from his pocket and placed it on the table.

Shaw leant back, balancing the stool on two legs.

'This is the mark left on Holt's car.' Valentine coughed, stubbed out the cigarette, played with the packet. 'Chinese name character for Joe. I asked some questions. He's a loan shark with a reputation for using muscle to collect. I think we can take it that daubing one of these . . .' he stabbed the Chinese character with his finger, 'on someone's car door is a final demand. A very final demand.' He knocked a fresh cigarette on the table top. 'Holt.'

'It's a motive?' asked Shaw.

'Yeah. Think about it.'

Shaw did. Holt needed the money – he was desperate; living in a slum down by the docks, supporting a daughter who couldn't work, a granddaughter. So James Baker-Sibley recruits him. Ellis too.

'There's more,' said Shaw. 'I've got Twine out at Holt's dentist. Night he was taken in the Queen Vic he lost his dentures – they had to be cut out of his windpipe. So when Tom's boys went round they must have taken a cast from an old pair.'

'The apple?' asked Valentine.

'Maybe.'

'I should have thought of that,' said Valentine, annoyed with himself.

'We both should have,' said Shaw.

Valentine stood and went to the raincoat hung on the pantry door. He took out a plastic evidence bag: inside was the toy eagle which had hung from the roof of Harvey Ellis's truck.

Shaw went to touch it, then stopped.

Valentine held up his hands. 'It's all booked out. No problems – it's been dusted, everything.'

He unpopped the seal and retrieved the toy. He found a tag on the underside with his index finger and a plastic door opened to reveal a slot for a single AAA battery. Against the light he held the plastic evidence bag. Inside was a battery.

'Hadden's team didn't check it. I did. It's flat.'

Valentine produced a TV remote control from the kitchen drawer and knocked out a battery, slotting it into the toy. Then he flipped a switch on the breastplate. The wings flapped, up and down, a jagged movement. Standing, he turned on the kitchen light and held the toy up to the bulb. Shadows danced around them – the kind of shadows Shaw had taken for movement that night on Siberia Belt when he'd first spotted the pick-up truck.

They sat in silence for a moment, Shaw laying both hands out flat on the table, palms down.

'I checked out the radio/CD, the gear in the pick-up,' said Valentine. 'It's a multi-CD system, but once the CDs have finished it switches to the radio. Ellis didn't switch the music off, it switched itself off. Then the radio ran down. Holt's lying. Ellis was dead when Holt went forward to speak to him.'

'Except that dead men don't drive pick-up trucks,' said Shaw.

'Then the killer did. Footprints, or no footprints.'

# 43

'We should do it now,' said Valentine, standing in the street. The road was flagged with stones, snow lying in the cracks between. 'Let's get him into St James's. It all fits. Holt takes his money as the backstop but Ellis gets cold feet. Holt kills Ellis. Forget how. Nothing else works,' he added, spitting into the snow. 'The stress gets him, his ticker packs up, then we turn up and fly him out of the crime scene.'

'We need the dental records, something solid to put him inside the cab. Tom said mid-morning. We can wait,' said Shaw, aware there was a combative edge to Valentine's voice.

The DS looked at his watch. 'It's wasting time,' he said.

'No, it's not,' said Shaw, angry now. 'How'd he kill Ellis on Siberia Belt *before* arriving at the scene himself? Houdini would be proud of that one. How did he strike the lethal blows? Where's the blood on him? Does the hitch-hiker exist? Is she an accomplice? How'd she get out of the truck without leaving prints? How many more questions do you need unanswered?'

Shaw felt a pulse in his pocket from his RNLI pager. Three 7s: the code for the hovercraft.

'It's a shout,' he said, pleased to be offered a route of escape. 'OK. I'll text when we're back on shore. Meantime, press Tom – nicely. We need the match on the teeth, then we'll hit Holt. And tell him to pull us a unit, we'll need to cover Holt's house down in town, on Devil's Alley, and the daughter's. We'll go in early afternoon – so find out where he is now. Don't spook him. This isn't over.'

The tyres on the Land Rover screeched as he pulled away. Valentine watched, humming the theme tune from *Batman*.

Shaw hit the inner ring road at a steady 80 mph. The coast road had been salted and the sudden sunshine had dried it out. He was the last one to the lifeboat house but made the crew as the only pilot, eye injury or no eye injury. He slipped forward into the cabin and checked the systems, redirecting the airflow from the fans down into the flotation skirt, lifting the *Flyer* over the concrete footings. Shaw cleared his head: tried to forget about John Holt, Harvey Ellis – and George Valentine.

An outbound trawler from Lynn, the *Scullion*, had spotted figures on Peter Black Sand, the wrong side of Snettisham Scalp, a mile offshore from Ingol Beach. The skipper had reported one adult, two children, possibly another being held or carried. It was a popular spot for digging worms, but a death trap in a rip tide because the long spit of sand held a treacherous secret – its lowest point was where it met the land, the highest point the furthest extent out into the Wash. Even in winter it could entice the unwary too far from the safety of the dunes. The trawler had got within 300 yards before the danger of grounding had made her swing back out to sea.

They had a visual contact within nine minutes.

'Jesus,' said the commander, a man named Driscol,

ex-navy with a hatred of the sea which seemed to draw him back to it. 'There – straight ahead. Looks like they're walking on water.'

The tide was still three hours off the full but had completely covered Peter Black Sand. The stranded family had been forced away from the coast, back out to the higher ground, but now even that was gone. They stood in the freezing water, footless, an adult holding a child, two other children clutching hands, beside them a large bucket, a deflated sack. The sea around them turned in whirlpools, seagulls picking fish in the shallows.

Shaw hit 60 knots, the noise of the fans deafening despite the ear protectors in the helmets. At 100 yards he throttled back, the note changing, the nose of the *Flyer* dipping, the craft slewing sideways slightly as the speed dropped and she began to pick up friction from the water surface. The gulls, hoping for a stream of fish guts, began to flock behind them. A sea wind was picking up and miniature waves clipped the forward skirt, spray arching over the crew.

Drifting, Shaw got her to within twenty feet of the man, then cut the down current, so that *Flyer* floated.

The man, a young father, perhaps thirty, was silent, tears running down his face, which was white with fear. He clutched a child in a papoose to his chest, his lips in its hair. A boy and girl, Shaw guessed five and ten, still held hands, the girl's jaw juddering with the cold, the boy glassy-eyed. The navigator jumped clear and put down a sand anchor; the crewman was already wading clear, calling: 'It's OK – paddle, just paddle.'

They clambered aboard but as the father swung his leg

over the apron he fainted, falling backwards instinctively to protect the baby.

The crew got him over the skirt and into the rear cabin, the papoose unclipped. Driscol radioed the station, standing down the inflatable inshore boat, and Shaw lifted the *Flyer* clear of the water, turning in a wide arc to pass the metal buoy which marked the edge of Black Peter Sands.

Shaw made himself concentrate on the view ahead. He dropped her speed, using sonar and radar as back-up. Looking shorewards he saw a metal buoy in the foreground, the beach beyond, marked to the north by Gun Hill, to the south by the oyster beds off Gallow Marsh Farm. The farm itself was almost lost in a stand of trees, but he could just see the dilapidated white wooden dovecote which had been lit like a beacon that night on Siberia Belt. Lining up the buoy and the dovecote Shaw saw that they marked a channel, a strip of open clear water between the muddled sandbanks, a passage to within a few hundred yards of Ingol Beach. He thought about the farmyard that night, the blizzard clearing to reveal the dovecote, lit a startling acid-white.

He pushed the microphone of the intercom away from his lips. 'Christ,' he said. 'It's a lighthouse.'

# 44

Valentine's Mazda was parked in a lay-by off the muddy track which led towards Blickling Cottages; the home of John Holt's daughter and granddaughter. Holt was clearly visiting, his Corsa – released from the police compound – was parked on the concrete forecourt. Shaw put the Land Rover behind the Mazda and jumped out, his hair still wet from the sea spray.

Bending his knees he dropped down to talk through the open driver's window.

'Did you get his dental records?' asked Shaw.

'Hadden says there's no match with Holt. Nothing like.'

'Shit!' Shaw wiped salt off his forehead with the back of his hand. He'd been sure, so sure. The cloudless sky was beginning to darken to the east, dusk slinking along the coast like a black cat.

So if they weren't John Holt's teeth marks, whose were they? The hitch-hiker's? Logic told them Holt was lying about finding Ellis alive at the wheel that night. But they had no evidence he was a killer. They weren't his tooth marks on the apple. It wasn't his footprint in the blood. Hadden had checked the boots and shoes of everyone in the convoy on Siberia Belt, and there'd been no match.

But they did know Holt had been borrowing money

from a notorious loan shark. He'd lied about Ellis being alive when he'd checked the pick-up. Shaw was convinced Holt was part of the plan to abduct Jillie Baker-Sibley.

'We're sure Holt's here?' asked Shaw, standing.

Valentine swished a single snowflake off the windscreen. The cottages lay in a small copse of trees amongst vast rutted fields. A narrow lane followed the gradient of a shallow valley. To one side lay a sports field, the snow cleared from the lines of a football pitch. By the road and a gravel car park stood a pavilion: whitewashed wood with two onion-domed turrets on either end of a wide stoop, the roof supported by carved pillars and free of snow. An exotic fragment of Russian romance in a snowy Fen field. The windows were half-shuttered and Shaw thought he glimpsed a light within, but it was gone as soon as he saw it out of the corner of his eye. A reflection perhaps of the low winter sun.

Just beyond the pavilion a farm track led over the hill. An unmarked Ford was obscured by snow-laden bushes. 'Twine got traffic to volunteer,' said Valentine. 'They've had Holt under surveillance since he left the hospital.'

'OK, let's do it,' said Shaw, walking round the front of the Mazda and pulling open the passenger-side door. 'We've still got more than enough to rattle his cage.'

John Holt was at the side of the house standing on a plank ten feet off the ground supported by two sets of stepladders. He wore a pair of new blue overalls, and heavy-duty boots. Two trees stood on either side of the door. Lopped branches from a magnolia tree lay on the path beneath. The sycamore had been pruned back already, pollarded so that the branches stuck out like the arms on a Greek statue.

Shaw stamped his feet in the snow to get his circulation back. Holt didn't look round and it occurred to Shaw for the first time that he might be deaf, but when he spoke he could see that his arrival was not a surprise.

'Is that wise, Mr Holt? Shouldn't you be resting?'

In a hospital bed John Holt had appeared diminished, weak, held down it seemed by the weight of the blankets. He didn't look a lot more robust now, perched on his makeshift scaffolding. The eyes still blinked warily from behind the thick lenses.

'I'm fine, thank you, Detective Inspector,' he said, peering down. Shaw sensed that discharging himself from hospital, completing the errand that was interrupted by Monday night's diversion onto Siberia Belt, was part of a ritual demonstration that old age had yet to defeat John Holt. 'Your people brought my gardening stuff back with the car, so I thought I'd better finish the job.' He pulled back a branch and lopped it neatly with a pair of secateurs. 'Sasha's not very happy, mind you. We've had tears.' Then he swung himself out onto the top rung of one of the ladders and climbed down, although Valentine noticed that he didn't drop a step before getting a double grip with his hands.

Back on earth he looked out over the garden. 'Pity about the snow, I had it all neat and tidy.' Shaw could see a precise row of roses breaking through a drift, the edge of a hedge trimmed to a topiary finish. A large vegetable garden stretched beyond the flowers, leeks in military rows breaking through the snow cover.

'Keen on the garden then?' said Valentine, as Holt packed up his tools.

'I'm a farmer's son. It's in the blood.'

'That's quite something,' said Shaw, looking out over the sports field to the pavilion.

'Local bigwigs gave the field to the village back in the 1880s – pavilion came with it. One of them made a fortune as a merchant in Moscow. It's listed, but the local kids don't seem to mind. Vandalize it pretty much once a month. I keep an eye on the place – unpaid night watchman. They've got one of those security firms checking it out – bloody useless.'

He took off his gloves and rubbed his hands. 'We better go in, warm up,' he said. The front door stood open, a fresh coat of red paint still wet. Valentine thought it was an odd time to paint a door.

Inside seven-year-old Sasha played on the rug, crayons scattered over a series of pieces of white paper covered in delicate lines of colour. A glue pot and paints stood beside a neat pile of sycamore seeds – the tiny winged 'helicopters' that children love. A book lay open on the floor as well, and Shaw recognized the cover – one his daughter had struggled with over Christmas. The little girl stood, holding the book by the corner, so that it hung down. A black cat lay at her feet, dozing.

'Bright kid, then?' said Shaw, nodding at a woman he took for her mother.

She sat in one of the armchairs and hadn't got up. She seemed startled that anyone had spoken to her. 'Yes. I don't know how that happened,' she laughed, trying to move some lank hair off her forehead. She fidgeted with her feet, crossing the swollen ankles. Shaw estimated her weight at fifteen stone, maybe more. She wore slippers, one of them crushed flat and threadbare, as though the one foot took all of her weight when she walked. She was only, Shaw reckoned, in her mid-twenties, but the swollen tyre of fat around her neck made her look older. Her face was an oddity, belonging to someone almost petite, and young still, the well-balanced features crowding together, the whole dominated by the narrowness of the nose between the vivid blue eyes.

The bungalow was furnished in second-hand furniture, cheap but sturdy. There was a flat-screen TV, but it appeared to be the only luxury.

'Yes, this is my Sasha,' said Holt, not introducing his daughter.

'This is Kit,' said Sasha, holding the cat like a baby.

Shaw smiled, working his way along the family snap-shots on the sideboard. There were more frames on the mantelpiece and a side table. He tried to memorize each picture, overlaying them one on another, establishing the family face. And then he found the one he was looking for, the picture of the gawky teenage Michelle, a slip of a girl, the limbs all elbows and knees, but the face a haunting echo of her father's. And another child, cuddling a black kitten. Shaw held the frame, tapping the glass, trying to age the child's face into an adult's. Wondering why she looked familiar.

'It's Michelle, isn't it – Michelle Holt?' he said, replacing the picture and offering his hand. He bounced slightly on his toes, trying to imagine what it was like to be dragged down by your own body, pinned by gravity to a joyless armchair.

Holt's wife brought him tea in a china cup and saucer, setting it on a side table which also carried a crossword puzzle book and a remote control for the flat-screen TV.

'It's not a coincidence, is it?' asked Shaw. 'Blickling Cottages. It's your middle name – Blickling.'

Valentine smiled. He knew the young DI hated coincidence, while for him it was the sister of luck.

Holt's eyes widened behind the thick lenses of the black-rimmed spectacles. 'Yes, that's right, Inspector. I built the cottages back in 1963. We lived here when we were married. As I said, I'm a farmer's son, but not a farmer's eldest son. So I had to find my own way in the world.'

He paused and Valentine wondered if he wanted a round of applause.

'We went bust two years ago – just in time for a leisurely retirement.' He smiled, but didn't make a good job of it.

Valentine got the obvious question in first. 'Who lives next door, then?'

'We sold that. It's rented. Tenants come and go.'

'And we've remortgaged this,' said Michelle, biting her lip.

'I'm sure Inspector Shaw doesn't want to know our business, Micky.'

Shaw went to the bay window and looked out into the garden of the house next door. Michelle sipped tea from a spoon she kept sinking into a large mug. 'Dad's very good to us . . .' she said. Shaw thought the voice was oddly juvenile compared to her bulk. The old man raised a hand but she went on.

'We don't pay rent. I can't work. I'm ill.'

Holt looked away, ashamed of her. Outside snow fell on the sports field. 'Should be a match this afternoon,' said Holt. 'But there's too much snow. I never miss when they play,' he said, sipping the tea.

Valentine interlaced his fingers and cracked the joints. Michelle ate cake, methodically, without any apparent enjoyment. The sound of her jaws working filled the little overheated room.

Shaw's temper snapped silently. 'I'd like to talk to you alone, Mr Holt – in private.'

Holt peered at him through the thick glasses. 'Anything you want to say to me you can say now.'

'Very well, Mr Holt. When you went forward to the pick-up truck that night on Siberia Belt, Harvey Ellis was already dead, wasn't he?'

Had Holt expected the question? He placed the empty side-plate carefully on a table, and his cup and saucer were steady in his hand.

'I don't understand.' He looked at his wife for support.

'John wouldn't lie to you,' she said.

Michelle shuffled towards the edge of the armchair and leant down to help her daughter glue helicopters to a piece of paper.

Shaw stood. 'Ellis was killed before the convoy of cars drew up on Siberia Belt – the spot where he died was about fifty yards back from where we found his body. He couldn't have been alive when you walked forward to the van. That's not possible.'

Holt licked a finger. 'I'm sorry. But he was. He was as alive as you are now, Inspector. That's the truth. If it doesn't fit the evidence I suggest you have another look at the evidence. And you had witnesses, didn't you? People who saw him move after we got stuck?' He sipped his tea, knowing now that something was wrong.

'The hitch-hiker – the young girl?' asked Valentine, trying to lead him on.

'I made her up too, did I?' said Holt, the voice just catching an edge at last. 'My, I've been busy.'

Shaw picked up the teenage picture of Michelle Holt. 'Hardly busy,' he said. 'This is the woman you described to me, isn't it? You changed the hair colour. Tried to make it someone else. But it's Michelle.'

Shaw turned the picture and held it to his chest. Valentine saw it too now, the likeness that they'd plastered across TV screens and newspaper front pages. Michelle held a tissue to her mouth, her eyes swimming with tears.

'I should have known. It's a classic mistake to make,' said Shaw. 'At first you struggled to give me the form of the face, but then your confidence grew and there was too much detail.'

'I don't know what you're talking about, Inspector.' Holt looked at his tea, blowing on the steaming surface. 'You've upset my daughter. I think you should go.'

Valentine put down his cup and Shaw saw the slight flush rise on his throat. A good sign – the DS didn't like being treated like an idiot any more than Shaw did.

'Have you met Joe?' asked Valentine. He took the piece of paper from his pocket and unfurled it on the coffee table.

Martha Holt jumped visibly, suddenly readjusting herself in the armchair.

'Joe who?' asked Holt, but he'd said it too quickly.

'Joe the loan shark. The one who left his calling card on the side of your car.'

Martha Holt stood. 'Do we have to deal with this now? John's not been well.'

'Leave it,' said Holt, not looking at his wife, slapping her down. Shaw knew then he could be a cruel man.

'Money's a problem,' said Holt. 'Of course it's a problem. But we'll be all right. I'm telling you, Inspector, that man was alive when I saw him at the wheel of the pick-up. I'm sorry, but he *was* alive, and the hitch-hiker was sitting next to him.'

Shaw tried one more time. 'So how did you solve your money problem, Mr Holt? Did James Baker-Sibley ask for your help? Did he pay for your help? Did you get the money? Were you on Siberia Belt that night to make sure the woman in the Alfa couldn't reverse back to the main road?'

Holt struggled to his feet. 'You really have lost me, Inspector. I think this has gone on long enough. I'd like you to leave now.'

They told Holt they'd be interviewing him again. He wasn't to leave the area without contacting St James's. Martha Holt took them to the door but little Sasha pushed through and handed Shaw a piece of paper on which she'd glued helicopter seeds in a pattern: a swirl of them like smoke rising from the red flames of a fire.

Shaw smiled. 'Thank you, Sasha. That'll keep me warm.'

As they drove away they didn't see her grandfather standing by the window, a phone to his ear.

# 45

*Sunday, 15 February*

Shaw woke a minute before the alarm at 5.30. He made coffee, and drank it outside. It was too dark to see the sky but the absence of stars told him the snow clouds had returned. He ran to the Land Rover along the still-frozen beach. By six he was on the towpath up-river of Boal Quay. Lights shone in kitchens and bathrooms in the tower blocks of the South End. Hedgehogs crept across the open concrete of the floodlit car parks. In mid-stream a Russian freighter waited to slip into the Alexandra Dock, its superstructure floodlit, the decks deserted, hot air drifting from vents in skyscapes of steam.

Shaw walked away from the sea. For the first time since he'd woken up he tried to think. When he'd handed over the Tessier file to DCI Warren he'd told him, promised him, that his role in the case was over. And he'd told Valentine the same. And he meant it. But then, when he'd got back to the station on Saturday afternoon, he'd found a note from Timber Woods.

*Peter,*

*The attached may help. I still think you should let it lie. But I'm not sure what Jack would do — so do with this what you think is right.*

*Timber*

'The attached' was Giddy Poynter's address. Shaw could have just added the information to the file he'd given Warren. But perhaps he did owe his father more than that, and perhaps he owed George Valentine more than that too, even if he'd never admit it to his face. If Warren said no to Shaw's request, then a last, clinching, piece of new evidence would be their only chance to get the file reopened.

Timber had set about finding Giddy Poynter with exemplary thoroughness. The child's ordeal in the rat-infested waste bin had been enough to disturb a mature adult, let alone a small, timid boy of twelve. So Timber Woods had gone to the record office at social services. Gideon Poynter had been an outpatient for three years after the incident in 1997, at the child psychology department at the Queen Vic. Absence from school on medical grounds was the hallmark of his academic career. He suffered from stress and anxiety, manifested by a series of uncontrollable phobias. Giddy, living now in sheltered housing in Lynn, attended a mental health unit twice a week. The patient suffered from profound claustrophobia, an irrational but almost tangible fear of being trapped. He had lived rough on the streets of Lynn for six months before the council was able to find him a flat in which each and every window could be opened. He'd wanted a balcony too, just big enough for a chair, on which he often slept if the weather was mild. There'd been a home number and mobile on the file for Poynter's social worker so Shaw had phoned. He promised he'd tread carefully, to respect Giddy's fears. In return he'd got an outline of Giddy's daily routine.

Ahead, along the river path, he could see the graveyard

of St Martin's church. Redundant now, the stained-glass windows were lost behind heavy grey mesh, the wooden lych-gate charred, graffiti over the tiles of the roof. The new bridge over the estuary had spanned St Martin's churchyard the year before, so that now the gravestones had a roof – the brutal concrete arches of the road a hundred feet above. In the echoing space beneath the pigeons clattered, and a single oak, a century old, lived a half-life in the shadows. The roar of the traffic rattled the medieval church, which was slowly but remorselessly crumbling. Stone flakes fell from the buttresses. The local paper had reported that when very heavy loads rumbled past on the flyover the old bells sounded: dull notes, as if from under the sea.

The morning was still dark so that the steady stream of traffic overhead, thrumming, traced a necklace of lights in a graceful curve over the water.

Shaw stepped through a metal gate and walked amongst the graves. There was a bench under a single lamp post which splashed a pool of jaundiced light on the snow. Above he could see bats flitting in the girders, roosting like black snowballs stuck to the rivets. He brushed the snow off the seat and sat waiting, emptying his mind, trying not to think of death.

When he saw the small shambling figure with thin, lank hair, he thought he must be wrong. Giddy would be twenty-three, twenty-four, a young man still despite the horrors of his short life. This man was as ageless as all those who lived on the streets, hidden from the world like a leper, wrapped in a formless heavy coat. Clutching a plastic supermarket bag to his chest with one hand, he held a bunch of flowers with the other, loosely furled in newspaper. At the grave he squatted down, fiddling with the flowers and a plastic urn.

It took him too long and Shaw guessed that he'd seen him and that he always sat on this bench; although there was another.

So Shaw stood. 'I'm sorry,' he said. 'I know this is your place at this time. My name's Peter. I'm a policeman. I just wanted a word, Giddy.'

The man turned, a knee on the wet grass. His face was fine, a thin nose, delicate cheekbones, and a high, brittle forehead. A miniature face, stunted. Acne disfigured the skin and a half-hearted moustache straggled over his mouth, hiding his upper lip.

He didn't respond and Shaw wondered if he was shivering or shaking. 'Giddy. Can I talk to you?' Shaw opened a small rucksack he'd put at his feet, taking out a thermos flask. 'It's tea, would you like a cup? Bernard said you liked tea in the morning.'

Bernard Parkin was the man Shaw had spoken to the previous day. He was Giddy's social worker, and the closest thing he had in the world to a friend.

A pigeon flapped around the headstones and Giddy stood quickly, walking sideways to the bench. He sat hunched against the armrest.

'I always sit here,' he said. 'It's under the sky.'

Shaw leant back and looked directly up. He was right, the edge of the roadway above was twenty feet to one side, giving a clear view of the clouds of dawn.

'Mum's grave,' said Giddy.

'Yes,' said Shaw.

'I don't mind the traffic.'

'I'm sorry, Giddy. It's about the boys who locked you up.'

Giddy tried to look into Shaw's face. The eyes were dove-grey, and one of them oscillated slightly, as if struggling to focus. 'I never talk about that.'

'I know. I'm going to speak to those boys soon – the three that were caught and punished. Do you want me to say anything to them?'

Giddy thought about it. 'Tell them I'm happy now. Better.'

Shaw nodded. 'And the fourth one – I just thought you might have known who it was. Did you, Giddy?'

Giddy looked at him then, the grey eye wandering. 'Stop following me.'

'I'm not following you.'

He stood, one arm jerking suddenly, the plastic bag gyrating. 'Fucking are.' He walked away, then turned. 'Dark glasses yesterday,' he said. 'But I know. You were in the stairwell last night, and then by the park this morning. I don't like it, it's like being trapped outside. Stop it.'

He walked back to Shaw, looked him in the face. 'Stop it.' He looked at the graveyard as if seeing it for the first time. 'I don't want you here, but I can't leave.'

Shaw nodded. 'I'll go. If you want to talk, or you need help, ring this number.' He put a card on the seat, and a £10 note, weighing it down with one of the limpet shells.

# 46

As Valentine drove east along the coast road, a hoar frost had the countryside in its grip, adding bone-white trees to a landscape of fresh snow. Shaw tried to focus on the events on Siberia Belt the night Harvey Ellis died. The central mystery remained: who had killed him, and how? They'd now interviewed everyone in the line of stranded cars at least twice: all except the teenager who had run from the scene that night as the helicopter had swung in to land on Ingol Beach – young Sebastian Draper. His solicitor had phoned to say he'd be available for interview at nine that morning – but that his client wanted to meet at a scrap-metal yard on the edge of Wells. He had something to show them, as well as tell them.

John Kimbolton & Sons was a graveyard for cars. It lay a mile out of town on the saltmarsh, the tottering piles of wrecked chassis only partly hidden behind an ugly hedge of leylandii tinted with frost. They flashed their warrant cards at a mechanic working with a welding torch by the entrance.

'Just looking for a vehicle,' said Valentine. 'Nothing to worry about.'

Draper arrived on the stroke of the hour in a powder-blue Bentley driven by his solicitor. The 18-year-old hadn't chosen his own clothes that morning: a charcoal-grey suit, the blue tie knotted savagely tight, the shirt as white as a ski slope. Without the baseball cap Shaw could see that his hair was dark, almost black, well cut, brushed back off the pale forehead, but falling forward despite the gel. Just eighteen; his face in transition, the eyelashes too long, his skin flushed, the over-long arms held awkwardly at his sides. The solicitor was called Barrett; black leather gloves, black brogues, and a skier's tan.

They shook hands; two detectives, solicitor and client.

'OK. Sebastian? Why here?' said Shaw, the snow beginning to fall. They stood by a little column of six crushed cars, one on top of the other. Shaw rested an ungloved hand on the nearest chassis, then pulled it back as he felt his skin freeze to the metal.

Draper had rehearsed his story, which didn't mean it wasn't true.

The gap-year idea had been a disaster. All his friends except Gee Belcher had left the village. He didn't want to travel abroad, not alone. His parents were in London during the week. Sarah, his girlfriend, had left for university at Durham. His father paid him an allowance but it wasn't much and so he'd got a summer job with the council, filling holes in the road. He'd made friends, the wrong kind of friends, and stayed on when winter came. He'd get into Lynn by bus, or if he could he'd borrow Rod Belcher's car, the BMW. They'd sus out likely cars, drink enough to overcome the fear they'd be caught, then pile in and drive out here to Kimbolton's. Never before seven, the only rule, and cash in hand: £100 per vehicle – any vehicle. They never knew what happened to them but it was easy to guess: there was a paint shed, a pile of number plates, stacks of second-hand tyres.

Valentine noted that the mechanic had stopped welding and was now on a mobile phone.

'They gave us the cash in an envelope. Twenties, always twenties. Then we had to go back and wait by the office for a lift into town. That was it, every time.'

The snow was heavier now, settling on the lawyer's cashmere coat. There was a partly wrecked bus parked by the leylandii – a double-decker, its windows out. Shaw led them on board and they sat on the stiff icy seats. It was out of the snow but somehow colder, like sitting in a fridge.

Draper told them what had happened that night on Siberia Belt. He'd stolen a car, got caught on Siberia Belt, panicked when the police arrived and fled the scene. One unexpected detail. Draper might have stuck it out for longer that night, but he said he'd recognized Sarah Baker-Sibley. He said she always picked her daughter up from the discos at Burnham Thorpe. It was a small world, he said. That was the problem with growing up in it.

The interview was, as Shaw had suspected, a depressing dead-end. He let Valentine take over the questions while he rang St James's and got put through to the car-crime unit. They'd need to check out every wreck on the yard before the management had time to cover their tracks.

Valentine was shivering now, holding his raincoat to his thin neck. 'That night – how'd you get home?' he asked.

'In the snow? I got down to the coast road . . . I fell

in – twice. A van stopped and gave me a lift all the way back to Gayton – right to the car. A Renault van.' He gave them the number.

'You memorize that?' asked Valentine, offering him a smoke.

Draper looked at his lawyer, then the Silk Cut, then took one. 'I don't need to. I can't forget numbers – not once I've seen them.' Shaw recalled Parlour's description of the teenage driver of the Mondeo on Siberia Belt; the T-shirt logo *Pi is God*.

'Why'd you take the steering-wheel cover with you when you stole the car?' asked Shaw, taking an interest now, realizing that Valentine had been right to probe.

'I didn't have gloves,' he admitted. 'I'd been along for the ride before, nicking cars. But they said this one was mine. That way I got the money – all the money. I didn't want to leave any prints. I used my T-shirt when I opened the door.'

Draper smoked the cigarette cupped in his hand. 'We don't need to go to the station,' said Shaw. Barrett nodded, catching his client's eye with a wink.

'I think you've been honest with me, Sebastian,' said Shaw.

'Seb,' he said, then bit his lip.

'Seb,' said Shaw. Valentine jiggled his dice key ring. But Shaw hadn't finished. Something about Seb Draper intrigued him. He wondered what it was like to have the kind of brain that couldn't forget a number.

'Seb, we're trying to find out what really happened out there on that road on Monday night. You know what we found?'

Draper worked a finger in between his neck and the white shirt. 'The guy at the front, he died, right?'

'That's right. We think he was part of a plan to divert the traffic off the road. Mrs Baker-Sibley's daughter was abducted that night – while she was stranded out on Siberia Belt.'

Draper's mouth opened to reveal perfect dentistry.

'I just need you to tell me precisely what happened,' said Shaw. 'You're good with details, Seb – that's what we want. That's where the devil is, right? You left Gayton in the Mondeo when?'

'Five. Five past. I left the BMW under the trees by the gate to The Walks. Outside number 56. I drove out towards Hunstanton – I took the old road 'cos it's always quieter. I got behind another car at the lights at Castle Rising. I kept my distance after that, 'cos, like, I didn't want some stupid shunt on the road. You need to keep it simple, nicking cars – no accidents.'

Barrett was looking at his client, his eyes hardening.

'I saw lights ahead turning down onto the sea wall. I got to the diversion sign, so I turned too. The lights were ahead, moving away from me. By the time I got round the corner the lights were ahead of me again – but they'd stopped.'

Shaw nodded. 'So you'd followed the same car from the lights at Castle Rising, to the turning, and then down the causeway until you came to a stop?'

'Well. Yeah. But that's an assumption right? For you. Not for me.'

'Why not for you?'

'Same model Morris, same number plate – KWX117. I clocked them at the lights.'

He didn't laugh because he wasn't joking, and Shaw felt the hair on the back of his neck rise. He thought about it. 'Because if you hadn't noticed the registration number and the make of the car it didn't have to be the same vehicle?'

'Yeah – I lost sight of it twice. Once on the coast road, and then when it went round the corner on the causeway.'

'Because in the time it was out of sight it might have pulled off the road, and another one pulled out to take its place?''

'That's it,' said Draper.

Out of the mouths of babes... thought Shaw. He pictured the scene that night on Siberia Belt, able at last to see the events unfolding, creating the puzzle which they'd been unable to break. Until now.

## 47

'Here,' said Shaw, tapping on the windscreen of the Mazda. Valentine pulled the car over where Siberia Belt met the track to Gallow Marsh Farm. Shaw kicked open the passenger door. The snow had stopped and the red disc of the sun was setting between banks of cloud the colour of theatre curtains. The air temperature was falling like a hailstone. It felt good, standing on the bank, now that he thought he knew what had happened that night.

He had to see if it worked on the ground, in the real world. So they'd come straight to Siberia Belt from Kimbolton's yard. En route St James's had radioed Valentine. They'd got a call at 3.30 that afternoon. One of Izzy Dereham's farm labourers had been walking down to check the oyster cages in the sea when he'd seen something in the dyke – metallic, floating in the tidal wash from the beach. DC Twine had told them to leave whatever it was, and wait for Shaw and Valentine. A fire-brigade hazardous materials unit was on its way too – just in case they needed specialist handling gear.

'Could be what killed chummy in the raft,' said Valentine, as the wind thudded against the offside of the Mazda. He wanted to get up to the farm, check out what they'd found in the dyke, get back to the station. What he didn't want to do was get out of the car.

'Come on,' said Shaw. 'It's not going anywhere. Let's check this out first.'

Shaw walked back to the turn in the road, then round the corner, leaving Valentine shivering in the wind. Once out of sight of Valentine Shaw could see down to the coast road; a bus lurching towards Lynn. Then he retraced his steps until he could see the Mazda again, and beyond it the rest of Siberia Belt, and the spot where the pine had been felled that Monday night.

'Check it, check it, check it . . .' said Valentine under his breath, annoyed at being kept out of the loop. He felt the damp insinuating its way down his throat and into his lungs, so he coughed, a deep hollow boom, like a goose. Shaw was upbeat, excited, but he hadn't shared whatever the good news was.

Shaw walked back. He stood still, then spun round, taking in the circular horizon of water, marsh and trees. He'd got it clear in his head now, and it made sense; at last, it made sense. He clapped his hands and listened to the echo ricochet off the farm buildings at Gallow Marsh.

'OK – the kid was annoying,' said Shaw. They stood together, looking out to sea. 'But bright. And he was right, George. We've made assumptions. We've assumed, and all the drivers have assumed, that the vehicles they followed round this bend were the vehicles they found when they got round this bend.'

'I guess,' said Valentine. He didn't see what difference it made.

A marsh bird made a noise like a 1950s football rattle.

'Two things are possible,' said Shaw. 'One of the

vehicles in the stranded convoy could have come out of Gallow Marsh Farm that night and slipped into the line. Or. A vehicle came up the road from the coast and slipped out of the line into Gallow Marsh Farm.'

Valentine spat in the snow. 'Well that clears things up.'

'Yes, it does.' Shaw beamed. 'I reckon we're pretty close, George – pretty close. The jigsaw's almost finished.' He smiled the surfer's smile.

'So what shape's the missing bit?' asked Valentine, acutely aware that the 'we' didn't appear to include him.

'I'm not absolutely sure, but it's got four wheels.'

# 48

Snow lay across the yard at Gallow Marsh, marred by tyre tracks, straw laid out in the worst of the ruts. The hazmat unit had beaten them to it, and was parked in the entrance to the barn, out of the wind. A blue light flashed, shadows dancing round the high rafters within. They walked past it and out through a pair of double doors on the far side. There was another yard here, bounded on one side by a deep arrow-straight dyke running towards the sea. A broken harrow stood rusting in frosted weeds, and a pile of sugar beet gave off a stench of damp earth. Two farmhands stood smoking in the half-light, standing on the snowy bank a hundred yards down towards the beach. Closer, three men stood in full protective gear, looking at mobile phones.

The dyke was a gullet of shadow about twenty feet across, the surface ten feet below them. The sound of water churning filled the dusk as the tide pushed in, swamping the banks of reeds and grass. One of the hazmat team produced a heavy-duty torch and scanned the dark channel below.

'She's here somewhere; I found it earlier,' he said. A corner of bright unpainted metal stuck up in midstream, the edge of a box, perhaps, an angle of reflective steel.

'OK,' said Shaw. 'When you're ready.'

'Right. But we think this might be dangerous, yes?'

'Maybe,' said Shaw.

The firemen began to unload a winch from the unit, a set of boat hooks. Valentine let the burst of flame at the end of a match warm his spirits as he lit a cigarette. This was tying up a loose end. They were making progress, and it felt good. Sunset soon, and then back to the city. The canteen at St James's did a roast on Sunday nights. He'd read the papers, then watch the live match on Sky at the Artichoke. It was the best week's work he'd done in ten years. Yes, it made him feel very good. It made him feel like a human being again.

One of the farmhands came up to Shaw; a teenager, swaddled against the cold, stamping his feet. 'Izzy said if we found anything we should get her first, but the kid's not well – flu, she reckons – so we thought we'd ring you lot.' They all stood back as a fireman in waders began to edge down the bank with a hook.

'Thanks, it might be important,' said Shaw. He scanned the horizon, trying not to look in the water, wondering what the chances were that whatever had come ashore that Monday night was still alive.

The fireman expertly snagged the metal triangle, then attached a chain back to the winch. The engine squealed, the chain tightened, water droplets flying off, and then whatever it was in mid-stream got sucked off the muddy bed of the dyke. Suddenly it was there beneath them, on the grass bank.

'Well that's solved that mystery,' said Shaw.

It was an AA diversion sign. Black lettering on a yellow background. Green weed, black under the light, knotted around one of the metal legs.

'Call Tom,' he said. 'Tell him we'll bring it in – we should get it dusted. See if you can get it in some shrink-wrap and get it in the boot,' he said to Valentine. 'I think it's time I gave Izzy Dereham another chance to tell the truth.'

The door to the farmhouse was on the latch, the hallway warm, full of shadows. Upstairs they could hear a child's voice, Izzy Dereham's comforting murmur running in counterpoint. Valentine shouted up that they were there, that they needed to talk. She said she'd be a minute, so they sat in the kitchen by what was left of a log fire, watching the clock creep towards six. Three rabbits, a hare and a brace of pigeon hung gutted from a rafter. She must be good with a gun, thought Shaw, and imagined her out on the marsh, the birds wheeling over her head. There was a child's drawing pinned to the door – a black cat again, on a raft at sea. Shaw walked to the window and shivered. Outside the clouds had finally closed over Gallow Marsh. The night snow was sporadic, in the wind.

When she appeared in the kitchen she seemed distracted, harassed. She considered taking the rocking chair by the Aga, but stood instead, leaning against the warm rail.

'Detective Inspector. Sergeant.' She tried to find pockets for her hands but gave up the struggle. She wore heavy-duty boots, green canvas trousers, a smock in blue, blotched with chemical stains.

'We found something in the ditch.'

She crossed her arms.

'The AA diversion sign. We wondered where it had

gone.' He left a beat. 'Did you wear gloves? CSI will get prints off it otherwise.'

'I don't understand,' she said.

'Was it just for the money?' He looked round the kitchen. 'The lease is up next year? Things must be tough. And then John Holt turns up on the doorstep one day – bringing a present for his godchild?'

She looked at her feet. Shaw thought how it was always little lies and omissions that were the real clues to guilt. Valentine got out his notebook and began to scribble a note.

'Holt's got your daughter's picture at his daughter's house. Bit like that one . . .' Shaw nodded at the snapshot framed on the wall.

She shrugged. 'John's my uncle. It's not a crime, is it? I'm a Holt too – I kept Pat's name after he died. It's all there was.'

Shaw braced both hands around his knee. 'You've been formally interviewed about the events here on Siberia Belt – you didn't mention the connection. Neither did he. What was there to hide?'

She ran her wrist across her lips and Shaw could see the rhythmic tremble in the fingers. Water began to pump out of her eyes and she grabbed a chair, the legs scraping horribly on the cork tiles.

'Your parents lost their farm, didn't they?' he asked.

'Yes,' she said, her head dropping. 'Dad couldn't take it – he killed himself, in the car with a pipe to the exhaust. I was seven. Uncle John helped Mum for a while, but it was no good. We gave it up.'

'And then it looked like it might happen again. Your

husband's dead. The farm's struggling. So Uncle John knew you were desperate. And he tried to help. And now you're going to let him carry the can alone? He's got a daughter too, you know.'

The line of her mouth broke, a sudden flush in her face squeezing out the tears, fully formed, like a child's crystal beads. 'It wasn't a crime,' she said, throwing her head back. 'No one was going to get hurt.'

Shaw winced at the cliché, because it was never true.

'John said James Baker-Sibley owned Shark Tooth – and Shark Tooth owned Gallow Marsh. I'd get a year, rent free, time to get back on top of things.' She stood suddenly, pacing the kitchen. 'All I had to do was put the sign out at the right moment, then fetch it back in. They had to do it on Siberia Belt because there's no phone signal – and it's the only spot on her route that's remote enough. It's always her route – that was something else I had to do, down on the coast road, I timed her each Monday for a month. Five o'clock, a few minutes either way. She never missed.'

She went to the mantelpiece over the fire. There was a family picture, framed in black wood; she turned it face down.

'It wasn't the only . . .' Shaw searched for the right word, '*enterprise* you were involved in, was it? You were already working for Colin Narr, helping get his smuggled merchandise ashore. The light on the dovecote to guide the boat in. Did they bring the stuff here?'

She nodded. Valentine scribbled.

'I didn't have a choice. Narr said he'd make it his business to push for the rent arrears on the farm. Get me out, us out, unless I cooperated. And again – it wasn't much. He ran the boat – the *Skolt* – over to Ostend. It was always timed so that they could slide back in to Lynn on a tide at dusk. They'd get in close – using the light on the barn – then drop the raft for the last few hundred yards. It'd be dark by then. I'd meet Terry down on the sands, stow the raft by the oyster beds, bring the stuff back here. Terry always had a lift waiting, up on Siberia Belt.

'He was due Sunday. The day after the consignment comes ashore Narr's men are always out on the delivery run – it's the only day I know they won't be here. That's why we timed Siberia Belt for the Monday – we knew the coast would be clear. But first Terry didn't appear, then you turned up looking for the drums. It was a nightmare, but we couldn't stop it happening.'

She rubbed her hands on the skin of her cheeks. 'We just had to keep our nerve. The plan was too complicated to ditch. If we wanted to get her off the road, and out of mobile contact, it had to be that night. Mr Baker-Sibley was ready as well, and the tides were right for him to sail before dawn.'

'Take me through what happened,' said Shaw.

'We met here first – me, Uncle John, and Harvey Ellis. Harvey was sick with worry over that kid of his.'

'Jake,' said Shaw.

'Harvey put the pick-up truck in the barn out of sight and we sat in the cab, going through it all one last time.'

'What time was this?' asked Shaw.

She shrugged, and Shaw noticed that her eyes had lost

focus. 'Four o'clock. I made us a flask of tea, some rolls and fruit.'

Apples, thought Shaw.

'Harvey was in a bad way. Nervous. He was sick, throwing up, shaking. He said he couldn't do it. We said he had to. John said it was too important to all of us. And no one was going to get hurt. Then they drove down to Siberia Belt in the pick-up – the two of them.'

The key. At last. Shaw sat back: 'So Harvey Ellis's van was *already* parked up on Siberia Belt – he didn't arrive there with the rest of the convoy?'

'That's right. They were going to switch the plugs – fake a breakdown. That's why John went: Ellis said he couldn't do it on his own. I guess they took the tree down to make sure. They were pretty nervous. Then John came back. Things were OK then – I could see it was going to be all right. John said he'd talked Ellis round, that once he was out in position he'd calmed down. Then it was our turn to get in place. When I got the van down to the junction just here by the farm I could see Ellis standing by the pick-up out on Siberia Belt – he waved. That's the last time I ever saw him.'

Shaw nodded. The confession had been smooth, almost effortless. Too smooth?

'Then?' asked Valentine.

'It was simple, really. We got in position on the coast road in a lay-by. When Baker-Sibley's Alfa went past John had to stay behind her, I got in front. When I reached Siberia Belt I had time to drop off the sign, then drive back here.'

'So Sarah Baker-Sibley followed *your* lights up the track?'

said Shaw. 'And by the time she turned the corner you'd turned off into the farm, and so she saw Ellis's lights ahead – but he'd been there for an hour or more. But she thought she'd followed *him* there, all the way from Castle Rising.'

The wings of a gull scuffed at the window and left a feathered imprint in the ice.

Izzy Dereham jumped at the noise. 'When I saw a few more cars go past at the junction I walked down, on the far side of the trees, and dragged the sign in. We needed to keep Baker-Sibley there for an hour – that was the deal. If she'd tried to reverse John was going to put his back wheels over the ditch and keep her in. But the snowstorm made it easier. We knew she was trapped for hours.'

Valentine closed his notebook. 'But when you and John Holt left the farm Harvey Ellis was alive?'

'That's right.'

'And alone?'

'No.' She turned to Shaw. 'It wasn't just the three of us. There was a fourth: someone to put the sign out at the other end of Siberia Belt. He was going to meet Harvey at the pick-up – just to double-check everything was OK. When I drove off there were two figures out on the track. John said this other man had planned the whole thing, and sorted the money side, but he wouldn't tell me his name. All he said was that he was James Baker-Sibley's man. His eyes and ears – that's what he said. Baker-Sibley's eyes and ears.'

# 49

They stood on the pavement outside the Artichoke in the steadily falling snow, Valentine using his mobile. Tom Hadden was in the Ark; he'd pick them up in ten minutes to run them to Sly's houseboat. Duncan Sly – 'the eyes and ears' of James Baker-Sibley, and before that of his father. They'd need uniform back-up. Shaw and Valentine had got scalding tea from the late-night burger van parked opposite the pub. Under a canvas awning they'd reduced the investigation to its stark core: if Izzy Dereham was telling the truth, the only person who could have killed Harvey Ellis was Duncan Sly. *If she was telling the truth.*

Valentine stood in the snow, his head sunk low on his shoulders so that the collar of the raincoat kept the back of his neck warm.

Shaw tried to call up an image of the boot mark they'd found in the bloodstain on Siberia Belt. Heavy duty, with a steel toecap, and the fern leaf burnt into the heel. It wasn't Holt's footprint, so was it Sly's? They needed to turn over the houseboat, find the boots. The footprint was the only physical forensic evidence that could put the killer on the spot. They had to trace it.

The snow was making little drifts on Shaw's shoulders as he stood under the swinging pub sign. He'd never really looked at the picture before: a gardener leaning on a spade, a line of artichokes still to be cut, a floppy white hat to keep the sun off his face, steel-capped boots, a freshly cut globe in his hand.

Shaw looked a long time at the boots.

'I'll catch up with you at St James's, George' he said suddenly, the excitement in his voice as audible as the snow was silent. 'I've got to check something out. Take Sly carefully, then bring him in to the station. Secure the site, leave the rest to Tom. The important thing is getting in the door before he's got a chance to destroy anything. Boots, clothing. I'll meet you at St James's.'

Valentine nodded, trying to see it as a vote of confidence, but knowing he was being cut out of something.

Hadden arrived in the CSI van with two uniformed PCs for back-up, and as they pulled away Valentine could see Shaw still looking up at the swinging sign of the Artichoke.

The streets of Lynn were empty, snow settling despite the salt. A neon kebab-house sign pulsed on Norfolk Street, the gyro inside turning as a man sliced off the cooked meat. They pulled up at Boal Quay and Valentine led the way to the footpath which ran to the houseboat jetty. The communal fire still burnt, despite the falling snow, but there was no one tending the flames. Valentine went aboard Sly's boat with Hadden and one of the uniformed PCs, the other skirted the hull of the boat, up on its blocks, round to the far side.

Valentine didn't have to knock. Sly opened the double wooden hatchway, blinking into Hadden's torch. He stood in his pants, nothing else, his skin as white as lard except where he couldn't cover it up on the sands – the hands and face as dark as tanned leather. Old tattoos, faded to a smudge of grey and blue, curled and intertwined on his forearms. Still powerful at fifty, but the skin tone gone, folds of tissue hanging across the broad chest. Valentine saw that Sly's hands were wet, the nails black, and that there were dark smudges on the white skin of the forearms.

'Jesus! What . . . ?' asked Sly, covering his eyes with a hand as if he were looking out to sea.

'Mr Sly? We'd like a word, and to look around.'

Sly looked back into the houseboat. Valentine sniffed, the cold air making his sinuses flood. 'Or I can be back with a warrant in ten minutes.' He'd give him one more chance, then they'd force a way through. Sod the warrant.

Sly didn't move, but seemed to settle on his feet.

Hadden opened his CSI bag and pulled on gloves. 'I need to look around,' he said, not waiting for Sly to give him permission. Valentine stamped the snow off his boots on the bare floorboards and led the way.

'Like I've got a choice,' said Sly.

'You'll need some clothes and a coat, sir. We have a car.' There was a strong smell in the room but Valentine's nose was blocked: peat perhaps, smoked fish?

'Now? This is crazy,' said Sly. 'I've told you I'd nothing to do with James's murder.'

Valentine, suddenly tired, felt sorry for Duncan Sly, so he decided to cut it short, spell things out. 'Mr Sly. We're going down to St James's. That's what's going to happen. It's got nothing to do with his murder. We understand you were on Siberia Belt the night Harvey

Ellis died. That's what we want to talk about. For starters.'

Sly stepped back again, and the single unshaded light bulb threw his face into relief. Valentine examined a large print of the Battle of Jutland on the wall. He thought what a defeat it must be, to end your life alone in a rotting houseboat, surrounded by the stench of tidal mud, when your dream was to be at sea.

Hadden was below decks, opening drawers, cupboards. The uniformed PC hovered. 'Can you get some clothes on, sir – we need to go,' said Valentine.

Sly stood his ground and Valentine wondered if they'd interrupted something. He walked to the sink. A box of firelighters stood on the shelf with a bottle of detergent, and the bowl had a black tidemark around it, a nail brush lying in the scurf.

Valentine turned quickly and caught Sly with his hands over his face. He took them away quickly and, realizing they were wet, he looked at his fingertips as if the water were blood.

'I didn't kill Ellis,' he said.

Valentine treated him to a blank stare. 'Fine. We'll take your word for it, shall we?'

Sly clenched then unclenched his fists.

'It's a tidy boat you've got alongside,' said Valentine. 'No more cockle-picking with scum on the sands, right? A bit of dignity, freedom. But at a price.' Valentine looked round the cabin, then up at the roof where a wooden patch had been nailed up to keep the old boat weather-proof. 'Perhaps it was worth killing for,' he said. He put a cigarette between his teeth but left it unlit.

Hadden reappeared with a clear plastic bag containing a pair of muddy boots. A single shake of the head. 'No match on these. I'll need an hour at least,' he said.

Frustrated, Valentine turned on Sly. 'What happened – did you argue about money? Did Ellis want a share of yours? Did he want you to sort it? Because you could, couldn't you – with James – your mate, the boss?'

'That's tosh. Jesus!' But Sly didn't move.

Valentine took a deep breath, a collarbone creaking as his shoulders rose. 'Just get dressed, sir. Now.'

Valentine went to the hatchway and called in the second uniformed PC, who was standing at the landward end of the gangplank. 'Accompany Mr Sly below please, Constable – he needs clothes, an overnight bag.'

Sly reluctantly went down, a cat passing him on the steps coming up. It brushed itself against Valentine's black slip-ons, then made a figure of eight between his feet.

By the time Sly was ready Hadden had six pairs of shoes and boots lined up on a plastic sheet. Two pairs had steel toecaps. But he still hadn't got a match.

'I take it you found some footprints,' said Sly.

'Just one,' said Valentine. 'Under the security van in the convoy of cars on Siberia Belt. But a deep one – because Harvey Ellis's killer was loading his body into the pickup's cab, and he was standing in a pool of Ellis's blood which had melted the frozen soil.' Valentine watched Sly's eyes, looking for signs of fear or confusion. 'Once the body was in the van my guess is it was pushed forward to the pine tree – but those footprints couldn't dent the frozen ground. We've got the one print, though, and that's all we'll need. Right, Tom?'

'If we're lucky,' said Hadden, unhappy with Valentine's methods: the hectoring, the implied menace.

'Why would I kill Harvey Ellis?' said Sly.

Valentine rolled the cigarette between his lips, tasting tobacco. 'Because he wouldn't do his job. And you worked out that he could do it just as well dead as alive.'

'It wasn't like that,' said Sly.

'No?' said Valentine. 'Let's go and hear what it was really like, shall we?' He nodded at the PC: 'I think we should cuff this one.'

The officer put Sly's muscled arms behind him and handcuffed his hands. Valentine was rewarded with a look of undiluted hatred.

Valentine swayed slightly on his feet, enjoying the moment. They'd find the boots. And if they didn't, they'd find blood. If Sly had struck the fatal blow then they'd find blood. Perhaps, he thought, there'd be time for the house on Greenland Street. The thought of the fan-tan table made his pulse pick up so that he nearly missed it, nearly proved for the last time that his career was over. But there was something about that smell, the smokiness.

He filled his lungs. 'Christ,' he said. 'The fire.' He threw open the double hatch doors, clattered down the steps and ran to the smouldering wood and rubbish, stumbling through the mud, splashing through the stagnant salt water. The heavy snow had almost put it out, the flakes sizzling in the embers.

He pulled out some wood, a branch, as Hadden joined him.

'There,' said Valentine. Under a piece of rotting timber they could see a piece of unburnt fabric, charred metal buttons, some cooked leather, as crisp as pork crackling, and an upturned tread of a boot.

'Got the fucker,' said Valentine.

## 50

Shaw unlocked the filing cabinet in the incident room and took out John Holt's file. The wad of scene-of-crime pictures was comprehensive. Holt's Corsa, interior, exterior, boot. And a black-and-white shot of the cast taken from his shoes. Slip-ons, like George's, with a criss-cross tread and diamond motif on the heel.

'Distinctive . . .' said Shaw, to himself.

The building was silent, even the drunks in the cells were quiet.

He pulled out the file on the footprint found under the security van by Tom Hadden's team. A boot, the steel toe-cap wide, the sole a grid-iron of raised squares, cracked and fissured with age, the imprint of the burnt-in fern, like a signature. Whoever had worn that boot had stood in Ellis's warm blood.

He re-read Holt's statement. He'd been on an errand that night, to his daughter's house, to cut back the magnolia tree that was knocking on his granddaughter's window. Shaw had seen him finishing the job when they'd called at Blickling Cottages: he recalled the gardener's jacket, the gloves and the heavy-duty boots. Holt had said the police had just given his kit back from the Corsa.

Shaw went back to Holt's file. Each car had been given a thorough forensic examination and each had a detailed inventory. Shaw read the one for the Corsa. The list for the inside of the car was predictable – mints in a tin, de-icer, an *A–Z* of Britain, a directory of builders' merchants in north Norfolk, two old copies of the *Lynn News*, both open and folded at local football reports. On the back seat a pot plant, a hyacinth, listed simply as 'gift'. A hatchback, so the list moved on to the large boot. A length of synthetic rope, a child's kite with a Mickey Mouse design, and a holdall, with zip, containing 'gardening kit'.

He rang Tom Hadden. The CSI senior investigator answered on the second ring. Breathless, the rhythmic thud of a heavy bag.

'Sorry, Tom – you can talk?'

'Yeah. There's a fire out near the houseboats, we're just checking it out. Some clothing, a shoe perhaps.'

'Tom. The night the convoy got stuck in the snow. Who took the inventories for the vehicles – specifically Holt's Corsa?'

Hadden left a beat. 'Er. Phil Timms. One of my best. Why?'

'I need to ask him a question – can I ring?'

Hadden gave him a number. Shaw rang. He let it ring ten times, waited a minute, rang again. Third ring it picked up.

'Hello? Phil Timms.'

The voice was thick, the acoustics muffled, Shaw guessed by bedclothes.

'It's DI Shaw, Phil. Look, I'm sorry, Tom gave me the number.'

'No, no problem. Go on.'

In the background Shaw heard heavy footsteps, a door

opening to admit the razor-edged pitch of a child's scream, then slamming.

'You did the inventories on the car contents at Ingol Beach?'

'Right,' said Timms. 'That was me.'

'John Holt's Corsa. You list a holdall containing gardening kit. What constitutes gardening kit, Phil?'

There was a long silence, and Shaw imagined him sitting on the side of the bed, trying to focus, trying to recall the details of a night a week earlier that seemed like a career ago.

'Trowel, hand fork, secateurs – you know, junk really. Oh, gloves, gardening gloves.'

Shaw willed himself not to interrupt.

'A torch – heavy-duty torch. Sorry, sir, I should have listed them. It was just we were looking for bloodstains, anything with blood . . . and there was nothing like that, nothing.'

First mistake, thought Shaw. He shouldn't have been looking *for* anything. Looking for anything was a good way to miss something.

'And boots,' said Timms, the voice suddenly dead. 'Steel toecaps, battered. Yup – that's it, right – boots. I didn't think. Sorry.'

Shaw winced. The English language's most overrated word.

'OK. Can you ring Tom – tell him what happened? They're on a job right now at Boal Quay. When they can, they need to get over to Old Hunstanton, Blickling Cottages. DS Valentine knows the address – he's with Tom. If these boots haven't been destroyed then that's where they are, either there or the town address in Devil's Alley, but we'll start with Blickling Cottages. OK – got that?'

'Sir.'

'Tell them I'll get a warrant for Holt's properties. I'll meet them there.'

He rang the number for the night-duty judge. Mr Justice Lamprey. A big house, a hobby farm, out on the silt fens at Wiggenhall St Germans, where the river cut under the walls of the old church. He'd be ready in an hour. Shaw needed to bring the paperwork for signature.

Shaw took out his mobile and swore. He'd left it off in his pocket, and when he turned it on it buzzed like a bluebottle. He scrolled to his inbox. He'd missed a message, an hour earlier.

## STOP

Just that. He rang the number back and it rang just once before it picked up.

''Ello.' The voice was loud, stressed.

'Hi. This is DI Peter Shaw, King's Lynn CID. You rang me an hour ago – I'm sorry, I don't understand the text you sent.'

'It's not my phone,' said the voice, then he heard a series of bangs as if it had been dropped, then the voice again, out of breath. 'It's Giddy's.'

Giddy Poynter's phone? 'Where is he?' asked Shaw.

'In the bathroom, but I can't get the door open.'

'You're a friend?'

'Not really. Flat next door. Did you say police?'

'Yes.'

'We need you. Some bastard's put glue in the locks on the front doors. I've just had the carpenter round to let us out – twenty-eight fucking quid. We looked at Giddy's and they'd done his too – so the chippy cut his lock out.'

'OK – look, I'll pop round. Just stay put. Wallflower House, right?'

Shaw ran down the back stairs and out into the yard to the Land Rover. Wallflower House was on the London Road, a fifties block on blighted ground beyond the city gate; a two-minute drive.

Frederick Armitage, the neighbour, introduced himself. He was wearing a jumper and running pants. He'd be sixty, wiry, the hair a wedge set at an angle, as if he'd just taken his head off the pillow.

'That's mine,' he said, nodding at an open door. 'This is Giddy's.' The door had been thrown back. The flat had a single living room in which Giddy had put one chair – wicker, with a cushion. A footstool lay on its side by the wall. There was nothing else except a TV, flat-screen, a pile of DVD games and a chessboard set on a tea crate.

Armitage took him down a short corridor to the bathroom door.

'Giddy?' said Shaw, shaking the handle. He turned to Armitage. 'What makes you think he's in there?'

'We heard him come in. At midnight. It's always midnight. Then out at three, back at five normally. He fishes at night, down off the Millfleet. Then out at six. That's Giddy. Clockwork.'

354

Shaw looked at his watch. He didn't have the time for this.

He thudded his fist on the chipboard. 'Giddy!'

'He's not deaf,' said Armitage, stepping back.

Shaw put his shoulder to the door and the hinges popped, screws lifting almost effortlessly clear of rotten wood. A toilet, the lid down, a washbasin, spotless, a shower unit with the curtain pulled back to reveal tiles in alternate black and white. A window stood open, a fire-escape beyond. He hesitated, just one second, before checking the bath. Spotless, empty.

'Nowt,' said Armitage.

As they walked back into the main room the front door creaked, a second hinge working its way loose, so that it began to swing into the room, revealing the hooks on the back.

Giddy was hanging from one of them, a piece of electrical flex round his neck. His toes, in socks, brushed the lino as the wood groaned with the weight. His face was distorted by the broken neck, one side compressed into a series of folds. The dove-grey eyes were open.

'Giddy,' said Shaw, moving forward, knowing it was too late. 'Call an ambulance,' he said, pulling up the discarded footstool and lifting Giddy's body clear of the hook, then laying it down. It was as light as a child's, and Shaw couldn't stop himself pressing it briefly to his chest. He knew it was pointless but he checked the pulse at the neck anyway, massaged the heart. The arms were still flexible, the joints free. He'd been dead an hour, maybe less.

Armitage stood his ground, beginning to shiver in his

bare feet. 'The wife said he'd do it one day,' he said. 'I better tell her.'

But had it been suicide? Had a random act of vandalism pushed him over the edge? Had Giddy locked the bathroom door to keep someone out? Shaw searched the flat looking for a note. Giddy was convinced he was being followed. Had someone seen him talking to Shaw in the churchyard at St Martin's? But he'd said he'd been followed before that. Or had an imaginary enemy become a real one?

Shaw didn't step into the bedroom, but viewed it from the threshold, the interior lit by the hall light. A single bed, and no other furniture; but this had been Giddy's special place: the walls were painted sea green up to head height, sky blue above, the horizon encircling the bed, the two windows open. But Giddy's glory was the ceiling: night-black, scattered across it hundreds, thousands of children's homework stars in silver. Constellations had jostled over Giddy's head.

He heard an ambulance siren and walked back into the living room. Now that Giddy's body was on the floor Shaw could see the letterbox. There was something caught in the flap. He walked to it, knelt down and felt his skin goosebump. He slipped on a glove and pulled it clear. It was a rat's tail.

## 51

By the time Shaw reached Blickling Cottages with the search warrant one of Tom Hadden's CSI units was parked in the lane by the sports field. The windows of the house were as dark as sockets in a skull. Shaw got out, the snow creaking underfoot. But the wind from the sea had lost its polar edge. The snowflakes were fat, spidery, falling lazily like leaves.

He'd left the duty DI from St James's at the scene of Giddy Poynter's untimely death. He hadn't had time to fill him in on the background to the case but he urged caution: it might look like a lonely and desperate suicide but the rat's tail had unnerved Shaw. It was too pointed a reminder of Giddy's childhood nightmare. Had Giddy been deliberately driven to his death? He remembered Giddy's fear, the figure stalking him from the shadows. Shaw left as quickly as he could, promising a witness statement when he got back to the station. Giddy's corpse had left at the same time, a life reduced to an anonymous black body-bag, shuffled into the back of a silent ambulance.

Headlights swept across the football field and settled on the front of Blickling Cottages. Valentine's Mazda rumbled along the lane at a steady 10 mph. His overcoat flapped at his knees when he got out but he didn't seem unhappy to be in the fresh air. He smoked a cigarette with enthusiasm, his shoulders hunched forward, his face turned away from the snow so that large flakes were left in his thin hair.

'There was a fire by the boat,' he said, looking Shaw in the eyes. 'Tom got to it before it was cold. Snowfall had saved a bit. Material – looks like a set of blue overalls. They're stained. Tom says it's definitely blood. In fact the material's soaked in it, and a belt. He's doing a type test now. He's got the stuff back at the Ark. And we can link Sly with the fire – there's ash in the boat, round the sink, on his hands.'

'Boots?'

'In the fire too. But there's not enough to get a footprint.'

'What's he said?' asked Shaw, trying to keep the inquiry balanced, trying not to let it turn into a lynching.

'Fuck all, really.' Valentine watched the smoke drain out of his nostrils into the night air. 'Denies killing Ellis. He wants his lawyer.'

'What's his story?'

'That they didn't go out on the sands on Monday – tides were wrong. Spent most of the day on his fishing boat down on the Boal, overhauling the engine. Says he didn't see anyone. Says he doesn't do friends. Bitter man, seems to think life owes him something.'

'Might he kill to get it?'

Valentine pinched out his cigarette and put it in his raincoat pocket. 'Yup.' He smiled, holding Shaw's gaze. 'What's the hurry here?'

'Holt had a spare pair of boots in the back of the Corsa out on Siberia Belt. Steel toecaps. We need to find them – even if it's to rule him out. Surveillance unit says Holt's here – but he ran the wife home earlier to town. I've got a unit down there too.'

Shaw told the CSI team to wait while they woke the family. Valentine knocked, the double rap bouncing back off the distant white pavilion beyond the football pitch: snow clung to its cupola domes, but the roof was clear, icicles hanging along the gutter.

In the cottage lights came on, one by one, voices in the hallway before the letterbox opened.

'Who's that?'

'DI Shaw, Mr Holt. And DS Valentine.'

Shaw shone his torch on the newly painted door. They could see the scratch marks now, despite the layers of paint; a perfect replica of the symbol etched into the side of the car. Holt opened the door on a chain. 'It's four o'clock in the morning.'

'Sir. I have a warrant for these premises. Can you open the door?'

Holt had a camp bed by an open fire where logs burned, the winter-red flames reflected in ceramic tiles. Upstairs they could hear a child asking sleepy questions. Valentine walked quickly to the fire and used a poker to pick amongst the ashes.

'Stay in bed,' called Holt up the stairs. 'Sasha's upset,' he said by way of explanation. 'So I said I'd stay over. She likes that.'

The CSI team bustled, collecting shoes from the hallway.

'They're going to have to go upstairs, Mr Holt.'

Holt's shoulder slumped and he sat on the edge of

the camp bed, his pyjamas damp where he'd been sweating in the night.

'What are they looking for?' he said, adjusting the glasses. The eyes, magnified, were bloodshot and rheumy.

A spark flew from the fire. They both watched it turn to ash on the carpet.

'Mr Holt,' said Shaw. 'You and I and DS Valentine are going back to St James's. We've been talking to Izzy Dereham. Your niece. So you'll need an overnight bag.'

Holt's face crumpled and he rested it in his hands. 'Can I get dressed? I'd like to walk for a while, could we? I'd like the air before we go to the station.'

'All right,' said Shaw. 'Five minutes, Mr Holt – no more.'

They heard running steps on the stairs and Sasha burst in. She was laughing, but she stopped when she saw her grandfather's face. Michelle Holt followed her in, and gathering her hand took her to sit in front of the open fire.

She looked at her father. 'Dad?' she said, the tears already flowing.

Holt stood. 'I need to dress. I'd like some privacy. Take Sasha to bed, Micky. Now.' She lifted his granddaughter up and carried her out. Shaw and Valentine waited out in the snow.

'George, do me a favour,' said Shaw. 'That sports pavilion.' He nodded across the snowy football field.

'What about it?'

'Why's there no snow on the roof?'

Valentine shrugged. 'It fell off?'

'Too shallow. Snow's still stuck to the domes. Just check it out. Force the door if you have to.'

Valentine set out on what he clearly judged to be a fool's errand, his shoulders hunched against the damp.

Shaw went back to the Mazda and used the radio to check with the murder room. Hadden had phoned through some preliminary results from Gallow Marsh – no joy on Izzy Dereham's boots, but her teeth matched the apple from Ellis's pick-up exactly.

Holt appeared wearing a full-length beltless overcoat, which looked new. They trudged down the cleared path to the lane and through the gateway into the playing fields. The snow was a foot deep, reflecting the cold light of the stars.

'The wood's a good walk,' said Holt, setting off uphill towards a line of dark, leafless trees. The stars overhead brightened as they got away from the CSI lights. Holt walked stiffly, his breath coming hard.

'We know what happened that night on Siberia Belt, Mr Holt,' said Shaw, his footsteps crunching now on the twigs beneath the trees. 'Izzy Dereham has made a full statement. Sly organized it – recruited you and Harvey Ellis. You knew each other through football, right? You run the club here – and Harvey Ellis played for the TA team. Did he bring his kids? Did they play with Sasha? And Duncan Sly runs the works team for Shark Tooth – Wootton Marsh. It's the same league – I checked.'

Holt didn't say he was wrong. The starlight lit the path ahead like crazy paving. 'And then – the final piece of the jigsaw – you recruited Izzy.'

Holt didn't look back but Shaw heard what he said, almost a whisper. 'She'll never forgive me.'

'James Baker-Sibley was a rich man, and one who wanted his daughter at any cost. What did he promise you?'

'He cleared the debts,' said Holt, turning. 'An interest-free loan. But it was a loan. And I'll pay it back.'

'Who to?'

The old man shrugged.

'The real question,' said Shaw, 'is who killed Harvey Ellis. You were down there with him. He did lose his nerve, didn't he? And you were all smart enough to realize that he could fulfil his part of the bargain just as well dead as alive. The body would be found – but so what? There was nothing to link him to you, to any of you.'

'When I left him, Harvey was alive.' Holt licked his lips. 'We saw him waving as we came out of Gallow Marsh. But I'd told him it was dangerous – what he was doing, what he planned to do.'

Holt walked on and within a few hundred yards they emerged on the crest of the hill. Over by Blickling Cottages members of the CSI team were in the upstairs rooms, the curtains pulled back.

'What was he going to do that was dangerous?' said Shaw, recognizing that he'd been invited to ask the question. He reminded himself that Holt and Izzy were family. Sly was the outsider, the fixer, the boss's man.

Holt spat, took an extra breath. 'Some people are greedy once they get their snouts in the trough. Harvey was a fool. His children made him a fool, anyway, and they're all he cared about. He knew there was money to spare, so he said he was going to screw them for it.'

Shaw watched the last of the snowflakes falling, outsized and feathery. There was a wind up on the hill and it promised rain.

Holt laughed, adjusting the spectacles. 'He said he'd put it to Duncan Sly, that he hadn't realized the risks. He wanted ten thousand – double what we'd agreed. I left him about four thirty. He'd been in a mess all day, kept saying he was putting his arse on the line, whatever Duncan said, and he deserved a bigger cut. Harvey said if he got caught he'd be inside when Jake died. That's what really freaked him out. That was the big risk, the only one he really cared about. But if he was taking it, he wanted paying for it.'

Holt's top lip curled back to show the ill-fitting dentures, the first time Shaw had seen the old man sneer. 'If Duncan didn't promise him more he said he'd reverse back, take the sign down, stop her coming up the lane.'

Shaw took in a breath of the air, damp now. To the east dawn was bleeding into the sky.

'I saw Duncan coming along Siberia Belt,' said Holt. 'He'd walked up from the far end. He had his car down there ready to put out the no-entry sign. I didn't want to be there for that. Harvey was a weak man, I reckoned he'd toe the line. Duncan could switch the spark plugs. So I left them to it.'

Shaw imagined Ellis and Sly in the cab of the pick-up, dusk gathering, the toolbox between them, the young father delivering his threat.

Shaw touched the dressing on his eye, the nerves behind suddenly jumping, making his jaw tremble.

Holt stood, shaking his head. 'Harvey didn't deserve to die like that. He loved that kid, all of his kids, and Jake most of all.' He gazed out over the field. 'He used to bring them to matches – they're good kids, they deserve a father.'

He looked back at Blickling Cottages. 'I couldn't have done that, lived with that kid's illness, knowing he was going to die, and not hating him for it.'

The rain was falling now, sheets of water like net curtains. They walked through the slush on the field. In the garden the carapace of snow had shrunk back, the dead stems of Brussels sprouts stuck through, the line of bricks which marked the path, a border of globe artichokes, the blackened fern-like leaves arching out of the snow and back to earth.

John Holt trudged to the door not looking back.

Hadden stood on the step, gave Shaw a quick shake of the head – no boots.

Shaw stood his ground in the rain. 'Ten minutes,' he said to Holt.

Holt climbed the last two steps an old man.

Shaw's mobile beeped. A text from Valentine.

### BLOOD AB

Shaw smiled. They had Sly now: they'd get a DNA match as well. He had the victim's blood on his clothes. Ellis had threatened everything Sly wanted – his own boat, his own life, and freedom from a low-life existence out on the sands. He might have been an honest man, an honourable man, but he'd kill to stay one. However, something about Holt's story made Shaw hesitate. He'd told so many lies, and told them so well, that Shaw was reluctant to believe he'd finally been able to spit out the truth.

## 52

Shaw walked Holt to the squad car. Through the rough tweed material Shaw could feel the warmth within, the old man's body over-heated by the exertion of the walk in the woods. Rain fell from clouds the colour of gunshot, behind which the day was breaking. Each drop left a miniature crater in the soft snow. The old man reached the car, and leant on the door for a second look back at Blickling Cottages, as if for the last time.

'Wait,' said Shaw to the police driver. 'I'll get George – we'll follow you back.'

He checked his watch. Valentine had set out to check the sports pavilion half an hour ago. Where was he?

Shaw padded through the slush of the football pitch, thudding up the wooden steps to the veranda. In the silence he could hear his heart beating.

'George! George!' An echo bounced back off the hillside and some rooks clattered out of the winter branches.

But otherwise, silence. Shaw cupped his good eye against the window but could see only condensation within. The central double wooden doors were padlocked – the locks new, brass, and shiny. He noticed that one window had recently been replaced, the putty still white and unweathered.

'George!' He looked around. Something about the

condensation on the glass made the hair on the back of his neck bristle. He followed the veranda around to the side and found a single reinforced metal door with a padlock and Yale. The door had been forced. As he stood before it a security light came on over his head and he felt the sudden surge of heat. A sign said: SECURITY BY RYNE GROUP. But the door was open by an inch. He pushed hard, so that it thudded back against the wooden wall.

'George!'

Still nothing. He flicked a light switch but nothing happened. It was a kitchen, a utility sink, a hot-water urn, a row of mahogany-brown teapots. And a hatch, closed, but on the serving surface a set of plastic tubs and a measuring spoon, some heavy-duty mechanics' gloves and several plastic dishes. He picked up one of the tubs and prised off the lid. Within, mealworms wriggled against each other, soft, translucent, the colour of pale butter. Overhead he could hear rainwater glugging in a drainpipe.

He crossed to the next door and pushed it open. The heat surrounded him like a duvet. A soft, wet heat. Despite the dawn the room was in shadow, and he stood motionless, letting his eyes change to night vision. Somewhere an electric motor hummed and a light came on – the light he'd seen that first day he'd come to Blickling Cottages – and he saw that it was on the control panel of a portable humidifier under the window. The open door behind him let in the cold air and he heard a thermostat clicking as an electric heater whirred on. Over his head fly-catchers hung from the wooden rafters, little sticky strips turning.

He searched in his jacket for a torch then let the light flood across the floor. It was covered with a cracked lino in black and white, like a chessboard. There were two large glass-topped wooden seed boxes on the floor – from a greenhouse perhaps, each about ten foot by four foot. George Valentine lay sprawled across one, the glass smashed, his face down amongst the splinters of wood.

Shaw ran to him, turned his body over, then lit his face. He stepped back, almost falling, unable to control his leg muscles. On the bare skin of Valentine's neck a spider the size of a small plate flexed one of its fur-lined legs. Its body was black and plump except for what looked like a circlet of white fur, like a jacket. Mandibles shivered where the mouth must have been, cleaning, extending, then folding away. The rest of the smashed box appeared empty, except for shards of glass and splinters of wood. Forcing himself to kneel again Shaw used his torch to brush the spider aside. It dropped lazily, with an audible thud, to the lino, and began to walk slowly towards the shadows by a raised stage, its movements arthritic, jerky. It paused in one of the white squares of the lino, then reared, two legs probing the light which fell through the window.

'Indian white jacket,' said Shaw.

'I fucked up,' said Valentine, his voice a rasp.

Shaw switched the torch back to his face. Valentine's skin was white, bloodless. 'Don't move, George. Keep still.' He examined Valentine's neck – which seemed unblemished. But then he saw his hand, palm up, and within it the tell-tale double incision of the bite. Clear pustules were already erupting in a ring around the wound.

'I bent down to look in the cabinet,' said Valentine, his eyes moving in and out of focus. Blood dripped from a wound on his forehead where he'd crashed into the glass.

'Spiders.' He splayed a hand, indicating the size. 'I jumped. Tripped, fell into the other one. More spiders.' He closed his eyes and a thin line of saliva spilt from his mouth.

Shaw flicked his mobile open and stood. The retreating spider had switched direction and was now ambling back towards the door and the hatch by the kitchen. Shaw was on hold for the St James's control room. Impatient, he counted out loud. 'One, two, three, four . . .'

Then he stopped. He'd let his torchlight fall on the hatch: it was covered in spiders, sensing their food beyond the flimsy wood on the kitchen counter, a dozen, maybe twenty, and as the light fell on them they all moved at once, a single ripple of flexing legs.

'Control room,' said a familiar voice, but Shaw couldn't speak.

## 53

Valentine's pulse was a fading tattoo, so Shaw didn't wait
for the ambulance. He carried him, unconscious now,
across the sports field, shocked by how light he was; just
a sack of fragile bones. He used one of John Holt's
kitchen knives to open the wound, squeezing out as much
of the clear poison as he could, then bandaging the hand
with a tea towel. The ambulance finally appeared out of
the teeming rain, and he carried him into the back.
Valentine's face was dotted with sweat so Shaw helped
the paramedic get his raincoat off. Grasping the collar,
he'd been oddly moved to glimpse a name tag inside: G.
VALENTINE – like a child's.

He'd left a PC guarding the pavilion, the doors locked,
with orders to leave it that way until a unit arrived from
Linton Zoo, near Cambridge.

John Holt was waiting in the squad car.

'What's happened?' he said.

Shaw wasn't in the mood to soften any of the blows.

'He's been bitten by one of your spiders. He may live,'
he said. 'He may die.'

Holt buried his head in his hands. 'Tell me,' said Shaw.
'Tell me quickly.'

'They're Indian white jackets – fifteen hundred pounds
a time. It was Terry Brand's last consignment. Izzy found
the canisters floating down by the oyster beds that Monday

night. She didn't tell Narr and Lufkin – she thought we could take a fair share for a change and they wouldn't be any wiser. So we brought the canisters up here. I did a bit of work on the pavilion. I told the security firm I'd check out the building – so they gave me the keys. I found a dealer in Manchester. No questions asked. I just needed to get them to him,' said Holt. 'I'm sorry, we –'

'Save it,' said Shaw, cutting him off.

He watched them drive Holt down towards the coast road, and he noticed the old man didn't look back. One of the murder squad had brought Shaw's Land Rover out to the scene and he unlocked it now, slid into the seat, turned on the heating and closed his eyes. From here he could see the sea in the light of dawn, brown, like over-brewed milky tea. It was a sepia world, sand brown and salt white.

He should get back to St James's. He'd have to make a report to DCS Warren. He put both hands over his face and rubbed the skin. What would he *feel* if George Valentine died? That's what Lena would want to know. At the moment he felt nothing. Shock? Maybe. Loss.

He had to get a grip. Duncan Sly would be ready for an interview soon at St James's. They had the forensics, his blood-soaked clothes were damning enough without the evidence of Izzy Dereham and John Holt. It would be tough; but he couldn't see how Sly could escape a murder charge. And yet . . .

He couldn't forget that pathetic name tag on Valentine's collar. It was as if the jerky handwritten capital letters were the only way the world could know who he was. He let that idea just float; an image swimming in and out of focus. Memory, like an escalator, took him down into the basement of the past. He was back on Siberia Belt that Monday evening, leaning into John Holt's car to check his pulse just as he'd checked George Valentine's. There was a name tag on the collar of the heavy blue jacket Holt had been wearing: RFA.

He jerked back into the present, rubbing cold hands into his face, shivering. RFA. Royal Fleet Auxiliary. Not anyone's initials at all. Why hadn't that jarred at the time? He pressed knuckles into his eye sockets. Then the first thing he saw when he opened them was the picture Sasha Holt had given him, stuck to the passenger side of the dashboard: sycamore helicopters rising from a blazing fire. He touched it with a finger where the flames were red, and felt his blood surge, his heartbeat racing.

He heard an engine race and saw Tom Hadden's 4x4 coming down the track from the cottage. Rainwater, coming down off the hill, had filled the ditches on either side. Plumes of water rose from the tyres as he rode through puddles. Shaw flashed his lights. The two stopped door-by-door and Shaw lowered the window.

Hadden did the same.

'Jump in,' said Shaw. 'And bring your box of tricks.'

Hadden splashed his way round to the passenger side of the Land Rover. Inside, the door closed, the sound of the falling rain was deafening.

'Any news on George?' said Hadden.

'He's with the paramedics. There's nothing I can do.'

'OK,' said Hadden, backing off, hearing the stress in Shaw's voice.

'I think I know what happened,' said Shaw, taking a breath. 'That night.'

He put the Land Rover into first and pressed on towards the cottages, negotiating the water-filled potholes and ruts until he could park beside the darkened house.

'When I found Holt slumped at the wheel of the Corsa I loosened his collar,' said Shaw, killing the engine. 'There was a name tag on the jacket– at least that's what I thought it was. RFA.'

'Right. Royal Fleet Auxiliary,' said Hadden. 'Merchant Navy.'

'Yeah. Except Holt was never in the Merchant Navy. It wasn't his jacket – it was Duncan Sly's. The blood-soaked material you found outside Sly's boat was Holt's jacket.'

'I don't get it.'

'They swapped at the scene. Holt had to stay around, get his car out on the coast road to box in Baker-Sibley's Alfa, play his part. But Sly could get away from the scene. All he needed to do was walk to the far end of Siberia Belt and take in the AA no-entry sign. So they swapped jackets. It was *Holt's* that was covered in blood. So he was at the scene after the fatal blow was struck – which means Izzy Dereham lied when she said she'd seen Ellis alive on Siberia Belt when they drove away from Gallow Marsh. I think she and Holt tried to frame Sly. They were family, and they were doing it for the kids. Sly was a loner. No family, no ties. Why not let him go down for it – especially as he'd planned the whole thing, recruited them, bribed them?'

'It makes sense,' said Hadden.

'And it buys some valuable time.'

'Why do we need time?'

'Because it's getting warmer,' said Shaw. 'And we still need to prove Holt was on the spot when Ellis died.' He got out of the Land Rover and met Hadden in the headlights.

Hadden shook his head. 'But I've told you – we didn't find the boots.'

Shaw placed both hands on Hadden's shoulders and smiled. 'But I think I can find you the footprint we need.'

He looked up at the side of the house. The sycamore and the magnolia stood in the lee of the storm, both stunted now they'd been pruned, like scarecrow's hands.

'Your boys couldn't find any footprints here because the ground's frozen – has been since Monday night. But remember that on the Sunday Holt was here, pruning the sycamore, to make sure his little granddaughter didn't have any more nightmares. Spring was in the air, it was mild and sunny.'

Shaw gave Hadden the surfer's smile. Rain dripped off the end of Hadden's nose.

'If he's our man, he pruned the tree wearing the boots he wore on Siberia Belt. And he did it before the frost bit. It doesn't matter if he's destroyed the boots, dumped them, whatever. Because we know what the print looks like.'

They both dropped to their haunches by the bole of the tree. Snow still lay on the ground, pockmarked with raindrops.

'It's under the snow,' said Shaw. 'Right here.'

Hadden flipped open the aluminium CSI case and extracted a tub of dental stone, a fixative spray and a gel releasing agent, and a battery-operated hairdryer.

'What do we do?' asked Shaw.

'Try and keep the rain off while I apply some warm air – I use this to shift dust. But it'll do.' He played the dryer on the snow.

Shaw fetched a tarpaulin from the Land Rover and they hung it over the spot from the lower branches of the tree. Within minutes black, frost-shattered clods of earth had begun to poke through the white crust of the frozen ground.

'There,' said Shaw, pointing at two depressions beginning to emerge. 'That's where he set the ladder.'

Then a pair of footprints began to appear. Hadden used the fixative spray, securing the friable sandy soil in place as the ice melted. He prepared the dental stone to pour into the print and make a cast. The first footprint was useless – the boot had slid in the wet soil and smeared the pattern. But the second was stable, once sharp, but softening now the frost was melting. Until the last moment Shaw thought he was wrong. The heel was the last part of the print to be revealed: but finally the impossibly delicate bone-structure of the imprinted fern leaf emerged, as unique as a blood-soaked fingerprint.

'There,' said Shaw. 'At last. The truth. Holt was there when Ellis died. And he's told us nothing but lies ever since.'

# 54

*Monday, 23 February – a week later*

Shaw walked slowly down the line of flowers, wondering why the blooms never seemed to have any scent at funerals. He was late, and from the chapel came the sound of an organ and uncertain voices. At the door one of the ushers stood, handing out an order of service, and Shaw took one and slipped into the back row. Up at the front the coffin stood on metal rollers, ready for its last journey through the velvet curtains. Oak; Shaw always thought it was a waste of a good tree.

On a side pew sat Paul Twine, Jacky Lau and Mark Birley. Beside them, still in a wheelchair, was Fiona Campbell.

The congregation stood for the first hymn.

*Abide with me, fast falls the eventide*

Shaw looked up at the eggshell-blue ceiling, trying not to think of the fire beyond the curtains, the plastic anonymous pot for the ashes.

*The darkness deepens, Lord with me abide*

Shaw shifted from foot to foot. His good eye swam with liquid, and if he blinked the image edged across his retina, slightly ahead of the point of focus. He'd had the stitches taken out that morning by the consultant, the dressing removed without ceremony, then the sutures, and he'd been left with the nurse who showed him how to bathe the eye; the water comforting, trickling over his cheek where she dabbed at the wound. Then they'd left him alone. He rebathed the eye. Waited; tried again. On the third try the lid parted, and he felt the stickiness of his eyelashes unmeshing. When he opened the eye he saw a strange darkness full of hints of colour – purple, and shifting green, and from the left a definite sense of sunlight. His heart raced. With both eyes closed he listened to the sounds in the hospital. In the corridor a pail was shifted by foot, the water slopping inside. He opened just the injured eye again and saw less. The light was still there, but the colours had faded. The third time there were no colours, just the light. He thought it was the window but when he stood, turning his head, the light stayed on the left side.

He crossed to the hand basin in the consulting room, gripped it and looked into the mirror above. The scarred skin was healing fast, and the red stain which had seemed so raw and angry was now dry, the dead skin peeling away. And the left eye was still tap-water blue, but the right was bled of colour, dappled like a moon rising in the evening when the sun is still up.

'A moon eye,' he whispered to himself.

The chemical had attacked the cells of the iris, burning away the tendrils of the optic nerve. He'd be blind in the eye for life. The consultant thought there was little hope he'd get any sight back.

*When other helpers fail and comforts flee*

He breathed deeply. Until then it hadn't been a bad day. First thing he'd briefed DCI Warren. Holt had been charged with the murder of Harvey Ellis shortly after his arrest. They'd separately interviewed his wife and daughter and built up a clear picture of the campaign of terror waged by the loan shark Joe. Holt had been pushed to the edge, and over. Sly would face the lesser charges of attempting to pervert the course of justice. Izzy Dereham was still being questioned but would certainly face a charge, with Sly and Holt, of attempted kidnapping and false imprisonment.

Holt had refused to talk, but Sly's testimony – and the little Izzy Dereham had been able to tell them – confirmed the picture they had built up of the killing. When Sly had arrived on the scene that night Holt was trying to get Ellis's body into the pick-up. Holt had been in a state of panic, his chest was hurting, his vision blurred, his coat caked in blood. Sly got the truth out of him, holding the shaking man by the shoulders.

They'd sat in the cab of the pick-up, Holt and Ellis, arguing it through. Ellis had said he wanted more for his family than some pathetic trip to see a bird of prey. That's when he'd switched on the toy: ranting, demanding more money: £10,000, £20,000, just more. Holt had said no, so Ellis had got out, saying he'd walk back, warn Sarah Baker-Sibley. Holt had snapped: confronted with this weak man, who even if he did lose his son to cancer still had a family to go home to, another son and another daughter. And what – Holt had asked Sly – had *he* got to go home to? The loan shark's warning had been stark. Pay up, or someone was going to get hurt. He'd never shake them off, with their knives, the threats, haunting their lives. And there was no way out, no money saved, or to be earned.

His life would be a nightmare until he died. But that didn't make him kill. What made him kill was that Sasha's life would be a nightmare too.

The toolbox had been on the seat, so Holt had taken the chisel and gone after him. He'd caught him, swung him round so that he lost his footing, put him down on his knees, in free fall, sobbing, pleading. If they got caught, cried Ellis, he'd go to jail, and even a short sentence was the rest of his son's life.

It was the selfishness of that single thought which unleashed the violence: that this pathetic excuse for a man would throw away everything just because he might be in prison when his son died. And so Holt had struck the blow that killed him. He'd held his shoulder with one hand and thrust the chisel towards his face with the other, into his face, not aiming for the eye. It was over, he'd told Sly, before he knew he'd done it. The weapon had slipped into the soft tissue, into the brain. The horror of it had made his weak heart convulse. There hadn't been a struggle. It had been an execution. And now it was over.

Sly had taken control. He'd seen men die before, and in the carnage then he'd kept his head. They didn't know where Ellis had put the spare spark plugs so he adapted the plan: they cut down the pine tree, edged the truck back to Ellis's body and lifted him straight into the driver's seat. Then they shut the door, and pushed it forward. Ellis was dying, but not dead. They decided not to touch anything: it would look less suspicious if the lights were on, engine running, CD blaring. So they'd left the wings fluttering, the exhaust pumping out into the freezing air.

Then Sly made them swap jackets, focused on the plan, and the rewards that would be theirs if they stuck to it.

Holt could see it then – that just because Ellis was dead didn't mean everything was lost. They'd leave him in the cab and they'd trap Baker-Sibley. They'd get their money. So what if Harvey Ellis's body was found? There were no links between them and Ellis. No rationale for the killing. If Baker-Sibley went to the police she'd never see her daughter again. They were just innocent witnesses, trapped with everyone else. All they had to do was keep their nerve.

But Holt's breathing had refused to return to normal. They fished in his overcoat for the pills he always carried, medicine for his erratic heart.

*Help of the helpless, O abide with me.*

When Holt got back to Gallow Marsh Izzy Dereham knew that something had gone terribly wrong. Holt sat in the kitchen, drinking malt, his hand held over his straining heart. They'd cleaned his hands and face of traces of blood, and she found him one of Patrick's old shirts. Despite Holt's distress, he'd still tried to save his own skin. He'd told his niece that Sly had killed Harvey Ellis, but that they had to stick to the plan. It would still work: they'd delay Baker-Sibley, Ellis's body would be found, but there was nothing to link any of them to the crime. So she'd driven the farm van down to Siberia Belt. They could see the pick-up in the distance, Sly walking away towards the far end of the track. Then they'd gone to the lay-by, in place at exactly 4.45, to wait for Sarah Baker-Sibley's lipstick-red Alfa Romeo.

Days later, after Shaw and Valentine had made their

first call on John Holt at Blickling Cottages, they'd agreed another version of events on the phone. Holt told his niece, again, that he was innocent of the murder, but that Sly would try to implicate him as the killer if the police cracked the case. If that happened there was a way to stop him: with a lie, just one. They had to say they'd seen Harvey Ellis *alive* as they'd driven away from Gallow Marsh. And so Izzy had lied, but she'd never known the truth until now, that the killer was really her uncle. And the lie might have seen Duncan Sly on a murder charge if Shaw hadn't found physical proof Holt had been there when Harvey Ellis died: the single footprint under the sycamore tree.

Shaw blinked his good eye, snapping out of his reverie. The coffin was being carried out of the chapel and along the gravel path between the guards of honour. He joined the shuffling line of mourners.

At the graveside there was a wreath from the Police Federation. On the grass a floral message stood, set upright with wire stakes, the letters spelt out in blue irises.

## JAKE WE LOVE YOU

Grace Ellis held a paper tissue to her lips like smelling salts.

# Epilogue

Despite being on the eighth floor of the Queen Victoria hospital George Valentine had found somewhere to smoke. A whip-round in the murder inquiry room had purchased the DS a new mobile phone with a built-in camera. The picture on Shaw's mobile screen, passed on from Jacky Lau, showed a steel platform on a fire escape, the northern suburbs of Lynn beyond, Valentine leaning against the railings blowing a smoke ring. His faded blue dressing gown blew in the wind. The hospital car park lay 150 feet below, rain puddled on the tarmac.

Shaw flicked the mobile shut. He was sitting in the waiting room for the juvenile courts. White walls, blue carpet, a child's playpen in one corner. He checked his tide watch. High water at home, and he wished he was there. The case he was waiting for would be up in the hour. Sooner. When it was over he'd drive straight to the beach, meet Lena and Francesca, catch the sunset. He closed his eyes and tried to imagine himself running.

When they'd got Valentine into A&E Justina Kazimierz had been waiting for them with the serum from the US laboratory which had identified the venom in Terry Brand's blood system. When he'd regained consciousness he'd been able to explain more fully what had happened. Taking his torch into the pavilion, he'd bent down to peer into one of the glass cabinets. That's when he'd seen the spiders. He'd stepped back too quickly, his phobia kicking in, his black slip-ons skating on the floorboards so that he fell, crashing into the other cabinet. He'd put out a hand, felt it lacerated by the glass; then felt something else: a double incision of something very sharp, and very small. Valentine's recovery would be slow but uncomplicated: a fortnight of blood transfusions to clear the poison, then a diet to boost vitamins and resistance to infection. For the duration he'd be off alcohol – *if* he followed the consultant's advice.

The doors of the court came open. The next case was called. A girl in jeans and a ripped T-shirt went in, a woman in a suit holding her hand.

Shaw checked the court list. The one he wanted was next – T. G. Maddams.

CCTV footage outside a corner shop had given the street-crime unit at St James's the information required to track down the vandal who had superglued the door locks in Giddy Poynter's flats, and the cars in the street outside. Fifteen-year-old Thomas Maddams, of Wilberforce House, Westmead Estate, was identified purchasing the glue six hours before the offences took place. His home was three miles from the shop, which was 100 yards from Giddy's block. Maddams's fingerprints had been on several of the vandalized cars. Shaw had talked to the prosecuting officer and Maddams had been asked, under caution, if he was responsible for the added torture of the rat's tail through Giddy Poynter's letterbox. He denied it. There was no evidence that he was anything more than a vandal.

Shaw tried to focus his good eye on the court clock.

Then he searched in his pocket and pulled out an envelope, re-reading the brief message inside.

Peter,
Just a note, you'll get an official letter from my office. I've read the file on Tessier very carefully. I agree the new forensics are interesting but nothing points, as yet, to Robert Mosse. The report on the spray paint found on the boy's clothes is intriguing, but hardly compelling. The resources which would have to be invested in taking these leads any further are prohibitive.

Peter, this case is now twelve years old. I cannot recommend the inquiry is reopened. Furthermore, I have to ask you not to personally pursue the case. Given your links to the original inquiry – through both your father and George Valentine – I'd find it very difficult to deflect charges that you were undertaking some kind of vendetta. The same goes for George. I'll send him a note separately when he's back on duty.

I've returned both the file and the SOC box to Timber Woods. He will release them only on my signature.
Kindest regards
Max

He could go to Warren and tell him about Giddy Poynter's suspicious death. But what did it amount to? The sudden, convenient, disappearance of a key witness, certainly. A potential witness, Warren would counter.

There was no evidence to link the gang's attack on Giddy and the death of Jonathan Tessier – no evidence that wasn't circumstantial. The inquest on Giddy had been as bleak and brief as his life. Death by misadventure. There was no note, but the patient's psychiatric report included several references to suicidal tendencies. The doors of eight flats had been glued that night, and eighteen motor vehicles on the streets in the district. Although there'd only been one rat's tail. Shaw was convinced Giddy Poynter had been harried to his death, but he could no more prove it to Warren than show him an evidential link between the two cases. If he was to make any progress on the Tessier case, it would have to be on his own. Ignoring Warren's orders could cost him his job. So he needed to step carefully, subtly, and work alone.

The heavy wooden door to the juvenile courtroom opened and one of the ushers gave him a nod.

The court was carpeted, the wooden seats polished, a single royal crest over the bench. The defendant was already in the 'dock' – in this case simply a table and chair to one side of the room. He looked fifteen, edgy in a school jacket, one hand constantly unclipping then reclipping a silver wristband. Shaw wondered why he'd bothered with this case. It was unlikely to reveal anything he didn't already know. But something his father had once said had made him attend: if you can, he'd said, always take the chance to see people face to face. Up close.

A single magistrate sat with a clerk. A police prosecutor outlined the case and evidence. Maddams pleaded guilty to twenty-six separate charges of criminal damage. The brisk pace, the conveyor-belt justice, was depressing, despite the bleak spring sunshine on the fire escape.

Maddams's solicitor stood. He said that there were circumstances the court should consider, although Maddams accepted full responsibility for what he had done. The solicitor had good skin with a winter tan, and blue eyes, not washed of colour like Shaw's, but the vivid shade of a Greek sky. He was thirty perhaps, perfectly at ease in a sharp suit, one hand holding a statement, the other casually in his trouser pocket. His face had a cartoon symmetry which might have made him handsome, but his features were too bland. It was his movements that marked him out: languid, unhurried, almost entirely devoid of stress.

Maddams's background was as bleak as a bus shelter. Low IQ, learning difficulties, excluded from three schools, his mother a registered heroin addict. His father, one of the original residents of the Westmead, had died that year from throat cancer. Thomas had been badly affected by his father's death, and this was his first offence.

But the solicitor didn't let it go at that. 'I knew Bill Maddams well, and indeed I've known Thomas many years. It was a family which, until recently, was part of the local community on the Westmead which helped hold together some semblance of a civilized society. A society in which I too had to grow up.'

He had them now. The magistrate leant forward, the clerk's head nodding.

'I agreed to represent Thomas – in fact I'm happy to represent him – not because of some misguided sense of solidarity but because he is a young man worth standing up for. I don't want to waste the court's time, but I have submitted a list of testimonials from teachers and neighbours. I hope you've had a chance to read at least some.'

The clerk nodded, touching a file on his desk. The magistrate leant back in his seat.

'This offence was a bizarre aberration. He can't explain it, and neither can I.'

Maddams shifted on his chair, trying to look the magistrate in the face.

Shaw could accept that there was no apparent explanation for the crime, but why had he walked three miles to commit it?

The magistrate stood. He'd confer with the clerk in the small office to the rear – or more likely share a cup of coffee, thought Shaw. Meanwhile he sent a text message to Lena: HOME SOON. Then he stood at the back, uncomfortably aware that if he was supposed to be following Warren's instructions to the letter, he should be back at St James's on his next case.

Warren's letter. He'd photocopied it and taken it in for Valentine to read. His first bedside visit had been his last. Valentine was propped up, making the pillows look grey. They'd got halfway through the pleasantries before the DS asked if Warren had made a decision on the Tessier case.

'Nothing formal,' said Shaw, handing him the copy.

'So it's a no, then.'

'Yup.'

'So that was worth it.'

'It was the right thing to do.'

'That's nice to know.' He'd put a cigarette between his lips, unlit. 'Don't let me keep you.'

Shaw had given him the camera phone, wrapped by Jacky, the paper dotted with images of dice. Then he'd left without a word.

A door opened and the court usher asked all to rise as the magistrate returned. The chairman started with the bad news, a sure sign he would end on the good. The value of the damage caused by Thomas Maddams was estimated in the thousands. Residents in the flats had been terrified by their ordeal – and in fact one had committed suicide that very evening, a fact which could not be completely disentangled from Maddams's juvenile vandalism, although the court had to accept he could not have foreseen such a consequence of his actions. The use of the glue had been cowardly and reckless. But it was a first offence and there were extenuating circumstances. A custodial sentence was not, therefore, appropriate. Maddams would undertake one hundred hours of community service and pay a fine of £1,000 in twenty monthly instalments. He would report on a regular basis to the probationary service.

The solicitor shook hands with Maddams, who embraced him awkwardly. Shaw followed the sharp suit out into the lobby.

'Can I have a word?' he asked, flipping open a warrant card.

The solicitor nodded, the hand slipping into the trouser pocket, the weight switching to one leg. 'How can I help?'

'Why those flats? They're miles from his manor.'

'I'm not sure Thomas can give a logical breakdown of that night's events. I could ask . . .'

Shaw thought he was supposed to be charmed by the frankness.

They stood, at an impasse. 'Look. My next case is up. Ring any time, obviously. Thomas is keen to help the police if he can.'

The solicitor took out a card from a small silver case. 'Just ask for me. Robert Mosse,' he said. 'Mosse, Devlin & Parker. We're down on College Lane.'

As Shaw took the card their fingers touched, the static from the cheap pile carpet making an invisible spark jump.

He stared at the embossed lettering, trying to keep his face in neutral. Mosse flicked a fringe of hair out of his eyes and Shaw wondered what his father had thought of him that night he'd gone to the flat in Vancouver House. Had he detected the arrogance? The self-regard? Was the twenty-year-old law student from Sheffield University anything like the successful young solicitor?

Shaw zipped up the lightweight RNLI jacket, trying to work out the connections – from Mosse, to Maddams, to the Westmead, to Giddy Poynter, to Askit's tractor works, to Jonathan Tessier. And he tried to work out what he could say. Warren's warning had been explicit: the Tessier case was closed. But he wasn't on the Tessier case. He was on Giddy Poynter's case.

Mosse looked back towards the open door to the court, a ballpoint between his teeth. When he turned back Shaw had the warrant card out again, at eye-level this time, where he couldn't miss the name.